Narratives of Class in New
Irish and Scottish Literature

NEW DIRECTIONS IN IRISH AND IRISH AMERICAN LITERATURE
Claire A. Culleton, Kent State University, Series Editor

Contemporary Irish Republican Prison Writing:
Writing and Resistance
    by Lachlan Whalen (December 2007)

Narratives of Class in New Irish and Scottish Literature:
From Joyce to Kelman, Doyle, Galloway, and McNamee
    by Mary M. McGlynn (April 2008)

Irish Periodical Culture, 1937–1972:
Genre in Ireland, Wales, and Scotland
    by Malcolm Ballin (August 2008)

Joyce through Lacan and Zizek:
From A Portrait of the Artist *to* Finnegans Wake
    by Shel Brivic (forthcoming, September 2008)

Narratives of Class in New Irish and Scottish Literature

From Joyce to Kelman, Doyle, Galloway, and McNamee

Mary M. McGlynn

First published in 2008 by
PALGRAVE MACMILLAN™
175 Fifth Avenue, New York, N.Y. 10010 and
Houndmills, Basingstoke, Hampshire, England RG21 6XS
Companies and representatives throughout the world.

PALGRAVE MACMILLAN is the global academic imprint of the Palgrave Macmillan division of St. Martin's Press, LLC and of Palgrave Macmillan Ltd. Macmillan® is a registered trademark in the United States, United Kingdom and other countries. Palgrave is a registered trademark in the European Union and other countries.

ISBN-13: 978–0–230–60285–4
ISBN-10: 0–230–60285–1

Library of Congress Cataloging-in-Publication Data

McGlynn, Mary M., 1970–
    Narratives of class in new Irish and Scottish literature : from Joyce to Kelman, Doyle, Galloway, and McNamee / by Mary M. McGlynn.
        p. cm.—(New directions in Irish and Irish American literature)
    ISBN 0–230–60285–1
    1. English fiction—Irish authors—History and criticism. 2. English fiction—Scottish authors—History and criticism. 3. English fiction—20th century—History and criticism. 4. Working class in literature. 5. Sociolinguistics in literature. 6. Working class—Language. 7. National characteristics, Irish, in literature. 8. National characteristics, Scottish, in literature. 9. Discourse analysis, Narrative. I. Title.

PR8803.M33 2008
863'.91409352623—dc22   2007036440

A catalogue record for this book is available from the British Library.

Design by Newgen Imaging Systems (P) Ltd., Chennai, India.

First edition: April 2008

10 9 8 7 6 5 4 3 2 1

Printed in the United States of America.

Contents

Preface and Acknowledgments

The last several years have spawned many discussions about the shapes cities should take and the place of the working class within them. Because of a number of unfortunate occurrences, we are now able to speak of "should" as a reality. From the collapse of the World Trade Towers in Lower Manhattan to the destruction wrought by the broken levees in New Orleans and the burning of the banlieues in metropolitan areas across France, a combination of architecture, city planning, and politics fused to amplify manmade devastation. All three events showed the tension between moneyed areas and poorer ones, forcing the reconsideration of social class, among other issues. The question of how best to reconstruct these areas has made urban planning an armchair sport; the death of Jane Jacobs in the spring of 2006 further focused the public on the interaction of class and space on city streets. This dynamic is one that has been of interest for as long as there have been cities, and its exploration in fiction has served as reflector and predictor.

But novels can do so much more than act as sociological case studies or philosophical tracts; they can show us how an individual interacts with space and language, shaping them and being transformed by them. *Narratives of Class* will look at novels that see living on the outskirts of cities that are themselves considered peripheral as such major forces in the lives of their characters that the form and vernacular of these texts must necessarily respond to it.

I have institutional gratitudes to express: my thanks to Columbia University bookends this project. First of all, the English Department was good to me when I was a graduate student, and as I have wrapped up my writing, the Columbia University Seminars program has provided me a grant aiding in permissions and indexing. Baruch College, and specifically the Weissman School of Arts and Sciences, has provided regular research time, travel grants, and research support. Libraries—amazing things—have been gratifyingly accessible and electronically amazing, from the Newmann Library at Baruch to the unparalleled New York Public Library. The CUNY Research Foundation and the PSC-CUNY program in particular have also been invaluable in securing time for me to research and write. The Whiting Foundation funded an irreplaceable semester's leave. And I am grateful to the readers at Palgrave MacMillan, series editor Claire Culleton for her input, and Julia Cohen on the editorial staff for her patience with me throughout our interactions.

So many friends expressed interest in my project along the way, asking questions and offering ideas. Those with the longest attention spans include Mark Reilly, Darran Foster, Emmet Wafer, Graham Zuill, Andrea Coleman, Kate Fitta, Jennifer Bradley, Tara Kirkland, Jennie Germann-Molz, Anne Howe, Mary Hatfield. Treasured colleagues from both sides of the Atlantic have been inspirational and supportive: Dudley Andrew, Abby Bender, Paula Berggren, Mary Burke, Stephanie Brown, Clare Carroll, Lilian Carswell, Mike Elliott, Elaine Kauvar, Joseph Lennon, Robert Mahony, Michael Malouf, William McClellan, Catherine McKenna, Cóilín Parsons, Diane Negra, Marilyn Reizbaum, Dermot Ryan, Clair Wills, Nancy Yousef. My students, especially at Baruch College, have been eager readers of narratives of class and deft interlocutors of my ideas about language, elitism, and the working class. Alexis Logsdon has been more of a colleague than a student. Tracy Riley's efforts as research assistant were invaluable. The Columbia University Seminar in Irish Studies heard and critiqued much of what is here, both formally and informally, and provided a scholarly community—Ed Hagan and Marty Burke have been especially generous. Leon Wieseltier made a gift to me of Kelman's *How Late*, the reading of which launched my investigation. As my dissertation adviser, David Damrosch knew exactly when to push and when to hold back. Certainly, without his guidance and support this project never would have taken shape. Ursula Heise kept me honest and made me careful when I was inclined to be hasty. Louise Yelin made me feel like I was the right person on the right track. John Brenkman suggested the development of the urban angle that has become central to my argument; his broad-sighted suggestions have been invaluable. Shelly Eversley provided a careful set of eyes, an intelligent perspective, and much joy. My sisters, Sara Platz and Lizzy McGlynn, have kept me laughing and worked to offer perspective. My parents, Richard McGlynn and Ann Palen McGlynn, both rigorous thinkers and brilliant conversationalists, gave me a hunger for exploring ideas as well as concrete tools and values to shape my approach.

I used to call this book my baby, until my children were born; it has been to my great delight to learn that children and scholarship can have a symbiotic relationship, each making the other appear to be a luxury and a relief. Tomás and Sally have left their marks on this book, both in inspiring a move to the urban peripheries known as the New York suburbs and in educating me about how lack of narrative fixity plays out in everyday life. But no one has had more of an impact than my husband, Conor O'Sullivan, whose ideas and attitudes have influenced me in my writing much more than he knows. I am grateful for his conscious input as well as his constant assistance, support, and love. I dedicate this book to him, and, consciously foregrounding my own marginalized vernacular, to all y'all listed above.

Earlier versions of portions of this book have appeared in prior publications:

Portions of Chapter Three were previously published as "Pregnancy, Privacy, and Domesticity in *The Snapper*: Roddy Doyle's Barrytown Family Romance" in *New Hibernia Review*, a journal of Irish Studies published by the University of St. Thomas in Minnesota.

Portions of Chapter Three were previously published as "Why Jimmy Wears a Suit: White, Black, and the Working Class in *The Commitments*," in *Studies in the Novel*, 36.2 (Summer 2004). Copyright © 2004 by the University of North Texas. Reprinted by permission of the publisher.

Portions of Chapter Four were previously published as "Janice Galloway's Alienated Spaces," in *Scottish Studies Review*, 4.2 (Autumn 2003), Association for Scottish Literary Studies.

Portions of Chapter Two were previously published as "'Middle-Class Wankers' and Working-Class Texts: The Critics and James Kelman," in *Contemporary Literature*, 43.1 (Spring 2002). Copyright 2002 by the Board of Regents of the University of Wisconsin System. Reproduced by permission.

Portions of Chapter Three were previously published as "'But I keep on Thinking and I'll Never Come to a Tidy Ending': Roddy Doyle's Useful Nostalgia," in *LIT: Literature, Interpretation, Theory*, 10.1 (Spring 1999).

Portions of Chapter Four are based on "'I Didn't Need to Eat': Janice Galloway's Anorexic Text and the National Body," *Critique* 49.2 (Winter 2008) 221–236.

Excerpts from *A Disaffection* and *How Late It Was, How Late* by James Kelman, published by Secker & Warburg. Reprinted by permission of The Random House Group Ltd.

I express appreciation to the University Seminars at Columbia University for their help in publication. Material in this work was presented to the University Seminar on Irish Studies.

Chapter One

Introduction: The Poor Mouth

"Fuck off, he couldnay drive man that was how he didnay have a fucking license: he couldnay fucking drive. He had never fucking learnt" (138). So we discover, midway through James Kelman's *How Late It Was, How Late*, that Sammy Samuels botched his potential to escape a criminal job gone awry. The free indirect narration offers Sammy's critique of the narrative arc of the numerous "true-life tales of woe" (136) he has heard from others who have done time; the stories are always identical in their structure and self-pity, a literary insight that leads Sammy to see himself not as victim but actively responsible for his own downfall. But Sammy misinterprets: it isn't mainly his "stupidity" (139) that results in his prison sentence. As much as Sammy is certain individuals hold the reins of fate in their own hands, that his inability to drive is responsible for his misfortunes, Kelman emphasizes throughout the novel not just that social conditions sculpt individuals, but that preexisting narrative structures direct storylines as well. Sammy cannot drive because his economic and geographical positioning combines with his entrapment in a mode of storytelling that offers few options to him. Repeatedly in the novel, physical circumstances stand in as not just analogues for but indices of Sammy's fate, until at last this marginalized character escapes the constraints of narrative expectation and literally vanishes from the page.

And so it is revealing that so many protagonists in the novels in *Narratives of Class* cannot drive. Like Kelman, Roddy Doyle depicts a character who falters in criminal activities because he can't drive: while Sammy gets seven years in jail, Charlo Spencer dies. Both moments take place in the final decades of the twentieth century, in an era in which driving is an assumed ability of any adult (outside of Manhattan). Eoin McNamee's murderous Victor Kelly spends formative time as a child "behind the wheel of an old Ford Zephyr on blocks at the edge of the dock" (*RM* 5), with his immobility overdetermined by age, absence of wheels, and lack of direction. In her depictions of Joy Stone and Cassie, Janice Galloway uses driving as an index of a woman's independence, a gesture antiquated by American standards, but very much alive in a world where many people do not drive or have telephones. Why are these characters still struggling with such elements of early modernization?

Class provides a major part of the answer. The novels I will discuss, published between 1983 and 1997 in Scotland and Ireland, depict mainly working-class characters.[1] Both Sammy and Charlo are from the working class, the part of it that can't always find work and has been left behind in the modernization schemes of the United Kingdom and Ireland. Both turn to crime in times of economic desperation; both fail even to rob the modern system, so remote are they from the late twentieth century. McNamee's choice to set his novel in the 1970s likewise removes it from the contemporary. Meanwhile, gender complicates the relation to class for Galloway's women, also left behind by the progress of technology. In each case, the role of class in these disconnections is obscured by conceptions of nation and nationalism not operative for these characters or their neighborhoods. The inability to drive, a literal lack of control of modernity's technology and a powerlessness to navigate through the national space, indicates estrangement from the economy benefiting from cosmopolitan prosperity via the Chunnel and the European Union.

Both Ireland and Scotland historically contained a large, deeply poor underclass kept at a distance from a small body of wealthy land and business owners. Ireland's position as a destitute outpost on the edge of a more prosperous Europe extends back at least to the early eighteenth century, when Swift wrote of "the streets, the roads, and cabin-doors crowded with beggars" (439), his word choices emphasizing the spatial, geographic circumstances of poverty. Following the drastic population decline due to death and emigration during and after the Great Famine, absolute poverty declined somewhat throughout the country but endured in a few pockets, parts of Dublin in particular (Frazer 485). Still, the number of impoverished remained high not only in absolute terms but also relative ones until 1997, when the combination of Ireland's GDP growth and drop in unemployment meant that for the first year on record, the living standard of the average citizen in Ireland was higher than that of the average European consumer (Bradley 21, Clinch, Convery, and Walsh 19–21).

Meanwhile, Scotland, along with much of the industrial North in the United Kingdom, saw a rapid decline in manufacturing jobs with the recession in the early 1980s: 1.5 million manufacturing jobs were lost, and unemployment rates ran between 15 and 20 percent in the North, Scotland, and Wales. Fintan O'Toole's summary of the situation ties it directly to regime change, noting that "In the three years after Mrs. Thatcher came to power in 1979, Scotland lost more than one-fifth of its manufacturing jobs and a tenth of its industrial output" ("Imagining" 69). As the recession lifted after 1983, the large percentage not prospering under Margaret Thatcher's policies became obscured by economic improvement, a phenomenon exacerbated in Glasgow in particular, where the unemployment rate in 1987 was 18.1 percent and over 30 percent were out of work in some areas (Raines, Furlong et al. 16). The infusions of "wealth deriving from the extraction [of oil]" from the North Sea and the so-called Silicon Glen tended not to "trickle down," despite the Tory embrace of Reaganomics.

Prosperity was rare in both Scotland and Ireland in the period I discuss, with even middle classes struggling economically. But as statistics indicate, the gap between struggling and destitute grew the longer that Thatcher and John Major's Conservative Party remained in power in Britain, with similar conditions prevailing in Ireland. Housing estates in both nations came to be seen as zones of poverty. In cities across the British Isles, and notably for my interests in Dublin and Glasgow in particular, post–World War II housing shortages had combined with moves toward city-center slum clearance in the 1950s, especially to push entire populations to the edges of metropolitan areas. O'Toole notes the use of the dainty term "decanted" to refer to this mass relocation ("Imagining" 67). While government-sponsored housing often combined both utopian good intentions and cutting-edge urban planning, the assumptions of predominantly middle-class reformers that underlay the choices made in relocating the urban poor revealed a "a culture transfer amounting to a cultural colonization" (Ravetz 4) and inadvertently created virtual ghettoes isolated on the fringes of society without access to opportunities for workers or consumers.

As *Narratives of Class* will explore, the segregation of the underclass created deep pockets of poverty and privation but also lay groundwork for new voices to redeploy certain narrative forms. This introduction will offer a synopsis of the literary and historical contexts giving rise to these voices, ending with an exploration of the legacy of James Joyce in particular. Chapter two will turn to the radical critiques made by James Kelman's novels, which link working-class voices, experimental forms, and reconceptions of the local—here, Glasgow. Chapter three turns to the less-overtly experimental novels of Roddy Doyle, examining his renegotiations of national identity in terms of the ways gender and class affect use of space and language in peripheral Dublin. The novels of Janice Galloway, taken up in chapter four, foreground their physical concerns as linguistic ones, using visible textual innovations to emphasize the restrictions on lower-class subjects, both linguistically and geographically. In his Belfast setting and his formal choices, Eoin McNamee's project departs from the patterns I set out in the prior chapters, but I hope to demonstrate in chapter five how his curious narrative style unearths conceptions of urban spaces and local language more in line with Kelman, Doyle, and Galloway than a first reading might suggest. An afterword, addressing the subsequent move toward engagement with history in the work of all four novelists, will bring my account of the spatial components of textual experimentation and working-class voices to a close.

Working-Class Voices

Such economic and physical estrangements as seen in the 1980s correspond to a long-standing literary estrangement of certain sectors of society on the British Isles, namely of these same peripheral working classes. This is not to say that the novel never represented the working class before; what I intend to trace in the pages that follow is a new direction in that representation and the formal evolutions it has evinced. Kelman has noted that working-class characters "were confined to the margins, stuck in the dialogue, kept in their place. You only ever saw them or heard them. You never got into their mind. You did find them in the narrative but from without, seldom from within" ("Importance" 80). Kelman's remark, in his collection of essays *Some Recent Attacks*, identifies a change in perspective in the decision to place working-class characters at the center of a novel, with working-class culture as the frame of reference rather than a foil for a standard, more intellectual, or less bathetic culture.

As Bruce Robbins explores in *The Servant's Hand*, when the working class is depicted at all in most texts, parallels between the upper class and the servant class predominate—servants a sign of their masters' wealth and status, remaining as fixed types rather than evolving characters. Even more troubling to Robbins, instead of grappling with the newfound roles for the working class outside servitude during the Industrial Revolution, the nineteenth-century novels he reads "reinscribe and rejuvenate the literary conventions of a servant" (xi). Robbins works throughout his study to resist the tendency toward reading servants in a purely mimetic manner, suggesting that "the novel casts its lot with rhetoric rather than with realism" (6). That is, looking for accurate portraits of the lower class is less insightful than recognizing that servants in such novels function as instruments of narration, as plot devices, as mechanisms of parody. He notes that "realistic details...are only a pretext" (90). While Robbins usefully offers routes to noting the nonrealist tendencies of even the most staunchly realist fiction, the novelistic conditions he describes are a vastly different thing from those I will discuss here, the latter being openly estranged from the establishment, cautious when leaving contemporary working-class neighborhoods, and actively defining their characters beyond binary oppositions with or foils for, their social superiors. This shift distinguishes the novels of Kelman, Doyle, Galloway, and McNamee from those of their predecessors.

The presence of these voices, again, is not new. Bakhtin and many since have been quick to laud Dickens and other nineteenth-century writers for the multitude of voices in their texts. This heteroglossia "is the basic distinguishing feature of the stylistics of the novel" ("Discourse," 263). The structural basis of such heteroglossia Bakhtin calls "common language":

> ...the average norm of spoken and written language for a given social group....the author distances himself from this common language, he steps back and objectifies it, forcing his own intentions to refract and diffuse themselves through the medium of this common view that had become embodied in language (a view that is always superficial and frequently hypocritical). (301–302)

The common language Bakhtin sees as parodied by the author is by definition that of the mainstream, meaning that in the history of British and Irish literature when peasant, servant, or other proletarian voices have been represented, it has been largely with the goal of "exposing...common opinion" (307). The working-class perspective becomes a tool, not an end in itself.[2] The novels I will examine here take as their common language (with the double-voiced articulation and parody implied by these terms) the speech of urban neighborhoods of Dublin, Edinburgh, Glasgow, and Belfast; the presence of other voices—teachers, government workers, mass media, and so on—is set against this backdrop, often highlighting the way that the competing discourses may be unaccustomed to their nondominant status.

Franco Moretti has called the polyglossia present in nineteenth-century novels "dialogic polyphony," distinguishing it from what he sees as "cacophonic polyphony," which reveals the tensions among various voices rather than emphasizing their harmony. The former is "critical and intelligent" (*Epic* 58), while the latter can be "just an incredible din...a tumult of discordant voices" (58, 59). Moretti identifies cacophonic polyphony as the solution Joyce, Goethe, Melville, and others find to characterize the experience of living in modernity: "many things are as yet unclear; and it is necessary to learn to live with noise: to represent it—and, indeed, 'feel it'" (59). While cacophony may be frightening, it captures the multitude of the modern experience, positive and negative. Indeed, dialogic polyphony might be open to the charge that it is liable to perpetuate what cacophonic polyphony critiques, the comfortable ideal of a level playing field and equal opportunity to communicate. Just as Victorian London was not a level playing field, neither are unemployment-torn Thatcherite Britain and Ireland. The difference between a hegemonic dialogic polyphony and a critical cacophonic one is then crucial here: despite an appearance of polyphony, many dialogic nineteenth-century novels actually exerted a centripetal force, helping to eliminate the cacophony of regionalism and create one national voice.

The examples of nineteenth-century England are instructive because they coincide with a period of imperial expansion for the United Kingdom, and indeed, critiques of the national voice have come in part from those voices throughout the British Empire suppressed via colonization. Like Bakhtin's dialogism, the notion of social hybridity contains the potential to afford cultural fluency and flexibility to the colonized. Hybridity of this sort is seen by Homi Bhabha to be a deeply positive condition, conferring advantages on its possessors unavailable to their monocultural colonizing counterparts:

> Hybridity is the sign of the productivity of colonial power...it is the name for the strategic reversal of the process of domination through disavowal...displays the deformation or displacement of all sites of discrimination and domination. It unsettles the mimetic or narcissistic demands of colonial power...reimplicates...enables...escapes. (Bhabha 34–35)

While Bhabha recognizes hybridity as a consequence of the colonizer's force, his verbs here indicate how optimistically he views hybridity's powers. And indeed, heteroglossia can have positive consequences as well, as it "permits a multiplicity of social voices" (Bakhtin, "Discourse" 263). But each condition bears material limitations that can often be overlooked by sanguine critics. Bakhtin cautions us about the productive power of dialogism and heteroglossia, emphasizing the limitations and continual sense of incompleteness inherent to such stylization. David Lloyd's radical critique of Bakhtin conceives of these limits and incompleteness as part of the inauthenticity of a colonized culture, that which creates uncertainty, and he reads this illegitimacy as threatening to nationalist and colonizer alike. For him, street ballads in the nineteenth century thus contain a subversive potential and any reading of hybridization must recognize the instability of the colonized (distinct from "the postmodern subject" [111]).

This reading of the class component in hybridity and heteroglossia dovetails with the work of Raymond Williams. As the end of the postwar boom was hitting the working class hardest across the British Isles, Williams delineated his influential theory of dominant, emergent, and residual cultural forms, arguing that in nineteenth-century-working-class writing, "the fundamental problem...is the effective predominance of received literary forms...which already conditions and limits the emergence" (*ML* 124). For Williams, if working-class fiction were to be seen as a viable form, it could not escape the realism dominant in narrative at the time of its emergence, and this formal constraint led to fiction that was "incorporated" into dominant culture, validating rather than challenging the status quo. Indeed, the central problem of working-class narrative for him is that "much incorporation looks like recognition, acknowledgment, and thus a form of *acceptance*. In this complex process there is indeed regular confusion between the locally residual (as a form of resistance to incorporation) and the generally emergent" (124–125). The mainstream gives an appearance of accepting working-class fiction when in reality this gesture conceals an attempt to subdue and control such texts. Local efforts to oppose this absorption can appear reactionary, relying on rejected or obsolete forms in a manner that suggests acceptance of prevailing tendencies. A new working-class narrative, then, must resist incorporation, through the shifting of perspective and through use of emergent, rather than dominant, formal techniques. Contrary to Williams's formulation, then, which predicates itself on an ideal of a global proletariat, the local, rather than being residual resistance, can, through its refusal of the dominance of the metropole, offer emergent forms.[3]

At the intersection and revision of these ideas from formal, Marxist, and postcolonial critics, then, we can see a space carved out for a form of expression that draws on innovative techniques and a hybridized, even cacophonic voice, a shifting of narrative center and narrative perspective that functions in part through a departure from narrative norms. While it is difficult to say exactly what could constitute a narrative norm in the late twentieth century, with widespread modernism and postmodernism, we can characterize certain formal decisions as symptoms of this emergent local literature that retreats from nationalism and working-class stereotypes. For instance, the authors discussed here decline to use quotation marks, transliterating dialect on the page; all include dialect—including profanity—within any normative narrative voice; and all favor less plot-driven novels, regularly privileging mundane, local, everyday experience through elliptical endings and unfinished sentences. Narrative voice is not straightforward, revealing tonal shifts, competing discourses, and challenges to notions of standard or proper English. Each of these textual techniques can be seen to challenge, invert, or demolish the conventional hierarchies governing our reception of novels, and the combination of these formal innovations with a working-class reinterpretation of national identity is what draws my attention to them.

Form is the crucial category here; the novels I analyze differ from English fiction less importantly in the biographies of their authors than in the sorts of textual shapes they assume. *Pace* Ray Ryan's assertion that "[Joyce's] model is most obviously taken up at the level of theme (no fool would try to match Joyce's innovations) and geography" (145), I will argue that theme, form, and geography interact in the creation of a class-based critique of economic history and literary history. Through the deployment of their new, local language, the authors considered in the chapters that follow unbalance a number of traditional linguistic hierarchies, with an eye to critiquing social ones. Yet we must recall that Bakhtin's polyphony can be either harmonic or cacophonic, and that hybridity is not the uniformly positive force Bhabha might have it, as well as how easy it is for the dominant ravenously to incorporate the emergent. In recognition of space-, gender-, and class-inflected heterogeneity complicating constructions of nation, writers in this book adhere to an underrecognized angle in an unexpected strain of Irish writing, the class-based critique made by Joyce via his modernist innovations, creating texts suffused not only with hybridized language but the recognition of the hardships necessarily accompanying this manifestation of linguistic dialogism under the status quo. As Lloyd has written about the Irish context, "both popular and literary forms map a colonial culture for which the forms of representational politics and aesthetics required by cultural nationalism begin to seem entirely inadequate, obliging us to conceive of a cultural politics which must work outside the terms of representation" (89). One example of this comes in the conveying urban dialect on the page, as nonstandard spelling must be used, giving texts a visually distinct appearance. Rendering a sociolect visually "accurate" via the transliteration of Scottish and Irish pronunciations into text evinces a curious paradox: the reader is faced with a simultaneous pose of realism (the supposed "accuracy" of the spellings) and an estranging device (the language becomes distinct from transparent, easily comprehensible, standard written English).[4] As Lloyd suggests, we see a move beyond authenticity/representation, and hence, beyond the homogenizing tendencies of an overarching cultural nationalism. It is therefore to the question of the relationship of region, city, and nation that I now turn.

Creations of Nations

To begin with, it is important in this context to point out that both Scotland and Ireland complicate any definition of the word "nation." Ireland has been split since its struggle for independence from Britain over 80 years ago into the 26-county sovereign Republic of Ireland and the 6-county province of the United Kingdom, Northern Ireland. While the Constitution of the Republic of Ireland no longer calls for restoration of the 32 counties to one state, after being amended in 1998, even many of those in the North who seek no union with the Republic consider themselves Irish. Scotland, meanwhile, joined with England in the United Kingdom via an Act of Union in 1707, which came at the end of a long struggle with overlapping monarchs. Even in union, Scotland retained separation of its education, judicial, and state religious institutions, maintaining a distinct cultural identity. Paradoxically, many Scots early in the union acted to efface the difference between themselves and the English, working energetically to construct a "British" identity and becoming highly visible proponents of the British Empire, financing, for instance, "investment trusts that bought and developed land, mines and railways in the Americas, Asia and Australia" (O'Toole, "Imagining" 70). But with the decline of shipbuilding, of coal and steel, and of heavy manufacturing, this century has seen a series of nationalist movements that finally, in 1998, resulted in the beginnings of devolution.[5]

Just as both nations were absorbed into a larger political corpus, historically, both Scottish and Irish literatures have been assumed into an overarching "British" canon. Still, critics have discovered tendencies to diverge from the norm marking Scottish and Irish novels since their inception. Writing from the peripheries was regularly placed in the position of defending, defining, and translating an alternate language and culture, trying to make an uncomfortable form fit with their narratives. Katie Trumpener traces the evolution of the novel in Scotland and Ireland, noting that "the English-language novel's cultural energy and formal innovations stemmed largely from peripheral practitioners, who developed the genre in interesting and hybrid ways" (170). Luke Gibbons identifies the "proto-modernist" tendencies of nineteenth-century Irish literature (*Transformations* 6), while Declan Kiberd notes "the paradox of a modernist literature and cultural politics in a country too often noted for its apparent backwardness" (*II* 24). Formal innovations arise precisely because existing genres are inadequate to the needs of the margins.

According to Robert Crawford, whose evocatively titled seminal work *Devolving English Literature* was followed up by the even more suggestive *The Scottish Invention of English Literature*, since union with England, Scottish writers have variously worked to create, explore, or deny the concept of British identity. During the Enlightenment, for instance, which in English owes so much to Scottish intellectuals like Adam Smith and David Hume, most Scottish writers sought to downplay their regional differences from England, to lose their accents, to learn works of the English canon so as to foster an equal relationship of the newly united countries and create a British identity. While Benedict Anderson suggests (rather uncritically) that Scottish "Anglicization was essentially a byproduct" rather than a "selfconscious policy" (90), both historical and contemporary Scottish critics sense an insecurity in linguistic choices of their ancestors. Speaking in 1921, Professor W.A. Craigie looks at eighteenth-century Scottish writing and concludes that "No Scottish writer of the eighteenth century who had anything important to say in prose attempted to say it in the language of his countrymen. He did it in his best English, and all the time he was haunted by an uneasy feeling that even his choicest English was not free from those dreadful solecisms known as Scotticisms, which would assuredly be pointed out and laughed at when his book had penetrated into the sister-kingdom" (15). In keeping with Craigie's rueful remarks (which use the escape clause "in prose" to allow room for Robert Burns's outsize impact), Crawford sees the study of English literature, as well as the creation of a British literature that examines an island identity, as stemming mainly from the efforts of Scottish writers and teachers. Wealthy and educated Scots in particular began to think of themselves as British, and the ethos of Enlightenment self-improvement, efficiency, and knowledge reinforced the sense of the Scottish tradition as archaic and obsolete, not to mention linked to undesirable class identifications. Hence, numerous Scottish writers participated in the creation of a British national voice—Scott, Stevenson, Barrie offer illustrative cases.[6] By the time that G. Gregory Smith publishes his *Scottish Literature: Character and Influence* in 1919, the source for the oft-referenced notion of Caledonian antisyzygy, T.S. Eliot breezily notes in his review of the book that "there is no longer any tenable important distinction to be drawn for the present day between the two [English and Scottish] literatures" (McCulloch 9).

Scottish modernism is a tiny phenomenon. Virginia Woolf's choice of the Hebrides as the backdrop of *To the Lighthouse* may be the best-known participation by Scotland in modernism. As this less-geographically centered international modernism followed its course, Hugh McDiarmid's Scots-based, technically sophisticated poetry and Lewis Grassic Gibbon's vernacular novels suggested routes for a local literary evolution, but neither took hold. Despite admiration of what was seen to be a highly developed national revival in Ireland, the reading public expressed unwillingness to engage with McDiarmid's pan-Celtic visions. On the other hand, ongoing shame at the excesses of sentimental "kailyard" literature of the late nineteenth century (from Barrie's contributions to such travesties as *Wee MacGreegor*) mingled with wariness of Gibbon's Marxist leanings to deem his regional patios suspect; his untimely death ensured his obsolescence.[7] With reactive mid-century efforts to write with little to no reference to Scottishness yielding little, Muriel Spark being a notable exception, and the decline of a powerful Labour voice making social realism seem unsuitable, a new literature, a new form, would be required to represent inner-city lives.

Meanwhile, Irish literary history reveals a distinct trajectory, intersecting culturally more than politically with the Scottish literature while building toward a similar conclusion. In the early 1700s, contemporaneous with the fusion of English and Scots identity into a British one, Conor McCarthy notes that Jonathan Swift sits "ill at ease in Ireland (resentful of his loss of influence in London) but critical of its treatment by the English government" (144). Swift writes in standard English, his most famous protagonist an Englishman, with his depictions of his compatriots certainly sympathetic but also unflattering. Richard Brinsley Sheridan may be the first Irishman to present stereotypic Irish characters for the amusement of London sophisticates; Sir Lucius O'Trigger's name and strongly accented dialogue mock and marginalize him for the benefit of a cosmopolitan audience. Within 40 years of the discomfiting Irish/British Act of Union in 1801, the notion of a "Stage Irish" persona was well in place, anticipating the kailyard. Certainly Maria Edgeworth, William Carleton, and George Moore, as well as Sheridan Le Fanu and Bram Stoker, represent what are now seen to be critical perspectives on Ireland, steadily innovating novelistic form, but as Lloyd emphasizes, at the time, none was seen as the national genius or voice that a nation hungering for authenticity and a spokesperson sought.

From this yearning for national representation come two distinct responses, a look to the past and a move toward the future. This dual-front assault on the British canon arises in the form of a deep lineup of textually rich poetry and drama in the Celtic Revival of the turn of the century and the dominance of Joyce's modernist voice, the combination placing Ireland at its furthest distance from Scotland, a distinct national voice with prominent and prolific practitioners. Cairns Craig's analysis of the relationship between the two nations maintains that "As Ireland's cultural capital grew with the successive achievements of Yeats, Synge, O'Casey, Joyce, Scotland's declined" (Craig, "National" 59).

Edward Said has read Yeats in particular as recuperating the "barbaric" West in an act of nativism designed to resist colonial mindsets. What results is an apotheosizing of "the landscape, culture, language and people of the Irish West" (McCarthy 149). Formally, this literature distances itself from the modernism contemporaneous with it: "while Ireland produced, as has been noted, an ambitious literary modernism,...even in the literary field the cultural dominant in Ireland during the decades between independence and the end of the twentieth century was not modernism at all but rather naturalism" (Cleary, "Towards" 232–233).

Representations of the poor in particular become compromised throughout the post-Independence period as class perspectives were subordinated to national ones in the 1916 uprising and subsequent struggle for independence. While socialists James Larkin and (Scottish-born) James Connolly drew working-class supporters to the nationalist movement, their vision was supplanted by Éamon de Valera's religious nationalism, downplaying class-inflected points of view in its conception of the Irish people. The self-imposed exile of Joyce and Samuel Beckett, combined with/resulting from this privileging leads to, in prose, a long, gritty period of realism largely based on rural voices and stories, some working in concert with a hegemonic national imaginary, but also, it must be noted, some resisting its constraints. In either case, Irish literature had largely negative urban images by mid-century; the paradigm tends to be as in Liam O'Flaherty's three Dublin novels, that protagonists "suffer tragedy largely because they have been corrupted by the city" (Martin 48).[8]

As economic liberalization in the late 1950s combines with a relaxation of a censorious culture, Irish literature experiences "a removal of the cultural reference points which had shaped its earlier period. With neither nationalism nor its concomitant ideology of rural life to act as a binding force, it became impossible to think of an Irish literary movement" (O'Toole, "Saints" 22). The shadows cast by such literary heavyweights as Yeats, Joyce, O'Casey, and Beckett, combined with a sense of unmooring from traditional definitions of nation, left Irish writers doubly inhibited.

In both Scottish and Irish contexts, then, the exploration of national literatures does lead us back to class. The onset of prosperity in the early 1950s in Britain is tied to the postwar boom and reconstruction, while economic growth comes later in Ireland, following T.K. Whittaker's economic programme, published in 1958. This economic development leads to new levels of material comfort for working-class citizens, whose underrepresented voices and spaces begin now to find expression, whether in those who resisted the epithet Angry Young Men, like John Braine, John Osborne, and Alan Sillitoe, or a playwright like Henno Magee, or—although he publishes the work far later—Jeff Torrington, who begins *Swing Hammer Swing!* in 1961.[9] All of these writers articulate discomfort with grand narratives of nation, much of their uneasiness arising because the position of the working class is absent or insufficient.

Indeed, the relationship of the demands of class and nation is often tense. National identification often has been supposed to supersede class concerns and has been evoked in an effort to pacify disgruntled workers (and to discourage international unity of the workers of the world). In his pivotal *The Breakup of Britain: Crisis and Neo-nationalism* three decades ago, Tom Nairn saw the "grotesquely uneven nature of capitalist development" (128) as one of the major motivations of nationalism: "In the general history of nationalism, material under-development has always has cultural and ideological overdevelopment as its companion. Faced with the culture of deprivation and enforced ruralism, rebels have always had to compensate with forms of militant idealism" (205).[10] Historically, then, nationalism has taken root in an unindustrialized countryside, often defining a bucolic life as the cornerstone of national character. Ryan sees this final characteristic as one that links Ireland and Scotland in particular, noting the "urbanized centres, and benighted rural hinterlands...the creation of a mystique of Irishness and Scottishness traceable to these depopulated zones" (10).[11] Northern Ireland's own constructions of nation are clearly contested but also rely on the pastoral in both their Loyalist and Republican guises.

Yet while the mystique of the breathtaking green vista endures on both sides of the Irish Sea, patterns of development have reconfigured. While we are accustomed to associating modernization with urbanization, paradoxically, much of the technologization occurring on the British Isles is taking place outside of traditional metropolitan centers, avoiding the decaying inner cities industrialized in previous eras. Stereotypes of backward country yokel and sleek, urbane citymouse do not apply in settings where industrialization shuns its customary urban locations.[12] Gibbons has noted that efforts in the 1980s to bring foreign (specifically American) capital to Ireland used romantic rural images to encourage industrialization in the countryside, a nonurban modernization. (This campaign relied on the absence in rural areas of trade unions, making them more economical places to develop.) (*Transformations* 89).[13]

This relocation of the locus of technical innovations has led to a recasting of efforts to come to terms with the primarily rural nationalism that marked the emergence of modern Ireland, and somewhat differently, contemporary Scotland. Suddenly Dublin's buildings and streets seem quaint and de Valera's mid-century visions of a cozy rural nation no longer register, much as kilts and clans had long been alien to urban Scots, and residents of the heavily industrial Glasgow, in particular. Belfast has seen a similar transformation from manufacture to service economy. In the new modernization, tractors dot agricultural regions, and country folk can drive, while their urban counterparts cannot. Working-class urbanites in particular become the least touched by modernization, inverting traditional rural and urban associations. Submerged class visibility and a national definition that downplays all but the historical dimension of its cities converge to place geographic pressure on the urban poor. I seek, therefore, to connect a reading of the interaction of class and nation to one of space. In this, it will be important to bear in mind Craig's contention that "*class-based* analyses of cultural capital are effective only by suppressing the extent to which they themselves are re-investing in a cultural capital which is specifically *national*" ("National" 44); that is, many readings that take class as a centerpiece ultimately reinforce a national context. In part, in anticipation of this issue, I draw on the suggestion of Glenda Norquay and Gerry Smyth that reading Irish and Scottish writers in the context of their respective contemporaries, and, even more importantly, more in comparison with each other, can evade their "congeal[ing] into some species of marginal essence permanently at odds with metropolitan practices [and thereby] consolidating the divide between centre and periphery" ("Waking" 36). Within the last decade, the trend to read Irish and Scottish texts in light of one another has grown exponentially.[14] My contention here is that analyzing class with an eye on this comparative framework necessitates attention to the outskirts of the cities where Scottish and Irish working classes are concentrated.

Urban Peripheries

If the rhetoric of nationalism reveres place, part of the project of the writers I examine is to modify such reification. Kelman has noted that in his attention to Glasgow, accuracy of detail paradoxically diminishes veneration of a location: "Glasgow can be any other town or city in Great Britain, including London, Edinburgh, Cardiff, Cambridge, Newcastle, or Ramsgate" (*SRA* 80). Terry Eagleton makes a similar point when he writes that *Ulysses*, in its very specificity, suggests "with its every breath just how easily it could have done the same thing for Bradford or the Bronx" (*NCL* 15). A local identity is not a romanticized, national one; rather, it acknowledges that there is nothing special to elevate it above any other city, a significant leveling of traditional national and colonial hierarchy. As Enda Duffy reads it, "*Ulysses*, dealing with Dublin and not the whole island, educates us, I suggest, in how to think our way out of the territorial imperative that nationalism demands" ("Disappearing" 37). Writing in the same volume, Marjorie Howes sees Neil Smith and Benedict Anderson each aware "that the national is to be grasped most fully in its relation to other scales, rather than in opposition to them…these other scales are structurally, simultaneously, both necessary and inimical to the national" (63). What emerges here is an underacknowledged countertrend to recent tendencies to read texts primarily in national contexts. Rather, regions, and more specifically cites, will become a primary frame of reference.

Therefore, even the city is not yet a specific enough category for examination of those omitted from definitions of nation. In many historical European cities, and certainly in Dublin and Glasgow, "the urban core is made up of neatly tended architectural treasures and disorder is pushed to the periphery" (Caldwell 28). Whether this has arisen via a Haussmann-style urban planning or in reaction to post–World War II housing shortages, ring suburbs in Europe may more accurately take a different name. For many English speakers, the riots and protests throughout France introduced a new term, banlieues, to label such areas. This word is "not a translation for suburb because it lacks the bourgeois cosiness of the English term... Although banlieue only means an area at the periphery of town, in recent years it has come to designate more specifically the working-class past of such an area" (Konstantarakos 133). Etymologically, the word literally means place of exile (134). Historically, as Johanna X.K. Garvey notes, women find themselves exiled in a like manner: "In city literature, especially until the latter part of this [the twentieth] century, female characters frequently appear on the margins, in domestic settings far from the power or in liminal spaces where boundaries are blurred" (116). These links of class and region and of gender and space are ones to which the novels in this book return repeatedly, both through an underdiscussed interest in spatiality and through an exploration of its linguistic corollaries in accent and dialect.

In invoking these peripheral regions of cities themselves considered peripheral (both to the own national self-characterizations and more overarching dynamics of metropole and outpost), the novels in *Narratives of Class* disrupt a long-standing organizational binary of both fiction and criticism—that of urban versus rural. As discussed in the "Creation of Nations" section preceding this one, both Scotland and Ireland saw the manufacture and maintenance of this duality as they groped toward national identities, often leaving questions of class by the wayside. Insistence on peripheries, then, is a way to force class back into the discussion. Kiberd's chapter in *Inventing Ireland* "The Periphery and the Centre" traces a distinction between rural/real Ireland and the inauthenticity of the urban Ireland, pointing out that "Dublin was in 1904 a classic example of a periphery-dominated centre, that is to say, a conurbation dominated by the values and mores of the surrounding countryside" (484–485). This reading of the Dublin of *Ulysses* sets the stage for a series of productive but ultimately incomplete analyses of both that novel and its consequences, and indeed, by the 1980s, this binary certainly no longer operates. As Smyth has noted, "the growth of the suburbs necessitated the reconstitution of the traditional dualistic urban imagination" ("Right" 26).

The peripheral novel therefore develops specific ideas about working-class spaces, using a vocabulary different from bourgeois conceptions of public and private, nation and community, productivity and usefulness. In this, it meets repeatedly with resistance, seen "as one aspect of a cultural degeneracy, wherever it was encountered, and as a challenge to a unified national language" (Snell 48). I shall turn in a moment to this challenge to language, but first will note the focus on place as well. Let us recall Michel de Certeau's distinction in *The Practice of Everyday Life* between space and place, which Andrew Thacker has usefully compared to Henri Lefebvre's: "Place thus resembles Lefebvre's official representation of space, while 'space' is closer to a combination of Lefebvre's representational space and spatial practice" (31). Not fixed terms, place can be seen to correspond to a map as space does to a walking tour, one being fixed, immobile, and formal, while the other is characterized by movement and unofficial use. Through everyday actions, "ordinary practitioners of the city" (de Certeau 384) reinvent the areas they move through, thereby serving as active creators as well as subverting efforts to control from above. As David Harvey notes, "Superior command over space has always been a vital aspect of the class (and intra-class) struggle" (232); spatialization is linked—positively or negatively—to power and control.

For Thacker, the instability of spaces calls to mind Foucault's notion of heterotopia, a real but alternate space that by its difference from everyday places unmasks their constructedness. Foucault sees them (somewhat confusingly) as existing on opposite ends of a spectrum:

> …either their role is to create a space of illusion that exposes every real space, all the sites inside of which human life is partitioned, as still more illusory (perhaps that is the role that was played by those famous brothels of which we are now deprived). Or else, on the contrary, their role is to create a space that is other, another real space, as perfect, as meticulous, as well arranged as ours is messy, ill constructed, and jumbled. This latter type would be the heterotopia, not of illusion, but of compensation…

Among the spaces that he suggests display heterotopic functions are prisons, brothels, colonies, cemeteries, fairgrounds, museums, libraries, and Scandinavian saunas. Presumably referring to the positive manifestations, Harvey calls them "particular spaces of resistance and freedom from an otherwise repressive world" (213). It is crucial then to pay attention to how spaces function for those most in need of resistance and freedom; hence I will reference not only the role of urban planning in these novels but attend also to the creation and maintenance of spaces with both liberating and restrictive potentials, from the jail cell that encloses Sammy to the doctors' offices that serve as sites of official reprimand for so many characters here to the role of the pub and the exotic (and seldom-reached) travel destination.

One further aspect of heterotopia deserves attention here. By connecting the material to the metaphoric, Foucault expands his explicitly geographic notion of heterotopia to encompass "a form of writing that undermines an ordering of knowledge" (Thacker 27). Not specifically writings about place, heterotopias can then be seen to "dessicate speech, stop words in their tracks, contest the very possibility of grammar at its source" (qtd. in Thacker 28), a move that reconnects his ideas with de Certeau's. The insistent analogy for both Foucault and de Certeau is between negotiating space and writing, a logical connection, since writing is the translation of language into space. "The act of walking is to the urban system what the speech act is to language or to the statements uttered" (387). What, then, of those who cannot walk?

James Joyce and the Urban Periphery: Toward a Working-Class Modernism

The link of spatial, class, and regional explorations to form is what connects all the writers I cover here, distinguishing their projects from other writers throughout the century and forging a bond with Joyce. While other antecedents are clearly important and will be referenced within particular chapters (Burns and Beckett for Kelman, for instance, Kafka for Galloway, and Dickens and O'Casey for Doyle), Joycean traits are part of what link these writers in their attention to space via local language. Like them, Joyce used textual innovation to distance his texts from reductively national identifications, aware of the constraints consequent to geography, class, and colonial status. Clearly, the novels of all the writers I discuss, and especially *Ulysses*, which I will soon turn to, engage with a multitude of ideas beyond the ones I refer to here, but the convergence of innovation and localism merits careful attention, especially in the case of Joyce, whose texts have been seen through so many prisms it's hard to know which ones best characterize what the text cares about.

In keeping with larger critical moves to reconceptualize representation in literature, recent Joycean readings have distanced themselves from Leavisite suggestions that Joyce's politics mirrored those of Stephen Dedalus, who viewed nationality, language, and religion as "nets flung" to hold the soul "back from flight" (*Portrait* 203).

Stephen's politics, it is reasoned, are supplanted by those of the texts he occupies, in particular of *Ulysses*. Critics still tend to see *Portrait* as marked by the sort of quietism and aestheticism that used to be regularly associated with all of Joyce's work, often hailing *Ulysses* as the "solution" to the first novel's presumed elitism.[15] Such a formulation, of a developing Joyce progressing from immature and unpalatable views to reasoned and balanced awareness of Ireland's postcoloniality and the virtues of mass culture, ignores the class readings and textual experiments so present in *Portrait* (and *Dubliners*) that anticipate the larger political and formal shifts that are played out in *Ulysses* and *Finnegans Wake*. Far too much criticism isolates in *Ulysses* itself a "*Portrait* section," similar in its modernist but relatively straightforward voice to Stephen's *Künstlerroman*. To do so ignores the radical experiments that take place throughout *Portrait*. The opening pages conjure "Oxen" and the *Wake*, for instance, quotation marks and other punctuation marks are absent (as they were in *Dubliners*), and neologisms arise from words imploded into one another, known as portmanteau words.[16] What links this career is the question of class, which is presented by Stephen in the opening pages of *Portrait* and influences his actions and Bloom's throughout June 16, even figuring into the "litter" in *Finnegans Wake*.[17]

As with *Dubliners* and *Ulysses*, *Portrait* shows itself to be invested in explorations of spaces, both urban versus rural as well as within homes and institutions, exploring notions of public and private and the class associations they carry. Stephen's epiphanic moments repeatedly take place outdoors, for instance, seemingly outside social constraints that connect home to social status quo. As Pericles Lewis has stated, "The role of language itself in *Portrait of the Artist as a Young Man* emphasizes the lack of a dividing line between the household and society at large" (95). Hiding under a table cannot spare young Stephen from the social pressure to "apologize" (8) for instance, setting the precedent for tensions explored via the blurring of boundaries.

Stephen's first encounter beyond his family is with boys at school. Nasty Roche engages with him by asking about his strange name.

> And when Stephen had not been able to answer Nasty Roche had asked:
> —What is your father?
> Stephen had answered:
> —A gentleman.
> Then Nasty Roche had asked:
> —Is he a magistrate? (9)

The second question here, like the inquiry into the origin of the name Dedalus, is left unanswered. The first question anticipates Stephen's impending discomfort with nation and origins, while the second engages with the class status of the Dedalus family, which declines markedly through the novel. Stephen replies with a dodge when he calls his father a gentleman, as such a term tells its hearer little about the bearer's actual status, so Roche retaliates by linking class and nation, wondering if Stephen's father holds an imperial post.

Formally, the exchange between Roche and Stephen is most notable for the austerity of its tone. All the sentences are brief, and the narrative voice is practically absent. Colin MacCabe has written that the absence of metalanguage in *Dubliners* forces the reader to produce meaning for the text (13). This leveling of distinction between artist and audience also challenges the standard hierarchy of the omniscient or first-person narrator whose perspective controls the text. As in the Christmas dinner scene soon after, in which the narrator recedes and a diegetic mode of pure dialogue dominates sequences where Dante and Uncle Charles fight, this scene declines to give us clues to how it is to be read. The speech tags—"said" throughout the dinner, and "asked" and "answered" in the magistrate scene—further retreat from comment. (Only the use of the past perfect, as in "had asked" gives us any indication of a narrative presence recalling a moment at all.)[18]

By declining to interpret the scenes for his readers, Joyce places the responsibility of a class-based reading on them, in marked contrast to the heavy-handed narrativizing later in the text, as when Stephen experiences his "bird-girl" epiphany: "Heavenly God! cried Stephen's soul, in an outburst of profane joy" (171). The narrator's input in this latter moment inflects our reading of Stephen's epiphany; more than that, it creates our reading, making sure that we sense both the intensity and the irony of the moment, the replacement of religion by art and the inability of Stephen to articulate his commitment to the latter except in terms of the renounced former (hence "profane"). But as John Paul Riquelme has pointed out, throughout the text, "[t]he ambiguous merger of voices makes it difficult, even impossible, for the reader to distinguish between the cunningly combined voices of character and narrator" (54). We cannot tell here if the narrator is some iteration of Stephen himself, someone using Stephen's own language to frame the scene, or a voice that Stephen himself will emulate. This merged voice—a clear cousin to the collective voices of *Ulysses*—diminishes narrative hierarchies through rendering all voices potentially equal.[19] The same result can come, paradoxically, from the narrative sparseness of the Nasty Roche exchange. Curiously, Joyce's class commentary often occurs in the austere mode, almost an analogy between textual and linguistic poverty. While the soaring language of epiphany may call more attention to itself, the everyday sections with their sparser qualities bear as many Joycean signatures.

One aspect of the nonepiphanic sections of the novel that simultaneously seems childlike in its affectlessness and foreshadowing of more radical Joycean experiment is the use of portmanteau words. The use of portmanteau words is linked in *Portrait* to everyday moments—to draw on Moretti's vocabulary of literary evolution, the moments of epiphany in *Portrait* are an artistic dead end for Joyce that he does not repeat in *Ulysses*; rather, his experimentalism is at its height in the everyday sections. In *Ulysses*, "sanctity will be offered to ordinary experience" (Tóibín xiv) and it is these moments of everyday that most closely resemble in form and subject matter the direction taken by *Ulysses*.[20] This investment in the everyday connects Joyce to de Certeau, who reads users of culture not as consumers but as active producers, inventive and innovative. Looking at such quotidian activities as talking, shopping, and moving through space, de Certeau notes their creativity: "Conversation is a provisional and collective effect of competence in the art of manipulating 'commonplaces' and the inevitability of events in such a way as to make them 'habitable'" (xv). In such an interest, de Ceteau redirects attention away from climax, conclusion, permanence, and propriety and toward the makeshift, the fragmentary, the temporary. This sort of interest in anticlimax and disorder conflicts with both Aristotelean conceptions of dramatic form and the novels taking shape in the wake of his neoclassical revival. The denial of reader gratification through indefinite endings and other thematic disruptions—Tóibín writes as matter of fact that Joyce "was against plot-lines and character development and closure" (xiii)—merges with formal challenges at the level of language to undermine traditional novelistic expectations. In tying these aspects in *Portrait* to domestic scenes in particular (the scene at Christmas dinner ends abruptly, for instance), Joyce also begins to make a statement about public and private spaces.

If there is a tendency to link women to home and thereby to contain them, in reference to *Ulysses*, Catherine Whitley pertinently links such choices to formal decisions. "Joyce experimented with various ways to interrogate these power relations by playing with concepts of interiority, both of people and places...specifically...connect[ing] women to interior spaces and to the 'interior monologue' in his efforts to craft a prose less intrinsically repressive" (35). Certainly throughout

Ulysses, women's appearances are disproportionately indoors; by looking at a woman we see only on the public streets of Dublin, I want to extend the discussion of form, spatial peripheries, and class.

Dilly Dedalus's Working-Class *Ulysses*

Ulysses is regularly cited as the "classic" novel of Dublin, a text in love with its setting, as much about place as character. Curiously, for such a novel, a great deal of it takes place or stems from *outside* of the city, whether the nearby Martello tower where Stephen begins his day, the Howth Hill where Bloomsday imaginatively ends, or the distant lands that so many characters fantasize about throughout the day, from Gibraltar to Palestine to Paris. Joyce famously wrote the text outside of Dublin, far outside, after having lived for a time on the outskirts of the city. Like so many young people with artistic ambitions after him, he was unwilling to live with his family and was forced by lack of finances to live on the urban periphery.

So, a concern with the margins, borders, fringes of the city—once it is articulated in this way it makes sense that *Ulysses* is a novel of physical peripheries, since it cares so much about other forms of liminality, from religious difference to physical disability to colonial status. Garvey notes that women are another instance of liminality, "a limit, a border site, and women can be pushed beyond the limit, out of the spaces of action and power in the patriarchal city" (111). This connection of gender to physical spaces recurs throughout the book. The geographic edges are not mere analogy for these other liminal spaces but important in their emergent status as suburbs. Drawing on Victoria Rosner's notion of suburbs as a "generative site" (2) for a new form that picks up on the class element that never got fully played out in modernism, I turn to the link of periphery and class, focusing on one episode in the novel—the tenth, conventionally known as "Wandering Rocks"—and particularly on one character in that chapter, Dilly Dedalus, Stephen's younger sister.

There are a number of reasons why it is tidy to focus on "Wandering Rocks" in particular. First of all, "Wandering Rocks" begins, in parallel with the entire novel, with Father Conmee heading away from the town, an emphasis on the undercurrent of centrifugal forces in *Ulysses*. In addition, "the episode itself is neatly closed off by a summary of its events and then a return to its opening scene, as the male actors never fully accept the fluidity that runs through, around, under Dublin" (Garvey 113). Moreover, like the novels of *Narratives of*

Class, "Wandering Rocks" does make experiments, but its form of experimentation is not on its surface radical. Unlike "Circe," say, "Wandering Rocks" allows itself to be read conventionally, as do, for instance, Doyle's novels; it is only after some reading of his early novels in particular that the charged nature of their rebellion from the norm becomes evident. Indeed, while analysis of some episodes of *Ulysses* inevitably revolves around form, critics tend at most to note the depersonalized style of this episode. (The historic critical obsession about "Wandering Rocks" focused on realism, the naturalistic promise that with a stopwatch and a map, the movements of various characters can be timed to intersect precisely.) Karen Lawrence detects in the style a "defamiliarization through meticulous facts"; the "narrative mind exhibits...a 'lateral' or paratactic imagination: it catalogues facts without synthesizing them" (83). She goes on to write that such "verbatim repetition imparts a curiously mechanical quality to the narrative" (85). In general, those critics treating form cannot resist reading a moral quality into this style—something of the scrupulous meanness of *Dubliners*, although the voice is not the same—and most detect in the chapter a pessimism. Anne Fogarty characterizes this line of analysis as a consensus that the style represents "fragmentation, confusion, and misinformation...mirroring the alienation and moral errancy of Dublin life. In particular, a generalized perception of early twentieth-century Irish society as lacking in political direction and enervated by colonial rule seems to inform the negativity of such conclusions" (61). While Weldon Thornton, ever the contrarian, concedes the naturalistic "narrator's agenda about the city [is] designed to demonstrate the confusion and loss of identity inherent in the urban environment" (*Voices and Values* 140), he sees this effort at objectivity not only laced with irony and sarcasm but undermined at the level of plot by the "many acts of charity and kindness, large and small, that run through the episode" (138).

There are indeed acts of charity and kindness, pointing to, in many cases, just how much their recipients are dependent upon the goodwill of others due to their own economic desperation. Mark Osteen points out that although "Wandering Rocks" takes place in the middle of the working day, between 3 pm and 4 pm, few of its characters are at gainful labor. "Virtually every one of the sections of 'Wandering Rocks' details an economic exchange—begging, borrowing, purchasing food, pawning, gift giving, gambling, auctioning—in which one party receives more than the other...[which] must be partially attributed to the economic deformations produced by the imperial presence in Ireland...Dubliners can no longer conceive of equal economic relations" (176). Michael Tratner reads this economic multiplicity more positively, seeing *Ulysses* offering many liberations, including "the normalization of being in debt, the freedom to spend first without saving" (19), opening with Stephen and Buck comfortably not paying what they owe.

But the freedom to be in debt is a gendered one, as is the freedom to move. Stephen and his father are both able to borrow during the day, while the Dedalus sisters repeatedly fail to participate in the exchange economy. Don Gifford and Robert J. Seidman have divided "Wandering Rocks" into sections of "progress" and "fixed locations." "[P]redictably, no women make it into sections of 'progress'" (141), notes Bonnie Kime Scott. The three Dedalus family scenes in the "Wandering Rocks" episode are all static scenes; unlike so many episodes during the day, and in particular contrast to the progress of Father Conmee and the Viceregal whose movements bracket the chapter, these scenes take place at fixed locations. Given that we see both Simon and Stephen on the move elsewhere, and that this is the only section in which the Dedalus daughters appear, the fixity of their scenes underscores their immobility, their entrapment within their poverty-stricken life. Class mobility may be a possibility for those who are a part of the capitalist system of currency and exchange, but the girls—who fail to sell Stephen's books and receive food via donation rather than purchase—have no commodities to offer (unlike Stephen, whom we see being paid by Mr. Deasy; Simon's borrowing from Jack Power is closer to the girls' dependence, but he is still able to engage with the exchange economy, getting drinks and a shave with his money). Along these lines, Peter Hitchcock points out that the washerwomen in *Finnegans Wake* are not technically proletarians because they do not produce goods but rather exchange "a use value (as service labor) for a use value (as money) within a relationship that Marx terms 'simple circulation'...the washerwomen's labor is important but in terms of class does not 'exist' except in the ghostly presence of a folded sleeve or a spotless collar" ("Joyce's Subalternatives" 32).[21]

Certainly Dilly's clothes are not folded or spotless, and her impact on the Dublin circulation of commodities is spectral. Bloom has passed Dilly at the beginning of episode eight, when she is waiting outside the auctioneer's to meet her father (who is late because he is drinking); Bloom remarks on her appearance, and mistakenly assumes that she is making a sale, attributing to her an economic status she cannot attain. The fact that Dilly does not move between Bloom's sighting of her and her meeting with Simon accentuates her financial immobility. This static female character has precedent in Joyce's oeuvre: Howes reads the peasant woman standing at a half door near Clongowes and again in Davin's stories, both in *Portrait*, as a way for Stephen to "see himself as part (however problematically) of the national community... his conflation of these women and Ireland consistently involves versions of a contrast between a stationary woman and a traveling man" (74). In a like manner, Joyce obscures both Dilly's movements, and those of her sister Maggy, while the Dedalus men have directed movements. If Howes reads such stationary women as helping Stephen to locate himself within some version of Irishness, however, then the fact that the Dedlaus sisters are not seen in motion points to the exclusion of the poor from constructions of nation.

Our first mention of Dilly in "Wandering Rocks" is in a scene in which she does not appear; Maggy has returned home following her effort to pawn the books, followed by Katey and Boody's return from school. The Dedalus kitchen is described as "closesteaming" (186/10.259), an example of Joyce's tendency, rampant throughout *Portrait*, toward "portmanteau" words: the kitchen is close and steaming. The creation of portmanteau words here moves beyond the expression of the everyday as the site of new forms into the sort of multidimensional punning that will mark every sentence of *Finnegans Wake*: for not only is the kitchen close, crowded, hot stuffy, enclosed, and steaming—full of steam, hot, stifling, maybe smelly—but it is also a place where *clothes* are steaming, being boiled.

This boiling of shirts comes as bad news to Boody, who was hoping for food, but according to Kimberley Devlin, it is likely to be a source of income for the strapped family. Given that Bloom's earlier sighting of Dilly honed in on her physical condition—"Dress is in flitters. Underfed she looks too" (125/8.41), it seems improbable that it is the family's own wash on the stove. Rather, the presence of clothing where food should be, being stirred as though a soup, requires the girls to get food from another source, and indeed, the pea soup they hungrily down has come from the nuns. The Dedalus sisters can thus be seen as antecedents to the gossipy washerwomen in Anna Livia Plurabelle not just in their status as alienated nonproletarians but as voices of women engaged in manual labor in order to survive. Though Hugh Kenner calls their poverty "genteel squalor" (qtd. in Osteen 193), both their own father and a divine one have failed to provide and their "material and physical struggles" correspond to genuine "human misery" (Fogarty 58, 76).

The failure of the father is further emphasized when Dilly reprimands and begs Simon in a scene soon before her encounter with

Stephen, knowing by his intoxication that he has money in his pocket. He originally gives her a shilling, eventually parting with almost another shilling, but Dilly suspects he has five total, one more at a minimum (196/10.711). Simon expresses concerns about Dilly's body ("Stand up straight girl, he said. You'll get curvature of the spine. Do you know what you look like?"), then calling his daughters "an insolent pack of little bitches" (195/10.681) when Dilly asks for more money. Simon sees women's bodies in terms of their appearances, assuming that like bitch dogs, the girls can as a group fend for themselves. Dilly leaves her father with her pittance, while Simon, clearly in possession of enough money for at least a few drinks, heads to the Ormond bar for an afternoon of song, drink, and reminiscence. It is of course his path, not Dilly's, that Bloomsday tourists pursue. Indeed, for all its specificity, the novel does not make explicit where the Dedalus family lives as it does Bloom or Stephen, even though its mention, in "Ithaca," takes place immediately after the giving of multiple other exact addresses (670). Whitley's generalization that "in *Ulysses* women and children traverse the city and appear in public spaces without quite the same sense of danger or displacement as was present in Joyce's earlier work" (38), but this is followed up with the astute reading that the text seems to be "[a]dmitting that the public/ private distinctions upon which the modern family are founded are artificial and unrealistic" (38); city is no longer the animus so much as the father with whom they share their home.

Although Simon tells Dilly to buy herself a bun and some milk—physical sustenance—with the extra pennies he gives her, the girl instead browses some bookcarts, where she will encounter another member of her family whose financial situation, while uncomfortable, is not nearly so dire as her own: Stephen.

> —What are you doing here, Stephen.
> Dilly's high shoulders and shabby dress.
> Shut the book quick. Don't let see.
> —What are you doing? Stephen said.
> A Stuart face of nonesuch Charles, lank locks falling at its sides. It glowed as she crouched feeding the fire with broken boots. I told her of Paris. Late lieabed under a quilt of old overcoats, fingering a pinchbeck bracelet, Dan Kelly's token. Nebrakada femininum.
> —What have you there? Stephen asked.
> —I bought it from the other cart for a penny, Dilly said, laughing nervously. Is it any good?
> My eyes they say she has. Do others see me so? Quick, far and daring. Shadow of my mind.

He took the coverless book from her hand. Chardenal's French primer.

—What did you buy that for? he asked. To learn French?

She nodded, reddening and closing tight her lips.

Show no surprise. Quite natural.

—Here, Stephen said. It's all right. Mind Maggy doesn't pawn it on you. I suppose all my books are gone.

—Some, Dilly said. We had to.

She is drowning. Agenbite. Save her. Agenbite. All against us. She will drown me with her, eyes and hair. Lank coils of seaweed hair around me, my heart, my soul. Salt green death. (*Ulysses* 10.854–877)

As in *Portrait*, elements of narrative flatness direct our attention away from narrative voice: Dilly's initial question has no question mark, and Stephen's first question receives the tag "said" rather than an interrogative tag. The discussion of the textbook highlights the fact that Stephen and Dilly are of different classes because of different genders, that Stephen is not providing financially for a family very much in need, and that all discourse involving books is necessarily financial. As much as they represent "symbolic goods" (McGee 73), they also are physical goods, actual commodities. Dilly's respect for their symbolic status rests on desire for the physical. For Dilly, learning French is a way to imagine acquiring the currency, if not the comforts, of a middle- or upper-class life (which she has heard about from Stephen, who has lived in Paris). It is interesting that Joyce chooses to use language acquisition as the site for Dilly's efforts. While Stephen, like all the men through whose eyes we have seen Dilly so far, sees her frail body and recalls her inadequate footwear, Dilly is interested in the trappings of education that have no physical corollary; she knows that a poor girl studying French will gain only signs. Dilly's interest in French thereby ruptures the linkage of money and cultural capital, making external signs like appearance unreliable.

In Dilly's purchase of a book instead of food, a book whose physical condition, like her own body, is dilapidated (note in particular that the book is also inadequately dressed, "coverless"), Joyce challenges the association of men with the mind and women with the body that both Dedalus men assert. Given Dilly's class position, the unconcern for comfort or appearances lays claim to French and learning and other emblems of privilege for the poor as well. Our last actual glimpse of Dilly (she will haunt Stephen for the rest of the day, each reference to her connected either with food or clothing) shows her reading as she heads home to the margins of the text.

Class, gender, and space are again linked in the "Circe" episode, when the lower class women of Nighttown seek to support themselves through the bounty of the gentlemen they entertain, be they English soldiers or the Irish middle class. Crucially, Nighttown is the site of some of Joyce's most radical experiments, including the changing of Bella to Bello in the playscript representing Joyce's biggest challenge to realistic representation and a full-scale blurring of boundaries of inner and outer. The staging of the scene places women in doorways or entirely inside rather than on the street, a parallel to Molly's containment throughout the day. The gender shifts that take place once Bloom enters Bella Cohen's establishment has a slight parallel in the Dilly scene above, as Stephen sees both himself and Charles I in her. The link of formal innovation to concern with the working class is a major part of Joyce's project. Tratner: "the unconscious is identified with the working class and women, and the emergence onto the public stage of these previously invisible social groups is coded within the works themselves as entwined with, if not the cause of, the disruption of narrative form" (16).

The interdependency of the female and working-class voices and the formal innovations of the text is not the most often-noted of Joyce's varied legacies, but the connection of a nation, class, popular culture, and form in Joyce does provide a new voice and tradition. Admittedly, beyond Flann O'Brien's continued link of social criticism to local literature, most of Joyce's progeny in the decades following his death followed other innovations he made or ignored his political edge, and indeed, within Dublin, Joyce became an oppressive symbol for certain writers, paralleling his ensconcing by the mid-century critical establishment. For instance, in 1990, Ferdia MacAnna rails against the shadow of Joyce on the literary landscape, suggesting that Joyce "had hijacked the city and imprisoned it in his writings, out of the reach of ordinary people and other writers" (18). Here MacAnna uses a spatial metaphor, rendering Joyce's crime physical; ironically, he identifies issues of place and class that many critics had yet to address. Claiming that widespread writer's block arose because Dublin had already "been captured in its entirety—from its pub characters down to the shopfronts in Joyce's masterwork" (18), MacAnna posits two arguable points: first, he suggests that Joyce's project was representational, when his attention to facsimile served, paradoxically as I have noted, to challenge the power of realism.[22] Moreover, MacAnna's reading of Joyce casts a Dublin static in time, ignoring the reality that Dublin by the mid-1980s was, at least in some locations, a "vibrant zone of creativity" (Kiberd 609). Granted, MacAnna is right that Joyce casts a big shadow and he's both insightful and funny in noting that bildungsroman, short story, and experimentalism, as well as Dublin's geography, had all been effectively claimed by one Joyce oeuvre or another; he seems less aware that his description of the varied media at last given a forum in Doyle's drama, which he sees as "more influenced by local environment and modern pop culture— television, advertising, rock and pop music, pub life, etc" (25), marks a modernizing of the ephemera Joyce as well sought to recuperate. MacAnna's essay achieves in part at least its polemical goals, making the case for the need for new forms of writing (after having dismissed experiments in form, it must be admitted) and making explicit critiques of the literary establishment that anticipate some strands of postnationalist criticism. But if his interest is in part to waken Dublin from the nightmare of its history, he instead fosters debate about the relationship of past to present in a nation where such conversations do tend to be fraught, and his critics have shown themselves to be reasoned, articulate, and delightfully pointed despite his assertions of a dull and monolithic academia.[23]

In making the claim that the so-called dirty realism of the 1980s and 1990s offers an alternative to Joyce, MacAnna is complicit in an ongoing construction of Joyce as elitist and inaccessible. Rather, the attention to the intersection of class and geography in his works reveals Joyce to be an influence in his link of national and class critique with emphasis on local language and formal innovation. Indeed, Linden Peach contends that "[a]part from unhelpfully eliding the work of very different authors, the concept of a school of writing devoted to the dirty realism of Dublin, developed by Ferdia MacAnna and traceable to the 1960s, can underemphasize...geographical location...for the Dublin suburbs are themselves zones of contested meanings where 'relocation' and 'reinscription,' the utopian and the dystopian, come up against each other, sometimes violently. In writing about working-class suburbs, Doyle locates his text in a place that literally has no stability and sense of certainty" (149). Despite his dependence on spatial metaphors and investment in "reclaiming Dublin," then, MacAnna's insistence on firm definitions and categories overlooks the blurriness of the peripheries and fails to do justice to the very spaces he would invest with such significance.

In recognizing that Joyce does speak to ignored spaces and voices, Margot Norris writes "Joyce's lyricizing of the working talk of lower class Irish women in 'Anna Livia Plurabelle' can be glossed historically against the gamut of prevailing poetic practices in modernism" (5). Similarly, Hitchcock argues *Finnegans Wake* is aware of the inadequacy of language and gives voice to the washerwomen in acknowledgment of their subalterneity. Joyce then writes in opposition to the very practices MacAnna sees him representing. Some of his stylistic choices work directly to avoid any quietism ascribed to modernism in general and to empower multiple discourses. "In *Ulysses* the discourses of British colonialism, Irish nationalism, lowbrow popular magazines, the Celtic twilight, Catholicism, and other belief systems all have their say, yet all are unmasked and demonstrated to be 'inadequate to reality.' ... no one discourse is privileged or indeed has any meaning except in dialogue with other discourses" (Fairhall 60). Fairhall's suggestion is that no single discourse is adequate, and his list focuses on powerful voices, but Joyce works not just to debunk a monologic presumption of superiority but to enfranchise those silenced. His inclusion of the female and working-class voices and the formal innovations of the text together provide an example to the writers I discuss. While this strain of writing is not the most often-noted of Joyce's varied legacies, the connection of a nation, class, popular culture, and form in Joyce provides a new voice and tradition. But with the development of localist writing, Joyce can be seen as an influence in his link of national and class critique with emphasis on local language and formal innovation.

Connecting Kelman, Doyle, Galloway, and McNamee to perhaps the most dominant voice in high modernism recuperates the highly political statements Joyce made, validates the use of experimental form toward political ends, and renders continuous a trajectory of engaged and innovative literature throughout the century. This notion of historical continuity is especially important in the context of romantic nationalism, which relies on disconnection from the past to support its isolationist claims. "[I]f regional power without European integration runs the risk of neotribalism, an integrated Europe without devolution runs the risk of neoimperialism" (Kearney, "Postmodernity" 590–591). For Kearney, localism avoids the dangers of both nationalism and imperialism, via political innovation. Similarly, both cosmopolitan formalism and realism are mediated by a localist literature drawing on both as filtered through its own language. Old forms and traditions are not so much rejected as reinterpreted, made multivocal.

The mid-century career of Flann O'Brien, seen by many to be Joyce's heir in both his wordplay and his sentiments about Irish nationalism, offers insight into the roots of recent neonationalism and antecedents of contemporary urban literature. O'Brien's choice to write his 1941 novel *An Béal Bocht* (*The Poor Mouth*) in Irish (he did not allow a translation to be published during his lifetime) emphasizes the significance and limits of writing in one's own language. (The phrase "to put on a poor mouth" means "making a pretence of being poor or in bad circumstances in order to gain advantage for oneself" [O'Brien 5]). While he was bilingual and published a number of brilliant novels in English, O'Brien chose to address issues of class and national identity most explicitly in Irish. M. Keith Booker suggests that *The Poor Mouth* exposes the poverty of monologism, whether purely Gaelic or purely English ("O'Brien" 179). Rather, it is the hybrid of the two languages, the interlinguistic puns made for the benefit of bilingual readers that captures what O'Brien characterizes as Irish identity. Rather than reflexively condemn English's prevalence, an incontrovertible aspect of Ireland's history, O'Brien makes the positive move of discovering the advantages of control over both languages. His narrator, for instance, with his fluent Gaelic and poor English, is able to garner government subsidies and mock a government worker.[24] Like Doyle's 1987 blend in *The Commitments* of Dubliny lyrics and African American soul music, such a combination confronts traditional hierarchies through creative use of multiple discourses. O'Brien's novel depends on a bilingual readership for its humor and meaning to assume their full depth; in the same way, the rural setting requires an urban corollary in the minds of its narrator and reader. So, while *The Poor Mouth* takes place in the countryside, it can be seen as a predecessor to the novels of the urban periphery in its construction of city.

O'Brien's send-up of the veneration of poverty-stricken Gaelic villages mocks the validation of a culture based on its authenticity, which precludes the possibility of change. "O'Brien's novels are generally set in deromanticized contexts and comically undermine the standard revivalist opposition between the country and the city...which idealized the rural landscape as a timeless and primeval idyll where the noble Irish peasant could live his life uncomplicated by the social and commercial relations of contemporary urban existence" (Kearney, *Transitions* 86). In both Ireland and Scotland, with its often similar romanticizations and a similar contained urban underclass, by the end of the twentieth century, the political and economic focus shifts from the rural West and Highlands to the urban environment. For many, however, the concept of nation remains fixed, "embalmed," in Gibbons's formulation, still distinct from the working class. Just as the intentional maintenance of a poor, premodern way of life for the surveillance, study, and amusement of urban gentlemen underlines the constructedness of national identity, and the poverty of O'Brien's

Gaels leads to their enshrinement as national emblem, the poverty of the Dublin northsiders excludes them from national definition and points up the constructedness of class divisions. Yet as exterior to nation as the working class is seen to be in Ireland or Scotland, it experiences its own romanticizations. O'Brien and Doyle both redefine Irish identity to expose the poverty of reliance on myths of authenticity.[25] With an eye to O'Brien's depiction of the ongoing economic oppression of his hybrid, dialogic protagonist, *Narratives of Class* recognizes that the blends of realism and modernism, of cosmopolitan and local forces, and of national and postnational/postcolonial identities established in these texts are not merely emancipatory or constraining conditions; rather, they are responses to the cultural conditions of the British Isles at the end of the twentieth century.

A poor mouth, then, is one that can speak only one language. Narratives of class on the urban periphery, by virtue of their exteriority, call attention to the poor-mouthedness of aggrandizement or romanticizations based on national origin or social status, revealing the richness of local identities evolved beyond constructions of nation, engaging in international discussions and maintaining their own distinctive sound. The stories they tell are specific and universal, rejecting the privilege accorded to certain sorts of characters through their dissolution of narrative and speech hierarchies. These authors represent a new movement on the British Isles, drawing on and reacting to modernism and postmodern experimentation. The pages that follow seek to explore the richness that can spring from refusing to put on a poor mouth.

Chapter Two

"Ye've No to Wander": James Kelman's Vernacular Spaces

The first time James Kelman was nominated for Britain's prestigious Booker Prize, in 1989, he skipped the awards ceremony. Kelman's excuse was a writing course that he would not cancel, but his decision to stay at home acted as a physical corollary to his disconnection from the literary establishment as well. His wariness was confirmed in 1994, when one prize committee judge, Rabbi Julia Neuberger, resigned in protest as Kelman's *How Late it Was, How Late* was named the winner. Conflating discomforts with regional patois, profanity, and stylistic experimentation, Neuberger said she found that the novel, in "broad Glaswegian dialect, littered with F-words...was too much, too inaccessible, and simply too dull...the novel does not appeal to me, I do not find it amusing—and it never changes in tone" (Neuberger 27).[1] Essentially, Neuberger's objections to tone, character, and action in the novel suggest a thwarting of both her literary expectations and her expectations for a realist working-class novel.

This sort of opposition is no surprise—postmodern fiction is regularly rejected by the public at large as unreadable, humorless, or over the top. Yet curiously, Neuberger's evaluation resembles contemporary academic criticism of working-class literature, even in the work of some of Kelman's staunchest advocates.[2] Where Kelman himself takes pains to interrogate nationalism, and more importantly, idealization of the working class, both types of essentialism have sometimes been wistfully reinscribed by his supporters, who often ignore in particular the effects that geographic spaces have on the politics and potential of Kelman's characters. Kelman's novels consciously place themselves on the periphery, mainly through their stylistic signatures and physical rootedness, drawing on modernist, realist, and regional ancestors to make stylistic innovations that level linguistic hierarchies; the novel's reworkings of narrative control, genre conventions, and lexical norms, generate a form that inextricably links critiques of physical banishments of society's undesirables to the snobbery of both the social and literary establishments.

News reports from the day after the Booker awards ceremony repeatedly pick up on versions of Neuberger's remark that Kelman "is deeply inaccessible for a lot of people" (Majendie, Winder, Llewellyn Smith). The physicality of the critique, the idea that Kelman's prose (or he himself, as some quoting Neuberger relate it) cannot be reached, constructs Kelman's oeuvre as remote, hard to get to, distant. If Kelman is condemned by some readers and lionized by others for his unreachability, it is exactly this remoteness that his novels repeatedly return to as the source of their protagonists' woes. Certainly the stylistic choices that alienated Neuberger themselves develop in part to characterize and depict the plight of Kelman's peripheral, isolated men. Kelman's formal experiments with punctuation, speech tags, and quotation marks, combined with his thematic concerns with immobility, entrapment, the everyday, and bureaucracy, not to mention the overlap of these two categories in attention to clichés, narratability, and language hierarchies, all center around the dynamics of accessibility.

Rejecting Realism

The roots of the British public's hate and love of Kelman's prose come from fluency with and expectations of several novelistic traditions, all being challenged and violated by fiction that resists easy classification. *How Late it Was, How Late* uses standard English only when it must, opting to rely instead on Scots, specifically Glaswegian, dialect; the novel seems anti-English on a number of levels. Contemporary England, with its (post-)Thatcherite budget cuts and continual deindustrialization, represents for Kelman an unacceptable status quo, a continuing system of exclusion and repression. At a 1988 conference in Glasgow, he connected his critique of Britain's class system to his simultaneous discontent with "literature" and "pulp":

> Ninety per cent of the literature in Great Britain concerns people who never have to worry about money at all. We always seem to be watching or reading about emotional crises among folk who live in a world of great fortune both in matters of money and luck...Or else we are given straight genre fiction...The unifying feature of all genre fiction is the way it denies reality. This is structural—in other words, if reality had a part to play in genre fiction then it would stop being genre fiction. (qtd. in C. Craig, "Resisting" 99)

Kelman rejects the tastes and norms of the British metropole he is "supposed" to please. He writes instead for a local audience, his prose showing as well a studied application of both the techniques and ideas of continental European modernism. His unwillingness to fulfill the reading public's desire for easily consumable working-class Scottish voices places him at the epicenter of a movement shifting literature from the universal to the local. Diasporic voices and those rejecting metropolitan norms have sprung to the forefront of global literature; the work of the "Glasgow School," including Tom Leonard, Alasdair Gray, and Janice Galloway, epitomizes this move to the local, the nonstandard, the fractured. Along with Jeff Torrington and Liz Lochhead, and most notably publicized in the *Trainspotting* frenzy of the mid-1990s, Kelman articulates the distance of a majority of Scottish voices from a mainstream British language and identity.

In many of his theoretical pronouncements, Kelman calls for a more realist fiction, but his novels reveal a nuanced awareness of the oxymoron regularly overlooked in that term. Kelman makes us aware that although we have come to accept certain modes as "more realis-tic" than others, any act of writing involves so many conventions that the claim of approximating reality may be misdirected. Moreover, he questions why realism ought to be the continuing project of the work-ing class. With Kelman's reworkings of a stream of consciousness and his disavowals of a single, verifiable truth, he operates on the level of realism as a goal, rather than a style.[3] As Cairns Craig puts it, "Kelman's working-class realism is tactical rather than essential" (105), that is, realism not a product of an uncritical belief in an author's ability to accurately reproduce a fixed, knowable external reality. While his rendering of working-class life offers a fresh approach to reality and may for a time seem "more realistic" than earlier forms, Kelman plays on the limits of realism. Such a realism works to create not the most representational prose, but one that, As Joseph Valente notes about Joyce, "offers a representation of the *act* of representation" (190). This writing at one remove from representa-tion includes a number of devices and modes of storytelling generally undefined by the conventions of realism.

Still, despite his technical artistry, Kelman is regularly seen as a "mere" realist, a spokesman of his class. Fay Weldon has claimed that Kelman's novels are not literature because their language of "rough recorded vernacular" could be overheard on any night in a Glasgow pub. Relating this story, Angela McRobbie laments that because of assumptions about "high" and "low" literature, "the writer whose material is working-class life is destined to be understood only as a realist." I want to leave aside for the moment the disparaging of real-ism implicit in both Weldon's and McRobbie's remarks[4] and suggest that Kelman's novels defy both realist and genre expectations, achieving at a formal level a simultaneous pose of realism and sense of estrangement through their narrative innovations and their transliterations of Scottish pronunciation and dialect.[5] *How Late, A Disaffection, A Chancer,* and *The Busconductor Hines,* Kelman's Glaswegian novels, employ various techniques to buck expectations of narrative control, genre conventions, and lexical norms, not to mention political and national poses, creating a language and a form free from overt hierarchy, expectation, or nationalism, ready to critique with one gesture Britain's class system and literature's class system.

The two class systems are to Kelman interchangeable in their romanticizing of class distinctions, making such differentiations seem natural, inevitable, and aesthetic. Kelman has noted that historically, the working-class characters whose language is so quaintly garbled have been equipped with an equally inaccessible inner life:

> Every time they opened their mouth out came a stream of gobbleydy-gook! Beautiful! Their language a cross between semaphore and Morse code; apostrophes here and apostrophes there; a strange hotchpotch of bad phonetics and horrendous spelling—unlike the nice stalwart upperclass English here (occasionally Scottish but with no linguistic variation) whose words on the page were always absolutely and splendidly proper and pure and pristinely accurate, whether in dialogue or without, and what grammar! Colons and semicolons! Straight out of their mouths! An incredible mastery of language...the narrative belonged to them and them alone. They owned it....We all stumbled along in a series of behaviouristic activity, automatons, cardboard-cut-outs, folk who could be scrutinised, whose existence could be verified in a social or anthropological context. In other worlds, in the society that is English literature, 80 to 85 percent of the population simply did not exist as human beings. ("Importance" 82)[6]

By reading punctuation as a physical presence on the page, Kelman casts it as one of the forces explicitly employed to keep working class characters, literally, "in their place." Casting consciousness not as a state but a location, Kelman depicts the *place* deep thought inhabits as having geographical corollaries, a characterization that implicates space in one's ability to be understood. Keeping this in mind will act as a corrective: whether laudatory or disparaging, discussion of Kelman's work—and of *How Late* in particular—tends to focus on form to the extent that content is ignored. The plights of Kelman's benighted characters, not to mention the environments implicated in their agonies, are crucial determinants of the stylistic choices he makes. The tendency to analyze the resistance Kelman makes via his prose is meaningless without reference to location.

For this reason, it is particularly significant that the opening scene of *How Late* takes place in a trash-ridden vacant lot, where, as the novel opens, Sammy Samuels awakens from his drunken sleep to the gazes of prosperous tourists. Kelman begins the novel with a reference to waking in a corner, an explicitly physical placement of the body that anticipates the emphasis on the interaction of self and environment throughout the novel. On the littered ground, a site that mirrors Sammy's throwaway status in society, Sammy becomes part of the scenery for what he concludes to be foreign tourists, a parody within the novel's first pages of the gritty realism expected of an urban, working-class novel, the "beautiful female publicity officer" a stand-in for a civilized narrator "obliged no to hide things" (2) from the tourists whose gaping gaze parallels that of the reader. Sammy, lower-class and disgusting, on the margins of the margins of society, is exactly the sort of character Kelman sees as usually having no more than a "stock character" role, never getting a break from social services or society at large. Not only does he have no job and no prospects, his fortunes take continual turns for the worse. Unable to remember where he has been, he vaguely recalls elements of a two-day drinking binge. Almost immediately, he has a fight with passing "sodjers" (police),[7] and is thrown in jail, only to wake up blind from the beating he has received. The remainder of the novel traces Sammy's efforts to recall what has happened, resist the coercive assertions of the police that he is involved in political terrorism, and figure out how to carry on his life, especially given that his girlfriend seems to have disappeared. We are inside Sammy's head for the entire novel, free associating with him as songs and sayings and memories direct his consciousness, deciphering with him the voices and inflections that must replace visual cues.[8]

This fact that Sammy is blind both underlines his alienation from place (in the Lefevre-ian sense, as distinct from space) and exerts a particular weight on the novel's voices—they are responsible for conveying all of a Barthesian "world effect" themselves, with no third person omniscient narrator providing descriptions of the scenery. Like a reader reduced to the typographical, dependent on imagination to construct images and voices from the words on the page, Sammy relies largely on his hearing, his perception limited to interpreting voices and pauses. Kelman parallels the novelty and estrangement of Sammy's state by omitting from his text most of the descriptors or speech tags his readers are accustomed to. In scene after scene, we experience the same disjunction as Sammy, uncertain of who is speaking, where the voices come from:

> Voices at last. He kicked the kerb again. Could ye give me a hand across the street? he said.
> What?
> I cannay see.
> ...
> I'm blind.
> Ye're blind?
> Aye.
> Sammy heard the guy sniffing like he was making up his mind if it was true. I left my stick in the house, said Sammy.
> Aye right pal, okay, hang on a minute till the lights change...Then the guy whispered something and somebody whispered something back. And Sammy's bottle went completely. A sudden dread. There was more whispering. What was it christ he knew the voice, like he knew it; and it wasnay good man it wasnay fucking good: it could be any cunt.[9] (53)

Especially this early in the novel, the dialect and the pauses combine with sporadic punctuation and the lack of quotation marks, attributions, or narrative tags to make the passage tough reading, a parallel to this period in which Sammy's blindness is brand new to him. There seem to be at least three speakers in this scene (plus limited narrative interjections), but the text never lets us know who they are any more than "they" tell Sammy who they are. Instead, we are confronted with vagueness ("somebody" and "something"), as well as slang ("his bottle went completely," i.e., lost his nerve). This colloquial speech acquires regional valence with the presence of words like "cannay" and "aye," which locate us specifically in Scotland.

Kelman's use of such regionalisms would seem to place him in a tradition of provincial literature; at the same time he intersects with the bulk of the modernist canon in his treatment of urban space and the disaffected individual. A third clear influence is the realist tradition and its proletarian tendencies. Early criticism of Kelman has tended to notice two of the three legs of this "triangle": "urban realism and existential modernism are not mutually exclusive in Kelman's work" says Simon Baker (245), while Robert Crawford's reading of modernism as provincialism/regionalism allies these two phenomena in the "barbarian, but also sophisticated" voices Kelman creates (285).[10] And from the social realism of the 1930s to the present, the connection of realism and regionalism has been common, a link that class-based readings of Kelman enjoy noting.[11] Yet Kelman repeatedly expresses discomfort with these labels, his refusals and reinterpretations of them appearing both within his fiction and in other forums such as interviews, speeches, and nonfiction essays.

To examine how Kelman contests constructions of working-class literature, let us revisit briefly the idea of realism as a style. Glasgow's working class has long been the object of efforts to render language and scene accurately on the page; Anette I. Hagan cites a 1866 novel, George Mills's *The Beggar's Benison*, as an early effort notable in part for its intent to "disapprove of its speakers and to show the middle and upper classes' disdain for both the dialect and its speakers" (218). This sort of representation of the poor for their social superiors was not uncommon in Victorian fiction, often censorious and didactic. Because written by outsiders with less of an investment in accuracy than mood, similar work over the next one hundred years tried to balance the appearance of authenticity with readability.[12] While the now-famous *No Mean City* (1935) was originally composed by an unemployed man from the Gorbals slum district, Alexander McArthur, it was only brought to press once it had been reworked by a journalist, H. Kingsley-Long. "Evidently produced for a readership unfamiliar with the living conditions portrayed in the novel, it has an unsympathetic third-person narrator who records events chiefly for the sake of sensationalism…the use of dialect supports an impression of the outlandishness of the setting" (Hagan 229–230). The use of a third-person narrator is in keeping with the goal of placing the Gorbals residents on display; the goal of realism here is to present an authentic image of an exotic otherworld.

Dialect literature is regularly invested in such a goal; contemporaneous to the publication of *No Mean City* and in response to work like it, we see the rise of writers circles within the working class, their practitioners often dedicated, according to Christopher Hilliard, "to correct[ing] the stereotypes and distortions produced by authors from other classes…As well as rebutting middle-class 'sneers' and 'caricatures,' plebian authors tired to provide authentic portrayals of working-class people that would displace outsiders' accounts. Many of these texts had middle-class readers as their implied audience, and the narrative voice occasionally shifts into an explanatory mode for reader unfamiliar with the industry or trade in question" (118–119). With this didactic aim and the privileged addressee, such work retains the formal characteristics of the fiction it strives to supplant.

According to Peter Hitchcock, who draws on Raymond Williams's terminology, novels of the working class retain a residual form because even 200 years into the project of working-class novels, "literary expression is bound by a dependence on received or traditional forms.... [not] ... autonomous or specific in purely formal terms" (Hitchcock, *Working Class Fiction* 101, 108). In other words, a working-class novel uses forms first developed in other novels; it is distinctive mainly on the levels of plot, setting, or character conversation, assumed, as McRobbie points out, "to be unconcerned with experimentation and even with shape" (40). Alan Sillitoe's *Saturday Night and Sunday Morning* exemplifies this sort of working-class writing that uses a residual form. *Saturday Night*, a novel about a boozing, rakish, factory worker named Arthur Seaton, retains a narrative in the third person and firmly conventional plot development and narrative sequencing. Ironically, even a working-class novel in part about how the working-class seldom speaks for itself does not let the main character narrate the tale. Rather, the narrative voice uses standard English, nearly all regional and class dialect relegated to the space between quotation marks. Arthur would never say that the "wood smelled of primeval vegetation," which is how the narrator characterizes an outdoor lovemaking scene, an episode in which Arthur himself declares, "'We's'll be comfortable 'ere'" (45). The ancient and almost condescending sound of the word "primeval" even suggests a speaker who feels more highly evolved than his narratees.[13]

In the words of Barbara Foley, at stake here is whether or not "proletarian writers who worked in the form of the realistic novel ended up confirming the very world order they originally set out to oppose" (48), whether realism is wedded to a world view.[14] Kelman, unlike Sillitoe and other prior working-class writers, rejects the inherent linguistic superiority of narrator over character. Moreover, he avoids equating narrative progress with economic advancement, even shunning the notion of plot development. David Craig credits Sillitoe with writing what may be "the first passage ... which evokes a factory worker's from the inside with ... finesse" (D. Craig 103), yet the novel still seems to emphasize the "tragic impossibility of escape from the working class for those with special gifts ... [and] the implication of a lost potential" (C. Craig 100). Middle-class consciousness and status remain norms and even goals, implying the desirability of a trajectory or progress in much the same way as plot resolution is desirable in conventional novels, radically different goals than Kelman's choice to disintegrate narrative hierarchies as a means of critiquing social ones.

Christian Mair brings up a relevant point in his comparison of Caribbean writers, Sam Selvon and V.S. Naipaul, who both create narrators emigrated from Trinidad to Britain. Naipaul's narrator in *Miguel Street* speaks standard English while sentimentally looking back at the Port of Spain slum of his youth: "the narrator's mastery of the literary standard becomes an outward sign of his personal growth...[whereas] Selvon refuses to place his fiction within the 'diglossic' sociolinguistic framework of Caribbean society...[and] develops 'nonstandard' Creole into the language of the third-person narrative" (Mair 145–146). In novels like *The Lonely Londoners*, to which Mair refers here, Selvon uses Creole outside passages of direct speech, while Naipaul, more in line with Sillitoe, contains such dialect within quotation marks and opts for an assimilated normative narrative voice that uses standard English. In this way, even novels that deal sympathetically on a thematic or plot level with marginalized populations may, on a structural level, reinforce the exteriority of nonconventional speech and speakers.[15]

Such exteriority is seldom absolute; in *Saturday Night*, the narrator occasionally shifts into free indirect discourse, allowing Arthur's speech rhythms and slang into the narrative framework. For instance, Arthur suspects that his affair with a married woman is evident to her husband: "[Jack] must know: no man could be that batchy" (Sillitoe 46).[16] Mainly, however, Sillitoe again seems wistful; it is the anarchist thoughts that Arthur has that are allowed to bleed into the narrator's discourse, such as "They think they've settled our hashes with their insurance cards and television sets, but I'll be one of them to turn round on 'em and let them see how wrong they are" (115). Sillitoe does want his characters to seem to be in control of their lives. The final chapter, ceded entirely to Arthur's mode of expression through free indirect style, shows Arthur deciding to marry and join the status quo. Arthur sits alone, thinking about how "you couldn't concern yourself too much"(188) with fears of war, his only hope of escape from his working life coming in a vague rumbling of anarchy. The moment of capitulation to societal expectations and norms is enacted in the character's own voice. Yet the choice of free indirect discourse here is revealing. We never enter a realm of direct free thought; there is no first-person narration. While Sillitoe clearly hopes that Arthur will take action someday (a point reinforced by the handing over of narrative reins to Arthur's language), he seldom allows his character an entirely unmediated voice in the text, this choice unconsciously paralleling the passive containment of the working class in the comfortable and ever-rising standard of living of the late 1950s in Britain.

While Sillitoe obviously wrote with a political agenda, he repeatedly declined classification as a working-class writer, resisting the likelihood that his sentiments would be attributed to the working class as a whole. Sillitoe wanted people to see Arthur as "an individual and not as a class symbol" (qtd. in Hitchcock 80). Rather, in John Kirk's astute analysis, "The working-class text is defined as such not because it speaks a working-class consciousness in some monologic and unified sense, but because the narrated dialogics—the clashing styles and voices, which represent class relations rather than a single class utterance—signify the existence of class antagonisms" (Kirk 72). Still, his voice has come to represent the postwar generation's teddy boys, a group who, as Dick Hebdige points out, "acted out" on weekends with elaborate dress while ultimately conforming entirely to society's expectations (51).[17] The tension between creating a portrait of an individual and speaking for an entire class too often already presumed to be monolithic in its tastes and desires leads Sillitoe to downplay the class elements in his work and instead emphasize the personal, his insistence on the individuality of his characters itself becoming a political statement.

Kelman's position is made possible by this earlier refusal. Indeed, Kelman's novels build on the individuality of Sillitoe's characters but work as well to dethrone the normative narrative voice, refusing to translate for middle-class readers. Previously, Kelman argues, working-class characters "were confined to the margins, stuck in the dialogue, kept in their place. You only ever saw them or heard them. You never got into their mind. You did find them in the narrative but from without, seldom from within" ("Importance" 80).[18] In freeing his characters from quotation marks, Kelman makes it very difficult for us to distinguish between passages of direct speech, passages of narration, and passages of interior monologue. Drew Milne points out that this blurring "offers neither a representation of speech as speech, nor an authoritative written register which might distinguish author from character" (Milne 395). Unlike the authority of Naipaul's or Sillitoe's narrators, no one portion of the text seems dominant or can act as the "key" to understanding the rest.

Milne's remarks posit a hierarchy of modes of expression, a range of registers from pure to patois, raising the question of who controls speech and language in narratives. For instance, nineteenth-century realist fiction, as Hitchcock aptly describes it, "articulates social relations through the construction of a hierarchy of discourses [which] appear to present history without a narrator while confirming omniscience as the guiding principle of subjectivity" (*Working Class*

Fiction 96). An invisible omniscient narrator exists on a different textual level than a novel's characters and has access to their thoughts and vocabularies. Of course, Kelman's rupturing of such hierarchical language boundaries is not new: William Faulkner, James Joyce, and others have not only challenged the conventions of omniscient narrative, but have done so in a working-class context. In *As I Lay Dying*, Dewey Dell, Jewel, and Vardamon will occasionally speak with language that they clearly would not realistically have knowledge of or access to. As Stephen Ross explains Faulkner's technique, the valuation of "'substandard' dialect over 'correct' English" (106) works precisely because a hierarchy exists. Without prior knowledge of the perceived superiority of standard English, readers would not be able to appreciate its displacement, a fact that ultimately reinforces the existence of a hierarchy of linguistic registers. Drawing on Bakhtin, Ross states that "The mimic always remains in some sense superior to the speech (or gestures) imitated, for he or she possesses mastery of both the originating and the mimicked voice" (108). Additionally, the reader's place in social hierarchies is presumed—he or she must be someone who is capable of recognizing and understanding both standard and nonstandard language. Ross argues that for Faulkner, this would mean readers are in the position of well-off whites, able to mimic and understand black and lower-class characters who could not in turn mimic standard English. "Transcribed speech, the product of mimicry, always occupies an inferior position in relation to the diegetic discourse of its production. The mimetic voices we hear are always secondary, indulged and condescended to by the reader who hears the author's power over all the voices" (108).

Kelman upends this analysis of how language hierarchies function. His characters, like Faulkner's, can access language likely to be beyond their purview. Yet while Faulkner's tendency to attribute "sophisticated, highly figural rhetoric to ordinary or even uneducated dialect speakers" served to "fulfill narrative goals" (Ross 85) such as the creation of a collective psychic mood, Kelman uses momentary disruptions of narrative hierarchy as places to contest our assumptions regarding the limitations of working-class minds, reconfiguring conventional hierarchical distinctions between narrator and character, between educated and uneducated speech, and between written and spoken forms of expression. While in jail for the second time in the novel, Sammy recalls a cellmate who died in prison, perhaps from a beating by guards. Thinking of his unexplained estrangement from his girlfriend, Helen, he conflates his situation with the other man's: "yer man, lying cold in his lonely room, a dark cavern of mental solitude. That was definitely the line from a song man, no question" (190). There appears to be no distinction between the narrator's voice and Sammy's in this paragraph: the sentence begins in Sammy's own voice and idiom, "your man" ("that guy"). Sammy himself recognizes the lyrical phrase that follows as a departure from his own voice, but unlike credited song lyrics throughout the novel, this one is not set off via indentation on the page. Rather, it is incorporated into the main body of the text, implying that it is part of the body of country music lyrics that Sammy aspires to create someday. Sammy's identification of the phrase as a song lyric may even imply that he is aware of its melodramatic excess, implying a sophisticated grasp of the concept of varied speech registers (something the police, Ally, and all social service employees fail to detect in him). His scan of his own words places him in the role of interpreter, not just interpreted.

This shift enables the conclusions that follow if we accept that a narrative voice with Sammy's limited education and background can generate phrases like "cavern of mental solitude," or later, "So all in all he had entered a new epoch on life's weary trail" (214). Again we see a full sentence in standard English, again with an ironic tinge to it. Sammy, it seems, is not only able to mimic standard speech but also to parody it. Contrary to Ross's reading of Faulkner, Kelman's reworking of speech hierarchies questions the assumption that those who mimic speech must necessarily see "standard" as the norm to be deviated from. Rather than calling attention to the author's power over all the voices in the text, Sammy's momentary use of standard English reveals the traditional conception of the relationship of dialect to normative language to be limited in its failure to see that dialect speakers have the capacity to be multivoiced as well. By using demotic as the lingua franca, Kelman furthermore unsettles the traditional placement of the reader near the top of a social hierarchy.

Thus the presence of demotic beyond quotation keeps Kelman's text close to its characters, to the point that a shift to first-person narration might actually create a hierarchy or insert distance between reader, writer, and character, all of whom seem to be the subject of the second-person often used in especially emotional moments in the text. On the other hand, when Sillitoe moves into free indirect discourse, the shift is always clearly marked; it is evident that Arthur is supposed to be speaking. When the narrative voice resumes, it is again formal and controlled, distinct from Arthur's voice, with none of the slang he would use. Kelman's text is permeated with slang throughout; there is no point at which a nondemotic narrative voice is in control.

In his review of *How Late it Was, How Late*, Denis Donoghue mentions that he thought at first that "Kelman was using standard English to denote authority and demotic to give Sammy the only freedom he enjoys, freedom of speech" (46), but this pattern turned out not to hold up. Seeking normal narrative hierarchy, Donoghue sees the inconsistency first as problematic, then as nihilistic.[19] But Kelman defies such an easy compartmentalization of his narrative or his characters—letting Sammy speak only in nonstandard English would actually rob him of the very freedom Donoghue implies he could retain and would replicate centuries of narrative condescension. Rather, an inconsistent concentration of dialect ensures an unpredictability that encourages us to consider all languages in the text as equally qualified to express a particular thought. Moreover, the novel with dialect outside the quotation marks makes "a broader attack on the claim to objectivity of the class which controls writing" (Milne 396), undermining the foundations of consistency.

In a fashion similar to the use of demotic throughout the text, Kelman's decision not to use quotation marks at all in his novels works in tandem with regional speech and slang to prevent the establishment of a traditional narrative hierarchy:

> [T]he interweaving of spoken and written forms is made more emphatic by Kelman's refusal to use inverted commas as speech markers. The text is designed to visually resist that moment of arrest in which the reader switches between the narrative voice of the text and the represented speech of a character,…to create a linguistic equality between speech and narration which allows the narrator to adopt the speech idioms of his characters or the characters to think or speak in "standard English" with no sense of disruption. (Craig, "Resisting Arrest" 103)

Through the absence of quotation marks, then, narratorial clout is undermined as the distance between narrator and character is diminished, making it less likely that we will see the narrative interjections as more authoritative, as passing judgment on the characters.

Of course, Joyce was another metropolitan colonial writer who sought to destabilize the reader's experience, like Kelman in part through his disinclination for quotation marks. Ellmann: "[Joyce] was eager to preserve one typographical feature of the manuscript, the use of dashes instead of quotation marks, on the grounds that the latter 'are most unsightly and give the impression of unreality,' in short, 'are an eyesore'" (353). Joyce's call for realism here resembles Kelman's; neither seeks an established realism so much as a way beyond it. Also as with Kelman's prose, in Joyce the lack of quotation marks works simultaneously to liberate traditionally underrepresented modes of expression (whether dialects, inappropriate thoughts, or fragments of advertisements) and to suggest that the notion of the individual is flawed, that we are all, in fact, collections of voices and phrases. As Andre Topia points out about *Ulysses*, "The disappearance of quotation marks from the stream of consciousness is crucial...Nothing permits [one] to know *a priori* if the sentence 'belongs' to Bloom or not" (108).[20] Indeed, the idea of "ownership" of sentences, even phrases or words, is what is being explicitly interrogated.

This seems in part to be why Kelman relies less and less on speech tags in his later work. While *A Chancer*, *The Busconductor Hines*, and *A Disaffection* have no quotation marks, their narrators still offers us lots of direction: people say, reply, ask, exclaim, grin, smile, nod, chuckle, mutter, glare—all words that offer more or less subtle instructions to the reader. In *How Late*, however, not only are there far fewer attributions at all, but—in another parallel with Faulkner—the tag is recurrently "said." Sammy will occasionally sigh or sniff or smile, but he is the only character for whom we regularly have such details. The "said" ensures a narrative levelness.[21] In a related technique, Kelman most often eliminates all speech tags entirely in extended dialogues, making it extraordinarily challenging to keep track of who is speaking. Together, these practices leave the reader unmoored, far removed from a comfortable position of narrative knowingness. Part of this effect is again a consequence of trying to render us as blind as readers as Sammy is in his world (both he and we are used to far more cues than we are given) and part of it is an attempt to render all voices and moments potentially equal. These stylistic choices work against plot or development of story, creating a static, redundant feel and preparing us stylistically for the denial of narrative satisfaction at the novel's end.

As in *Ulysses*, where Bloom's stream of consciousness places a variety of external discourses on the same level, equating the authority of a line from a book with that of a music-hall song fragment, in Kelman's work, a number of discourses attain authority in the text, the traditionally "subservient" regional dialect now on par with the Queen's English. For Kevin J.H. Dettmar, it may be the refusal to remain consistent within a style that matters most. Dettmar characterizes current literary criticism as plagued by "modernist readings" even of nonmodernist texts. By a modernist reading, Dettmar means an interpretation that accords highest value to an aesthetic of continuity and inner formal logic, which he characterizes as primarily a modernist concern. Current critics, he argues, stress such cohesion even when it is not a major feature of the text, his main example being *Ulysses*. Dettmar suggests, for instance, that Joyce tried to downplay the novel's mythic overtones and continuity by leaving the Homeric titles out of the final draft (i.e., chapter one instead of "Telemachus").[22] Dettmar wants criticism to move beyond a "modernist" reading of *Ulysses* that praises—even insists upon, "discovers," or invents— formal cohesion to one that allows for and even valorizes inconsistencies of style. The strength of *Ulysses*, he feels, lies in its variety and chance discoveries.

This interpretation of *Ulysses* dovetails nicely with Franco Moretti's notion of literary evolution, in which "rhetorical innovations...are the result of chance" (*Epic* 6). Old forms discover new functions by accident—experiment generates solutions to textual problems: in the case of *Ulysses*, a multitude of styles is the solution to the question of how to characterize modernity, and stream of consciousness is the answer to the question of how to critique the notion of the individual. Moretti emphasizes the intervention of the fortuitous in the development of new techniques; here I want to look more at the element of problem-solving, at the question of why the use of a new form. Kelman opts to use demotic outside quotation marks, a studied randomness of style, and thus solves the problem of how to write a working-class novel that does not merely replicate the style of the dominant class. The decision to evade traditional language hierarchies and maintain a chaotic style throughout a novel enacts Kelman's challenge to traditional authorial authority.[23]

Through his innovations, Kelman builds on what Bakhtin perceives in *The Problems of Dostoyevsky's Poetics* as Dostoyevsky's success: "A character's word about himself is just as fully weighted as the author's word usually is; it is not subordinated to the character's objectified image as merely one of his characteristics, nor does it serve as a mouthpiece for the author's voice" (6–7). We sense less certainty, an "eschewal of the author's privileged position for himself, his own voice, a turning loose of his book to his characters" (Dettmar 32). Indeed, a number of critics have noticed Kelman's willingness to allow his characters ample space and control of the narratives they occupy. Ian Bell observes that "Kelman removes himself from the scene entirely," remarking upon the fact that Kelman's characters are "apparently unsupervised by an authorial presence" (232, 231).

But this ceding of control is complicated by the issue of class in Kelman's writing in a way not emphasized by Bell, nor in Bakhtin's analysis of Dostoyevsky. Literary merit is rarely a criterion for works by members of the working class, obliging Kelman to establish his artistic expertise while turning over his text to voices that would presumably lack his elegance, being "almost wholly unmotivated, inarticulate, and marginalised" (245). Kelman's position poses an interesting paradox: he needs to demonstrate that contrary to conventional assumptions/prejudice, working-class writers are capable of rhetorical heft and stylistic verve, yet this point is somewhat in tension with his political and technical desire to allow control of his narrative by his characters, whose voices have long been the defining counterweight to notions of learning and eloquence.[24] As Keith Dixon asks, "How do you contrive a literary link with a predominantly non-literary, and often anti-intellectual cultural tradition?" (99)

Certainly Kelman, more than his critics, sees the need to balance his stylization with his politics. His novels give the appearance of dialogic freedom through an extreme stylization. Kelman's use of spelling, for instance, reveals a strategic use of Glasgow dialect, his rhythms impersonate oral speech, and his supposed realism flouts realism's conventions. In each case, what seems to be casual (to Kelman's supporters) or incomprehensible (to his detractors) turns out to be a highly literary choice, down to the commas: "Every comma in my work is my comma. Every absence of a comma or a full stop or semicolon or colon is my absence" (qtd. in Lyall C20).[25]

This consciously literary quality of Kelman's writing is part of what helps him to escape the pitfalls of stereotypic urban realism, "caught as it usually is between the limited scope of the strictly urban voice and the intrusive commentary of the urban narrator" (Baker 247). His language is neither fully slangy nor anthropological. Rather, an English inflected by Scots becomes the lingua franca for all speakers in Kelman's novels. Drawing, then, on Kelman's negotiation of working-class literature and his stylistic expertise, what we see emerging here is the wedding of antihierarchical prose to regional identity, simultaneous to the divorce of realism and authority. The regional, working-class speech in Kelman's novels, realistic and disordered, confronts the neat conventions of realism as a style.

Breaking with Britishness

Kelman's explorations of working-class themes, settings, and characters via dialect have stretched existing critical frameworks, not the least paradigms of nation. Literary critics have sought to draw on elements of postcolonial theory to account for this longtime assumption of Scottish writers into the British canon and what has been deemed by Robert Crawford the invention of British literature.[26] According to Crawford, following the 1707 Act of Union between England and Scotland, terms like regional and provincial acquired negative connotations and any mention of Scotland at all took place under the presumption of a metropolitan readership. When writers did invoke their Scottishness or insert Scottish characters into their texts—Crawford mentions Smollet and Boswell as examples here—they played on English stereotyping of Scots. Allowing English prejudices to express themselves, Boswell and Smollet gently mocked them, but while neither man ever fully effaced his spoken Scots accent, both wrote in standard English, containing all dialect within quotation marks, within the mouths of characters like Smollet's Lismagaho, who is at once a figure of fun and a slight tug toward tolerance. In their efforts to assimilate, the Scotsmen who were the "first British" citizens/subjects marginalized an identity they saw as outdated.

More recent manifestations of Scottish identity in British literature include Sir Walter Scott's creation of a mythical Scottish past safely devoid of modern nationalism, the bathetic kailyard stories of the late nineteenth century, and Hugh MacDiarmid's reintroduction of Scots language into poetry. Unlike any of these, Kelman's writing comprises a seemingly contradictory blend of distinctively Scottish speech rhythms and an utter disavowal of Scottishness. In this vein, we can consider that perhaps more like Robert Burns than any Scottish writer since, Kelman is aware of his connection to a tradition he would shun. Burns exploited his regional identity as a way to avoid, but ultimately dominate, a nascent British (as opposed to English) literature. Not actually of the extremely humble birth often attributed to him, he allowed himself to be perceived as a peasant, a "mere child of nature" (Crawford 97). He appropriated (though with extreme, if unnoticed, irony) the degrading term "Scotch bard." The presence of extraordinarily learned images in his poems was regularly overlooked by those wishing to emphasize his racy Scots dialect; such emphasis could come both from those proud of their Scottish identity, or more regularly, those wishing to reinforce a sense of Scottishness as a throwback to a romantic earlier age. What both contemporary supporters and detractors of Burns generally failed to note, however, was his cagey use of a range of dialects from standard English to educated Scots to peasant Scots, as well as a blending of classical allusions and folk ones.

In "To a Mouse," for example, Burns speaks to a mouse whose nest he destroys with his plow; the whimsical device of addressing an

animal combines with the scenery of the field to create the image most
often seen of Burns, the clever rustic. Yet, the metrically perfect qua-
trains confront issues of mortality and perception, realizing a crucial
distinction between humans and other animals to be an understanding of the passage of time. While the occasional elevated word, such
as "foresight," ("But Mousie, thou are no thy-lane, In proving foresight may be vain") seems colloquial in the context of so many apos-
trophes and slang words, the mock-heroic tone contains a level of
irony often overlooked in Burns.

This mastery of multiple registers simultaneously is of a piece with
Burns's juxtaposition of his peasant language to his classical references. Burns can be explicit in revealing his learning, as in his Scots
"translation" of a passage from Ecclesiastes:

> The rigid righteous is a fool,
> The rigid wise anither:
> The cleanest corn that e'er was dight,
> Mat hae some pyles o' caff in;
> so ne'er a fellow creature slight
> for random fits o' daffin. (190)

The form of these lines as well as their theme addresses Burns's placement in a British tradition. The passage acts as an introduction to one
of Burns's critiques of ecclesiastical hypocrisy and points out the
impurities present in all of us, a commentary that could easily extend
to the inevitable corruption of language as well. Burns cautions
against an overemphasis on one's own righteousness or wisdom, here
repudiating his status as holy fool, a bearer of truth. His blending of
languages—the words are drawn in part from the King James version
of the Bible and in part from Burns's native Ayrshire dialect—mirrors
the mixing of "corn" and "caff."[27]

Burns, then, inadvertently serves as "one of the major figures in
the Scottish invention of British literature" (Crawford 109) through
his use of a combination of standard English, Scots dialect, and
even Gaelic. Kelman's relationship to the British tradition is similar. Like Burns, he writes in "English energized with Scots"
(Crawford 127). Like Burns, he firmly and clearly draws on a lower-
class Scottish identity, complete with a rejection of middle-class
morality. And Kelman is received, again much like Burns, as a
working-class scribe, despite the careful allusions in his novels. Yet
Kelman's allusions actually suggest where in the Western literary
tradition he thinks he belongs, avoiding English references in favor

of specifically Scottish ones, as well as European Enlightenment and modernist ones.

Unlike most writers of his class or subject matter, Kelman has clear connections to a European modernist tradition, in terms of influences, formal techniques, and mode of allusion. Such an aesthetic pedigree would seem to contradict the critical resistance to *How Late* in particular. But while Kelman's influences are highly canonical, his use of them often goes against mainstream readings, emphasizing the exteriority and class tensions present in texts sometimes lauded for aesthetics alone. The way Kelman comments on the Scottish social system, for instance, owes a great deal to Kafka's sense of the absurd, inflecting it with a class-based critique of bureaucracy: schoolteacher Pat Doyle, in *A Disaffection*, receives a transfer that he does not remember applying for. He refers to the principal of the school he teaches in by a number rather than a name, and he continually suspects surveillance by various authorities. Pat himself consciously alludes to "The Metamorphosis," when he compares his state to Gregor Samsa's, offering an intertextual connection within the plot. Cairns Craig has noted in reference to *The Busconductor Hines* that its setting is a "real Glasgow, but it is a Glasgow which exists to put [Hines] on trial, and that trial it is transformed into a Kafkaesque distortion by which Drumchapel becomes 'the District of D'" ("Resisting" 106). In *How Late*, Sammy is required to reregister with the employment bureau after being beaten to the point of blindness by the police, but first he must get a doctor to certify his loss of sight. Unwilling to grant him an appointment, the state medical system eventually refuses to confirm that he is blind. Sammy is removed from the rolls of his original work program but is not allowed access to openings for the visually impaired without a doctor's corroboration of his claim, because, as a Social Service representative who interviews Sammy tells him "Some jobs demand the capacity of sightloss dysfunction" (108), a reversal that makes his disability seem like an advantage, even a privilege! Sammy's blindness makes literal the concept of faceless bureaucracy that Kafka saw around him.

But Kelman's frustration with bureaucracy has a more explicitly political edge to it than Kafka's, making its location and the class positions of its characters explicit, largely through reference to accents. The cunning language games of those in power constitute one of the most Kakfaesque elements of Sammy's world at the same time as they form the center of Kelman's social commentary.[28] One of the major doublespeak debates throughout *How Late it Was, How Late* is about when and how Sammy became blind, the police and doctors all happy to contend that his condition is self-imposed, psychological, or false.

> At the police station: "I wouldnt be at all surprised if his allegation were to prove unfounded. I suspect there's nothing fucking wrong with them at all...Are you sure you're suffering sightloss?" (181)

And at the doctor's:

> Aye sorry for interrupting doctor but see when you say "alleged"?
> Yes?
> Are you saying that you dont think I'm blind?
> Of course not...In respect of the visual stimuli presented you appeared unable to respond.
> So ye're no saying I'm blind?
> It isnt for me to say.
> Aye but you're a doctor.
> Yes.
> So ye can give an opinion?
> Anyone can give an opinion. (225)

Just as the text offers no anchors through punctuation or attribution, the bureaucrats Sammy encounters offer nothing he can hold on to. Even phrases that would seem fixed ("of course not") here are ambiguous: does the doctor mean he is or isn't saying Sammy's blind? Recalling Foucault's textual and physical heterotopias, if language is a "non-place" (Foucault, *Order of Things* xvii), and heterotopias are "disturbing, probably because they undermine language" (xviii), Sammy confronts in the doctor's office both a language that has been destroyed, evacuated of the very properties of language, and an analogous physical space. Not only are doctors and police paralleled by their interchangeable state-sponsored skepticism, but the jail and medical office both operate as outlets for an evident yet hidden authority.

Authority is represented in part by accent; the police officer in the scene above has an English accent, while the SS person bears an educated Lowland Scots accent, implying a complicity of the upper classes and the British in maintaining Sammy's marginality; the difference that he perceives in their speech collapses into ultimate resemblance. Sammy's blindness and dependence on his hearing become more than just stylistic experiment here; his condition ironically parallels the discrimination he encounters when others hear his accent and are unable to "see" beyond it. Reflexively regarding his strong local accent as "provincial, vulgar, uneducated and unrefined" (Hagan 135), the interlocutors assume that Sammy's low social status means that he will be easy to manipulate verbally, and anytime a response is seen as inadequate, he is upbraided for not "knowing his place":

> [W]hat did you call him?
> Tam Roberts.
> Tam Roberts, the political, that's correct.
> …
> Eh?
> It's you the sarjeant's talking to Mister Samuels.
> Sorry.
> …
> Well?
> What?
> Tam Roberts, he's a political?
> Sammy smiled.
> What then?
> I didnay say that.
> Aw, must've been somebody else.
> …
> So what did ye say?
> I didnay say he was a political.
> We're no asking what ye didnay say, it's what ye did say, that's what we want to know. (169)

In this passage we see how what Sammy says, as well as what he does not say, can be used against him. His wary refusal to affirm the statements of the interrogators is read as an indication of his complicity in a terrorist plot. Silence is not an allowable response, yet all words are twisted against him. The Kafkaesque run-around here is not so much about bureaucracy as about how language works, the gymnastic contortions that words can be forced into. This betrayal by the language one must use to express oneself suggests as well a connection to the works of Beckett, who seems a likely inspiration for Sammy Samuels's name.[29]

Beckett is certainly a presence in *How Late*, not just in name, though the novel's title echoes the rhythms of *How It Is*. Sammy's difficulties walking, the ill-fitting shoes that are not his, his love of a wet and rainy countryside, his bleak yet funny insights—these elements evoke Molloy, Moran, Knott, Vladimir, Estragon. On a textual level, as well, the text has a Beckettian feel to it, its stream of consciousness, its cadences and pacing, and its repetitions and contradictions calling to mind one of Beckett's novels: "Even getting from here to the house, ye couldnay take it for granted. Ye couldnay. Ye thought ye could but then ye found ye couldnay" (329). The passage reads like Beckett spoken in a Glaswegian accent.[30]

Stylistically, thematically, Kafka and Beckett are Kelman's most prominent literary forefathers, though Goethe, Balzac, and Dostoyesvsky all receive mention in *A Disaffection*, and the subject matter of Dostoyevsky's *The Gambler* offers a point of comparison to *A Chancer*. Worth noticing here is the complete absence of any immediate British influences, less a nationalist or isolationist statement than a question of necessity, according to Kelman. In his readings, he found that no one had ever written from anything like his own experience before. "So because of this dearth of home-grown literary models I had to look elsewhere. As I say, there was nothing at all in English literature, but in English *language* literature—well, I came upon a few American writers" ("Importance" 83) as well as writers in Russian, German, and French. Robert Crawford sees much of the textual innovation of modernism as a consequence of provincialism, marked by the work of outsiders, "their most characteristic effects gained by combining materials on the outer edges—slang, foreign, dialectical—rather than simply rearranging the common pool with the literary and colloquial. There seems to be a geographical correlative of this, inasmuch as most of the High Modernists did not come from the centre of English culture" (Crawford 270). Operating from the periphery himself, Kelman derives major modernist influences from Crawford's "provincials."

Indeed, Deleuze and Guattari go even further in asserting the power of periphery. Kafka is the classic example they use in their exploration of the idea of a minor literature,[31] and Beckett, writing as an Irishman and then in French, occupies a peripheral position as well. Both wrote in languages not exactly theirs (echoes as well of Stephen Dedalus and his tundish), in countries not exactly theirs. The political situation of one's homeland is taken to be crucial in one's ability to rework inherited forms. Yet neither Beckett nor Kafka draws explicitly on a sense of place; their existential explorations tend to gain force from the seemingly generic quality of their settings. Further, their intertextualities are seldom so explicit as Kelman's. His use of both writers takes place mainly in his use of a modernist style of voice or rhythm, and more specifically, on a philosophical level, insofar as he explores the same issues of alienation.

While the solitude of Kelman's protagonists, from the loner Tammas and the isolated Rab Hines onward, connects him to Beckettian bleakness, and his explorations of the irrationalities of the structures of power riff on Kafkaesque absurdity, in the ethos motivating his stream of consciousness, Kelman's writing more closely resembles Joyce's. Joycean references and roots constitute a frame and point of reference that provides a structure both in terms of how Kelman uses allusion and in terms of how he negotiates a sense of identity within a nation whose language is both necessary and unacceptable. Some of the Joycean intertextualities are quite clear: "The penis floats on the sudsy surface of the water...Masturbation could never be a possibility here" (*D* 108–109), thinks Pat Doyle, incapable of a Lotus-Eaters moment of relaxation. Certainly, the anxious and irritating Pat is much more of a Stephen Dedalus figure with his pretensions, his distaste for humanity, and his aesthetic theories. He fantasizes about meeting, or even being, Hölderlin, philosophizes to his students, and frets in a ponderous stream of consciousness. We regularly hear echoes of Stephen in Pat Doyle and Rab Hines, from disillusioned efforts of the former to teach adolescents to a lack of respect for the schoolmaster and other authority figures down to the strained communication with siblings and awkward weak teas with parents.

Sammy has much more of the peripatetic Bloom to him: thirty-eight years old, sentimental—even mawkish, unaffected in his appreciation of songs, ambling quickly and superficially through a million received images and memories and allusions. The country music fragments in *How Late* offer the most Joycean instance of exchange, though paradoxical, between an individual and a collective mind, Sammy's friendly-hostile interactions at the pub calling to mind the Cyclops episode while his descriptions of failed efforts to connect emotionally with his girlfriend evoke Bloom's own physical awkwardness and touching missteps with Molly. This now-vanished girlfriend is named Helen, a Trojan allusion presenting a further connection with *Ulysses* as Sammy embarks on the wander of his life at the end of *How Late*. While the specificities of Kelman's geography of Glasgow are not nearly as exhaustive as the Dublin rebuildable from the pages of *Ulysses*, the specific mentions of bus lines and pubs and the negotiation of the city space evoke a Joycean sense of urban space as well as continually underline their evocation of a local identity.[32]

For Kelman, grounding his novels in a local setting involves negotiating between often conflicting definitions of the Scottish and the Glaswegian. While it is productive to talk about Kelman as a Scots writer in order to emphasize his similarities to Burns, he would hardly prefer this label to that of Britishness, a point he's made clear in repeated speeches and essays.[33] Certainly, "[t]he city rather than region or nation is the key analytic category" (Milne 394). The urban elements of Glasgow writing are significant on at least two levels. First, in response to the critical tendency to emphasize Kelman's Scottishness, Simon Baker offers the interesting theory that Kelman should not be viewed as Scottish because his native Glasgow, as a city that came of age in an industrial and imperial boom long after Scotland ceased to exist as a nation in 1707, is alien and even antithetical to the imaginary Scotland critics draw on (endnote 255). The patterns of immigration to Glasgow even render it ethnically distinct from the idea of a Scottish race. Second, "[i]n the cities, many Scots saw the real Scotland in terms of a proletariat whose identity was with other proletarians around the world, rather than with a 'people' or a nation in which the industrial city happened to be situated." (C. Craig, "Introduction" 5). Kelman's very existence as a writer shows the strain of an overarching nationalism, suggesting its historical exclusion of Glaswegians in particular presents opportunities for other allegiances.

If the best approach to Kelman is through a Glaswegian, rather than a Scottish, or certainly a British lens, we must deal with a host of especially Glasgow-based problems. "Glasgow is domestic, historyless, unimagined; there is no narrative to its existence, and consequently its life cannot be translated into artistic forms which depend on narrative for their effects" (Craig, *OH* 33). On a structural level, then, a Glaswegian novel would not conform to conventional notions of plot—authors including Alisdair Gray and Christopher Whyte have made similar arguments. Such a novel would have a distinctive linguistic traits as well: the introduction to *The Scottish National Dictionary* questions the value of Glaswegian as a dialect, arguing that it is constructed rather than natural, bastard rather than legitimate: "Owing to the influx of Irish and foreign immigrants in the industrial area near Glasgow the dialect has become hopelessly corrupt" (qtd. in Morgan, "Glasgow Speech" 195). Not a national capital like Edinburgh and certainly not an imperial center/metropole like London, Glasgow sits on the margins of history and of linguistic uniformity.

This state parallels the peripheral condition of other nonmetropolitan urban centers as well. Stefanie Lehner compares Glasgow to Belfast, noting both are "former imperial cities whose increasing poverty has been screened off in their official representation, as apparent in their respective 'City of Culture' campaigns" (7). Indeed, as once-prosperous cities hard hit by the decline of heavy industries, the two metropolises have both experienced first a decline in comparison to the rest of Scotland and the island of Ireland, and then a rapid gentrification of some neighborhoods that further widens the gap between the affluent and the marginalized. According to Luke Gibbons, urban marginalization in countries with a powerful sense of mythic history stems in part from the supposition that the locus of authentic culture is always the countryside; city is always corrupt, suspect, and "inauthentic."[34] Moreover, the very size of the population leads to inevitable dilutions of dialect, forcing the idea of place to come from other elements. Nationalism is hence denied to city dwellers, as one cannot be an "authentic" nationalist on the periphery of nationality, a condition characterized sarcastically but pertinently by Tom Nairn's criteria of "ethnic purity, rural bliss, ancestral gemeinschaft, [and] ineffable idiom-truths" (qtd. in Kane 178).

Disavowing this sort of genuine, pure identity motivates Kelman's own reading of where he is from. He suggests that the idea of Glaswegian identity is a late-twentieth-century construct, the state from which he inevitably must write rather than a glorious or burdensome condition. But because Glasgow, the "New York of Scotland" (Prime 47),[35] is only tangentially related to the rest of the country, rougher, distinct from it, it is Glasgow, specifically seen as an urban space, rather than Scotland, which anchors Kelman's prose. Although he steeps his text in region-specific language and grammatical constructions, Kelman's understanding of municipal geography leads him to downplay any unique qualities of his hometown. Versus a belief in an innate talent for blarney or the gift of the gab, he declares "There is nothing about the language as used by the folk in and around Glasgow or Ramsgate or Liverpool or Belfast or Swansea that makes it generally distinct from any other city in the sense that it is a language composed of all sorts of particular influences, the usual industrial or postindustrial situation where different cultures have intermingled for a great number of years" (Kelman, "Importance" 83). Kelman's catalog does not evoke images of cosmopolitan centers of fashion, high culture, and learning. Instead, the circumstances that generate this view of interchangeability seem to arise in connection with working-class areas of cities in particular. An urban identity is cast not as a romanticized, national one; rather, nothing special is seen to distinguish laboring cities beyond their hybridity. Terry Eagleton remarks that the specificity of *Ulysses* suggests "with its every breath just how easily it could have done the same thing for Bradford or the Bronx"

(*NCL* 15); again, the chosen areas, both of the Dublin of *Ulysses* and the industrial centers of New York City and Yorkshire, are scruffy underbellies rather than portraits of prosperity.[36] The Catholic victims in Eoin McNamee's *Resurrection Man* are deemed by Fintan O'Toole to be easily exchangeable for "Jews or blacks,...for these streets to be those of any European city, for Victor [Kelly, McNamee's homicidal protagonist] to be English or French or Italian" ("Darkness" 10). Whereas nation isolates what is special, class marks out the universal.

The voice from nowhere that so offended the Booker public, then, has clearly traceable roots, from a realist working-class tradition, from a European modernist one, and from Glaswegian and modified Scots identities. Geography shapes structural, stylistic, and linguistic choices, while class gives ideological meaning to these choices. If, as Frederic Jameson has suggested, "urban alienation is directly proportional to the mental unmapability of local city spaces" ("Cognitive Mapping" 353), Kelman's move to write within the consciousness, voice, and locale of Glasgow's periphery is designed not so much to convey alienation to middle-class readers as to combat that alienation.

"Middle-Class Wankers" and Working-Class Spaces

Kelman explores the issue of working class identity most fully not, as in classic social realist texts, at the level of plot development, but at the level of a character's or narrator's language. For example, the choice in *A Disaffection* of a working-class born teacher allows him space, like Selvon, to undermine the notion of "mastery" of standard English as a sign of personal growth. For one thing, Patrick Doyle is not more personally grown than the blue-collar characters in the book. A teacher of working-class adolescents in Glasgow, Pat experiences ongoing existential crises that he seeks to resolve through an attempted affair with another teacher, through musical creativity in the form of a homemade wind instrument, and through reconnection with his estranged family. None of his efforts is totally successful, however, suggesting that perhaps the solution lies beyond the personal, that it is the isolation of modern industrial society that causes his anomie. Within Pat's self-styled *Weltanschauung*, then, lies an indictment of the hearty individualism and companion work ethic that turn out not to function in contemporary Glasgow. An earlier or

more standard working-class novel might follow one of two predictable plotlines: either the success of the hero would show the advantages and freedoms offered by an education and a good job, or failure
would end in bitter disillusionment in expectations not met. With
Pat's disaffection, however, Kelman manages both to point to the
limitations of progress through social mobility and to make a critique
of such progress as a goal.

If anything, Kelman seems to imply that Pat's education and
supposed insights have led him only to a form of bourgeois ennui in
place of the more physical suffering of his family. Though Pat does on
occasion make use of sophisticated linguistic or grammatical forms,
such as the subjunctive mood, for the most part even his "intellectual" ruminations take place in part in his boyhood vernacular; a full
range of thought inheres even in "uneducated" argot. "[T]he world
ceases to exist when I shut the fucking eyelids. Okay! I'm going to
fucking wipe you out yous bastards" (221). Pat's existential questioning, reminiscent of Piaget and Descartes among others, yet slangy and
profane, implies that "deep" thoughts are not just the territory of
sophisticated speech.

But Kelman does more than merely point out that educated speech
is not unique in its access to complex ideas. There's a further twist in
Pat's musings: not only does the use of slang demolish the idea of
appropriate forms for certain subjects, the subject itself here critiques
the very terms of the philosophical debate Pat would enter. In fact,
reality is the exact opposite of Pat's philosophical fantasy. In his
thought experiment, closing his eyes would wipe out his aggressors;
in reality, their relentless rules and conformities are wiping *him* out.
Again, the value of a good education in the face of such an overwhelming System is questioned, both at the conceptual level and at a
linguistic one.

To complicate the matter, Pat himself is aware of the disjunction
between the language he grew up with and the one he now speaks, his
egalitarian politics confronted by assumptions about the superiority
of educated speech that are seemingly contained within language
itself. During a strained visit to his parents, as Pat contemplates his
guilt in avoiding them, the narrative moves toward their grammar:
"He should have gone straight home after the match. He just shouldni
have come here? How come he came? He shouldni have fucking came"
(114). From a proscriptively proper use of a past conditional, the language shifts to a slang, shouldni, and then slides into an incorrect
construction, "have . . . came," perhaps brought on by the intrusion of
the demotic, or perhaps by the presence at the dinner table of parents

who would say "have came," who Pat senses would feel awkward in the presence of their son's learned (in both senses of the word) speech. In either case, the move within so few sentences and within one voice calls attention to its leveling of speech hierarchies. In his attention less to a mimesis-directed representation of authenticity via voluminous respellings in local accent than to a grammatical challenge to accepted standards, Kelman's use of a narrative voice so likely to be demotic liberates slang to the level of true polyglossia. For centuries working-class and folk voices have been represented in novels, no doubt, but their place has always been tightly controlled by a narrator, by a hierarchy in which they were at the bottom due to the "continuing—and probably inevitable—presence of Standard English as a language of power" (Mair 137). Kelman challenges the inevitability in this pronouncement.

Yet like the scene with his parents, Pat's relations with his brother confirm that while Kelman may be more willing than earlier writers like Sillitoe to cede control of his narrative, he is simultaneously less idealistic about a working-class call to action. Where Sillitoe's working-class Arthur stood alone at his machine, Gavin, Davie, and Arthur—Pat's brother and his mates in *A Disaffection*—sit together at home. All three are unemployed, drinking the afternoons away, collecting their dole, wishing for work. This shift away from the historic settings of working-class texts, those workplaces that needed explanation for middle-class readers, emphasizes the plight of these characters at the same time as it declines to provide a tour guide for ethnographic observers. In a glancing connection to the proletarian fiction of earlier eras, these men do define themselves as workers, thinking Marx is "fucking great" because "he was for the workers and that's that, end of story" (274). The endorsement of Marx here by the lads is so casual as to render it dismissive on a textual level. Obviously wary of the "implausible 'conversion' plots" (Foley 46) marking previous proletarian novels, Kelman seems aware as well that his characters, while not insincere, lack conviction. The nod to Marx is a platitude, not a dogma.

Indeed, the scene highlights the "illusoriness of traditional modes of solidarity" revealed by the "destruction of the traditional Scottish industries" (C. Craig, "Resisting" 101) like the construction work Gavin is trained to do. Discussing working-class life in the 1980s, John Kirk points out "The spatial displacements of class became a distinctive feature of the period, as working-class communities, often based around traditional industries of coal, steel and the shipyards and docks, were closed down in rapid succession" (105). Notable in

Kirk's formation is the mention of specific industries linked to the identity of working-class characters. By the late 1980s and early 1990s, even trace allegiances to these professions have vanished— Kelman's working-class characters are displaced spatially and psychologically from a factory, shipyard, or mine-based identification. Their difference from Arthur Seaton in mindset and prosperity could not be greater.

The definition of characters in terms of work is therefore highly problematic, and Kelman's text is suspicious of traditional Marxism because although they are united, its so-called workers remain disempowered, with nothing to lose. Yet, such a reading of *A Disaffection* as a critique of Marxism falls short of the commentary that Kelman makes. Certainly, Kelman in no way discounts the presence and power of class tensions in modern-day Scotland. Pat has been trained as a teacher and had access to a university education that his older brother did not. When he arrives at his brother's house, mid-afternoon, it is because he has decided to leave his stable teaching job although he has no clear plans in mind. Throughout the scene, Gavin expresses anger and resentment: "More than half Scotland's no got a job. So you dont start treating it with impunity if you're lucky enough to have one" (255). Even jokes bear sharp edges, to the point that "The levels of irony were become slippery" (255). Tensions finally reach a head when Gavin calls teachers "middle-class wankers" (281), a charge indubitably directed at Pat. Gavin sees nonmanual labor as pointless, as evidenced by his substitution of "wanker" for "worker," which links the nonproductivity of masturbation with class standing. Pat, who wants to quit teaching expressly because of his powerlessness to effect changes in the lives of his disadvantaged students, cannot bear to hear the accusation he would likely level at himself coming from the mouth of his exploited brother. He begins to hope that Gavin's friends will "step into the fray and fix things so that all would be okay again and they could all be muckers and just sit back and I dont know christ anything, tell stories or something, wee yarns about going over the sea to Skye and Heraclitus and genies" (282).

Pat's response, then, is to return to the working class (and here he embraces and appropriates the usually degrading term "mucker"), swathe himself in regional speech—the word "wee" in particular has a Scots feel to it—and enter the world of myth. The first myths he thinks of are those of the island of Skye, a locus of Scottish national, and in particular, the more "authentic" Highland, culture. He then moves to Heraclitus, a seeming stand-in for a European or Western tradition, and then to genies, the exotic representatives of the rest of the world.[37] His list is significant in a couple of ways: first, he leaves Britain out of his geographic progression, implying the irrelevance of that category. Second, Pat ends up in the international sphere again, wanting to exchange myths with the workers of the world. In both his need for local myth and his internationalism, Pat seems to want or need to reromanticize the very working class about whose future he is so cynical.

Even more ironically, the scenario Pat hopes for, the sitting back and trading stories, is precisely the scene taking place, a scene more possible in the world of the unemployed. In romanticizing the workers, Pat eliminates work from his fantasy, using the term mucker for all of its connotations of fraternity while ignoring its implication of coarse (even disgusting) manual labor. Not unlike Gavin's uninformed embrace of Marx, Pat's supposedly more educated view, in its failure to account for labor, misinterprets what it means to be a worker. Here, then, we see the limitations of Craig's reading of the scene as social critique. Like Milne, McRobbie, and others, Craig lauds Kelman for eluding the very essentializing and proselytizing that such criticism can recapitulate. The idealism Kelman takes pains to critique with his slippery irony is wistfully reinscribed by both romantic Pat and sanguine Craig. "Once again the question is raised as to what discourse might provide sufficient force to emancipate the workers;…this is often quite literally an absence in Kelman's writing, a mode of response he refuses to write" (Kirk 131). Much as Kelman's characters make ineffectual nods to Marxism, Kelman's advocates approve the endorsement of Marx they find on one level without accounting for the critiques taking place on other levels.

What other levels? This is one crucial point at which Kelman's formal choices begin to interact with and influence thematic and narrative ones, with location acting as the basis for linkage. Amidst his longing for the Highlands and his wish for universal identification, Pat remains rooted, like all of Kelman's early protagonists, in distinctly unromantic Glasgow. Tammas, Rab, Pat, and Sammy all talk about leaving Glasgow, but we never actually see it occur.[38] A recurring allusion in the book is to Wilson's *Tales of the Borders*. This anthology of traditional stories is "a folklore, bonded to a particular landscape" (Crawford 140), which nursed for J.G. Frazer, for instance, "the fires of piety and patriotism in my Scottish heart" (qtd. in Crawford 157). The *Tales'* chief proponent in *A Disaffection* is a substitute English teacher who lacks the irony of the permanent faculty, most of whom scoff at the book's "unspeakable sentimentality" (12). Yet the pervasive presence of the *Tales* in the novel attests

to their continuing presence in Scotland as a source of national identification while the titular reference to boundaries underlines Pat's
entrapment in the local. The border turns out to be holding the
Kelman protagonists back, the physical corollary to their psychic
entrapment.

Pat's containment has a lower physical, material cost given his
improved economic standing, his status as a former member of the
working class—much like Hoggart and Williams—giving him an
authenticity at the same time as it opens him up to charges of romanticization, both of which he is acutely aware of. His modernist
narrative exposes the limitations of this line of discourse—or any
preexisting form, Kelman appears to suggest—to account for postindustrial working-class life. The reconsideration of geography throughout Kelman's oeuvre provides him with a means to develop a form
that addresses the challenge of avoiding romanticization. As the novel
with the greatest contrast in class standings among major characters,
A Disaffection is most explicit in its association of place with power.
According to John Kirk's astute reading, the novel:

> constructs an opposition… "sealed" in place geographically—Gavin
> located on an outer-city housing scheme, Pat ensconced within a
> wealthier part of the city itself. There may be a divide here between the
> periphery and the centre, but it is established within a wider hierarchi-
> cal structure of colonization and capital… The control and commodifi-
> cation of space rile Pat and, worse still, he recognizes his own duplicity
> as an agent of the imperialist state he so despises. (Kirk 125–126)

The spaces in which action occurs structure interaction and perception, reaffirming class differences and widening the gap between
those without power and those who benefit from the status quo.

In a move to combat both physical and social enclosure, it occurs
to Pat to drive away from Glasgow and from predictability, though
this possibility seems unlikely to his narrator/his consciousness:

> Hang onto your hat! He will not do it. He'll never get beyond the
> reaches of greater Glasgow. Such a thing is scarcely possible. He has
> always lacked a certain bon vivre, a certain affirmatio, a certain
>   Patrick Doyle, drove right out of Glasgow, late that Friday
> evening. (69)

Within this short passage, there are layers upon layers of languages.
Pat mocks the clichéd, upbeat mood of early newsreel reporting: hang
onto your hat. The passage becomes cosmopolitan, redundant, and

novelistic, passing through British, French, and Latin characterizations of his problem. Then it trails off, leaving the sentence grammatically and thematically unfinished, the condition undefined. When the voice resumes in a new paragraph, it becomes temporarily, parodically formal, traditional, and pedantic, sticking in extra commas and using Pat's full name.

Just as the surplus commas create grammatical errors, however, this authoritative final voice is wrong. Pat does not leave Glasgow, this night or any other in the novel. Like Sammy, Rab, and Tammas, Pat may repeatedly wish and plan to leave, but he is contained entirely within Glasgow. The only possibility of escape is offered by the multitude of unfinished sentences in the novel, the gaps and pauses that the narrative voice has left for him. More precisely, it is the absence of any dominant narrative voice that allows for this freedom. Indeed, the fact that the narrative voice is mistaken raises the possibility that much of what happens does not happen as described. Unlike novels where a patently and visibly unreliable narrator is often so undermined and mocked by his or her own text that careful readers can distinguish the "real" and "true" story, what "actually" happened beneath or around the lunatic rantings, the text here seems to invalidate the possibility of any narrator or reader being correct all the time. A character can escape the generally prescriptive power of narrative trajectory through actions that belie the narrative voice. Less illusory than myth or Marxism, grammatical freedom and formal change here have the possibility of generating a way out through emphasis on the local. Whether this is a genuine freedom or not is arguable—Pat's escape of the narrative voice equals his failure to escape Glasgow—but Kelman's formal decisions allow him to depict working-class Glasgow without reverting to clichés of gritty realism.

Throughout the novels, we observe tension between knowable and unknowable spaces, in which knowable does not correspond to public. Precisely because of Sammy's class status, the various government offices he visits remain foreign to him, and because of his blindness, which seems in many ways a symbol for his poverty, even supposedly free public spaces are figured as opaque and hostile. And yet we cannot automatically correlate private to knowable either: Pat's cold flat alienates him, as do Rab's collapsing tenement and the temporary arrangements come to by Tammas and Sammy. Destabilizing the stereotype of the warm, working-class home as refuge, Kelman indicates ways in which trying economic circumstances can render spaces on all levels of Edward Soja's "nested hierarchy of scales"

(*Postmodern Geographies* 200), from the body itself through housing and public city spaces to the conceptual space of the nation-state, as alien and unwelcoming.

This alienation from the urban seems set up in distinction to the escapism of pastoral depictions conjured by each of Kelman's protagonists. Rab seeks a job farming in Australia, while Tammas contemplates moving north to greener employment prospects. Pat is more than conscious of the cliché aspects of his bucolic fantasies, noting that "[m]any years have come and gone since those far-off days of the sun-drenched uni" (171) and thereby placing temporal distance between his current situation and the *Brideshead Revisited*-style of idealizations occupying the bulk of contemporaneous British fiction about young men his age.

For Sammy, as for Rab, freedom from Glasgow's oppressive spaces involves the idea of emigration, though Sammy's escape is patently fantastic and particularly dehistoricized—Sammy's preferred destination is Texas, a mythic place where he can enjoy the music and company of Wille Nelson and Waylon Jennings. He even writes his own country songs. In each case, the alternative to Glasgow is nonurban and unreal, inaccessible, but touchingly and tellingly, for Rab and Tammas at least, the rural idyll offers not so much a therapeutic refuge as economic stability.

In this context, the role of place in the concluding episodes of each of Kelman's Glasgow novels takes on a political resonance. Having failed to definitively leave his job or retain it, Hines reports to work: "Hines shifted his position, he wiped the condensation from the back window and looked out" (*BH* 237). Tammas hitches a ride with a truck driver, his gambling personality opting to ride as far as the life will take him, which turns out to be London: "Yeh, four days I been away Jock, four days—four days too long! Tammas nodded" (309). After waiting in a rundown bus stop for a bus that appears never to be coming, Pat begins running through the rain, which appears to inspire two policemen to give chase: "It was dark and it was wet but not cold; if it had not been so dark you would have seen the sky. Ah fuck off, fuck off" (337). And Sammy's famous exit, boarding a bus to London: "Sammy slung in the bag and stepped inside, then the door slammed shut and that was him, out of sight" (374).

Two characters apparently headed to London, the other two in motion as well, but their destinations and outcomes left unspecified. Jeremy Scott reads Sammy's final moments as "'out of sight', at last, of the prying eyes of the reader, who at times is made to stand in for the eyes of the ubiquitous system which Sammy is helplessly fleeing—the shadowy 'powers that be' who desire and need to know all and the omniscient narrator of classic realism who accedes to these demands" (3). Scott's reading parallels the "system" oppressing Sammy and the classical omniscient narrator, a claim resembling one I have been making throughout this chapter. But the ending lacks the openness and optimism implied by the idea that Sammy has somehow escaped. The door slamming shut is yet another imprisonment for Sammy, just as Hines is looking backward, merely shifting in position rather than moving positively. As readers we cannot know what is to come for these untoward characters, but nothing that happens to any of Kelman's Glaswegian protagonists suggests that their movements at their novels' ends are anything positive. Rab Hines will not emigrate to Australia; Tammas may spend some time in London but he will return to Glasgow, gambling problem intact; Pat Doyle seems more suicidal than the others, more unaware of the inescapability of his situation; and Sammy's exodus, if it succeeds, resolves none of his problems and offers no real opportunity to start over, given the link of English and Scottish social services and police data. These endings in motion, then, must signify something other than optimism about looming change. Rather, it would seem that they suggest a continual restlessness among Glasgow's disenfranchised, an understanding that their conditions and their environment are linked.

And we do see throughout all four novels continual recurrence to the theme of the (im)possibility of movement. *The Busconductor Hines* begins with Rab's wife, Sandra, preparing to bathe. She pours boiling water from a soup pot into a portable plastic baby bath situated on the hearth of the couple's kitchen, one of two rooms in the flat they share with their four year old son. An episode in which Rab and his work-mates are seeking a place to finish an evening's session of drinking emphasizes that public space is as limited to these characters as private space is; they are kicked out of a pensioners club into which they have fled from the rain. "What we need's a roof over the head" (11) asserts one of the men, his remark immediately following a moment at the end of Sandra's bath in which she seems to wish for privacy. The couple wake at night to hear a mouse rummaging in their garbage, and they frequently discuss whether to move or wait for the building to be condemned, which would bring with it a buyout. In introducing us to his characters and story, Kelman intersperses scenes of the crowded, infested flat with scenes of Rab's work life, suggesting by juxtaposition the entrapment and impossibility of change or escape endemic to both.

The recognition of the pernicious nature of the council housing is also evident in Pat's analysis of his brother's housing block: "The flats all had these verandas which were idea for parties to dive from" (252). The spaces in which Britain has chosen to house its poor are intentionally remote and appear designed to encourage despair, even suicide. Tammas, in *A Chancer*, experiences similar denials of appropriate spaces for him. He and his fellow shift-workers have to leave the workplace so that the next shift can begin, their gaming broken up by the absence of an appropriate space for them. Tammas lives in a room rented from his sister and her husband, an inopportune circumstance mirrored by episodes in which visits to a couple of different girlfriends cast him as the interloper on family spaces that have no room for him, either because adult women are still living with their parents or because they have families (husbands, children) of their own. He cannot take these women on dates because of his economic situation; although Tammas's gambling problem means that at least some of his poverty is self-inflicted, the continually shifting scenery of his employment, social, and personal lives underlines the lack of rootedness of his situation. "Thus, for Kelman, public space is often coded as some kind of dead-end: the corner café, the cinema are places where his characters kill time, filling the minutes and hours with the cheap commodities from the bottom end of the marketplace. Figures sit alone and alienated in cafés" (Kirk 119).

By the same token, Sammy's physical difficulties in leaving the police station and making his way home are not due only to his blindness. The place he lives, which, significantly, is not his own but his girlfriend's and thus offers yet another indication his placelessness in society, is inaccessible by subway: "it didnay go near where he stayed" (39). His struggles to get home run from not knowing where he is to being unable to catch public transportation to knowing that a taxi driver will not take him. The narrative blanks out on the details of Sammy's final approach to Helen's, recreating for readers the mental unmappability of the anonymous compound. Once Sammy arrives to the block of flats where Helen lives, he continues to struggle. Crossing the large open space to reach the buildings is nearly too much for him in his newly blinded state. The building itself is even more alienating—not only can Sammy hear the comings and goings of nearby neighbors, but the boundary between outdoors and indoors seems permeable, both features depriving tenants of privacy but failing to create community. As he exits the elevator, he can feel "the fucking wind blowing in from the corridor as usual. That was the trouble with this place ye were aye faced by the elements. Sometimes it made ye hear things. It did...it could even get a bit scary, there was a lot of shadows; and even just now, even though ye couldnay see shadows and stuff like that, it was still a bit funny, like there was somebody hanging about watching him, just dodging about out his footsteps" (58). Kirk, inclined to grant Kelman's characters power and agency, sees Sammy's position here as one he chooses, suggesting that "In his beaten state, disaffiliated from the class habitus and community, he opts for isolation" (132). Kirk's active verb—"opts"—overshadows his participle, "disaffiliated," a term that raises the question of what and who is responsible for the disaffiliation. Environment seems culpable. Sammy's next venture out of the building confirms this isolation, when his grand plans to hit the local pub for a drink are thwarted once again by the big open square, the roads, and ultimately and most tellingly, his lack of any cash with which to gain entry into the pub culture. "Nay point in being stupit. No after yesterday. Glancy's Bar! Who was he kidding, take him a fucking year to get there. And once he did, what was he gony do?" (77–78). Setting and status fuse here to keep Sammy in his place.

Specific Narrative Strategies

Sammy admires the pioneer mentality he senses in the musicians he loves, but their words do him no favors. The songs he quotes—by Dylan, Guthrie, Nelson, Kristofferson—are often about men who had love but lost it or had to give it up, who are nostalgic but bravely moving on, alone in the vast world. Sammy is even inspired to write his own songs:

> When Samuels went blind he was thirty-eight
> he was thirty eight years of age
> and the sun didnt shine
> no that old sun it didnt shine
> yeh he's going back down the road one more time
> poor boy
> going back down that road one more time (119)

What Sammy internalizes from his musical influences is a gutsy solitude, translated into his own language. His song fragment later recurs to him accompanied by a mantra of sorts: "Ye kept yer nerve, ye just kept yer nerve"(186), a philosophy that even in the pithy context of country music sounds reductive, simplistic. Indeed, the next time we see the phrase, Sammy has elaborated, though not in a constructive way: "Ye just had to keep yer nerve. Nay cunt was going to get him out of trouble; nay cunt except himself" (245).

Such assertions of the power of the individual are exactly what keep Sammy in his place, from society's perspective. The shopworn quality of the phrases further oppresses their speaker. Indeed, many of Sammy's clichés come from American country music, articulating a rhetoric of self-sufficiency and escapist fantasy. But rather than serving as comforting doxa, the aphorisms serve as mortar to hold together Sammy's entrapment by state and society. Indeed, the clichés can be seen to represent what Gramsci calls "common sense": "aggregated and internally contradictory forms of thought: the incoherent (not systematic) set of generally held assumptions and beliefs...has the force of obviousness [and]...'naturalizes' the social order" (qtd. in Bromley, *Lost Narratives* 137–138). The balancing of contradictions makes possible the simultaneous presence of Sammy's anti-idealist skepticism and his rugged individualism.

Richard Hoggart points out that cliché is regularly riddled with contradiction, this sort of repetition being less about meaning than rhythm:

> Old forms of speech...[I]f we listen only to their tone we might conclude that they are used simply by rote, flatly and meaninglessly, that they have no connections at all with the way life is lived, are used and yet somehow do not connect. If we notice only their subject-matter...we might conjure up a pretty picture in which old attitudes, simple but healthy, remain unaffected...[Actually,] tradition is harked back to, leaned upon as a fixed and still largely trustworthy field of reference.... The aphorisms are drawn upon as a kind of comfort...it should cause no surprise that these tags often contradict one another. (28–29)

Like Leopold Bloom's, Sammy's mental space is crowded by cliché, yet the clichés may have a recuperative power as well. Kelman's remarks in *Some Recent Attacks* about stereotype and cliché warn of the dangers of lazy and conventional writing, suggesting that stereotype is useful if turned on its head to reveal individual under the stereotype. The use of clichés in the creation of a sympathetic character by a writer so overtly wary of cliché has to be examined carefully. Part of what we witness in *How Late* is the transformation of our own perceptions of Sammy from stock character to human being. Sammy certainly fits the stereotypical urban scrounger ("Scroungers are in receipt of DHSS benefit" [*SRA* 19].) and his repeated clichés in this context take on a new meaning. By revealing the individual under the stereotype, Kelman also suggests the ability to turn cliché into a site for meaning.

Likewise, Kelman works through what is regularly taken to be impoverished language and punctuation to recuperate meaning where society would presume there to be none. Profanity becomes an expressive form rather than emblematic of nothing to say. Sammy tries to resist language in part through an abundant profanity, a feature Hagan sees as "characteristic of the style represented in recent Glasgow fiction" (209). Sammy acknowledges his vocabulary to be limited; he was a strong student but left school early. He works within the one he has, hence the use of "fuck" in every situation in every possible way, and Kelman takes pains to show us that even this finite lexicon is capable of expressing a full range of ideas. This is slightly different than the language of Herbert the revolutionary, whom Barthes introduces at the beginning of *Writing Degree Zero*: Herbert never began his newsletter without "a sprinkling of obscenities. These improprieties had no real meaning, but they had significance...here is an example of a mode of writing whose function is no longer only communication or expression, but the imposition of something beyond language, which is both History and the stand we take in it" (1). Essentially, meaning is secondary to mood, and obscenity here, as in Kelman, serves to locate one, both in a time period and in relation to existing linguistic norms. Alan Freeman suggests that profanity provides an extralinguistic ability: "[a]s well as being simply part of normal speech, swearing, like nick-names, serves to emphasize form over content, and the relational nature of subject status, undermining the concept of selfhood as a fixed element in social change" (255). Freeman offers several insights here—first, that the "how" is more important than the "what," that swearing works to devalue plot; second, that profanity challenges a connection between linguistic norms and a fixed sense of self; and third, that swearing does not always equal obscenity.

Certainly, "fuck" hardly ever means the sexual act for Kelman's characters (who do, incidentally, have a very hard time relating to women). Moreover, "fuck" works as every part of speech, including as one of the few infixes in English: "enerfuckinggetic" (*How Late* 174), which Milne aptly sees as points where "a sought for intensification of negativity ruptures the normative language of criticism" (395), which implies that "swearing is already a register set apart from intelligent discussion" (398). Language, able to fulfill multiple grammatical functions, belies the division of labor inherent in parts of speech and tones of voice. The literary use of profanity, while exposing the limits of Sammy's vocabulary, expands Kelman's expressive terrain.

Similarly, Kelman recuperates the exclamation point, a profane cliché of excess in the world of punctuation. Adorno says that after Expressionism, exclamation points degenerate "into usurpers of authority, assertions of importance…Their proliferation was both a protest against a convention and a symptom of the inability to alter the structure of language from within…a desperate written gesture that yearns in vain to transcend language" (93). An exclamation point tries to invest words with a power they apparently lack on their own, a fitting effort for the disempowered:

> Ye think about it but! Everything had went wrong! His whole fucking life! Right from the kickoff! It all went fucking wrong! Even the most stupitest things: they went wrong too! Ye felt like asking some cunt. How does it all work? How did it happen to me and no to him! him ower there, how come it didnay happen to him; that cunt, him ower there. (*How Late* 172–173)

The repetition here combines with the profanity to indicate Sammy's struggle to express himself, a groping for words to articulate his anger. The impoverished vocabulary and the exclamation points actually, perversely, render the passage powerful and moving as the effort to transcend language mirrors Sammy's frustrated efforts to transcend his desperate situation. Each exclamation point seems more excessive than the one before it as Sammy's vocabulary falls short of bridging the distance between thought and expression: "Exclamation points serve as tokens of the disjunction between the idea and the realization" (Adorno 93).

Sometimes idea and realization mingle and we are confronted by a narrative voice articulately and openly antagonistic:

> Ye blunder on but ye blunder on. That's what ye do. What else is there man know what I'm talking about what else is there? fuck the suicide rates and statistics, Sammy was never a huffy bastard, that's one thin. Know what he felt like? A can of fucking superlager. Aye no danger. He had a drouth, a drouth. Know what that means it means he's fucking thirsty. Fuck yer coffee and fuck yer tea and fuck yer fucking milk if ye're fucking lucky enough to fucking have any of the fucking stuff know what I'm saying. Plus nay tobacco. (319)

Beginning with the notion of "blundering," both a physical awkwardness in movement and a mental mistake, Sammy's outburst links language to space, evoking both as alien heterotopias where he feels

likely to falter. But he takes control here via the definition of the word
drouth, which seems specifically directed at readers who would not
know its meaning otherwise because of regional or class differences—
class especially, as the question of privilege enters into Sammy's tirade.
This passage marks a partial exception to my stance that Kelman
declines to define his working-class speech for middle-class readers.
But the aggressive act of translation coalesces here with the move into
a second person form of address to underscore the link of deprivation
and language. Grammatically, this passage is among Kelman's least
conventional—omitted letters, run-ons, fragments, uncapitalized
words. Sammy's distance from the dominant national language is
never greater, Kelman's link of class status and alienation from nation
never clearer.

Yet for all its political heft, the passage avoids idealization of its
wayward hero. While Sammy himself may have moments of self-pity
or self-romanticization, Kelman resists the temptation. Even the
essentially trivial subject of the rant above—beer and smokes—
diminishes our tendency to see Sammy as an emblem of the plight of
the working class. Indeed, the vernacular itself is rendered such that it
declines to offer "an ideal of the Scottish working class as maintainers
of a distinctive Scots language" (C. Craig, "Resisting" 102). The
spellings of demotic words are not consistent throughout the text, nor
do they follow traditional renderings of a generalized Scots accent.
Rather, the pronunciations are "specific," "geographic" (C. Craig,
"Resisting" 102), Glaswegian rather than Scots.[39] Kelman's use of
this specific urban dialect interspersed in a mainly English text forbids national generalizations and the nationalistic romanticizations
that arise from them at the same time as it deconstructs the notion of
a homogenized working class and implicates strategies of physical
containment in the creation and maintenance of the politicized shape
of the city. "The desolate landscape (full of bad memories, avoidable
disasters, personal despair) is a recurring image in Kelman's work,
giving it a distinctly 'scenic,' or spatial, structure of feeling in which
the urban is fragmented, or divided between declining and thriving
areas" (Kirk 115).

Kelman thus openly relates class organization to the politics of
language, nation, and space in a passage that captures the disintegration of plot into rant. Another form of disintegrated story can be seen
in Kelman's disinclination toward traditional plot development,
another marked similarity to Joyce. We cannot be certain how thor-
oughly Sammy's memory fails him; his relationship with Charlie is
left nebulous; his departure at the novel's end cannot be said to offer

closure. Traditional novelistic expectations of answered questions, mysteries cleared up, and loose ends neatly tied are overturned. Ian Bell remarks that "no clear plotting emerges to impose shape on the randomness of [Sammy's] life" (232). Rather, like Beckett, Kelman creates characters who seem destined to either stasis or repetition, in either case not generating a typical narrative trajectory. This is important—form is following function, style being engendered by the structural needs of the text. If Kelman's characters live in a world where nothing ever changes and hope is low, it makes no sense to have a novel with some sort of Aristotelian five-act structure. The social circumstances and physical surroundings call for a plotless plot; crucially, like Beckett's texts, Kelman's bear the appearance of plotlessness although a highly structured product, akin to his seemingly artless but carefully stylized rendition of Glaswegian dialect.

This deliberately shaped shapelessness arises from a leveling of plot hierarchies. While most narrative texts—novels, short stories, fiction, nonfiction—rely on the logical (if not chronological) ordering of major plot events (what Seymour Chatman calls narrative kernels), Kelman's texts increasingly decline to distinguish between kernels and satellites, the irrelevant events usually included for verisimilitude, rhetorical flourish, or comic relief. Barthes sees kernels as advancing the plot "by raising and satisfying questions" (Chatman 53).[40] But such a logic, which Jonathan Culler has pointed out must necessarily be retrospective and based on cultural models (Chatman 56n), is deprivileged in Kelman's novels, as Bell remarks about *How Late*: "Indeed, the novel is so persistently enigmatic about its constituent events that... it turns into a kind of anti-novel, refusing to lay bare the causal mechanisms which link its events, and refusing also to discriminate between the decisive 'core' episodes and more trivial ones" (232). While, as Barthes suggests, the narrative does raise questions (Where is Helen? Is Tam a political? What does Sammy know? Will he survive/live happily ever after? Will Pat? Does Pat leave teaching? Go crazy? Find love? What about Tammas?), later events do not satisfy these questions, meaning that the kernels do not quite act as kernels.

Culler's analysis is helpful here—a kernel only exists as one within a mind trained to read for them, and only in retrospect. With their absence of causation, their seeming randomness, and their sense of incompletion, Kelman's texts level the narrative so that even one trained to detect kernels cannot identify them, so that looking back offers no insight. In this, Kelman's novels are like *Ulysses*, in which millions of thoughts are not followed up: "[A randomly chosen] page, however, in no sense seeks to prefigure the hierarchy that will be

established in the course of the novel" (Moretti, *Epic* 139).[41] Peter
Brook has suggested in *Reading for the Plot* that all acts of reading
search for narrative gratification; the absence of gratification in
Kelman's texts seems to parallel the estrangement of his characters at
the same time as it asserts the power of non-kernels in shaping the
individual. If only kernels determine a story, he seems to suggest, then
a character is fixed into place, a condition that has led to the social
stratification that places Sammy and Tammas especially at such a distance from the reading public. By leveling story into events indistinguishable as kernels or satellites, even in retrospect, Kelman ensures
that the stories his novels tell are not seen to "make sense," to be
socially acceptable.

Theo D'haen has noted the postcolonial resistance to one story,
and by extension to one version of history, in his analysis of John
Banville's formal experimentation. For Scottish writers, however,
Craig suggests that the challenge is dual: to combat both the static
world so seemingly benignly offered by *Tales of the Borders* and Sir
Walter Scott and the postindustrial anomie (i.e., disaffection) that
characterizes Kelman's characters. For Craig, the nineteenth-century
historical novel in Scotland "leaves to the twentieth two forms of
the historyless: those who never entered the world of historical
narrative—the primitive in their world of magic—and those who are
becalmed in a world that has moved so far into history and then lost
its narrative dynamic" (*Out of History* 48). Both forms of historical
determinism depend on some sort of static language, a Bakhtinian
monoglossia imposed by the ruling class. The disintegration of narrative hierarchies through the polyglossia discussed above, as well as
such specific textual strategies as punctuation choices and use of foul
language and nonstandard spelling, work with thematic elements like
the reshaping of the idea of wandering and the power of learned and
popular allusions to evade the fixity of the officalspeak of the police,
the doctors, the educational system, and even the literary establishment. Kelman's novels resist incorporation into these spaces.

Writing about a parallel form of resistance, exile, Timothy Brennan
predicts the creation of stories that are functional, cosmopolitan writing that would seek to win favor with a metropolitan reading public,
likely to suit urban tastes, whereas Kelman's style contradicts this
formulation. Kelman's characters may feel trapped, but they are not
in exile; their forms of expression are designed to resist plot, to challenge the London they scarcely ever reach in any case. What emerges
instead of a metropolitan-friendly prose in Kelman's novels is a new
form that emphasizes the inevitable failure of a normative narrative

voice to articulate the local or the working class and indeed decries standard narrative dominance.

In Craig's discussion of historylessness and its particular Scottish context, he states that the ordinary is historically insignificant, as it does not make for good narrative. Having industrialized rapidly only to fall to the margins of economic power, modern urban Scotland, in its subsequent static condition, is "trapped in the aftermath of the industrial revolution it helped pioneer, yet no longer able to sustain its industries, it seems to have entered the world of historical change only to be cast out from it, to be left with an image of history as 'an infinitely diseased worm without head or tail, beginning or end,'"[42] hence the conclusion that narratives are illusory. This is why, like other Scottish writers such as Gray and, as I shall discuss in more detail, Galloway, Kelman generates plotless narratives. Scotland is not a place where narrative exists as a way to cope with the present, not a place where stories work. Rather, like those of the Joyce who was affected by Irish nationalism and the ravages of World War I, these narratives are open-ended, circular, pointless, plotless, unresolved. What we saw taking place on a linguistic level with unfinished sentences is recapitulated on a structural level with unfinished stories.

What emerges in Kelman's novels, then, is a form that emphasizes the inevitable failure of a normative narrative voice to articulate the local or the working class. Instead of an authoritative narrative control, marginal voices reign in a landscape of nonstandard forms that emphasize the effects geography has on his characters. Resisting a standard realistic style, Kelman reinterprets both what constitutes realism and what its status is. Kelman's reshaping of the genre involves an embrace of incompletion and fragments, textual experimentation, pastiche, antinovel, nonstory—the territory of the postmodern. He inflects this postmodern awareness of his text as a physical object with an awareness of the ways in which spaces impose on and sculpt the lives of the poor and working class, both exploiting and criticizing the effect environment can have. Operating from the periphery, he reveals the limits of writing from the center.

Chapter Three

Barrytown Irish: Location, Language, and Class in Roddy Doyle's Early Novels

When Frank McCourt's *Angela's Ashes* was to be made into a film in 1998, the crew went to Limerick in search of his evocatively described World War II-era slums in the dirty lanes. As the story goes, they found instead a local economy in the midst of Celtic Tiger growth that had long since eliminated the health hazards of open group lavatories and damp, unheated homes. The crew was therefore obliged to build its own filthy set, which McCourt, on a walk through it with *60 Minutes* reporter Ed Bradley, pronounced a perfect replica. The simulacrum is ironic given that controversy surrounded *Angela's Ashes* in Ireland because of its claims to authenticity. The power of McCourt's memoir for economically stable readers resides in part in its realism; its depiction of poverty by a narrator who has escaped destitution conforms to narrative expectations of the triumph over adversity, "an endorsement of bootstrap capitalism" (Whelan 194). The construction of a hyper-squalid hovel for the film is suggestive of the artistic choices underlying memoir's claims to mimesis.

By contrast, Roddy Doyle's novels resist mimetic representation; but paradoxically, crews for his "Barrytown" movies—*The Commitments, The Snapper*, and *The Van*—had no need to fabricate a setting, shooting on location at the thinly disguised poverty-stricken estates Doyle uses as his backdrop. The Barrytown films were criticized for overplaying the destitution of Dublin's Northside. One of the most controversial of such scenes, from *The Commitments* (1991), opens on Jimmy Rabbitte, Jr., musical agent hopeful, awaiting the elevator at the Ballymun high rises. A young man leading a horse waits alongside him, prompting Jimmy to ask, "You aren't going to take him on the elevator, are you?" The lad replies in an especially pronounced (and hence stereotypical) Northsider accent: "I've got to; the stairs would kill him." Doyle and his directors have explained that the scenes coming under the most fire, namely the horse in the elevator, were added to the script during scouting because they were actually observed to occur (O'Toole, "Working-Class" 36).

Barrytown is a fictional place on the Dublin's Northside, thought to be a composite of the real-life suburb Doyle grew up in, Kilbarrack, and Ballymun, notorious as the site of the Seven Towers that became emblematic of the failure of mass public housing in Dublin.[1] The novels named above and *Paddy Clarke Ha Ha Ha* (*PCHHH*) are explicit about their setting in Barrytown; *The Woman Who Walked into Doors* (*TWWWID*) does not specify what Northside council housing the Spencers move into, but its desolation is vivid. The high rises of Ballymun and the working-class neighborhood of Kilbarrack, several suburbs away, saw extremely high unemployment rates throughout the 1980s; Kilbarrack, while generally considered to be the more pleasant of the two places by a considerable measure, was dubbed, only half-jokingly, an "Irish Soweto" (Foran 64). The *Barrytown Trilogy* and Doyle's two other novels of periphery do not blame their characters' problems on their environments. As Paula Spencer says in *The Woman Who Walked into Doors*, about her criminal husband, "He started robbing. He shot a woman and killed her. Because he didn't have a job, was rejected by society. It would have been nice if it was that easy" (192). At the same time, the structural poverty faced by most of Doyle's protagonists comments on the way that the development of peripheral housing after the slum clearances of the City Centre in the first half of the century has shaped the lives of Dublin's working class. What Doyle does throughout these novels is critique the "slice of life" didacticism of much social realism via narrative techniques that downplay the marginalization of his characters. In tandem with this move, he suggests that the Irish national rubric is inadequate to account for Barrytown's residents, looking at how the intersection of their class and their relationship to metropolitan spaces shapes their stories.

As we have seen with the public and critical reception of James Kelman's novels, the demands of realism occupy the center of debate, with expectations for working-class texts often extending no further than a desire for authentic representation. The presumption that such works will provide an ethnographic window for more bourgeois readers further links reception of Kelman and Doyle. Fintan O'Toole writes that "Realism as a genre assumes that the audience lives somewhere safe and ordinary. It takes the viewer to places—the domain of the lower orders—that are assumed to be unfamiliar" (O'Toole, "Working-Class" 39). But "[t]o focus on Doyle's representation of an under-represented working-class Dublin without recognising that the quality of that representation is more complex than celebratory is to limit the significance to Doyle's achievement by confining it within a narrow mimetic pigeonhole" (D. McCarthy, *RD* 19). While Dermot McCarthy rightly notes that overattention to accurate representation ignores the complexity of identity issues, even more is at stake, as even a focus on such definitions (whether read as unabashedly recuperative or sensitively nuanced) retains realism as its organizing principle. More relevant to Doyle's project are questions of what other genres his work engages. Unlike Kelman, who challenges his status as nonliterary working-class writer by trying to be simultaneously high and lowbrow, Doyle works, even revels, in the middlebrow, willfully antipolitical and antiliterary. Not as overtly political or openly experimental as Kelman, less lyrical or sarcastic than Janice Galloway, seldom as stylized or violent as Eoin McNamee, Doyle's innovations and the underlying aesthetic and political messages of his novels ultimately reveal him to be more like these writers and James Joyce than the "comic-strip realism" (MacAnna 24) such advocates as Ferdia MacAnna seem comfortable classifying him with, a characterization he publicly welcomes.

Doyle's position is unsurprising given the development of Irish politics and Irish literature during the century, sketches of which appear in my introduction. Born in 1958, Doyle came of age in years full of symbolic landmarks that characterized momentous shifts in Irish life. The move from an insular nationalism of the early part of the century to an outward-looking construction of nation is in process at the time of his 1993 novel *Paddy Clarke Ha ha ha*. For most of the century, Éamon de Valera, who held a variety of public offices from 1917 to 1973, had envisioned and attempted to enforce an Ireland of moral restraint and artistic poverty, a land of interchangeable religious (Catholic) and nationalistic fervor. Economic stagnation mid-century brought interrogation of the myth of motherhood and nation complicit in protectionist trade barriers. With the naming in 1959 of economic activist Sean Lemass to the position of Taoiseach, the domestic head of state, the nation began to look outward, the fits and starts of the Irish economy of the 1960s and early 1970s providing the backdrop to Doyle's interpretations of cultural memory. Economic change coincided with revised attitudes toward Irish culture and national identity, the shifts often seismic. O'Toole suggests that "[t]he past only becomes problematic when it is being broken with, and in the Ireland of [the 1960s] there was an unprecedented break with the past in progress" (O'Toole, "Working-Class" 16). *Paddy Clarke*'s marital tensions serve as a microcosm for the tensions of the nation, in which the entering into adulthood of the boy enacts the entry of Ireland into a tumultuous period of history.[2]

This cultural isolation was costly to Ireland's domestic literary production. After the new Republic exiled many of its greatest writers and purged its shelves of immoral works, there was a disproportion of the sort of material that fills Paddy Clarke's fantasy world: lives of the saints, the poems and stories of the Revival, and imported American westerns.[3] To be an "Irish" writer mid-century meant, according to O'Toole, to write rural stories of a noble peasantry.[4] Declan Kiberd as well refers to the "largely ruralist canon" (*II* 653) of Republic writing. But just as the economic isolation of the country failed to make it productive, the yield of literary isolation was slim. Soon writers were critiquing and dismantling old myths, while T.K. Whitaker's 1958 *Programme of Economic Expansion* set the stage for urbanization, industrialization, and foreign investment. The change was immediate, reflected in the works of poets and playwrights—Thomas Kinsella, Brian Friel, Tom Murphy. All struggled to resolve the sense of schizophrenia generated by the collision of new and old. [5] As they wrote, Ireland saw the coming-of-age of the "generation which grew up in Ireland in the sixties and seventies—a changing culture where cinema and popular music exercised a more formative influence than the traditional pieties of revivalist Ireland," part of what Richard Kearney calls an "internationalized youth" for whom "the old ideologies of fixed national identity or insular salvation can never suffice again" (*PI* 185–186).

The new literature, the new youth, and the recast Ireland that emerged were all more pro-European, secular, and forward-looking, leading Peter Gibbon, Paul Bew, and Henry Patterson to write in 1980 that "'urbanization and industrialization have relegated the national question to the margin of Irish politics'" (Gibbons 83), replacing it with politics of class and of left and right. This industrialization may have come later to Ireland than it did to Scotland, but it arrived surrounded by the same optimism and confidence; the subsequent economic collapse and rising unemployment of Dublin in the 1980s gives it parallels with Scottish cities to a degree that was not possible before. Gibbons's list of Ireland's reemergent problems in the eighties could be applied without major revision to the Scottish case: "chronic unemployment...the growth of a new underclass, the reappearance of full-scale emigration, the new censorship mentality" and, perhaps predictably, a resurgence of nationalist sentiment and counterweight of apathy. "The equation of urbanization and industrial development with enlightenment values of progress, secularization, and cosmopolitanism proved no longer viable in the austere cultural climate of the 1980's" (Gibbons 84), whether Thatcher was one's prime minister or not. As we shall see, the similar economic problems and cultural ambivalences on either side of the Irish Sea can generate similar narrative experiments and cultural resolutions in the urban peripheries.

Doyle's writing, then, is taking place in a period of increased globalization and nationalistic rumblings, through the 1980s economic recession and 1990s economic recovery. Engaging with popular culture like few Irish writers since Joyce, he distances himself from political and nationalist issues at the same time as he obliquely works to resolve such questions through the invention of a regional voice. This voice stems from a combination of local language and innovative technique. The representation urban idiom relies not only on distinctive regional usages and slangs, but also on the representation of local accents, grammatical constructions, and pronunciations on the page. A number of critics, including Elmer Kennedy-Andrews, make the point that contemporary Irish fiction, "with significant exceptions—has been remarkable for the conventionality of its formal procedures" (*Irish* 9), while Norquay and Smyth observe that before Doyle and "Apart from Flann O'Brien, one has to go all the way back to Joyce...to find any sustained attempt to produce a meaningful written rendition of the Dublin accent" ("Waking" 35). Combining these ideas, we can connect Joyce's Dublin to Doyle's via the relationship of language to textual innovation. This chapter will examine the ways in which Doyle has used his Northside Dublin setting and dialect to challenge conventional notions of narrative hierarchy and plot structure and foreground questions of class status.

"Rednecks and Southsiders Need Not Apply": New Voices and New Form[6]

The novels of the *Barrytown Trilogy* share a number of common characters, elements and themes, namely the Rabbitte family, money troubles, and pubs, as well as their setting, the fictional, blue-collar Barrytown. The focus of *The Commitments* is the life and death of a soul band, moving in *The Snapper* to a pregnant girl's relationship with her father, with *The Van* examining the struggles of that father in the face of unemployment and entrepreneurship. Together they create a picture of Barrytown, constituting a trilogy on a thematic level as they address multigenerational unemployment and underemployment, the problematics of group identifications, and the dynamics of space and economics on Dublin's periphery. Moreover, they address the same questions of the place of Barrytown's dialects and profanities in the national and global hierarchy of languages, their textual experiments recapitulating structurally what the plots address thematically. In each novel, we see conflicting discourses leveled through an incredibly intricate ironizing of doctrine, as well as a decreased narratorial power.

The first place where we see the curtailed narrative presence is in the appearance of the text on the page. Given that most novels today that shun the use of quotes seem to be literary rather than popular, and that Doyle so consciously straddles this distinction, his decision to use dashes rather than quotation marks in his novels seems not to be a choice made out of a pure aesthetic preference. Doyle told Karen Sbrockey:

> "I do it [use dashes] because I saw it used by Sean O'Casey in his autobi-ography, and I liked this. I just liked the appearance of it; and [...] didn't want there to be too big a division between the narrative and the dia-logue. I thought by just using a dash it would advertise the fact that people were talking, but that there wouldn't be a huge gap between the narrative and the dialogue. I wanted it to be, at times, irrelevant." (537)

The reduction of difference between narrator and character via this stylistic technique parallels the choices by Kelman, discussed in chap-ter two, and by Joyce: "That there should be no authoritative narra-tive 'voice' is not unexpected: readers of Irish fiction, tutored by Joyce...have long been accustomed to such an absence" (Cosgrove 231). A further Joycean connection arises in the link of the role of Doyle's narrator to issues of that voice's use of slang.

While Doyle, like Kelman, may still use narrative tags to attribute speech to characters, by not setting these tags outside quotes, he makes it less likely that we will rely on the authority of narrative interjections, see them as insights or judgments on the characters. Moreover, the use of both standard English and regional dialect both inside and outside the quotes implies the interchangeability of these forms of expression. Where a narrator would normally speak a stan-dard English to bridge the divide between demotic character and "standard" reader, Doyle's narrator is not elevated in this way, using local speech rhythms. Indeed, the text even challenges and discour-ages the expectation of "translation" from a narrative voice. By avoid-ing an easy equation of narrator with standard English and narrated with the vernacular, Doyle avoids further linguistic ghettoization of characters already on the fringes of Irish society. In *The Commitments* in particular, Doyle may emphasize this leveling even more than Kelman, largely because he barely uses a narrator at all.

This diminished narrator is a crucial feature of Doyle's innovations, a complication of the traditional distinction between mimesis and diegesis. Composed almost entirely of dialogue, "preeminent enactment" (Chatman 32), his prose reads something like a script (and converted to one handily). In *The Commitments*, this near-total diegesis eliminates (after an opening page of explanation) most of the need for a narrator; indeed, throughout the novel, the narrative voice seems to have no more insight than the characters and isn't privileged or elevated. What's more, the narrator's role decreases further as the fusion of the band takes place, their discovery of a new voice seeming to supersede an existing one.

Early in the novel, we receive a number of explanations, some in free indirect discourse. Where most narrators obtain varying degrees of what Wayne Booth refers to as "privilege," generally through the possession of more knowledge as to the direction of the story or more grace of articulation, Doyle's narrator is denied omniscience, on a level narrative field with the characters. According to Booth, narrators are "privileged to know what could not be learned by strictly natural means or limited to realistic vision and inference. Complete privilege is what we usually call omniscience." Having an inside view of another character matters "because of the rhetorical power that such a privilege conveys upon a narrator" (160, 163). Booth relies on the discourse of class—"privilege," "power"—to articulate the narrator's position, which suggests that Doyle's leveling of a narrative hierarchy therefore can have real-world analogues and consequences.

Omniscience is not a possibility for the narrative voice in *The Commitments*. The neutrality of most of the narrative remarks, the preference for the word "said" even when questions are being asked—these facts render the narrator less a controlling personality or interpreter for readers than a minor player in the narrative. The reader's role begins to resemble what Neil Nehring sees as "the Benjamin-Brecht position" of making "every man and woman not necessarily an artist, but a critical thinker or 'expert'" (Nehring 70) controlling his or her own reception of a text, softening the distinction between artist and audience. In all of Doyle's works, "[t]he reader must become an active part of the meaning-making process, filling in the gaps and making choices deliberately left by the narrator" (Smyth, *NN* 67).[7] In a country where national myth has so long been a viable and powerful concept, Doyle's evasion of omniscience has a political edge, for as Gibbons has proposed, it can be the attempt to invest an omniscient narrator with authority, "denying the possibility of other voices or other ways of framing experience, that leads to cultural supremacy and other forms of fundamentalism" (*Transformations* 186 n46).

Descriptive speech tags—say, answer, ask, whisper, exclaim, grimace, nod, laugh, mutter, glower—offer the reader varying degrees of insight to narrative perspective. Such value judgments generally provided to a reader are diminished by Doyle (again, like Kelman); not only are there far fewer attributions at all, but the tag is predominantly "said," sometimes even in situations where characters ask questions: "—Are yeh sure? said Jimmy Sr" (*S* 145). Seemingly bland but a stylized choice, this technique ensures a level narrative, the most neutral, nonjudgmental tone available. Part of what is important about this effect is the way it works against plot or development of story—the flatness of the narrative gives it a fixed, redundant feel. (For Doyle, not unlike Joyce, boredom can be an aesthetic device.) But the most significant aspect of this stylistic choice is its attempt to render most voices and moments potentially equal.

Often, there are no speech tags at all, which creates a slightly different effect from the blandness of "said." If no attributions are given, it becomes difficult to determine who is speaking. Usually a careful rereading, a tracking of the alternation of the remarks, yields insight into who speaks which line, though often it seems not to matter. And if more than two characters are part of the conversation, or if it seems that two consecutive lines might belong to one character, we are firmly in the land of narrative ambiguity, not expected from such a straightforward text. Doyle's vagueness, then, must be strategic, making the words said more important than the speakers sometimes. Indeed, especially in *The Commitments*, which confronts the difficulty of integrating individuals into a collective entity, Doyle seems to leave lines unattributed explicitly to ascribe the sentiments to "the band." As Doyle himself explained in an interview, "it didn't really matter who said what very often. That was part of the fun, trying to figure out who's speaking" (Smyth, *NN* 104). The characters who most often speak clearly from their own voices are Jimmy, the band's manager, and Joey, its father figure and trumpet player, their prominence underscoring the tension between narrative democracy and managerial hierarchies. Besides their tags, the narrator gives us no way of figuring out who makes the following remarks as the band does its first dress rehearsal, a moment in which the narrator assumes a bigger role than usual, explaining and describing:

> They played better in suits. They were more careful and
> considerate...Dean swapped jackets with Jimmy. (—Why have you
> got a suit? Outspan asked Jimmy.
> —Soul is dignity, said Jimmy.
> —This is a great fuckin' group, said Outspan. —I must say. Even the
> skivvies wear fuckin' monkey suits.
> —I'm no skivvy, said Jimmy. I'm your fuckin' manager, pal.
> —An' don't you forget it, said James.
> —Fuckin' righ', said Jimmy.) There was more room in Jimmy's jacket
> so Dean could still lift the sax up high. (C 76)

In this passage, we see an interesting inversion. Where normally the narrative voice would make comments during a pause in the action, having the power to stop time, here the narrator gets paused, while the kids address a question that the narrator seems not to have realized might be asked: why is Jimmy wearing a suit? The kids themselves answer, inside parenthesis so that their remarks are a pause in narration rather than a part of narrative progress.[8] The narrator is thus revealed not to be the authoritative, efficient voice we might expect. Indeed, the very subject of the interjection, the difference between labor and management, occupies a central role throughout the text, implying that conventional narrative control may gloss over important issues. In contradiction of Jimmy's collectivist speeches, he has organized his group in a conventional capitalist structure and underscores his class anxieties by enforcing a normative dress code. The narrative voice not only sidesteps all discussion of the socioeconomic significance of the suits, it also ignores the jockeying for power between labor and management and the very existence of such a division.

Narrative units undergo similar modifications throughout *The Barrytown Trilogy*. The elements of most stories can be divided into two categories—the kernels, "logically essential" (Chatman 32) moments crucial to plot development and satellites, episodes included for other reasons (to give the appearance of reality, for instance, or to shed more light on a character's motivations in kernel moments).[9] In all of Doyle's novels, as in Kelman's, satellites and kernels blur, become indistinguishable. Moments that appear to be kernels turn out to be neither climaxes nor anticlimaxes, just parts of the daily lives of the characters. Very little effort is made through satellites to convey realism—this task is left, innovatively, to the language alone. Fundamentally, no particular technique that Doyle chooses is that new or experimental, but their combination here, especially when considered in light of his subject matter and aesthetic, asserts the arrival of a new, local mode of writing, distinct from a historically "Irish" voice.

Doyle actively repudiates in all of his novels the conventional emphasis on purity and Irish tradition in the creation of an Irish voice. Indeed, Doyle is as likely to convey his sense of place through coarse words like "wanker" that are used throughout the British Isles as through more specifically Irish terms.[10] Moreover, none of the Irish kitsch normally associated with attempts to define Irishness—ballad singing, fierce Republicanism, shamrocks and leprechauns—appears in Doyle's novels, not even to be mocked. Rather, though the characters never leave Dublin, much less Ireland, there are numerous references to cultures outside of Ireland: the Commitments follow the antiapartheid movement; we see the Rabbitte family interact with the rest of Europe through the World Cup; Paula Spencer of *The Woman Who Walked into Doors* participates in the "universal" religion through naming her son John Paul; and Paddy Clarke's geographical knowledge offers shaky connections to other former colonies as he dreams of a move to Africa and supports the Vietnamese guerrillas. Doyle explores with particular caution this relationship with the third world, something Ireland has been conscious of since Ghandi studied its independence movement; he is as wary of overarching political universalist claims as he is of the nationalist pride that would deny their existence entirely. The connections he cites are small but significant: Doyle's texts do not make overblown claims to the cosmopolitanism of his ghettoized characters, yet the international references are frequent enough to dispel any illusions of a reaffirmed exclusionary national consciousness.

Mostly, however, Doyle's characters *are* quite specifically rooted—not just in Ireland, which none leaves, not just in greater Dublin, whose environs act as an invisible border scarcely crossed, but more specifically in Barrytown. Like the locally peripatetic but island-bound Bloom, Paddy plays with an atlas, plans to move all over the world, and plots to run away, but in the end, his life and story are contained in Barrytown. We never even see him journey to Dublin proper. Likewise, when Jimmy Rabbitte, a working-class Dublin teenager decides to form a band, he makes several moves that indicate his sense of territory. "Rednecks and southsiders need not apply" (*C* 15), says his ad to attract musicians, restricting the applicant pool to others from the generally more impoverished Dublin Northside. Importantly, he distinguishes his locale not only from the posh part of town, often identified with the remains of the Anglo-Irish Protestant Ascendancy,[11] but also from the supposedly more authentic locus of Irish identity, the countryside. The use of the term rednecks, an Americanism, indicates that some cross-fertilization is inevitable and acceptable in the creation of identity, a contrast with the jingoistic exclusivity of the culturally conservative mid-century. As Smyth points out, "although quintessentially 'realist' in many ways, Doyle's work might also be described as 'postmodern' in the manner in which it juxtaposes the effects of mass international culture with a residual local culture" (Smyth, *NN* 97). In this context, Jimmy's ad not only designates the tendency toward a regional identity, it points to the sorts of issues important to youths segregated in their own neighborhood. Isolated explicitly because of geography, though as well by the distance of intervening years from an "authentic" Irish identity they might spurn in any case, they valorize their own territory at the same time as they become more cosmopolitan. The absence of "Ireland" in the creation of a hybrid local and international identity is noticeable.

The blend of local and international is especially pronounced in the choice of musical genre by the Commitments, even though the kids in the band aren't originally familiar with soul music, having grown up on pop. The musically and politically hip Jimmy Rabbitte critiques pop bands, "the way their stuff, their songs, are aimed at gits like themselves. Wankers with funny haircuts. An' rich das. —An fuck all else to do all day 'cept prickin' around with synths" (10), he declares, adding that their lyrics are "bourgeois" (12). Further linking economics and art, he turns to questions of profit, noting how many "units" Frankie Goes To Hollywood "shifted" (13) with their postbourgeois lyrics. It is in the wake of this marketing discussion that Jimmy makes the connection between his ghetto in Dublin and the plight of black Americans via the economics of consumption:

> —Who buys the most records? The workin' class. Are yis with me? (Not really.) —Your music should be abou' where you're from an' the sort o' people ye come from. ——Say it once, say it loud, I'm black and I'm proud.
> They looked at him.
> —James Brown, Did yis know——never mind. He sang tha'. ——An' he made a fuckin' bomb.
> They were stunned by what came next.
> —The Irish are the niggers of Europe lads.
> They nearly gasped: it was so true.
> —An' Dubliners are the niggers of Ireland, The culchies have fuckin' everythin'. An' the northside Dubliners are the niggers o' Dublin.
> —Say it loud, I'm black and I'm proud. (13)

From here, Jimmy moves to proclaim that the band will perform soul covers, altering the lyrics slightly to make them "more Dubliny." The move from audience through profit to politics is important, as it shows Jimmy's awareness of their interdependence.

The connection of Irish and black that Jimmy makes is arguable, as Lauren Onkey points out; moreover, the use of the word "nigger" bears a certain weight, and there's a slippage between Jimmy's words and the text's ultimate critiques of capitalism and postcolonial theory. But the passage also offers insights into the question of self-identification, of how Barrytown conceives of itself. The other lads have never even considered the postcolonial connection that Jimmy sets forth.[12] Once the analogy is set out for them, however, it brings to light the degree to which the Northsiders do feel themselves to be on the losing side of any binary opposition. Noting the connection that Jimmy makes between neighborhood and class we see the local for the Commitments will be an economic issue as well. McGonigle underlines this when she writes that the reference to culchies "has been occluded if not altogether omitted, an indication of how superfluous it is felt to have been" (165).

The foreignness of James Brown, emphasizing the kids' youth and isolation, seems both generational and geographical. When the lads don't recognize Brown through his music, Jimmy tries to make the connection through movies. *The Blues Brothers* doesn't trigger a response, so Jimmy mentions *Rocky IV*. While all present acknowledge "Tha' was a shite film" (20), it is significant that this is the allusion that clicks. Mainstream American movies, even the bad ones, are a part of an international youth culture's consciousness. The irony of music "abou' where you're from" coming from the United States itself emphasizes that American influences in Barrytown life are more pervasive and persuasive than traditional Irish ones.

Yet the stylistic level reasserts the local: Doyle's rendering of a Northside accent on the page incorporates pronunciation (tha'), distinctive vocabulary (yis), and actual slang (bomb). The combination locates the voice in a very specific place, making no claims to speak for the parts of Ireland whose perceived prejudice contributes to the Commitments's alienation. Moreover, the narrative voice, in this typically brief appearance, is in no way superior to or more articulate than the kids. Not only does it offer merely parenthetical, self-evident comments on Jimmy's speech, the narrative voice speaks in the same demotic register as its subjects, prone to the same hyperbole. Both "nearly gasped" and "so true" are comic overstatements, signatures of a particular generation, class, and neighborhood, as well as ironizing remarks calling Jimmy's postcolonial reading into question. Citing Elizabeth Butler-Cullingford, McGonigle dismisses Jimmy's pronouncements, as "intentionally 'spurious rhetorical distortion' and his homilies should not be taken at face value" (168). But this view oversimplifies a knotty issue; Doyle does not merely mock or discount his aspirational protagonist; rather, paralleling the physical incongruity of "nearly gasping," he suggests Jimmy articulates an analogy that *almost* works. For Jimmy's motives are profit-oriented and capitalist, despite his working brothers cant—he refers hopefully to his future fame and fortune, a pointed comment on the malleability of postcolonial rhetoric.

The postcolonial thrust of Jimmy's argument relies on a "rapid metonymic slide" (Piroux 3), which is further paralleled by the one that he makes generating a musical genealogy for the group. The band's previous name had been And And!, revealing traces of the art music scene of the 1980s (a la The the, Wet! Wet! Wet!, &c). But such influences are to be repudiated. Jimmy's interview of those responding to his ad often begins and ends with influences. U2, Simple Minds, and Led Zeppelin, seemingly stand-ins for the entangling nets of Irish music, Britpop, and classic rock, are responses that fail to impress. None of the band's influences are Irish; tradition is supplanted by discontinuity and Americanization. But there is a synthetic resolution of sorts through the introduction of the Dublin lyrics and the replacement of the irrelevant Irish tradition with a more meaningful, if exoticized, African American one. This is a significant reinterpretation, as Jimmy "evokes a discourse of class at odds with nationalist and racialist agendas which have dominated the Irish political arena since the nineteenth century" (Smyth, *NN* 71). Ironically, the interest Jimmy has in soul music is grounded in a class-based, not racial, analogy, as race would lead the Commitments back into the national essentializing that has excluded them in the first place. The word "nigger," then, becomes a class signifier rather than a racial one.[13]

This distinction between class and race is crucial. In the struggle for independence from Irish colonial rule in the beginning of the century, most rhetoric focused on the need for a formerly autonomous people to govern themselves, a logical extension of nineteenth-century agitations for Home Rule in a Dublin-based Parliament still loyal to the British Empire. Catholics and Protestants alike, mostly from the upper and middle classes, comprised this movement, which drew further strength from the Celtic Revival's cultural efforts to rediscover (and create) a lost Irish culture, language, and identity. While socialism and nationalism were not immediately seen as mutually exclusive, with the Irish Labour Party of James Connolly and James Larkin a significant force, but as the Free State was born, Connolly dead and Larkin in the United States, the idea of a socialist nationalism was subordinated by a religious one. Thus there has not been a strong Labour party in Ireland subsequently; discourses of class have been subordinated to ethnic and religious unity.

Alongside this substitution of concern for class with concern for nation, the history of the racial portrayal of the Irish offers insight into Jimmy's class-based allegiance with African Americans. Throughout the nineteenth century, in both Britain and the United States, the Irish were considered to be a "dark" race, a counterweight helping to define the whiteness of a supposedly less temperamental, more cultured citizenry. In the United States, Irish immigrants consciously distanced themselves from abolitionist movements in an effort to assert their whiteness, "an expression of race privilege" (Ignatiev 86).[14] But the Irish in Ireland never effected the same separation from blacks; 'the great liberator' Daniel O'Connell throughout his career linked his advocacy of the abolition of slavery and Home Rule for the Irish; Marcus Garvey met with members of Sinn Féin in the 1920s; and Bernadette Devlin McAliskey and other Northern Catholics borrowed rhetoric and resistance techniques from American civil rights leaders of the sixties.[15] For Jimmy to invoke a connection to black America is to reactivate such links at the same time as he distances himself from the homogeneity presumed by Irish politics and aligns instead with a notion of difference based on class.

In choosing soul music and repudiating Irishness, Jimmy redefines the construction of identity as something based not on ethnic ties, but on economic ones. This shift of perspective is most evident in the decision to substitute local lyrics for some of the words in the tunes the band covers. "We'll change the words a bit to make it—more Dubliny, yeh know, Jimmy told them. They were really excited now" (22).

—NIGH' TRAIN—...
                    EASY TO BONK YOUR FARE——...
                  NIGH' TRAIN—
          AN ALSATIAN IN EVERY CARRIAGE
                  NIGH' TRAIN——
            LOADS O' SECURITY GUARDS——
                  NIGH' TRAIN——
LAYIN' INTO YOUR MOT AT THE BACK——
                  NIGH' TRAIN——

GETTIN' SLAGGED BY YOUR MATES—
NIGH' TRAIN——
GETTIN' CHIPS FROM THE CHINESE CHIPPER—   (93)

The images are distinctly Northside Dublin here, as is the language, both instancing class-based identification. Piroux calls "Night Train" as "an emancipatory musical journey that transgresses class boundaries and freely explores both the wealthy and the poor areas" (7), but this view overempowers the song while it downplays the perspective of the slum dweller being "carried home." Rather, the night train sounds like a place that offers continual reminders of the way that poverty has forced Barrytowners to the edge of Dublin. Even in their musical journey, physical barriers like Alsatians and security guards exist to remind the Commitments that they are rooted in their neighborhood whether they like it or not.[16] The power in the song comes not from any physical boundaries it might imagine crossing so much as from the linguistic conventions it challenges.

Indeed, for as much as Jimmy says that Southsiders need not apply, when profit calls the Commitments out of their own neighborhood to the Southside, they answer. The Miami Vice pub, "a bit on the Southside, but near the DART" (106), offers the band an in-residence gig, every Wednesday night. The mention of location is narratorial—we have no perceptions from the band. Nonetheless, a narrative bias reveals itself in the "but"—the narrator is again seen to be on the same level as the characters, giving a new twist to free indirect discourse. The reason for the "but" is that the bar is outside of the gang's traditional territory, accessible by the public transportation system less used by the Southside Dubliners. Yet the total absence of further comment on the location of Miami Vice (whose name implies an unappetizing form of cosmopolitanism) indicates that the Southsiders and rednecks exclusion may be only a pose, something to be dropped once economics are at stake.

Indeed, the cautious Doyle doesn't allow leaving the Northside to acquire mythic status. Unlike revivalist tales where crossing a border leads one into either an idealized Ireland or a debased urban space, Doyle's regions have both positive and negative to them.[17] The Commitments play the above gigs on the Southside without incident in the book (though the film version would have them run into trouble). In *The Snapper*, Sharon leaves Barrytown to drink closer to town during a conflict with a friend, and Jimmy Sr has an escapade in *The Van* the night he goes to a Dublin club. The potential for adventure exists when a character leaves Barrytown, but the text doesn't pass judgments on such moments. Notably, the ventures inward hardly ever take place, and when they do, the shopping is a major motive, as though the partition into neighborhoods were as strong as the one that long restricted Dublin-Belfast interaction to the commercial and duty-free. Class boundaries turn out to be as significant and geographically indicated as national ones, both broken only by the power of the market.

Despite local identity, nationalism remains a powerful enough force that the Commitments do fall into a few nationalistic tendencies, significantly in a reference beyond Barrytown. Their innovative lyrics, for instance, draw on a reference to meeting by a clock outside the Dublin department store Clery's, just north of the Liffey. "—Only culchies shop in Clery's but, said Billy" (51), pointing out that the local color they strive for makes reference to a part of the Irish tradition that is not theirs. This poses an interesting dilemma for the band, as the inclusion of local lyrics was meant to give the songs a personal political meaning. The lyric remains in the song, however, because the clock is outside the building, on the street they all identify with, not the store they don't. As Doyle generates a peripheral aesthetic through his stylistic choices, the Commitments make a parallel engagement, converting their poor neighborhood into a site for creativity, for self-identification, and for appropriating and reworking the labels placed on them. Their invention is not unproblematic— racist stereotypes about blacks crop up, and the word "nigger" is used uncritically by several band members—but Doyle knows better than to invest his character with the sentiments he would hope they would have.[18]

Nevertheless, whenever the issue of race comes up, the younger Commitments show a reflexive awareness and tolerance. As the band receives its stage names, for example, Jimmy tells Outspan "we can't call yeh Outspan.... It's racialist.—South African oranges" (43).[19] Moreover, in an interview after the first gig, Jimmy excitedly blurts out that his band "ain't gonna play Sun City" (98). The concerns in both cases are irrelevant: the fact that blacks pick oranges doesn't make being named after these oranges a participation in oppression any more than it is a tangible and effective political statement for an obscure band to boycott a nation they're nowhere near, or near being commissioned to play. Still, these platitudes do suggest that the kids don't recognize their own racism or perceive the problems with their terminology and stereotyping. Like Bloom at the beginning of the century, the Commitments meld stereotyping and exoticizing with a sentimental and automatic sympathy and allegiance. The similarities in Bloom's and the Commitments's views offer depressing insight to how little has changed.

Perhaps it is our sense that those who understand American racial dynamics should know better which means that the remarks by Joey the Lips, twenty years older and supposedly well-traveled in the States, remain more problematic. Indeed, Joey may be present in part precisely to emphasize the contrast between racism and ignorance, as he is guilty repeatedly of essentializing statements. Most markedly, he dismisses jazz, because in contrast to the "ordinary...simple" music of soul, jazz is "abstract...emotionless," leading Joey to announce "The biggest regret of my life is that I wasn't born black...Charlie Parker was born black, a beautiful, shiny bluey sort of black...He turned his back on his people so he could entertain hip honky brats and intellectuals" (106–108). Miles Davis is deemed "the biggest motherfucker of them all" in this schema that adopts a conventional fetishizing and patronizing association of black skin with nature and white skin with the intellect.

But Parker's crime in his distance from soul is that he replaced "ordinary people making music for ordinary people" (107) with an audience of "middle-class white kids with little beards and berets" (108). The Bird's betrayal, then, is as much about class defection as it is about race. Joey axiomatically equates blackness with populism and whiteness with elitism. Like Jimmy's rejection of Depeche Mode because of their audience, Joey's contempt for "Jazz Purists" is about reception, containing within it the notion that only educated whites could appreciate jazz. The tautology here denies intellectual interests or prowess to both blacks and the working class. Ironically, of course, Charlie Parker's improvisations, while "experimental and apparently 'discordant,'" make a "rupture with the white classical music tradition [that] was quite deliberate" (Hebdige 147). Joey's interpretation of the history of black music misreads the mission of the Commitments as well, reinforcing their social status.

While isolation in Barrytown remains a far cry from apartheid or segregation, the class connection does account for the Commitments's stated allegiance with both American and South African blacks. In this vein, it becomes significant that the two references to South Africa—Outspan oranges and Sun City—are economic. The Commitments view themselves and these blacks in primarily class-based, financial terms. The band even goes so far as to rein Jimmy in when he tries to make too direct a link between the rhythms of soul and the rhythms of the factory,[20] responding to his romanticized, aestheticized "they could chain nigger slaves but they couldn't chain their soul" with "their souls didn't pick fuckin' cotton though. Did they now?" (38). The response, offered narratologically by the collective, unattributed voice of the band, again draws attention to the labor that ties working-class white to slave, then exploited, black.[21]

Still, in their own way, the Commitments develop an aesthetic that draws both on their region and on their politics, creating a group, creating commitment. As soul becomes a catchword for all deemed desirable, the band alters from an assortment of disconnected individuals into a group. There are some differences from most bands: cover tunes will be the norm, and expertise, or even knowledge of one's instrument is not a prerequisite. Instead, the Commitments make a statement about the elitism of art through their refusals to privilege originality or skill. The division of labor creates small pockets of expertise, but Jimmy works as the band's technician, and believes that "Anyone can play the drums, Billy" (111); soon after, Billy departs and the bouncer, Mickah, becomes the drummer. The group is not so much a collection of individuals as a collective, which is why lead singer Deco's self-importance and interest in his individual career are a major factor in the band's demise.

The band brought together by an ad becomes an entity: lectures and policy statements bring them together—art comes second to ideology, less the ideology of the sermons themselves than the aesthetic of the community they create. The collective mindset is expressed especially in the backup singers, the Commitmentettes, who always practice as a unit. The only women in the group, they are never treated by Doyle as distinct performers, just as soul music tended to have "girl groups" but few female solo artists. While the men listen to individual men at home, the Commitmentettes listen to "The Supremes, Martha and the Vandellas, The Ronettes, The Crystals, and The Shangri-las" (33–34). Doyle's own assumption here is that women seem not to have individuality: "they conform to a certain extent to what is expected of them, at the same time they refuse in many ways to conform...the language of the Commitmentettes is as coarse and courageous as the lads, in fact more so. They're more at home with themselves" (Smyth, *NN* 105).

Individuality, apparently, is not soul, as Dean finds out as he begins to push the envelope with his saxophone. Barely a beginner during the band's rehearsals, Dean discovers a talent and a passion in classical Jazz. Nothing could outrage Joey the Lips more, however, because "Jazz is the antithesis of soul ... intellectual music...It's anti-people music." (108). Joey feels that soul solos have "corners," rules. The spirals of jazz have no place in the box of soul, which suddenly turns out to be a bit constricting. While the reworking of standards, a cornerstone of jazz, parallels the project of the Commitments, the class context, as constructed by Jimmy and Joey, forbids the perceived individualism of jazz in favor of a communal reworking of earlier tunes.

This notion of cover tunes in itself becomes a politically charged statement, challenging the supremacy of originality in art, placing the process on equal footing with the product. Onkey's charge that the Commitments make a "backward look" (154) becomes problematic when we consider that, as Neil Nehring states, repetitions can be "expressions of solidarity with the discontent and insubordination of radical ancestors, whose voices remain significant sources for insubordinate forms in the present and future.... A 'revolutionary nostalgia' of this sort combines recovery *and* innovation in the same process" (306).[22] The notion that retro necessarily equals reaction doesn't stick, then, in part because of the Dublin-y lyrics, and in part because of the political rhetoric the Commitments adopt, although Doyle's slippery levels of irony do lend some credence to Onkey's skepticism. Though the band likes the "[g]ood, old-fashioned THE" (15) in its name, its revision of lyrics and reworking of soul move beyond the mere romanticization of the past that cover tunes could imply. Further, if Jimmy's theorization had led him already to black music, the 1960s would seem to offer a convincing template for a blend of politics and music, not a mere "look back."

Yet soul does not ultimately bring the Commitments fame, a political voice, or artistic fulfillment; the band does not alter its socioeconomic status. Dean's defection to jazz takes place alongside Deco's self-aggrandizing, Billy's retreat into nihilism, and Joey's romantic entanglements with all three Commitmentettes. Soul cannot answer the questions that Dublin youth put to it, or live up to the expectations they place on it. Throughout the course of the book, soul is, at various times, sex, politics, the rhythm of the factory, dignity, style, street, the people's music, escapism, integrity, revolution, feeling, no skin color, getting out of yourself, and so on, categories that sometimes even contradict each other. Doyle empties out soul by overinflating it. While soul is never fully discredited, as infighting begins, it cannot hold the band together, and its concepts seem irrelevant. In particular, Joey's philosophy of soul and dignity is discredited by two shameful moments: one, his false claim he is going to play soul in the States for Joe Tex, who Jimmy recalls is actually dead, and two, the exposure of this lie as a cover for his escape from Imelda, whom he believes he has made pregnant. Yet Joey's final words in the novel, a quote from the Bible ("... Make a joyful noise unto the Lord, all the earth make a

loud noise, and rejoice, and sing praise. —Psalm 98, Brother Jimmy"
(134)), affirm the value of the activity of making music, not just the
product. This is a message that Doyle's text would seem to confirm,
yet it multiplies ambiguity by placing the philosophy in Joey's
mouth.

At the same time as the philosophy deflates, the story fizzles. A
standard narrative might have featured a conventional romance, the
pairing off of Commitments and Commitmentettes. But not only is
this sort of matchmaking delayed in neighborhoods where adult children still live with their parents because of economic hardship, it
speaks to a sort of fairy-tale genesis of a rock band, where a band's
success parallels romantic success. Doyle upends, parodies the traditional trajectory by having all the Commitments "fancy" the same
woman (a problem of supply and demand), Imelda, but nobody ends
up with her. Indeed, a fight over Imelda helps to spur the band's
breakup. The band's final show and subsequent final fight would
seem to be the end of both the Commitments and *The Commitments*.
But the novel occupies several more scenes, in a couple of final jabs at
Aristotelian unity, revealing both Joey's flight and the formation of a
new band. The novel gives us no indication of how three ex-Commit-
ments come to be at Jimmy's house in this final scene, nor how much
later this final episode takes place. Yet the early direction toward soul
that Jimmy orchestrated in his bedroom acts as a structural bookend
to this scene, in which again "Jimmy let the needle down and sat on
the back of his legs between the speakers" (20, 136).[23] Instead of
James Brown, he plays The Byrds for a few band members and offers
them the new hybrid genre of "country punk." Nearly all of the former band will be included in the new band, including the women,
whose presence is deemed responsible for having held the Commitments
together and for having eventually broken them up. The country punk
band is given the name of "The Brassers," which is Irish slang for
"girls." This choice of local slang, perhaps the only gesture immune
to Taylor's charge that the band is "more gimmicky than political"
(297), detaches the local from the soul aesthetic. The retention of
Dublin aesthetics is buoyed by the unconscious choice of the band to
ally itself with yet another marginalized group, women, and may
ironically allude to the "brass" roots of the band, the soul origins that
are otherwise invisible given that Dean and Joey, the brass section,
are gone. As the commercial success of this incarnation of the band
seems unlikely, Doyle's interest here seems to be in exposing the
motives of his characters and in critiquing the substitutability of discourses (though the sparse narration refrains from judgment). The

speedy tempo of country punk suggests that it will, like soul, allow for only haphazard engagement, political or emotional; the band's modes of production and consumption limit their potential to construct alternatives to the status quo.

Moreover, the introduction of a "country" element, while again an American import, implies a reconnection with the rural half of Ireland's population. [24] Joey's politics and soul are replaced by a less overtly political genre, the country music that already is popular throughout the nation: "yeh know, Joey said when he left tha' he didn't think soul was right for Ireland. This stuff is though. You've got to remember that half the country is fuckin' farmers. This is the type of stuff they all listen to. —Only they listen to it at the wrong speed" (139). This move reconnects the band to the rest of Ireland, though with new motives and a heightened self-insight. Rednecks might be acceptable after all, and politics are forsaken for profit, which is revealed in this final twist to be the unifying feature the Commitments sought in their valorization of the working class. This new nationalism, based on economics, retains the local innovations the kids discovered earlier: their first tune is to be a country punk version of "Night Train." The localism and everyday aesthetic prevent an unadulterated reading of the new band as the embodiment of capitalist manipulation; at the same time, they represent a cynical realization that any discourse, whether political or aesthetic, is ultimately subordinate to economics.

Philosophically, the novel complicates the relationship of art and politics with the inevitable incursion of market forces impervious to both, while narratologically, it resists conventional plot emphases. A more hackneyed rendition of the story would show the efforts of the band as they pull together, the trauma of the breakup. But the novel's end and the band's end coincide, in that, neither is definite. The band is and is not defunct; there is and is not novelistic resolution. The same tunes will be played, with the same local innovations, in a new genre by Jimmy's new band, comprised of the core of the Commitments. On a narrative level, we see movement, if not resolution, in the exposure of the profit-motive what was concealed before and in the establishment of a rhythm of repetition—this band, or another, will always try to access the market via a new angle—the high hopes the novel sets forth early on turn out to be yet another means of production that capitalism can incorporate. Doyle's depiction of a working-class band willing to trade on stock images about racial, postcolonial, and class identity ultimately repudiates the stereotype of a lazy proletariat responsible for its own poverty at the same time as it expresses cynicism about the potential for change. By appearing to conform to the jolly images of a fun-loving working class that audiences can access without guilt, Doyle points out that contrary to supposition, class is alive and well in Dublin, that national unity is not monolithic or adequate to the needs of urban youth, and that in the absence of inclusive and plausible politics, capitalism stands ready to provide mobilization for the disenchanted.

"Barrytown Was Good That Way": *The Snapper*

In *The Commitments*, stylistic features such as dialect and profanity combine with structural choices like unattributed speech and indefinite plot development to create a local aesthetic that paradoxically removes the Commitments from their provincial inheritance. In a "cover tune" of his own first novel, Doyle revisits the Rabbitte household, retains his local innovations, retains several characters, and tells a similar story in a new vein in his next novels, *The Snapper* and *The Van*. These novels are far more interested in character exploration and more explicit in their analyses of space, retaining elements of many of Doyle's formal innovations. What emerge are more psychologically complex texts with a muted local aesthetic and increasingly pronounced class commentary.

Less diegetic, with less uninterrupted dialogue than *The Commitments*, *The Snapper*'s narrator uses free indirect discourse, adopting the speech of the character it discusses. The novel is marked by the intersection of all sorts of different languages—slang, grammatical, "unaccented," medical, profane—and by an interest in definition that underscores the novel's centerpiece: Sharon "wondered a few times if what had happened could be called rape. She didn't know. That was as much as she remembered. She wished she didn't remember more" (185). The first sentence here implies that we've been told the full story, but the second lets us know that we're not being informed of everything. The interplay of different stories and languages takes place against a backdrop of the daily rhythms of family life, in which the plot, insofar as there is one, is the transcendent/mundane experience of pregnancy, with the emphasis here often on the mundane.

In part because of the bonhomie of a story culminating in a healthy birth, many critics saw *The Snapper* as a heartwarming tale of a gutsy working-class family.[25] But the story raises uncomfortable questions about public and private space in contemporary Irish society. As Sharon tries to conceal that the baby's father is a neighbor and the father of a friend of hers, she must allay her own father's fears of his personal humiliation, which he eventually represses via an intrusive and biologically explicit interest in Sharon's pregnancy. Doyle shows a working-class family evading the traditional influences of nation and church, offers readers a pleasing view of collective identity, and endorses the validity of a variety of linguistic registers—all sentiments in keeping with the postnationalist socialism he articulates in interviews.[26] But at the same time, Jimmy Sr's focalization, as well as the pressures that economic stress places on domestic space in contemporary Ireland, undermine his open-minded collectivism and sanction the very middle-class constructions of privacy and privilege that the text purports to resist.

The Snapper's incestuous dynamics posit the behaviors and interactions of his working-class urban characters as a metaphor for contemporary Irish society. As Clair Wills points out, "... the relation between the public and private spheres, while always complex, is particularly entangled in the case of Ireland" (38); as such, Ireland can reveal the gender and class underpinnings of what is perceived to be normative political and social engagement. Sharon's willingness to take charge of her unwanted pregnancy becomes eclipsed, structurally and narratologically, by Jimmy's imperative to regain control of his household and social milieu. Only by submitting to public involvement in her private life, via a simultaneously liberating and repressive humor, is Sharon permitted to carry her child successfully to term. *The Snapper* discloses the logic by which what is private is converted to the public domain, suggesting that, for the working class, the distinction is not as rigid as domesticity theory would have it. Doyle reveals contemporary Irish family life to be self-consuming and subject to the very strictures he seeks to deny, such as the traditional stranglehold of family, the inevitability of gossip and public critique, and the denial of individual will or mobility.

Wills describes the cooperation in Ireland of church and state in advocating the adoption of middle-class nuclear family norms in the early decades of the twentieth century, noting "while the middle class ideals of domesticity were deployed in the service of Catholic nationalist hegemony, the concomitant ideal of privacy within the home was decried" (46). The Rabbitte household exists outside of and unfamiliar with bourgeois conceptions of privacy while at the same time striving to conform to models of appropriate domestic behavior. We see traces of class shame, efforts to better one's situation, and discussions of space in language that accepts the middle-class status quo to which the family has, at best, limited access. Although Ellen-Raissa Jackson may argue that "In Doyle's novels, the family is no longer the inviolate space of freedom and solidarity which the 1937 constitution revered and sought to protect" (228), external pressures do push the Rabbittes toward the appearance of exactly that sort of family structure. Though it depicts a community comfortable with out-of-wedlock pregnancy, *The Snapper* can be seen as a site for the suppression of nonnormative family structures and for anxiety about family dynamics, showing the way that class affects conceptions of public and private.

Unlike the adaptation of *The Commitments*, which substantially altered the themes of the book, Stephen Frears's movie addresses the same concerns as its source novel even when it adds or deletes scenes or shifts emphasis. The plot and dialogue are largely the same, though because the producer of *The Commitments* holds the copyright on the original character names, the film replaces the surname Rabbitte with Curley, as well as Jimmy Sr with Dessie. Doyle's major revisions as author of the screenplay, including the substitution of an older brother in the military for one trying to become a radio personality, effectively capture the tension between the novel's interest in giving voice to a working-class family and this family's own unconscious embrace of middle-class notions of privacy, an interaction underlined by Frears's repeated framing of shots through opening and closing doors. Considered together, film and novel address concerns with space and privacy that may arise in lieu of class politics.

As much as the novel may affirm bourgeois nuclear family structures, Roddy Doyle's characters don't have access to middle-class public sphere/private sphere distinctions. Rather, *The Snapper* can be read as a series of ruptures and interminglings of the purportedly distinct public and private spheres. For instance, in a scene that appears in both film and novel versions of *The Snapper*, a drunk Sharon envisions the reactions of people in Barrytown to her pregnancy, which range from mocking disapproval to disgusted condemnation:

——Sharon Rabbitte's pregnant, did yeh hear?
——Your one, Sharon Rabbitte's up the pole.
——Sharon Rabbitte's havin' a baby.
——I don't believe yeh!
——Jaysis.
——Jesus! Are yeh serious?

——Who's she havin' it for?
——I don't know.
——She won't say.
——She doesn't know.
——She can't remember.
——Oh God, poor Sharon.
——That's shockin'.
——Mm.
——Dirty bitch,
——Poor Sharon.
——The slut.
——I don't believe her.
——The stupid bitch.
——She had tha' comin'.
——Serves her righ'. (206)

The film stages this scene so that the population of Barrytown lurks in Sharon's bedroom, under her bed, along her walls. Gossip and rumor become standard methods of circulating purportedly confidential information, but the community here is not seen as an agent of a collective morality. Not only do the different voices in this scene express divergent and even contradictory points of view, but the different accents—Jaysis and Jesus, for instance—challenge any easy assumption that Barrytown is unified in any sense of "working-class unity" such as Richard Hoggart romanticized or that the Rabbittes are meant to be stand-ins for any/every working-class Northside family, much less any/every Irish family.[27] The entire text is suffused with such invasions of the private sphere, with personal matters aired publicly, and with a general dissolution of the public/private border, indicating that class-based practices shape the use of space.

Sharon, at twenty, shares a room with two younger sisters, her older brother with two other brothers. The bathroom door is never closed enough, and both this novel and *The Van* make the Rabbitte household feel like a space of constant movement, a sensation that the film captures particularly well. When Sharon goes to confront George Burgess about his locker-room chat about her, the doors in his house further emphasize how hard it is to keep a secret within the family— Burgess's wife disappears through one door as Yvonne, Sharon's friend, pops out of another. Characters are constantly reminded that they can be seen at any moment; the supporting posts of the banister divide the frame to suggest the perspective through the bars of a jail. Kilfeather points out that "the house open to hospitality and community is also open to surveillance" (87). Paradoxically, when there is so little privacy, the home itself functions as a public space, much as Wills and Kilfeather suggest about the Irish home in earlier periods. Kilfeather sees the "apparently transparent domesticity" suggested by open doors "riven with incongruity and contradiction" (87); the endlessly opening and closing doors of Barrytown similarly show resistance to the candor they pledge.

Only when Sharon finally quits her job, the week before she is due, does she experience genuine physical privacy: "Sharon got Linda to open the window a bit before she went down for her breakfast. Now she was alone in the bedroom" (324). With the cessation of external noise, anxiety sets in, and her response is to rush downstairs. Physical privacy makes room for mental solitude here, as throughout the novel, which is perceived as threatening—it is too connected to memory. A crowded household and dense family life allow characters to avoid unpleasant musings. Jimmy and Sharon, the novel's focalizers, both spend most of their reflective energy trying to deny their own motives or wishing others would behave differently.

Jimmy's denial evolves throughout the novel. At first, he appears to accept Sharon's news with neither pleasure nor displeasure; his concerns, as anticipated by Abbey Hyde's study of parental response to nonmarital pregnancy, focus less on the practical impact of the upcoming birth than on such issues as who the father might be and whether he could be expected to marry the girl. And like a number of fathers in Hyde's research, Jimmy's initial responsiveness is followed by "a period of social disengagement with [his] daughter" (286), arising in his case once rumors begin to spread about the presumed paternity of his neighbor, Burgess. "Negative reactions were almost always expressed in terms of the father's own personal hurt and disappointment" (Hyde 287). Jimmy certainly perceives Sharon's situation via its impact on him: "his life was being ruined because of her.... He was the laughing stock of Barrytown. It wasn't her fault—but it was her fault as well. It wasn't his. He'd done nothing" (278–279).

Jimmy adopts a belligerent attitude in public, first threatening Burgess and later going so far as to punch someone. He goes out of his way to make sure that Sharon sees his injury for herself, thereby forcing her to acknowledge that he envisions himself acting in her defense. "It appears that, as the fathers saw it, in their inability to control fertility, daughters had in turn failed and exposed their fathers as inadequate protectors of the daughter's sexuality" (Hyde 293). It is not just Jimmy's personal reputation at stake, but his masculinity. He fights after Sharon is pregnant to compensate for his inattention previously. But more than Jimmy's lax involvement as a parent is at issue.

Because, as Sue Sharpe puts it, daughters are seen to "belong to fathers twice over, as children and as females" (85, qtd. in Hyde 289), Sharon's pregnancy can be read not just as a consequence of Jimmy's inadequate masculinity, but also as a larger threat to the status quo. Hyde: "There are clear threats to patriarchal structures when a breakdown of traditional relations between men and women occurs, and the daughter's 'dangerous fertility' bypasses the male-controlled route of marriage" (292). Though the family lists other out-of-wedlock pregnancies as a way of diminishing the social significance of Sharon's, Jimmy's behavior throughout the novel, as well as that of other male characters, reveals a crisis of traditional male roles and masculinity in progress.

With unemployment in Kilbarrack, the "real" Barrytown, exceeding 60 percent for men throughout the late 1980s and early 1990s, manhood could longer be defined in terms of earning and providing. While Jimmy has not yet been made redundant—an event that occurs between *The Snapper* and *The Van*—one of his sons and several of his friends are looking for work and submitting to pointless and demeaning employment training. *The Snapper*'s male characters are absorbed into what had traditionally been a feminine world yet lack the power of the female characters. The disappearance of work outside the home removes one outlet for male public behavior, forcing men into front gardens, kitchens, and other spaces typically regarded as women's domain. Even more than the novel, the film takes particular pains to evidence the emasculation of Barrytown in a foreshadowing of *The Van* that not only infantilizes but castrates masculinity. When Sharon's oldest brother Craig (a character not present in the novel) arrives home from the armed services—apparently the UN peacekeepers—he is predictably macho, declining to embrace Dessie, showing affection only to the women of the family, then stereotypically flaring up at the news of Sharon's pregnancy. But Craig's bluster is derided in an innuendo-laced scene when his friends in the pub scoff upon hearing that his gun had no bullets ("But you had to look 'em in the eyes—the Arabs," says Craig in his own defense, this eye contact substituting for aggression; later in the scene, Craig flails under the gaze of Yvonne Burgess).

Significantly, the absence of privacy is implicated in the weakening of male roles. In a scene added to the screenplay, when Craig hears that Burgess is the likely father of the baby, he throws a trashcan through the Burgess front window, calling Burgess out and yelling to Sharon, "I'm doing this for you, you slut!" In his rupturing of the boundary between outdoor and indoor, public and private, Craig seeks to draw Burgess into the public sphere, yet he is unable to push Sharon's condition back into the private. David Lloyd has referred to the need for authenticity as the basis for "nationalism's consistent policing of female sexuality by the ideological and legal confinement of women to domestic spheres" (109). But as the entire block watches Craig's impotent gestures, including the way he passively waits for the guards to arrive but begins to struggle when they touch him, what is emphasized is the futility of divisions of public and private within the working-class community, which in turn implies the failure of traditional masculinity and of traditional definitions of nation in contemporary Barrytown.

Fintan O'Toole has argued that Doyle's writing is "firmly located within an Irish tradition" of "fatherhood and its failure," the Barrytown trilogy in novels and onscreen depicting "a working-class father's attempts to come to terms with the loss of his traditional role" ("Working-Class" 39). Indeed, Doyle's paterfamilias makes all sorts of futile parenting gestures throughout *The Snapper*, from wanting to tell his younger daughters that what Sharon did was wrong to trying to discipline a son alienated from the rest of the family. O'Toole argues that through Dessie's active interest in the baby, the film avoids stereotypes of nation and class; he recaptures fathering, paradoxically, through grandfathering.

Yet even when Jimmy/Dessie overcomes his own shame, his method of coming to terms with Sharon's pregnancy is one of roundabout avoidance. Sharon gets herself a book about pregnancy from the library; later, Jimmy checks one out as well. He talks to her about the baby in the book's clinical and technical terms: "it'll take some o' the pressure off the oul' diaphragm," (303) he tells her as he props her up in bed. His dialect blends with the terminology he learns as he makes medicalspeak his own, knowledge Sharon finds intrusive: "he was becoming a right pain in the neck. He'd be down again in a few minutes with more questions" (302). Even during her labor, he tells her to time her contractions so "They'll be impressed" (338) at the hospital. While Doyle characterizes this interest as positive, the product of the supposed benefits of reading and family togetherness, Jimmy seeks both to avoid and control the reality of Sharon's pregnancy. His involvement in the pregnancy can be read as a bulwark against threats to the patriarchy and as an effort to render typically female space his own.

On one level, then, Jimmy's acceptance of Sharon's pregnancy functions as an acceptance of a collective family identity, an emotional development that binds a family together; on another, it speaks to the larger problems of contemporary Irish society. In a scene that emphasizes Jimmy's difficulties in making the suggestion, he offers to be with Sharon in the delivery room. "There wasn't even a car going past. The pipes upstairs weren't making any noise" (327) as Jimmy approaches the subject in a roundabout manner, finally tentatively saying that he "wouldn't mind stayin' with you when—you're havin' it" (328), to which Sharon replies "Ah no" and the matter is dropped. The absence of noise renders this one of the few truly private moments in the text, and as usual, Sharon retreats. Jimmy's concern is portrayed as touching, but Sharon and her mother both feel that it is excessive, as when Sharon thinks "It was her pregnancy and he could fuck off and stay out of it" (303) and when the usually serene Veronica sarcastically mimics Jimmy by saying, "We don't want you bursting your waters all over the furniture, isn't that right, Jimmy dear?" (326) before storming out of the room. Both women's objections are phrased in terms of physical space, and both view Jimmy as infringing on their domain. In making Sharon's pregnancy his own through his reading and conversations in the pub with friends, Jimmy relocates it in the public sphere.

The story of a pregnancy serves as an ideal site to explore such negotiations as the place where private acts are rendered visible to the public. For a normative middle-class couple, pregnancy visually affirms their implicit bond, asserting their link and forging it. But for a single mother, a swelling belly signifies the opposite; it raises questions about who the father is. Not until her condition is on the brink of visibility does Sharon resolve to tell her friends. "She felt her stomach. It was harder and curved, becoming like a shell or wall. She'd definitely have to tell the girls" (175). The decision to do so triggers a series of thoughts about her lack of intimacy with anyone, the fact that she'd like to confide but confines herself to the level of "slagging." Such slagging, which also triggers Jimmy's discomfort with his daughter's pregnancy, is one of the most remarked-upon features of *The Snapper*, as it opened up the film in particular to the charge that, in the words of Charles Foran, it was "stage-Irish distortions to please foreign editors...reinforcing the image of the working-class Irish as happy-go-lucky slobs with sharp tongues and gutter vocabularies" (64).[28]

To be sure, Sharon's relationship with her girlfriends shows the imposition of public, "gas" narratives in place of any real intimacy. "She's often read in magazines and she'd seen it on television where it said that women friends were closer than men, but Sharon didn't think they were. Not the girls she knew" (183). Rather than merely dismiss their relationships—Caramine White charges that "she and her friends are shallow and immature" (White 69)—we can see the superficiality as an indictment of Barrytown social patterns, especially given the absence of any confidant for Veronica in the text and Jimmy's emotional reticence. Jimmy finds himself unable to express his emotions in front of any male characters. "He wondered if he should kiss Veronica on the cheek or something...But no, he decided, not with the boys there. They'd slag him" (180). The public face not only differs from private reality but stifles and changes that reality. In Doyle's Barrytown there is almost no such thing as the private sphere, and his characterizations of Jimmy and Sharon show them unsure how to reveal the self except through accepted public behaviors and prescribed gender roles. Rather than the portrait of a carefree working class he is accused of promoting, Doyle proffers a critique of an Irish society grounded in familiarity without intimacy, a paradox that Sharon's apparent rape itself signifies.

Ireland as a nation has a long and complex association with imagery of rape. From Declan Kiberd to Roy Foster, all stripes of Irish critics mention the ambivalence of Irish interpretations of English colonization: sometimes Ireland is the virgin raped by an aggressive invader, sometimes the slut that lifts her skirts, complicit in her own violation, what Elizabeth Butler Cullingford calls "the familiar background of the gendered analogy that aligns England with the powerful male, Ireland with the weaker female, and tells the story of the Union through the metaphor either of rape or of heterosexual marriage" (*IO* 7). The self-loathing willingness to blame the victim accounts in part for Sharon's shame and culpability.[29] But while Sharon does not acknowledge her rape, neither does she remain passive as rumors circulate in the public sphere. To maintain control of the story and erase the suggestion of intercourse with Burgess, Sharon begins to tell everyone that an anonymous Spanish sailor who had been docked in Dublin is the father of the baby. Because "guess the daddy was a hobby" (253) in Barrytown, an Irish father would have been too decipherable—and perhaps, too incestuous.

Sharon's attempts to control the scandal are well-matched by Barrytown's sense of humor: control of such a juicy scandal eludes her. Two conflicting stories battle for dominance—the one that Sharon can tell so she is not raped or disgraced, and the one that is funny. The "bigger piece of scandal and better gas" (267) of a Sharon/Burgess alliance is too funny for gossip to discount, and Sharon realizes she herself would hope for the funnier story except that "she was the poor sap who was pregnant" (267). This admission by Sharon exonerates the community; at the same time, Barrytown is implicated for its laughter-induced blind spots. The community's sense of humor glosses over the awkward or the painful, a pattern we see replicated within Sharon's limited understanding of emotional intimacy.

Doyle states, "I wouldn't personally consider it a rape. I do believe that he behaved very wrongly in taking advantage of a drunk woman. But again, does that make it illegal? ... I suspect that it is not the first time she has had sex against the car when she has been drunk. I wanted the circumstances to be left open to interpretation" (White 150–151). In the film, the choice of background music and the careful juxtaposition of the scene with shots of a weeping Sharon in her bedroom show the experience was traumatic, if not legally a rape—all we get is the muffled "no" when Burgess is already inside her. But the discussions of *The Snapper* that I found, mostly movie reviews in mainstream press, referred, like so many rape trials, to Sharon's drunkenness, her perceived availability, calling this a mistake she made, a "seduction" (Canby), in "less than romantic circumstances" (Carr), "submit[ting] one night to the impromptu ardor" (Stark), "a careless, definitely not rapturous moment" (Schickel), and so on. Allowing for freedom of interpretation in this situation results, paradoxically, in activation of narrative norms. Doyle does allow for the interpretation that Sharon is raped, depicting lack of consent: "they were kissing rough—she wasn't really: Her mouth was just open" (185). One more disgusting detail is then offered to us: "what he'd said after he'd put his hand on her shoulder and asked her was she alright. —I've always liked the look of you Sharon" (185–186), one of the numerous clichés that mark Burgess's speech throughout the story. When she staggers home, "She wanted to sleep. Backwards. To earlier" (185). Memory is revealed to be something created, much like a baby, or, more tellingly, the story Sharon invents to replace the awful memory.

Sharon's story skirts both rape and Burgess in favor of an invented Spanish sailor, and in doing so, reveals the slipperiness and dangers of memory, calling attention to the way that narratives are molded into conventional storylines. Such shaping of the past is of particular interest in Ireland as the nation struggles to shake off stereotype and cliché without denying its history entirely. Peadar Kirby, Luke Gibbons, and Michael Cronin deplore what they see as an economically motivated rejection of Ireland's history, calling instead for "an engagement with our past, rediscovering in its many muted voices values and aspirations contrary to those that dominate the social order of the Celtic Tiger" (200). Stories like *The Snapper* are to be criticized, in this model, for their "social and political evasions"(10) via a new, urbanized, romantic idyll (viz. the critiques of Doyle's characters as stage Irish) or, alternately (as seen in the perception of unsentimentality by reviewers), for their conformity to old models of "fatalism" re-emerging "in the contemporary guise of a gritty, working-class realism" (11).[30] What Sharon's possible rape suggests about contemporary engagement with the past is that interpretations are not so easily fixed. When Sharon hopes to return "to earlier," we can read this moment as one of regression (except that the past she wants to return to is not so idyllic), or we can read it as an indication that memory is not fixed or reliable. In either case, Sharon's unwillingness to confront the past does not equal Doyle's—here he asserts the unfixability of memory, emphasizing how expectations and assumptions render some stories impossible. Sharon cannot conceive of rape, so the forced jocularity of pub culture sculpts her story. In revealing the dynamics by which the men in the novel delineate public space as a means of attempting to control women, whether through paternalism or sexual advances, Doyle shows that private memory becomes public as it takes shape through story.

Indeed, the pull toward convention is pilloried in the character of Burgess, with an undertone asserting serious stakes. Part of what's important about the Sharon/Burgess scenes is the way that the older man continually exhibits an attraction for the norms that Sharon repeatedly repudiates; Doyle links these social norms to the mindsets accountable for her violation. When Sharon confronts Burgess, repeating the coarse phrases he has been using around the town about her: "you said I was a ride. Didn't yeh? ... You got your hole, didn't yeh?," Burgess flails in part because "he hated hearing women using the language he used" (223). Burgess's crass words may be formulaic, but they are made strange and new for him when spoken by a woman. Doyle shows Sharon relishing the power of bluntness, which she goes on to use to stand up to other male characters. Speaking directly violates Barrytown's pattern of avoidance via gossip, and moving away from pat phrases gives Sharon power.

For the most part, Burgess's responses to Sharon are very predictable. "Sharon knew what he was going to say next" (227), and later asks him "did you rehearse this, Mister Burgess?" (261). Cliché blots out insight, just as local slagging obscures the possibility of rape. From the phrases like "we both made a mistake" (226) and "I am, as the old song goes, torn between two lovers" (251) to his midlife crisis decision that he should run away with Sharon, Burgess represents the path of conventional narrative. Reliance on received storylines and clichés makes the revelation of the truth impossible. When Sharon opts to conceal Burgess's fatherhood, she removes from him a way to grasp what has happened, much as the suggestion of his rape of her is beyond either of their conceptual frameworks. Sharon's own muted sense of violation suggests just how much culture sculpts personal ideas, as well as pointing to her community's accountability for her situation.

The community in denial is reflected by individual shame about clear speech markers of Barrytown, and subplots show the Rabbitte family eagerly working to efface their "Barrytownness," a move the text itself resists. The star of *The Commitments*, Jimmy Jr., his role in this novel peripheral, pays forty pounds for lessons to acquire a proper radio accent. In Doyle's rendering of the new accent, Barrytown's pronunciations become the orthographic norm. "Hoy there…this is Jommy Robbitte, Thot's Rockin' Robbitte, with a big fot hour of the meanest, hottest, baddest sounds around" (316). Doyle's choice to respell "Jimmy" in reference to the Northside accent locates *The Snapper* in a political literary tradition as well as an experimental one. The reversal calls to mind, for instance, the way Maria Edgeworth, in *Castle Rackrent*, "does not convey regional speech through the Victorian convention of misspelling, devices which signals the speaker's ignorance and linguistic incompetence" (Butler, Introduction). Rather, the new accent bears the marked quality.[31] Edgeworth, Gray, and Doyle all indicate both the arbitrary nature of translating oral sounds into written language and the class assumptions regularly underlying such adaptations.

Ironically, *The Snapper*'s own comfort with Jimmy Jr.'s accent contrasts with his efforts to retool it. The insertion of Jimmy Jr.'s accent-experiments in the novels has several consequences. In Chatman's terms, these moments are certainly satellites. The fact that they are so clearly outside of the bounds of the storyline indicates a fluidity of plotline, that story is not the most important goal here, as well as implying that Doyle wanted in particular to introduce the issue that they foreground, namely the connection between class and language.

While Jimmy Jr. tries to elevate his speech through elocution lessons, Mrs. Rabbitte, Veronica, spends her time correcting the grammatical errors and demotic dictions of her profane family. When Sharon tells her parents the Spanish sailor story, she says, "Ah, look, I was really drunk…Pissed. Sorry, Mammy" (264). Sharon explains in standard English, then slang. Ironically, Veronica receives apologies throughout the novel for language slips while she is leaned on and taken advantage of in every other way. "—It's no wonder they talk the way they do, Veronica gave out to Jimmy Sr" (149). The narratorial "gave out" here is more informal than Veronica's own language, the narrator sitting beneath Veronica on any linguistic hierarchy we can detect. Veronica is both the moral and linguistic high ground of the novel, but it is made clear throughout that the characters have access to a variety of linguistic registers that they choose to deploy at various moments. Even the fact that the title word "snapper" itself is slang challenges Veronica's grammatical corrections.

Sharon herself refuses to accept the dominance of mainstream Irish English and the cultural hierarchy that it would imply. A prenatal visit she makes to the doctor stresses the difference between Sharon's language and the educated speech of Sharon's doctor: "She said she wanted to know me menstrual history an' I didn't know what she talkin' abou' till she told me" (214). The difference in the voices of these two women is in part one of vocabulary, menstrual history versus periods. The film plays up the different accents of patient and physician, indicating that the doctor's voice is a signature of her neighborhood and education, just as Sharon's accent is. Sharon goes out of her way to mention that the doctor looked really young, further calling attention to the fact this is a class difference rather than an age difference. *The Snapper*, however, doesn't let this hierarchy stand unquestioned, any more than Sharon does. Refusing to be cowed by the doctor, the film has her give sassy answers, even placing herself in the role of questioner. Even more important, however, is the fact that the scene is related via Sharon's narration in a voiceover to her friends in the pub. Sharon and her friends interpret for us, undercutting the presumption of education and making a clever pun along the way ("Menstrual history,...I got a C on that in me Inter").

Gerry Smyth has lauded *The Snapper* for being a "dialogue-based text, beginning and ending with spoken words rather than the narrator's reflections and opinions" (Smyth, *NN* 73). Doyle cedes control of his narrative to his characters, replaces the governance by one narrative voice with the presence of multiple voices. But both plot and narrative structure of the story ultimately moderate such positive heteroglossia. Although the novel is heavy with dialogue, Sharon and Jimmy alternate as focalizers throughout, as well as being the subjects of lengthy passages of free indirect discourse. And the growth of Jimmy's interest in Sharon's pregnancy parallels the growth of his free indirect discourse in the novel at the expense of hers. By novel's end, we read far more from his point of view than we did at the beginning; Sharon's perspective is eclipsed to the point that we see only a few seconds of her labor.[32] Ultimately, Jimmy oversteps his role, motivated as he is by his need to present a certain public face. "A strong active man in the house, a father figure, would be vital for Sharon's snapper" (320). Jimmy's solicitous involvement in Sharon's pregnancy merely replaces the colonial invader with Irish paternalism. Sharon never contemplates raising the child without her family—sweet, but also telling as to the degree of her dependency. "She didn't want to be by herself, looking after herself and the baby. She wanted to stay here so the baby would have a proper family and the garden and the twins and her mammy to look after it so she could go out sometimes" (287). And here we encounter the central problem of Doyle's method and of Jimmy's interest in the pregnancy—by rendering the individual the collective, the private is effaced by the public, further reinforcing the very culture of avoidance that Doyle critiques throughout.

At the novel's end, Sharon laughs at her own decision to name the baby Georgina, which leads to readings of the entire novel as a stereotyping of a carefree, fun-loving Irish working class. Such an interpretation is understandable if one reads the novel as a conventional piece of fiction in which character, plot, and time function more or less normally. But *The Snapper* is full of episodes that question the class system, gender roles, and the educational system. Most of them would be classified as satellites rather than kernels because Sharon is not a part of them and this is her story. Or so it would be if this novel conformed to narrative norms. Part of Doyle's project, however, is to challenge a narrative and social status quo. The supposed satellites further challenge the unity of story, emphasizing community rather than individual still further, making the family, not Sharon, the real main character here. In this light, Sharon's final laughter is only a fraction of the full response, certainly one she is entitled to. Her younger brother Darren, a slight presence, is the one who cries with joy at the birth of a healthy baby, his relief seemingly in response to Sharon's unexpressed anxiety that the baby "would be normal and healthy" (304). Darren's release of tension serves as Sharon's, the family acting like one consciousness.

As in his other novels, Doyle's narrative sparseness appears to withhold judgment of any sort, declining to comment on the right or wrong of his characters' actions and behaviors. At the same time, in ceding control of the text to the multiplicity of voices in Barrytown, Doyle reveals the power of middle-class norms as states the family strives toward. Rather than a move away from the sort of de Valeran family Doyle strives to reject, *The Snapper* actually shows the Rabbittes strenuously trying to integrate themselves into this conservative structure. For all of its efforts to portray Jimmy as a modern man open to being in the delivery room and timing uterine contractions, the novel characterizes him as motivated by very traditional concerns. The power and language gains the family experiences they ultimately use not to resist the status quo, but to attempt to emulate or join it. The burying of the truth is effected by the community's expectations and by the concurrent absence of intimacy—the public face is the only face.

The seemingly comic high jinks of the Rabbitte family encompass both the value and perils of working-class community for Doyle, revealing his wariness of private consciousness as well: "the family is inevitable...it's just part and parcel of the Irish package, really" (Smyth, *NN* 106), he says in an interview, the word "inevitable" suggesting both the comforts and constraints of family life. Doyle liberates the Rabbittes, placing them in charge of a variety of discourses and revealing how deftly they manipulate them, and his text highlights the change in traditional definitions of gender in the face of overcrowded housing and large-scale male unemployment in the working-class Ireland of the 1980s and early 1990s and the concomitant incompatibility of traditional distinctions between public and private. Yet his progressive notes sound alongside Jimmy's efforts to maintain a male-controlled household. Indeed, as Jimmy assumes the role of father, the text connects with the past and endorses the ersatz incestuous model of Irish society that Doyle would resist. Even though the novel defies stereotypes while depicting the strengths of a working-class family, it reveals the downsides of collective identity and shows, however inadvertently, the irresistible appeal of privacy and middle-class status.

Economic and Textual Transitions: *The Van, Paddy Clarke*, and *The Woman Who Walked into Doors*

While *The Commitments* focused on youth culture, *The Snapper* moved to an emphasis on peer group for both father and children, as well as on the family itself, an examination deepened in *The Van*. Throughout the trilogy, the use of local idiom is central, and we see drawn-out investigation of the way this vernacular interacts with the forms of speech offered as the norm. Convention is questioned again in *The Van*, where it becomes especially clear how Doyle's linguistic explorations connect to social, political, and economic ones. As Doyle continues to evolve his novels set in Barrytown, their interest in the intersection of class and space becomes increasingly pronounced, while their uses of narrative experiment explore the dynamics of memory and the power of narration. If *The Snapper* showed Jimmy Sr asserting his masculinity, in *The Van* we confront the failure of Irish economic revival and the concomitant failure of Irish manhood, both set against the limits of normal language hierarchies and narrative form. Where Doyle's first two novels upended form, showing the peaceful coexistence and jostling of languages, *The Van*, while retaining the humor of the earlier novels, reveals the high stakes underlying language battles and the downside of unresolved narrative. Unlike *The Commitments*, this novel is told entirely via free indirect discourse, a third-person narrator who uses Jimmy Sr's own words. Colin Graham takes note of the link between structural poverty and challenges to narrative structure: "Like the novels of Scottish contemporary James Kelman, Doyle's *The Van* is comfortable when almost narrativeless—indeed the same social context (unemployment) forces characters...into periods of apparently unhealthy stasis" ("Doyle" np). The narrative without trajectory therefore acts as a parallel to an unmoored life: Jimmy Sr finds himself laid off and deeply depressed. Reading and reeducation, a couple of common solutions that he tries, only emphasize how pointless he feels. Jimmy tries, for example, to read *David Copperfield*. "He was sure it was good, brilliant—a classic—but he fuckin' hated it. It wasn't hard; that wasn't it. It was just shite; boring, he supposed, but Shite was definitely the word he was looking for" (371–372). A British orphan's story does not register with an Irish family man. Colliding here are differing notions of the individual and the family, with national valences attached to each. Moreover, the rags-to-riches format may seem improbable or irritating to someone whose months of unemployment have educated him as to how difficult such bootstrapping can really be. Via Jimmy's dismissal of the novel, Doyle may also be making a tongue-in-cheek repudiation of the stereotype of colorful working-class characters said to populate his texts and Dickens's.

Jimmy's word choice is important here as well, as it challenges the value of specific or literary terms of analysis. The word "classic" does not guarantee readability and is revealed to be an arbiter of taste rather than quality, as empty of real judgment as the empty, everyday "good" and slang exaggeration "brilliant." Even the mainstream word "boring" is disallowed; where profanity is often written off as a thoughtless or unintelligent retreat from careful expression, Doyle here suggests that it can be a very careful choice.[33]

The roles and capabilities of language are foregrounded through-out the novel. In the novel's opening pages, Darren, Jimmy Sr's son and only a minor character, is completing a take-home essay ques-tion. Significantly for my interest in space in Doyle's novel, Darren displaces his father from the kitchen table so he can work; Jimmy ends up on the front step, fully part neither of interior or exterior world (Smyth, "Right" 23). Ironically, Darren must discuss how "[c]omplex-ity of thought and novelty in the use of language sometimes create an apparent obscurity in the poetry of Gerard Manley Hopkins" (349). The wording of the exam question establishes the oppositional and distant position of academic language to the working class, who may view writing as "a trap, not a way of saying something to someone.... exposing as it goes all that the writer doesn't know, then passing into the hands of a stranger who reads it with a lawyer's eyes, searching for flaws" (Shaughnessy 7). The word "apparent" in the essay question suggests that the difficulty in reading Hopkins's poetry is not real, implying that someone who finds it so is wrong.

Especially difficult for Darren is beginning to write, though not because he has nothing to say—he thinks to himself that Hopkins must have sniffed glue, for instance. But he knows "he couldn't write that in his answer though." Even the words he gets onto the page are a problem to him: "he shouldn't have written In My Opinion. It was banned" (349). What is banned is not so much the phrase in itself as it is a way of thinking that elevates personal tastes over institutionally agreed upon aesthetic qualities, conventions Darren does not recog-nize or have access to. The scene ends with Darren tearing out the page he was writing, having given up.

Jimmy has given up as well, unable for months to find work, depressed. "The good thing about winter was that the day was actu-ally short. It was only in daylight that you felt bad, restless, sometimes even guilty" (408–409). To kill time, he "went into town and wan-dered around...It had changed a lot; pubs he'd known and even streets were gone...He could tell you one thing: there was money in this town" (409). Jimmy's sense of the city begins with interior spaces, moving to ways of navigating the city and connecting the disappear-ance of both to a new prosperity from which he is excluded. In this, he acts as one "excluded from political and economic power offer[ing] viewers another construction of the city" (Konstantarakos 142). The pressures of purchasing power that bracket Jimmy's afternoon on a bench in town also diminish his pleasure, however, so that the section begins and ends with half-hearted denials of his uselessness: "You got used to it. In fact, it wasn't too bad" (408) and "He was happy enough" (411). "Too" and "enough," adverbs of sufficiency, indicate their opposites instead.

Entrepreneurial activity, traditional work like the sort that has always defined him, is the only thing that will cure Jimmy's depression. And as it turns out, Jimmy's thumbnail analysis of city center Dublin is insightful: Ireland's collective national mood is recovering from a depression at the same time, the thrill of World Cup playoff victories reasserting an old-style sense of national pride. Jimmy's friend Bimbo and his wife Maggie put up the money for a chipper van (fish and chips on wheels) and take Jimmy on as a "partner." The early success of the Irish team in the World Cup benefits the business. But traditional male relationships and traditional economics create tensions in a society where they no longer seem adequate. The fact that the van cannot at first move on its own foreshadows the limits of economic mobility. For M. Keith Booker, *The Van* recapitulates the trajectory of the *Dubliners* stories: "the main characters (stimulated by American models) develop glorious dreams of wealth and success, only to have those dreams collapse within the context of Dublin reality" (39).

While "[i]t was great having the few bob in the pocket again" (507), Jimmy becomes aware of the disparity between the word "partners," which "was the word Bimbo'd used at the very start" (556) and the fact that "Bimbo and Maggie were the ones in charge... he was sure they talked about business in bed every night" (554). The explicitly personal relationship of husband and wife and the ethos of friendship inevitably conflict with the profit-driven business, and Jimmy casts his anxiety about the female invasion of the male domain of business. Maggie not only keeps the books, she also acts as the force of planning and innovation, seeing ways to expand the business such as offering special occasion meals in the customer's home. They struggle with the logistics of having only one thermos but two courses needing temperature control until they realize one of them can "hoof it" (545) to Bimbo's home to fetch ice cream out of the freezer there, a detail which adds both comedy and a reminder of how local their business is. Maggie buys a white waiter's jacket with gold buttons— Jimmy feels "humiliated just looking at Bimbo in it" (546)—and targets couple celebrating anniversaries for candlelight service. Jimmy reads Bimbo's get-up as emasculating, a microcosm of Maggie's silly plans and meddling control, and the dinners-with-wine represents her ongoing efforts to merge home and public spaces, something he sees as inevitably castrating. Even the enclosed kitchen of the van, a feminine, private space moving through public ones, can be seen as a metonymic emblem of the inability of Doyle's working-class subjects to locate themselves in the new economy.

Concerns about space are at the intersection of *The Van*'s concerns about masculinity and class. As Smyth notes, much of the novel takes place indoors, working "on one level to produce a knowable community based around family and friends, [but] there is also a sense of a larger urban milieu which the characters cannot (fully) know nor the narrative (adequately) represent" (24). Smyth reads this urban space as a challenge to a rural community for which Barrytown stands in, but given that *The Van* takes place a full thirty years since the settling of such suburbs, it seems reasonable to read the unknowability and unnarratability Smyth notes as consequences of a space that has failed to create the prosperity it promised; instead, old forms appear inadequate and the novel strains against linear plot and character development as norms.

The dissolving of the novel's form is paralleled by the dissolution of Jimmy Sr's friendship with Bimbo. As the relationship deteriorates, the men head into the Dublin City Centre together, "away from the van, and Maggie, and the pressure and the rows and all the rest of the shite" (577). Space and women are implicated in male troubles. The scene opens with the men studying the timetable for the DART, their unfamiliarity with the train schedule bestowing a foreignness of the capital to residents who live only a 15-minute ride from the center, a fact made explicit when Jimmy Sr jokes, "Is there a duty-free shop in the last carriage?" (577). The suggestion of a long journey, and its link to capitalist consumption, when combined with the fact that Jimmy Sr and Bimbo are off for a night in the town to escape their own economic tensions, casts Dublin as safely and appropriately consumerist, while Barrytown struggles with financial modernity. The friends make a pub crawl through some of Dublin's most famous bars, we are told that "They were new places to Bimbo, and to Jimmy Sr although he'd walked past them and had a look in. He'd promised himself that if her ever had any money again he'd inspect them properly. And here he was" (579). Tourism and money are again linked, and while only six miles away, Dublin represents the cosmopolitan metropolis, prompting Jimmy Sr and Bimbo to dress in suits for the evening.

The evening takes a turn for the exciting when the men head away from the pub culture they recognize toward a nightclub, passing what seems to them a younger, hipper, posher clientele on Grafton Street. "These young ones were used to money...they had accents like newsreaders" (580). Despite Bimbo's visible discomfort with their environment, Jimmy Sr, who himself "hated this place, and liked it" (581), moves through the press of bodies in the hopes not of sleeping with a woman, but just "to know if he could get his hole" (582). References to the moneyed character of the clientele permeate the narrative, and as Jimmy makes clear that he believes he could success-fully seduce a woman in his own neighborhood, his agenda in the nightclub is, like in the pubs before, to validate his masculinity via economic prowess. Lower-class status, far from connoting manliness, indicates an absence; money and virility are interchangeable.

Failing to start conversations with women in the nightclub, the men repair to a pub. After a discussion about the general predilection of women for money over looks (Jimmy repeatedly coaxing acquies-cence from Bimbo), they attempt another nightclub, where, over expensive bottles of house plonk, they manage to hit on a couple of women. Surprisingly, given the narrator's repeated mentions of Bimbo's discomfort, awkwardness, and satisfaction with wife and home life, it is he who "gets off" with one of the ladies. Jimmy, drunk and embarrassed by his own rejection by the other woman, follows Bimbo to the toilets and hits him, underlining again his connection of masculinity and money when he blames Bimbo's mention of the chip-per for his own inability to score. As the argument moves to their conflicts over work, they back away from talking and leave the club, catching a (very expensive) taxi home. Leaving Dublin, which during the evening acts as a place where money flows freely and the unspo-ken can be openly expressed, the men head back to Barrytown, to inhibited communication, and to economic tension. For all his will-ingness to elide the difference between money and sex, Jimmy Sr is only capable of talking about the latter, and his efforts to use it as a coded method of reasserting his economic parity with Bimbo fail.

How big a failure becomes evident when, in the next conversation between Jimmy Sr and Bimbo, we learn that the men will no longer split profits; instead, Jimmy will be paid a weekly wage. Doyle structures the scene so we enter en media res, finding out the topic of the painful exchange only after several paragraphs of cryptic semi-communication, a technique that highlights the communication dif-ficulties that structure so many relationships in Doyle's novels. This new arrangement reminds Jimmy of "working in McDonalds or Burger King. Maggie was probably up at her sewing machine making one of those poxy uniforms for him" (603). The American emblems of global capitalism and the depersonalizing uniforms accompanying them, while hardly analogous to Jimmy's situation (as indicated by the hand-production of the imagined uniform), reveal the fundamental basis of class relations, the difficulty of personal relationships between employer and employed.

But the solution is not a return to an earlier form of small business proprietorship. For one thing, Bimbo's cash-basis van and Jimmy's noncontract labor, not to mention the success of a small start-up, hark back to a time before big business and government intervention in local enterprise. Moreover, Jimmy realizes

> he couldn't go back to what it had been like before they'd bought the van. He couldn't do that; get rid of the video [VCR] again, stop giving the twins proper pocket money and a few quid to Sharon, and everything else as well—food, clothes, good jacks [toilet] paper, the few pints, the dog's fuckin' dinner; everything. There was Darren as well now. How many kids went to university with fathers on the labour? (602)

Jimmy's list of the benefits of employment is touching in its triviality, but what matters about these benefits is his perception of their irreversibility. Being "on the labour"—receiving public aid—is not an option; the limits of the social welfare system so long the backbone to neighborhoods like Barrytown are recognized. While the capitalist future is unpalatable, the socialist past is inconceivable, neither a positive solution to Jimmy's condition.

As Bimbo begins to act like more of a boss and proprietor, seeming to enjoy Jimmy's submission, Jimmy pretends that he intends to unionize, claiming that he needs to protect himself and his family. Bimbo tells him that he'll no longer have a job if he pursues the union idea. The conflict that ensues is the final development in the novel, placing a certain blame on the threat of unionization. Economics have shifted in Ireland to the point that a union may often be a moot issue, that old-style collectivism breeds division. Even when Bimbo buckles and offers to go fifty-fifty with Jimmy Sr again, Jimmy declines, seeing that Bimbo seeks to repair a friendship via business, "desperate for Jimmy Sr to give him a sign that he still liked him" (630). The novel's end is another curious instance of a climax that is not a climax. A visit from a health inspector shuts the van down until it is brought up to regulation, a reminder that as much as Bimbo may be a proprietor and have economic control over Jimmy Sr, he himself is subject to larger regulatory forces. The two men again physically fight, and Jimmy Sr finds resolution impossible because Bimbo reminds him again that their stake in the van was never equal. But as conversation is never allowed to venture too far into the painful, the men go for a pint. Bimbo does try to talk through their meltdown, but Jimmy Sr had "no time any more for that What Happened shite...the No Hard Feelings wankology" (629, 630). Despite his facility with neologisms and witty turns of phrase, Jimmy Sr articulates a belief in the futility of communication, a signature of the lighthearted, superficial culture that he and Sharon both participate in. His use of capital letters and the suffix "-ology" indicate his sense of the institutional source of Bimbo's rhetoric, thereby labeling it suspect. Jimmy Sr's emotional remoteness does not stem from an essential national character; rather, this detachedness arises largely because despite Bimbo's gesture, there is no genuine economic parity here. A verbal exchange cannot be productive any more than an economic one can.

Recognizing that language will not be effective, Bimbo decides to drive his van into the ocean, to remove the irritant from the disintegrating friendship. He and Jimmy Sr continue to fight, never quite forgiving each other during the evening when this takes place. The van finally in the water, the two walk away, Jimmy repeatedly shrugging off Bimbo's friendly arm. Doyle ends the novel here, not telling us if the van is ever recovered, if the friendship is ever repaired, if the gesture is real or symbolic.

What is clear is that the economic undertone will not recede with the waves. While a drunken Bimbo is willing to sacrifice his business for his friendship, both men realize that such principles are too expensive for the lower class. As they walk away from the sea, Jimmy turns back to look at the submerged van, only to see that Bimbo had turned back ten yards sooner. In the wake of gesture, pragmatism reasserts itself: "You'll be able to get it when the tide goes out again, Jimmy Sr told [Bimbo]" (633). Most likely, the van will be saved, if not by Bimbo then by some other small businessperson with a dream. Like the cyclical nature of the tides, business cycles will spiral onward, always unfinished.

Other story lines in the novel do reveal progress in keeping with the aspirations articulated throughout the *Trilogy*. Darren begins the novel absolutely estranged from the language of education, which by the end he has mastered to the point that he gets honors on all seven of his exams. Veronica makes a trajectory as well, returning to school and passing two Leaving Certs. Both avoid the entrapment on the economic ladder of Jimmy's limited, outdated qualifications. Although their self-improvement is relatively conventional as well, its promise is not as compromised or undercut as that of the traditional capitalism of the novel's central story line, in which there is no clear progress.

Like both the earlier and subsequent novels, then, *The Van* closes somewhat arbitrarily, the "story left deliberately open. All the books are unended in a way" (Smyth interview, *NN* 108). This notion of "unended" stories leaves space for reader input, much as the unattributed dialogue allows the reader to contribute an interpretation. In the latter case, to continue to read the story, the reader must decide who is speaking; in the former case, to stop reading, the reader must accept the lack of resolution. These ideas are linked in Doyle's aesthetic of diminishing the distinction between artist and audience, which resembles what Nehring sees as the project of the avant-garde: "the volatile interpenetration of art and everyday life through a mutual activity on the part of artistic producers and recipients, with the latter putting aesthetic forms to uses creative in their own right" (89).

In inventing an entire community, Doyle makes a move similar to that of Kelman or Joyce, creating a place so awash in specificity that it becomes universal, that the same detail could be developed about any place:

> Barrytown is not Ireland; indeed, it is not even Dublin. It is a fictional construction of a working-class suburb on Dublin's northside, and as such it displays many of the characteristics of the suburban phenomenon...proximity to the city, knowledge of a rural hinterland, displacement of older communities into large population concentrations often without adequate civic or cultural support.... (Smyth, *NN* 67)

This characterization of the peripheral qualities of Barrytown emphasizes both the universality of its traits and some of its major drawbacks. In creating a new community instead of drawing on an existing one, and paralleling Kelman's vague Glasgow and invented pub names, Doyle refuses to offer his characters up as "types" for the tourist gazes of a middle-class audience. Indeed, as Doyle turns in his next novels to the birth of Barrytown and its blend of lower-middle-class and working-class citizens, we will see that his denial of specificity can serve strategic ends.

The Barrytown Trilogy novels offer relatively brief vignettes, stylistically similar in their diegesis, their retreating but humorous third-person narrative voices, their leveling of climaxes, their use of dialect, and their contemporary settings. Following these novels, Doyle makes a stylistic break of sorts. His next novel, *Paddy Clarke Ha Ha Ha*, retains the humor and vernacular but takes place entirely in the mid-1960s and is wholly narrated by a distinctive first-person. Similarly, *The Woman Who Walked into Doors*, while told from the present, consists mainly of flashbacks and again relies entirely on a powerful first-person narration. The coincidence of the two major shifts, from present to past and from third to first person, locate the novels as fictionalized memoir, raising interesting issues of how Doyle translates his regional identity and textual experiments onto this genre, at the same time as they more directly address the relationship of history and tradition.

Kevin Whelan argues that memoirs of 1990s are evidence of the "further splintering of national narrative" and "a deliberate privatization of memory, a return to bourgeois interiorization" (193). Essentially, discussing the individual inevitably dodges larger social and political messages. While some 1990s Dublin memoirs in particular do suggest bourgeois interiority, no doubt (and although the workings of memory could be seen as a definitive feature of memoir across the board), Doyle's reworkings of the memoir style resist the idea that giving a working-class character a voice necessarily incorporates him/her into a complacent middle class, in particular when formal resistance is in place. Indeed, place is a crucial aspect of the working-class voices Doyle uses to critique limited views of Irish identity.

Doyle's first person narration evokes another fictional memoir from the turn of the century, *Portrait of the Artist as a Young Man*, his choice of mainly monosyllabic words combining with simple declarative sentence structure to create the sound of a child's voice, a technique that gives his book a Joycean cant:

> My hot water bottle was red, Manchester United's colour. Sinbad's was green.... You didn't just fill it with water—my ma showed me; you had to lie the bottle on its side and slowly pour the water or else air got trapped and the rubber rotted and burst. I jumped on Sinbad's bottle. Nothing happened. I didn't do it again. Sometimes when nothing happened it was really getting ready to happen. (Doyle, *PCHHH* 33)

Ten-year-old Paddy Clarke moves from a discussion of the colors of hot water bottles into their uses and perils, ultimately making a statement very telling in the narratives of both the novel and Irish history. The echoes of *Portrait* are amplified here by the subject matter, or more specifically, the color of the subject matter. "Dante had two brushes in her press. The brush with the maroon velvet back was for Michael Davitt and the brush with the green velvet back was for Parnell" (7). These brushes introduce the young Stephen to politics at the same time as they alert the reader to the presence of nationalistic tensions throughout the novel, encouraging us to read back to the little green place of the opening page as an allegory for Ireland, and setting the stage for the traumatic Christmas-dinner conflict that will alienate Stephen from politics permanently.

Doyle's Joycean resonance, however, upends the process of allusion as it recasts a child's introduction to the adult world of politics. Paddy doesn't receive political indoctrination from his mother based on the colors of the water bottles; rather, she offers him practical advice about how to keep them serviceable, a reversal of the form-over-function emphasis on the decorative aspect of the brushes. Further, the frame of reference here has been dramatically altered. Where the Dedalus household divided over the relationship between church and state in an independent Ireland, the Clarke brothers Paddy and Francis (a.k.a. "Sinbad") fabricate a rivalry between the red-jerseyed Manchester United soccer team and the green-jerseyed Northern Ireland (their favorite player, George Best, plays for both). The passage, then, makes several crucial substitutions: sport for politics, and British teams for Irish men. The allusion to the Christmas dinner scene repudiates, more, ignores the issues raised by Joyce; so why make the reference at all?

Here we see the reduction of nationalism by the book's characters; the symbolism of colors once provided a point of mobilization and anxiety, but the world that Doyle's novel evokes of suburban Dublin in the 1960s feels itself beyond politics. Nonetheless, the author writing in the 1990s knows the years between him and this peaceful, prosperous past have belied this view. The allusion becomes not so much to *Portrait* as to Ireland's inability to escape the issues Joyce identified. Both nationalism and a Joycean influence seem submerged here, to the point that Doyle is able to assert that neither is an issue.[34] The color of the hot water bottles becomes a statement of Doyle's hope for a contemporary Ireland that will not think right away of Joyce's brushes, something of a paradox: he opts to use these colors to show that they don't have resonance any more. But "[s]ometimes when nothing happened it was really getting ready to happen," a foreshadowing of the hostility within Paddy's home, the "Troubles" in the North, and the collapse of economic progress in Ireland.

Brian Cosgrove has pointed out that setting the novel in the Dublin suburbs "implies an ideological stance" in which Doyle "becomes one of those disaffected Irish moderns who reject 'the old Irish totems of Land, Nationality and Catholicism'" (232).[35] Nevertheless, amidst a steadfast unwillingness to engage in romanticization of the past, we can detect the presence of nostalgia—for boyhood pranks, storybooks, mother's love. As Declan Kiberd puts it, the novel "evinced nostalgia for the 1960s in which it was set and at the same time checked that tendency with a portrait of a disintegrating marriage" (Kiberd, *II* 611). The frontier-like setting on the edge of Dublin reveals both the promise and perils of progress.

Similarly, in his next novel, *The Woman Who Walked into Doors*, Doyle explores the relationship of nostalgia to the processes of modernization through a strategic overlap of national and family histories. Paula Spencer's married life is a checklist of contemporary social problems—marital discord, alcoholism, child and spouse abuse, unemployment—all of which culminate for her husband Charlo in a botched kidnapping that leads to his own death at the hands of the police. As in *Paddy Clarke*, Doyle addresses the fragility of the domestic sphere, but he includes warm, happy memories in the text to resist the stereotypic bleakness of urban realist novels. Declining to wallow in local color or romanticization, he depicts a complex Irish suburban world. Along with the demolition of simplistic distinctions between urban landscape and countryside, his novels about the 1960s and 1970s challenge binaries of the Irish and the international, of a miserable childhood and a blissful one, as well as of realist and experimental techniques. Paddy Clarke's household is one disrupted as much by modernization as by his parents' strife, while Paula Spencer's life with an abusive husband reveals the misplaced optimism of early economic growth. Both novels mediate an uncritical embrace of modernity with a thoughtful nostalgia for the end of an era, suggesting that there is an evolutionary link of contemporary Barrytown to its past as a space undefined in the urban-rural dichotomy.

Doyle disrupts the idea of an origin and illustrates the ambivalences of nostalgia and history through the formal device of telling the same story several different ways. *Paddy Clarke* is suffused with contradictory versions of events, incomplete narration, and unresolved narrative tensions. Realism does not make space for these sorts of issues, technically or philosophically. Challenging novelistic norms acknowledges the processes of memory, as hinted at by Doyle's verb construction here, for instance:

"We lit fires. We were always lighting fires" (4). Even two sentences can reveal the overlap/interplay between documentable fact and nostalgic reminiscence. The simplicity of the verb in the first sentence would make the boys' pastime matter-of-fact, worth mention but not discussion. The insertion of the word "always" into the second sentence, along with the shift to past progressive, moves the tone from one of straightforward relation of events into one of nostalgic exaggeration (no one is *always* lighting fires). The first statement is the text of the child narrator, the second, a glance backward, indicating the existence of a covert adult narrator (an older, matured Paddy) narratologically separate from the overt narrator (Paddy the child). Throughout the novel, emphasis moves from child to adult within sentences, within ideas:

> The barn became surrounded by skeleton houses. The road outside was being widened and there were pyramids of huge pipes at the top of the road, up at the seafront. The road was going to be a main road to the airport. Kevin's sister, Philomena, said that the barn looked like the houses' mother looking after them. We said she was a spa, but it did; it did look like the houses' ma. (13)

The narrator here seems at first to be the covert narrator, remembering and condensing the scenes, but this summary contains elements of the overt narrative voice as well;[36] the word "spa" in particular acts as a clear sign of the child's perspective. The normal hierarchy of narrator and character is undermined by the constant interplay, just as the sentimental is denied by disruption of the domestic sphere and nostalgic memories are revealed as already corrupted. While skeletons suggest decay, they represent the future, as do the ancient/modern "pyramids" of pipe. The familial construction of the house/barn relationship conjures the national narrative enshrined in the 1937 Constitution.

But the barn burns down, problematic if it stands in for mother Ireland presiding over the new suburbs. Rather, it would seem an emblem of the rural is being destroyed, an obsolete ancestor "left behind" (11). Another relic, again suggestive of an overarching national family, is Uncle Eddie, a slightly mad farmhand, who reportedly perished in the blaze: "Uncle Eddie was burnt to death in the fire; we heard that as well" (14). The first part of this statement reads as fact; it is only after the semicolon that we discover that it is hearsay. And the past is so unwilling to capitulate to the Corporation that Eddie turns out to be alive. What is important about his survival and about the passage is the way that he is said to be dead but is resurrected, the way that the factual, the idea of progress as inevitable and incontrovertible, is thwarted by syntax and uncertainty about the future.

Incidentally, despite their pyromania, the boys are not responsible for the fire set to the barn, which raises the interesting question of who is, especially given that the barn remained after "the Corporation bought Donelly's farm" (11) and that somebody "found a box of matches outside the barn; that was what we heard" (13). Whether the rumor is true or not is irrelevant; what matters is that even the grown-ups see the fire as arson: "Everyone said someone from the new Corporation houses had done it" (14). This tension between older residents of the area and newer ones emerges again and again ("Slum scum" (118), Paddy repeats at one point). Indeed, the fires set by the boys tend to be on the building site of the new houses, a burning of the new as opposed to the barn-burning, which ignites and destroys the past.

Similarly, the road to the airport, connecting Barrytown to Dublin, and by extension, the rest of the world, severs the connection of the emerging subdivision to the land's more rural past. Grammatically, the past progressive captures the moment of expansion—"was being widened"—making it sound as though the widening is ongoing, continuous. Doyle's texts repeatedly focus on such instants marking the transition from past to future. In this vein, the nostalgia for childhood in *TWWWID* is problematized by its juxtaposition with the distinctly un-rosy scenes from Paula's adulthood and the apparent narrative present in which she is being informed that her husband was killed by police during a botched kidnapping/robbery. [37] As in *Paddy Clarke*, modernization, while laced with benefits, proves less than benign. The early picture, however, like the Irish economy, at first seems rosy. Paula, on the advantages of *not* emigrating: "We both had jobs here. There were housing estates being built all over the place, all around the city; the papers were full of ads for skilled labourers—just turn up at the site and ask the foreman. The city was bursting with people growing up and getting married. There were people coming home from abroad" (132).[38] Paula mentions marriage, the moment of transition from youth into adulthood; she seems to long here for the period of initial commercial development contemporaneous to her own marriage, when jobs were more plentiful.

While the 1960s in other countries saw the Age of Aquarius, Paula and Charlo wed under the sign of economic growth, following a conventional path despite early signs of their unsuitability. Soon, prosperity and expansion are conjoined as the young couple moves to the suburbs: "There was no bus to the estate; it didn't exist yet...There was still a farm house. Nicola [Paula's oldest daughter] waved at the farmer in his tractor...We didn't know where he was going with his tractor. His fields were gone" (193). The farmer leaves his fields, now buried by modern new houses, in the same years that Ireland becomes a predominantly urban nation.[39] At the height of Irish industrialization and development, this newness is supposed to be invigorating: "The smell of the new house would rub off on us. A new start...Charlo hummed the national anthem as I filled the kettle for the first time in our new kitchen" (194). Both Paula's quintessentially Irish display of domesticity and Charlo's hum underline the role of the nation in their temporary abundance.

Paula mostly recalls the promise and excitement of the family's move, though just as all of her memories foreshadow Charlo's unpredictable outbursts of violence, this reverie is punctuated by hints of the endemic problems of peripheral housing estates:

> It was all raw and bare, the edge of the world....I wondered how far it was to the nearest shop. I wondered if the place would always look like an abandoned building site. I couldn't imagine it changing, growing older and smoother. There was a cement mixer, turned over on its side, in the front garden two doors up. There were kids playing in front of the houses that were already occupied. I didn't like the look of them. They were rough-looking, even the girls, filthy language coming out of them." (193–194)

Similar to Paddy's use of past continuous, Paula here articulates a fixedness in time, an inability to envision the future. Interlaced with the impermanence are the qualities Paula identifies with suitable living—smoothness: of ground, language, access to transport and goods. Paula would like the suburbs to eliminate the roughness of lower class life, but she cannot romanticize the neighborhood or the neighbors. And just as we see in the work of Kelman and Galloway, public transportation is an unresolved concern. "there was no bus yet to the new estate—it didn't really exist yet. We had a long walk from the bus stop" (193). "Then we went to my parents' house—it was Sunday. Two buses" (195). Unfinished housing sites and unfinished transit routes reveal an estate already marked for disrepair and marginalization.

Shopping offers a view to how Paddy's estate, where children are advised to avoid newcomers like the Spencers, is on a more stable footing, in part because its ties to the past are not fully severed. In a semi-nostalgic evocation, Paddy is sent one Sunday to get half a block of ice cream on credit. Mister Fitz "wrapped the ice-cream in the paper he wrapped the Vienna Rolls in. He folded it up. It was already wet" (59). There seems to be something special about the trust involved in the payment and in the inefficiency of the packaging, the idea of ice cream in paper, paper that is used for many things and thus denies the division of labor. In an age suffused with mechanical reproduction and competition amongst brands, Doyle recalls the immediacy of childhood, linking it here explicitly to the less-market-oriented past.

Indeed, a number of Doyle's potentially nostalgic moments refer to the time before mass production—"There were no supermarkets yet, just grocers and shops that sold everything. Once, when we were out on a walk, Ma asked for the Evening Press, four Choc-pops, a packet of Lyons Green Label and a mouse trap and the woman was able to get them all without stretching" (156). There are a couple of important features to this moment: for one thing, the old shop represents a vastly different relationship to space, separating consumer from product and containing everything within an enclosed area. What follows from this is the implication that "everything" was available before the onslaught of supermarkets.[40] The significance of this fact comes immediately, as Paddy offers personal details about nearby shop owners. "[T]he people in the shops were friends with our parents. They'd all got married and moved to Barrytown at the same time. They were all pioneers, my da said" (157). The portrait of early Barrytown settlers paradoxically encompasses nostalgia and modernization, harking back to a bygone era, if to an era of "progress" and westward expansion in the American old west.

If there is romanticization, then, it is for a period of development and potential. We see this again when Paddy describes chips being brought "[a]ll the way from town in the train, cos there was no chipper in Barrytown then" (36). The word "then," like the "yet" in the supermarket sentence, indicates the existence of the covert adult narrator. The underlying presence of this covert narrator is responsible for creating the sense of nostalgia, the "cos" aping the child's voice that the "then" subsequently belies. The temporal displacement caused by the interplay of narrators complicates the feeling of nostalgia.

But Doyle's mediation of nostalgia does not exist merely on the formal level. The subject of this passage, the chipper, resists sentimentalization as well. If the sentimental "invokes the impossible desire to retrieve unified identity, a fantasy of original and pure Irishness in some pre-postcolonial unity, which, for Ireland, never existed" (C. Burns 237n), then Doyle's choice to reflect on the moment of transition escapes the trap of nostalgia. Chippers exist, though not everywhere. The era before chippers is gone, as is the era of uncommercialized suburbs, both only moments in an ongoing Irish history; the period Doyle evokes is already hybridized, impure.

One of Doyle's biggest critiques of an uncritical welcoming of modernity comes in one of Paula's most poignant moments, when she bemoans the blur that is her married life: "It's all a mess—there's no order or sequence. I have dates, a beginning and an end, but the years in between won't fall into place" (203). "I can't arrange my memories.

I can't tell near from far. I was married one day. I threw him out another day. It happened in between" (213). The tragedy here is the separation of past from present; Paula's memory gap renders the past separate, an unacceptable and immoral outcome to Doyle, in part because it opens up space for nationalist nostalgia, the idealized myths of origin. Combating the gap means filling in the blanks, and indeed, the act of composition of her own narrative is part of what renders Paula complete. This calls to mind Benedict Anderson's assertion that forgetting the continuity of national history "engenders the need for a narrative of 'identity'" (205). For Paula, as for Ireland, part of the challenge lies in moving beyond negative, disempowering constructions of identity.

Doyle does not allow for an easy convention to remain unchallenged. In the final pages of *PCHHH*, Paddy, ever a stand-in for the reader, is sure that "tomorrow or the day after my ma was going to call me over to her and, just the two of us, she was going to say, —You're the man of the house now, Patrick. That was the way it always happened" (281). But this moment never arrives, Paddy's expectations as learned from books and culture failing to account for the details of his own life. Rather, Doyle offers us an awkward nonending, a handshake between Paddy and his father when Patrick Clarke, Sr. arrives home for Christmas. Unlike the traditional novel where Paddy would become Patrick and replace his father as man of the house, Paddy's position is left unclear. We cannot determine if Mr. Clarke returns for good. The coming of age that we might expect from a conventional *Bildungsroman* is left uncertain. The novel ends because the protagonist's transformation has happened, though the traditional denouement of the conflict between self and society is left unresolved. Paddy realizes that adulthood does not follow fairy-tale format, but this realization offers no sense of resolution.

The final scene of *TWWWID* is one of thematic and structural uncertainty as well: Nicola and Paula have just violently expelled Charlo from the house, and Paula feels "I'd done something good" (226). Nowhere in the novel are we told whether this is Charlo's last time in the house, so no finality is derived from the expulsion, which all know is not a sure thing. Moreover, the event is chronologically two years prior to some things we hear about, so the expulsion cannot serve as a temporal end. Most significantly, the scene as it appears on the final page of the novel is a near word-for-word restatement of the previous page, undermining any structural ending as well. Rather, we enter the world of abused women, where each slap is meant to be the last, where the terror is never gone (even after Charlo's death, the scars and nightmares thrive), where the idea of "end" does not function. As Paula herself says, "I could rest if I believed that; I could rest. But I keep on thinking and I'll never come to a tidy ending" (192). Paula opposes closure to thought; she realizes that belief and faith create endings that inquiry refuses. Rather, in every place where Doyle would have the opportunity to provide closure, he declines to offer his readers or his characters historical, literary, and Irish needs for an ending.[41]

Between the first relation of Charlo's expulsion and the second (225 and 226), Paula places only one scene, one piece of information that she has as a storyteller held back until the final pages of the novel, the fact that Charlo

> couldn't drive. That was why he'd got out of the car again. The poor eejit, he'd never got round to it. The kidnapper who couldn't drive. He'd never had a license, he'd never had a car—he'd never learned how to drive. He saw the guards coming over the wall, he shot Missis Fleming and ran to get away in a car he couldn't drive. It was neatly parked, a green Ford Escort. He'd fallen out onto the path. The houses looked nice. He was far from home. (225)

The useless green Ford that stands guard at Charlo's death evokes the dual-edged changes in the Irish economy; while EC membership led to increased growth, it also resulted in the closure of the Ford plant in Cork, widening the gap between rich and poor. Via her use of the vernacular "eejit" here in the final words of the novel, Paula reestablishes the Irishness that Charlo had robbed from her. Through her repetition of the word "never," she takes control of her narrative, and by extension, her life and her home, while Charlo becomes distanced from his, stuck in the narrative, stuck in the past. The "nice" houses that surround Charlo, like the "incredible. Huge" (93) ones that Paula cleans for a living, emphasize the interchangeability of physical and economic distance.

Both *PCHHH* and *TWWWID* link past to present, asserting continuity where Irish revisionism would see a rupture. In placing this connection in the suburbs of the working and lower middle class, Doyle recuperates the role of these people in Ireland's history, making their stories central and suggesting that the narratives of the periphery require careful narration precisely because they represent a hybrid history. Both novels explore family dynamics at the same time as they map out a national identity. The breakup Paddy witnesses in the home accompanies major shifts in the cultural landscape of Ireland, while

Paula's halting, difficult move toward independence conceives of new ways to be female and to be Irish. What occurs on the family level is not so much an allegory for the national as an intersection with it, each causing and caused by the other. The overlap of family, national, and coming-of-age narratives requires compromises—hence the multiple time periods and voices—but they don't make for easy resolution. Rather, the compromises indicate a theory in progress, the possibility for change and growth. This kinesis is crucial, desirable, exactly the opposite of a sealed history. It is Paula's repeated ending, complete with narrative insert, that most explicitly compels us to question narrative and historical closure. Likewise, Paddy's story ends without resolution; he too must move forward into history. The repeated refusal to sentimentalize the past in either novel combines with their incompletion to insist on a present continuous with history. The preservation of the moment of transition from a preindustrial world to a modern one ensures that the past will never be severed from the present; the indefinite endings keep history in motion; the hybrid nature of the world Doyle recalls invites us to resist homogenizing nationalism in histories and in the future.

Doyle's texts are criticized repeatedly for their engagement with the past, but as I have shown, in each case, not only is the look backward an acknowledgment of a complicated history, but it also serves as a mode of activating the present. At the same time, each text can be seen to develop textual modes that challenge mainstream expectations at the same time as thematically, the characters strive to attain the trappings of middle-class economic stability and therefore articulate seemingly conformist stances. Much criticism of Doyle fails to note the tension between these two agendas. Doyle's investigations of class, voice, and space do not fit neatly into the radically ahistorical revisionism Ferdia MacAnna fantasizes about and Gibbons excoriates; neither, surely, do they represent an activist call to arms. Allowing for their subtlety and complexity opens up constructions of a working-class, local identity.

Chapter Four

"Make Out its Not Unnatural At All":
Janice Galloway's Mother Tongue

Local identity in the novels of Kelman and Doyle blends regional, working-class vernacular with wariness about constructions of nation. Several of Doyle's novels explore how gender inflects this recipe, revealing the expectations society places on its women as standard-bearers and national icons. Similarly, Janice Galloway's women are often aware of their secondary status in a male-centered society, depicted amidst their reaction to it. These Scottish women that Galloway depicts refuse to conform to historic women's roles, whether the Celtic symbol of motherhood and the land, the ever-enduring British wife, or the sterile, bitter old maid; instead, they articulate their rejection of these norms through formations of alternate families, through play with metaphors of ingestion, and through reconceptions of male-dominated Enlightenment history and philosophy.

These crucial themes in Galloway's work are addressed elsewhere in the contemporary Scottish canon, though their import is often undermined by the stylistic choices made by other writers. For instance, Irvine Welsh's story "Eating Out" relates a night in the life of Kelly, one of the few women in the ensemble of characters in *Trainspotting*, a scarcity that this episode in particular seems to seek to explain. Working her way though college, Kelly waits tables at a Leith restaurant/bar. Four men come in: "Ah can tell by their accents, dress and bearing that they are middle to upper-middle-class English…failed Oxbridge home-counties types" (302). Their first remark in Kelly's presence, a joke linking sexist and anti-Scottish sentiments, sets the tone for their treatment of her. "One sais:—What do you call a good-looking girl in Scotland? Another snaps:—A tourist!" (302). After more degrading remarks along these lines, Kelly's anger reaches a peak, yet "No cash, no Uni [university], no degree" (303), so she holds her tongue. In the position of silent servant, she is without power or means of redress. Her reaction is to lace their food with menstrual blood, urine, feces, and eventually rat poison. The men unknowingly ingest the products of Kelly's body while they devour their food and talk about profit margins and Hawaii, capitalism and imperialism.

Kelly feels powerful, "actually enjoying their insults" (305), her reaction similar to Doyle's Sharon when she confronts George Burgess in *The Snapper*. As she worries about possible consequences of her poisoning on the restaurant, she recalls a philosophy paper assigned to her about whether morality is absolute or relative. "In my essay, ah now think that ah'd be forced tae put that, in some circumstances, morality is relative. That's if ah was being honest with masel. This is not Dr. Lamont's view though, so ah may stick wi absolutes in order to curry favour and get high marks" (305). Poisoning one of her diners seems morally acceptable to the waitress who has been denied any other response; Kelly's only ethical qualm involves the owner. But the clear sense she has that her actions are justifiable will not enter into her academic discourse, mainly because she sees the same power structure that kept her silent at work to be operative in the classroom as well. Ironically, her absolute moral realization of the relativity of values is denied voice by a relativistic understanding that she ought to see morality as absolute. Kelly's short-lived and violent empowerment is overwhelmed by a male power structure that insists upon the categorical imperative and will determine her future beyond her waitressing job.

Especially important here is Welsh's linkage of class, Scottishness, and gender, and the way that he represents Kelly's voice as an alternation of her local dialect and the language she is learning to use at college. Yet this separation of voices reinforces the notion of separate spheres for men and women, an idea that the dissolution of language hierarchies, as practiced by Galloway, implicitly challenges. Kelly narrates in her own idiom, but ultimately, her place is in the kitchen in this story, and her dialect remains in a secondary status as well. (Even the title of the story, "Eating Out," retains the perspective of the customers: male, wealthy, linguistically dominant, sexually in control; their consumption of Kelly's body parallels the colonial consumption of local resources.) The title omits any hint of vengeance, suggesting that the act of revenge will not achieve parity of men and women or of local and "learned" languages. Further, the undermining of Kelly's revenge by her submission to the terminology of her professor suggests that confrontation may not be the best solution to differences, serving briefly to invert but ultimately to reaffirm this opposition of local to learned. Elsewhere in *Trainspotting*, dialect does move to a central and equal role, so the fact that its inability to escape marginalization occurs when a woman confronts the issue speaks to the extra layer of difficulty that gender can add to the question of the "poor mouth."

Like the angry woman in *Trainspotting*, though retaining more agency, Galloway's characters are aware of their condition as particularly Scottish:

> Scottish women have their own particular complications with writing and definition, complications which derive from the general problems of being a colonised nation. Then, that wee touch extra. Their sex. There is coping with that guilt of taking time off the concerns of national politics to get concerned with the sexual sort: that creeping fear it's somehow self-indulgent to be more concerned for one's womanness instead of one's Scottishness, one's working-class heritage, whatever. Guilt here comes strong from the notion we're not backing up our menfolk and their "real" concerns. Female concerns, like meat on mother's plate, are extras after the men and weans have been served. (*Meantime* 5–6)

Galloway's introduction to a collection of writings compiled in the interests of exploring the new millennium "and what it has in store for women" (dust jacket) speaks to an overlap of class-, sex-, and nation-based agenda, and more importantly, to the necessity of privileging "female concerns" in the face of these other matters. It is in this context, then, that she writes: a literary scene in which writing is complicated by postcoloniality and class, both of which she feels must be subsumed by the less-addressed needs of women.[1]

Problems of "writing and definition," while not unique to colonized nations, are often foregrounded textually in their writings. The recurrent emphasis on textuality receives a further dimension from Galloway's choice of metaphor to explain how being a woman inflects one's responses to class pressures and colonization: meat on a plate, the leftovers that a mother eats after serving men and children ("weans").[2] Women's writing is figured as innately secondary/supplemental, on one hand, but also as self-nourishing. Politics must be fed, and a danger is implied in that if the mother doesn't get enough meat, she will starve.

The choice of a food metaphor is especially apt in light of Galloway's own literary output, focusing as she does on people "consumed" with guilt, as above, and in particular, women whose responses to the issues and problems of day-to-day life are regularly figured in terms of stuffing, starving, purging, and cooking. Like Welsh's Kelly, Galloway's protagonists revel in and resent their status as cooks. As we will see, eating and its disorders serve

Galloway repeatedly as means to comment on nation, femininity, and class.

Dorothy McMillan has referred to the "overwhelming masculinity of the Scottish cultural tradition at least in the Lowlands" (96). Indeed, although the so-called Scottish renaissance of the past 20 years has brought a number of nontraditional authors to the public attention, many of them working class and critical of traditional notions of Scottish identity, women are underrepresented even within this progressive group; certainly none has had the exposure in the United States of male luminaries such as James Kelman or Irvine Welsh.[3] The image presented by the "new guard" in Scotland through the hip, glossy *Picador Book of Contemporary Scottish Fiction* is aware of and responsive to women writing in Scotland: one-third of the writers listed on the cover are women, an improvement from earlier eras that indicates nonetheless that women are still underrepresented even when the best of intentions abound.

It would seem, then, that a woman from the west of Scotland, being neither male nor clearly Scottish, would be faced with particular challenges in writing a feminist Scottish novel.[4] And indeed, many Scottish women are not seen as Scottish at all, whether by their own choice to ignore/deny their Scottishness, out of a publisher's decision for marketability, or because of a society's lack of awareness (Muriel Spark, for instance, is most often characterized as British; Miss Jean Brodie herself is a paragon of European-ness). Marilyn Reizbaum points out in reference to contemporary Scottish writers that "one might name them without knowing that they are Scottish since they have been publicized through and often appropriated by British, specifically English, sources" (169). Furthermore, she accurately emphasizes the "phenomenon of 'double exclusion' suffered by women writing in marginalized cultures, including here examples of Scotland and Ireland, where the struggle to assert a nationalist identity obscures or doubly marginalizes the assertion of gender (the woman's voice) … the historical interaction between the marginalization of culture and sexism" (165, 182).[5]

The interplay of a marginalized nation and a marginalized gender expresses itself in Galloway's texts via a parallel focus on the inadequacies of family and on the perils of inhabiting threatened spaces, from the female body to remote housing estates. Both concerns are grounded in Galloway's interest in the constraints of a woman living within a society that is sexist, colonized, and, as a result, nationalist in a manner that forecloses on the participation of women and the lower classes. The formal features of her texts suggest that style as well is affected by one's spatial placement and one's position in hier-archies of nation and gender. Galloway's texts use their nonstandard modes of representation as a means to emphasize how socioeconomic class can place restrictions on a woman's access to and use of space, assiduously linking homes, council housing, cities, nation, and body in her protagonists' struggles.

Galloway's anorexic/bulimic text, *The Trick Is to Keep Breathing* (1989), with its obsession with houses, its modes of rejection, its ques-tioning of hierarchies (linguistic as well as human), and its constitu-tion of novel frameworks for family and sanity and alternatives to blood family, as well her next novel, *Foreign Parts* (1994), through a combination of stylistic experimentation and critical evaluation of hierarchies, explicitly and implicitly confront the role of women in Scottish society, in particular the idea of "Scottishness" itself as it is affected by inherited stereotypes and recent nationalist/devolutionary movements.

This final return to issues of nation, while often oblique in Galloway's fiction, is crucial. The traditional notion of family is sus-pect, rejected as damaging, much as traditional notions of nation and Scottishness are called into question. For one thing, all of Galloway's characters are urban in a world alien to and yet bounded, defined, and stereotyped by the Highland region and the kitchsy film *Brigadoon*; for another, their inherited conceptions of Scottishness are tied to stoic Calvinist and Presbyterian inheritances no longer operative. The value of the past, on both personal and national levels, is repeatedly called into question. The novels examined throughout *Narratives of Class* repeatedly deny the primacy of the past on a national level, yet excepting Galloway, the authors valorize personal origins through recurrent, if often ironic, focus on father-son rela-tionships. Galloway's disavowal of inherited family structures strikes a powerful blow against the pitfalls of nationalism as well, avoiding the paradox that has plagued theorists of nationalism from Fanon until today: if nationalism looks to precolonial origins to restore char-acteristics erased by the presence of the colonizer, the very narrative of origins risks reproducing the colonial logic it opposes. This is a point at which writing as a woman and in an urban Scotland, modern and heterogeneous, outside of the national original myth, offers Galloway the opportunity to skirt nationalism.[6] As Dorothy McMillan points out, the devolution movement of the late 1990s is "one of the crucial moments in Scotland's continuing quest for national defini-tion, a quest complicated by the uncertainty about *whether the aim is revivification of an old sense of nationhood or the creation of a new*"

(80, italics mine).[7] Revivification often seems to be the goal of the tourist board and movies like *Braveheart* or *Rob Roy*, while Kelman and fellow novelists like Alasdair Gray and Iain Banks seem more interested in the creation of a new nation that will challenge the very terms of national identity. Galloway's own response moves beyond even Kelman's, challenging the gender roles, origins, and family dynamics that have underpinned any number of nationalist movements.

Like Kelman, Galloway is critical of Scotland but resolutely and recognizably Scottish, sitting easily alongside her inspiration and mentor.[8] Like Kelman, she focuses on characters normally sketched only as "stock characters," in her case reworking the young school-teacher, the old maid, the depressive. And like Kelman and Roddy Doyle, she integrates global popular culture into her novels while maintaining their local valences. Linguistic hierarchies are leveled, giving space to women, to pop culture, to dialogue between levels.

Yet there are major differences between Galloway's project and those of Kelman and Doyle, both in terms of gender and class. Galloway differs from Doyle and Kelman in that her characters are not as marked as working class, seem to come from what we might call the lower middle class.[9] As in Dublin, poor Scottish women, excluded from heavy industrial and manual jobs by their sex but still in need of an income, furthered their education and were able to continue to find employment when their male counterparts were hit with recession; the discrepancy between male and female unemployment rates was at its greatest in the late 1980s. But stable work does not equal security. Though Galloway's protagonists appear to be college educated and at least one of the jobs each works to make ends meet is white-collar, they don't drive, grew up without telephones, and worry about money obsessively. Their lives on the margins of Glasgow provide Galloway space to explore the relationship of nation, gender, and formal experiment, making a case for the reconception of the first two via the third.

Janice Galloway's Alienated Spaces

The idea of being an external observer of one's own life structures much first-person narration, but at the same time, narrative conventions usually place that narration in an often unspecified moment beyond the boundaries of the text. The opening line of *The Trick Is to Keep Breathing*—"I watch myself from the corner of the room" (7)—violates these expectations in two ways. First, its present-tense verb: ongoing narration in present tense belies the idea of a structured story, lending realism to the scene at the same time as it departs from the realist practice of narrating in the literary past. Second, the idea of watching oneself from a corner of a room suggests that the self is also present in another, more central part of the room, a logical contradiction that splits mind and body, perhaps, or fragments the body or consciousness. Whatever we take this statement to mean, the narrator, Joy Stone, establishes an exteriority that persists throughout her story and acts as a backbone to it.[10]

Joy's emotional retreats are represented physically, as her body wastes away. Moreover, her mental distance from others is reflected in her geographic distance. Throughout the novel, we hear about her difficulties with transportation and about how alienating the outskirts of Glasgow are. Edwin Morgan remarks in passing that *Trick* "is not specifically a book about Glasgow, but the Glasgow background which it uses, a postwar estate on the outskirts, with a poor bus service and few car-owners, graffiti everywhere, slaters slithering in the porch, seems perfectly designed to be of least help to someone trying not to go mad" ("Glasgow Speech" 91) and indeed, the novel opens with a discussion of the shortcomings of Joy's house, moving within pages to the failed city planning that is responsible for her neighborhood.[11] In the constant interplay of internal and external throughout the text, body, home, housing estate, city, nation, and family are both setting for and cause of her drawn-out, viscerally painful, seemingly inescapable anxiety.

The nexus of problems contributing to Joy's condition is both acutely specific, drawing on regional language, relying on local geography, and tracing the decline of one body, and more general, characterizing female bodies, Scottish identity, and the condition of peripheral estate poverty. Like Joy watching herself, the novel is both object and observer. Through her relationship to her body, as well as in her interactions with the urban and suburban environment she inhabits, as well as her own living spaces, Joy searches for meaning and works to heal herself outside traditional structures, a tendency that the novel itself structurally parallels.

Galloway takes pains to delineate the ways that Joy's specific environment shapes her story, carefully implicating what Soja calls the "nested hierarchy" (*Postmodern Geographies* 200) of house, housing estate, town, nation, and body in her inability to cope. The history of council housing, especially the hasty enforced movement to Glasgow's perimeter following World War II, and the concurrent reentrenchment of class structures in Western metropolitan culture under the guise of shifts of notions of personal space, trouble Joy's relationship with her body and gender roles even before Michael has died. David Harvey contends that the significance of "spatializing practices in architecture and urban design" hinges on the defining of "what exactly is the right time and right place for what aspects of social practice" (217). In short, spaces create and enforce social norms. Standards of appropriate gender interactions and behaviors, in particular, arise from the limitations of spaces designed to maintain certain ideas about postwar class structures and domesticity. The lower middle-class domestic spaces so central to *Trick* structure the novel's central relationship, which shapes the novel in turn.

Both the language to characterize human relationships and the spaces that bound them are slow to abandon traditional definitions, often trailing in the wake of demographic shifts. Joy is in her late twenties, having never been married but recently having emerged from an emotionless, stagnant, and contained live-in relationship of seven years, a relationship marked by traditional gender roles (Joy's boyfriend Paul "ate my meals and let me make the beds, do his washing and attend to the Superflat" [42].). Joy's subsequent lover, Michael Fisher, was ten years her senior and married with two children. Joy never provides terminology to make reference to Michael simple (a parallel, significantly, to the non-naming of the anorexia and bulimia she suffers from throughout); the closest she comes is to call him "a man I was living with" (62), which misrepresents their arrangements in any case. The text avoids referring to Michael as a "lover," which might not acknowledge that he is still married, or as a "married man," which privileges that prior union over Joy's and Michael's. Even the term "wife," for Norma Fisher, implies more than it ought to, as would "ex-wife," given that the separation was not final at Michael's death. This indefinability plays out in particular in Michael's death, in a swimming pool in Spain, where the small boy who tells her what has happened, apparently chosen because he can speak English, refers to Michael as Joy's husband. Some things, it is suggested, are untranslatable, not so much from Spanish to English as from existence to language.

Just as language misnames Joy's relation to Michael, architecture has not caught up to the evolving social structures. Michael's council house, which Joy inhabits throughout the present events of the novel, built for a nuclear family, has too many rooms for a single man expecting occasional visits from his children. Most of the spaces within the house lack definition. "It's too big really. There are four rooms. One is decorated as a bedroom and the others randomly. There isn't enough furniture to go round" (19). The emptiness of the house accuses its inhabitant of failing to be appropriately domestic. Especially once Michael is dead and Joy secures permission to stay in the house, she is engulfed by the space.

Kerstin Shands has remarked that, from subway seats to the workplace, "Men tend to expand physically, while women shrink in order to take up less space" (44). While such a remark overgeneralizes, it does seem apt in light of Joy's diminishing physical frame and Michael's overlarge house. A single woman does not need or belong in a home of this size, apparently. There are exceptions, however, namely, Ellen, the mother of Joy's best friend Marianne, who acts as a maternal figure for Joy. Ellen lives in a big house on a hill that overlooks the town. "The street looks like an old movie shot through a vaselined lens" (95). "Ellen is always having a spot of lunch/supper/a little something when I call…. The house is full with the smell of cooking" (85), and Ellen knits after meals. Her solicitous behaviors make it reasonable for her to occupy such a large home; Joy even spends a night in Marianne's old room, complete with nine-year-old fashion magazines. The home cooking, home production of clothing, and references to how the house seems to exist in the past all point to an earlier version of housing in which self-sufficiency and caregiving factored heavily and justified the consumption of space. Without these behaviors, Joy cannot fill Michael's home. Her efforts, including the preparation of food she never eats and the sewing of clothes, reveal how deeply the notion of home is intertwined with ideas of female domesticity, a model Joy resists and yet enacts throughout the novel.

The only time that Joy has ever lived alone was in a small cottage after she left Paul, a home into which Michael had then briefly moved. Once Michael inhabits the home, it becomes a traditional domestic space: Joy refers to the couple eating, cooking, and cleaning together, emphasizing both his sharing of household chores and the extreme closeness of the relationship at this point. "When we washed dishes, we'd watch our reflections in the night-blacked window, kissing" (64). In contrast to all the discussions about independence, Joy reenters a conventional male-female union. As appealing as this sort of companionate bond sounds, the site of her autonomy becomes a place for her to once again participate in the habits of marriage. At the same time, the house is revealed to have interior flaws. The revolt of this space, embodied by the reclaiming of the house by spores and molds, implies the power of structures like marriage, so long considered natural, organic, inevitable, normal. The cottage, small and intimate, creates a cohabitation based on long-held social norms.

All the homes in *Trick* comment on the social interactions they try to sculpt. Just as important are the forces responsible for the neighborhoods shaping the homes, which emphasize the restrictions that economic status can place on the consumption of space. The home Joy takes over upon Michael's death is located in a housing estate called Boot Hill, in a part of Ayrshire once known for its mining. Few specific details are provided to the reader about either the village or about Glasgow itself, some thirty miles away. This omission speaks to several parallel phenomena. First of all, let us recall the lists of cities made by Eagleton, Kelman, and Doyle, always industrial and working-class centers, in their desire to deprivilege the specific.[12] While specificity may dissolve into the general, working-class texts in particular can use their local region as a means of indicating commonality with other peripheral communities. What would normally be dismissed as mere regional variation reveals patterns and continuities, demonstrating the potential power of the simultaneous presence of the unique and the universal—of course, one can distinguish a Liverpool accent from a Glasgow or Belfast one, but what Kelman and the others posit is that such a particularity matters less than what is shared, a working-class, urban, yet nonmetropolitan identity.

And yet the exact place matters nonetheless. Peter Barry's study of *Contemporary British Poetry and the City* identifies a trope of urban poetry in the presence of both setting and geography, where setting is a "generalized impression of the urban or the metropolitan, while geography is *loco-specific*, giving a rendition of specific cities" (48–49). In this formulation, setting acts as an index of a character's or speaker's mood, geography relating the text to the "real" city it describes, allowing readers to connect their knowledge of a city to what a poem says about it. Galloway's mentions of Glasgow are few in *Trick*; her discussion of Boot Hill is more developed but again on the surface appears to be peripheral to the novel's explicit themes. I want to suggest that *Trick* depicts a space that is at once general and specific—that a few of its elements suggest a general urban feel (most of the novel takes place in dystopic suburban spaces), but that, more importantly, it evokes not so much a specific city as a specific *sort* of city. Boot Hill *could* be on the outskirts of Bradford or in Swansea, because it constitutes a particular set of responses that various British councils and housing authorities tried to make to specific economic and social conditions. Beyond this economic context, there are elements of the text that are regionally specific as well, outlining a notion of Scottishness consciously at odds with stereotype yet perceptibly different from other British identities, adding another layer to the creation of the loco-specific.

In order to examine the urban dynamics of the novel, it is necessary to cite one lengthy passage in particular, as it so aptly characterizes Joy's state and indeed, is one of the few places where we are given such detail:

It takes two buses to get where I have to go.

ooo

On the map, it's called Bourtreehill, after the elder tree, the bourtree, the Judas tree; protection against witches. The people who live here call it Boot Hill. Boot Hill is a new estate well outside the town it claims to be a part of. There was a rumor when they started building the place that it was meant for undesirables: difficult tenants from other places, shunters, overspill from Glasgow. That's why it's so far from everything. Like most rumours, it's partly true. Boot Hill is full of tiny, twisty roads, wild currant bushes to represent the great outdoors, pubs with plastic beer glasses and kids. The twisty roads are there to prevent the kids being run over. The roads are meant to make drivers slow down so they get the chance to see and stop in time. This is a dual misfunction. Hardly anyone has a car. If one does appear on the horizon, the kids use the bends to play chicken, deliberately lying low and leaping out at the last minute for fun. The roads end up more conducive to child death than if they had been straight. What they do achieve is to make the buses go slow.... The buses take a long time. (Galloway, *Trick* 13)

The first thing that Joy tells us about her neighborhood is the ambiguity surrounding its naming, which is not uncommon with housing estates, a sort of fuzziness about which Alison Ravetz has remarked, "It is often impossible to find them [council estates] in street atlases under the names they are known by" (179). Joy's area itself has two names, and the tree that it is named for at least three. The not-so-simple relationship of signifier to signified is further complicated by issues of translation. The word bourtree evokes Scotland, "bour" being Scots for pipe, the plant having inspired a Robert Louis Stevenson poem written partly in Scots dialect, "The Bour-Tree Den." At the same time, the tree has negative associations: "this mangy, short-lived, opportunist and foul-smelling shrub was once regarded as one of the most magically powerful of plants" (Mabey).[13] The plant can also be used as hedgerow material, which would evoke an earlier, more rural image of the developed area. Galloway ranges quickly through these meanings, citing the name Judas tree as well; elder, or honeysuckle, is credited with being the tree upon which Judas hanged himself after his betrayal, yet another layer of meaning for a woman contemplating suicide and fighting guilt at surviving her lover. While later we are told that Boot Hill is composed in part of tower blocks, which would not lend themselves to the simulation of a bucolic environment, Joy suggests that the developers as well sought to link present to past as well through the installation of "wild currant bushes to represent the great outdoors"; even the profusion of "tiny, twisty roads" seems meant to suggest organic material.[14] The coopting of the pastoral to create a suburban housing estate unifies an antiurban ethos with elements reminiscent of some notion of Scotland's romantic past, a move in keeping longstanding trope of a timeless countryside.

But these associations are submerged entirely in the locals' renaming of the place, Boot Hill. Boot Hill is a road name, replacing the natural with the man-made; moreover, it conjures images of a masculine space, boot camp. And it replaces the Scots word "bour" with English ones, revealing, perhaps, the resistance of residents to the mythologizing of their homes.[15] Not that local elements are suppressed entirely: the slang word "shunters" and the peripheral presence of Glasgow root the description in a very specific area and class. Most other insights we receive to the character of Boot Hill situate it economically as well. We're told that "hardly anyone has a car" in a place where buses are infrequent and "take a long time," suggesting a financially disadvantaged population with little power. The "pubs with plastic beer glasses" divulge just how rough the neighborhood is, plastic cups being not only cheap but a hedge against violence. (Elsewhere, Joy refers to "lunatics" (130) who hang around the estate and discloses the information that for a while she carried a knife to fend them off.) The graffiti covering the shelter, not to mention the kids hanging from it, perhaps the same kids who play chicken with the cars, suggest a bleak environment where parents exercise little control. The winding streets, possibly part of postwar efforts to move streets away from a grid system, are deathtraps. The detachment from Glasgow does not promote suburban bliss but a feeling of isolation. The conjunction of poor public transport and distance from not just the city, but any village amenities suggests an ill-conceived design for the housing estate, one that presumed greater prosperity in its residents. Joy's own problems, like those of Kelman's or Torrington's narrator in *Swing Hammer Swing!*, are as much sociological as personal, so the urban development plans of Glasgow and the issues surrounding council housing in the twentieth century come into play.

This shift in Glasgow's profile from industrial giant to depressed economy coincided with a major postwar housing crisis, in which half a million people were forecasted to require housing, both due to a population boom and a high concentration of unfit houses. With the mass return of women to the domestic sphere, new homes were required in new spaces. The Clyde Valley Regional Plan in 1946 proposed relocation of 250,000 to 300,000 people to areas outside of Glasgow, the so-called "New Towns." As Andrew Gibb has explained, the sense of urgency to house so many resulted in a decision with far-reaching consequences:

> Services and amenities could wait, in the prospect of a successful national economy generating sufficient surplus for the provision of the growing New Towns, once the all-important houses had been built. The eventual result was economic downturn, subsidy, and rating base restriction, and in terms of provision of the most basic elements of social support, far too little, far too late. (Gibb 161)

In his sweeping study of constructions of country and city, Raymond Williams notes that "Housing clearance and housing shortage are alike related to the altered distribution of human settlement which has followed from a set of minority decisions about where work will be made available, by the criteria of profit and internal convenience" (Williams, *C&C* 294).[16] Irvine, the town that Bourtreehill is a part of, was one of the fifty-seven towns contracted to receive excess residents, referred to throughout discussion as "overspill." The "overspill from Glasgow" that Joy refers to is part of the tail end of these relocation plans.

The dehumanization present in the term overspill itself spilled over into planning calamities throughout the development of the peripheral and overspill estates: new dwellings were not ready by the time inner-city slums were torn down; worse, estates never received the public transportation their inhabitants required because of the belief that car ownership would become universal, leaving many residents stranded in poor neighborhoods that were unable to sustain what few local markets and shops had opened. A cycle ensued in which estates were evacuated by all except the poorest tenants, which in turn led to businesses closing and further cuts in transportation. Indeed, Boot

Hill is afflicted by similar troubles; one must cross a gothic-sounding "moorland" (130) on foot to get to the town: "... estates were almost willfully cut off from their surroundings...the commonest situation of all was the placing of estates where no one would ever choose to live" (Ravetz 178).[17] Planning mishaps merge with the design to isolate undesirable tenants.

Urban blight means that in Boot Hill, "every fourth house in this estate is empty. Kids break the windows and the council have to pay to repair and maintain them empty so rents go up all the time. Every time the rent goes up more houses become empty, some overnight" (18). Paradoxically, the interaction of poverty and delinquency means that tenants' costs are higher, not lower, a dilemma not uncommon in the dynamics of housing estates. Gibb remarks that "Over large areas of public sector housing, particularly in peripheral estates, a deadly combination of insufficient maintenance, high levels of environmental pressure, and concentrations of multiply deprived households generating no retail stream accelerated the growth of the new slums in the 1980s" (179). More than an unfortunate circumstance, Joy's struggles with the council are endemic to the system, structurally a part of it. In discussing a parallel period of precipitous urban growth, Williams emphasizes that, "much of the physical squalor and complexity of eighteenth century London was a consequence not simply of rapid expansion but of attempts to control that expansion" (145).

Efforts at social control endure, for Joy's neighborhood in Boot Hill may be uninviting and partially vacant, but this does not mean that the Housing Authority are willing to allow her to live there without a fight. Her struggle is both gendered and economic. Because Michael was technically the only resident of the house, the council representative Mr. Dick reminds Joy that "Strictly speaking, we're under no obligation to house you at all, not when you were never registered as a tenant. We needn't do anything at all, strictly speaking" (18). The Kafkaesque hints of bureaucratic nit-picking and corruption here are made all the more obscene because of their unnecessary cruelty: the estate needs tenants to help control costs, and there is plenty of room to spare. Even the language, with its repeated references to strict speaking, registration, liability, and other legalistic lingo, seems interested in catching Joy in a technicality. "Strictly speaking, you're breaking and entering every night" (66).

Galloway structures the novel so that the encounter with Mr. Dick marks our first clear indication that Michael and Joy were not married. To use another word, the text studiously avoids, it is Joy's station as "mistress," that places her outside of the legal framework within which the housing authority operates. Her problem is at once linguistic and physical; as Glenda Norquay has put it, Galloway "writes against the grand narratives and mastering discourses which shape us. These mastering narratives are directly related to the materiality of people's lives: "... Joy's attempt to sustain a domestic environment without social legitimisation, her refusal to work within 'binary oppositions,' almost results in homelessness" (135–136). While people are welcome to emulate the dominant patterns of gender role organization, only full participation in them guarantees the protection of (and from) the state.

Joy goes to all of this trouble to secure a house she does not particularly like—we read of how cold it is, how dirty the porch is, how little it matches her imaginings. Her previous house had been one that she cared about, yet it, too, betrayed her. Leaving Paul, Joy had moved into the small cottage, "tiny but cheap. There was a bus stop right outside the door...buses starting and stopping right outside my door for whenever I needed to go somewhere. It made me feel free" (63). As opposed to the isolation that Joy feels from neighbors and shops in Boot Hill later, the cottage offers social interaction and endless possibility, mainly through the liberation of easy mobility, a feature Williams identifies in *The Country and the City* as key to twentieth-century images of the city (240). Even more, the word cottage sounds cozy in comparison to council house, seems to predate it, to sound more rural.[18] But connection with the land and the past turns out to have an insidious edge, as Michael discovers: "I found him in the kitchenette, right at the back of the cottage, turning lilac in the cold. He was kneeling on the concrete looking at something. I kneeled down too and tried to see what it was. There was a mushroom growing out of the skirting. LOOK he said, LOOK" (64). The cottage is being invaded by mushrooms, one of the most primeval of plants; the boundary between indoors and out has been ruptured.

Michael begins to obsess after it becomes clear that the first mushroom was not alone:

> I saw another mushroom...LOOK I said and we both looked again. This one was more securely attached...It left a little pink trail like anaemic blood where it had been growing. After a month there were little shoots all along the hallway...baby mushrooms appeared overnight...Every so often, I would find him in the hall or the kitchen, peering down and scratching with a pen knife, then trying to hide it when he saw me coming. (64)

Joy goes on to mention Michael's repeated handwashing and his library research to discover that the problem is dry rot, which will eventually consume the house and its structure from within. Michael's hasty eviction from his own home has enforced a marital form of domesticity on him and Joy, forcing them into the older model just as the house represents a "landscape of origin," as Martin Conboy has put it in another context.

The fact that all of the homes we learn about are beset by both emotional and spatial traumas links Joy's psyche even further to the place that she inhabits. Much as Joy's house must be perfectly clean before a social worker she calls "the health visitor" arrives, her body must be scrubbed and cleansed before the lover she refers to as "the night visitor" arrives. "I clean till my hands are swollen from cold water, red as ham. My knuckles scrape and go lilac till the kitchen looks like they do on TV and smells like synthetic lemons and wax" (18). Not so different is the bathing ritual: "When I finish [the bath], the skin sizzles: my whole surface sings.... I rub my skin hard with the flat loops of the towel till it hurts" (47). Just as both callers are referred to by common nouns rather than proper ones, Joy distances herself from her body by using the article "the" for her own skin rather than the possessive pronoun, referring to her skin as an almost disconnected covering. Combined with the emphasis on surface appearances, the effort to strip anything personal from the smell of body or kitchen, and the compulsion to inflict pain through scrubbing, the use of indefinite linguistic constructions further underlines Joy's dissociation from what surrounds her and from notions of identification and place. The reference to Joy's lilac hands links the passage to Michael's efforts to remove the first mushroom he found, a scene that precedes this one temporally but follows it in the novel's sequencing and ties her obsessive behavior to his, behaviors linked by their concern with surfaces, interiors, and exteriors.[19]

The history of the consumption of the house by something inexorable within it is related via analepsis while Joy's sister Myra is invading her Boot Hill home, connecting the asexual spores to the parasitic family presence of Myra. The overtaking of the house by the land thus hints at the choking inevitability of Scottishness in Joy's behavior. As she and Myra drink together, Joy adopts "This cheery intonation I get when I'm well on: something to do with a race memory of New Year" (63). Her responses come from within, from the land and climate, just as much as the spores that destroyed her cottage. The phrase "race memory" credits Joy's response to a genetic overdetermination that makes her sound cheerful in response to Myra even when her feelings are otherwise. When family issues arise, Joy makes reference to the role she sees Scotland playing in their dynamics, viewing nation as both an analogue for her family problems and a prime mover behind them. While Scotland's presence in *Trick* is muted, Joy's negotiation of her tragedy is bounded by if not actively engaged with her nationality. Joy articulates a sense of betrayal by her own nationality and the land that infects her house, underlining her ambiguous relationship to Scottishness, much like her ambiguous relationship to domestic space, as a place she does yet does not belong.

It comes as no surprise, then, when the ugly room in the creepy house in the rough town in the dysfunctional nation all reveal themselves to be analogies for the most horrifying of Joy's inner/outer issues, that of her eating disorder and the disintegration of her body as a consequence. Recognizing the link between spatial boundaries and metaphorical ones, Shands has noted that "Women, food, and boundaries have much to do with introjection, invasion, and expulsion" (48). Joy's moment of discovery comes when, absorbed by a sewing project, she forgets to eat. Opening a tin of soup, she begins to play with the condensed "jelly, dark red…watery stuff like plasma started seeping up the sides of the viscous block" (38). Ultimately, she inadvertently cuts herself, moving to the sink to rinse. "I was learning something as I stared at what I was doing; the most obvious thing yet it had never dawned on me till I stood here, bug-eyed at the sink, congealing soup up to my wrists. I didn't need to eat. *I didn't need to eat*" (38). The blood-like qualities of the soup render it indistinguishable from her own blood once she is cut, suggesting that there is no boundary between what is inside and what is outside. This insight leads to the realization that food perpetuates the distinction between inner and outer, one that Joy has been ignoring since the mushrooms invaded the cottage and needs to elide to perpetuate her sense of her own death alongside Michael's. Moreover, the fact that she feels herself "bug-eyed" at the moment of epiphany, as the soup "slithers" down the drain connects Joy to an earlier epoch; like the ancient spores, the primordial soup retreats from the binaries and divisions part of the modern, urban world.

To a certain extent, this symbolic move backward in time is recapitulated by the novel's own temporal organization. We begin months after Michael's death, working backward through the funeral to the affair to Joy's prior relationship with Paul to her family dynamics, each connection explored parallel to the discussion of the space in which it took place. With Joy's decision to enter a psychiatric hospital, the novel continues to flash back through Joy's memory, but more of it takes place in the present, ending in the present tense it began with. While the past is painful and must be moved beyond, the future, as represented by the housing estate, is equally unpalatable. Literally unpalatable, it is a space where Joy cannot and does not eat.

Joy ceases menstruating as well in Michael's house, most likely a consequence of her self-starvation. While one clueless doctor suggests that perhaps she is pregnant without knowing it, her lack of blood contrasts Michael's house again with the cottage, where the mushrooms had at least produced "anaemic blood" (64). Indeed, all of the physical features of Michael's house suggest emptiness and mortality, from the bird's skull he found before his death to the "withered leaves in the porch" to the "shell of something dead that's been there for weeks now" (14). Joy's revulsion about insects springs from the fact that they "have their skeletons on the outside, too many eyes, unpredictable legs, and you can never tell where their mouths are" (15). Her own body resembles that of the insects, from the ribs she counts during her bathing ritual to her eyes that can watch her from another part of the room to her own unreliable mouth. (During a binge, "Chocolate and biscuits...blot out everything but my mouth" [183].)

These intersecting interests in death, skeletons, and anorexia find formal correlatives in the text's structure and organization. The text replicates the pathologies of anorexia and bulimia; namely, it withholds information, refusing, most significantly, ever even to use the words "anorexia" or "bulimia," and it suggests bulimia in the way that it spews disconnected pieces of prose (playscript, magazine snippets, italicized passages, etc.) of varying styles. Moreover, in certain passages, words bleed into the margins and get cut off by the physical boundary of the page. As David Harvey has noted, "the written word abstracts properties from the flux of experience and fixes them in spatial form" (206). As means to resist the confinement of spatial form, Galloway draws on irregular typography and unconventional formal devices, challenging textual conventions. Given that Joy repudiates the confinements of body and housing estate, the use of formal innovations implies a *strategic* experimentation, disruptions of form for a purpose; just as physical spaces try to contain Joy and determine her actions and behaviors, a traditional rendering of her story would distort it, be inadequate.

Indeed, this refusal to be contained by narrative norms makes significant statements about the links between the dynamics of housing estates and gender roles. If housing estates are part of the maintenance of the division of space into public and private spheres that has, within this century, been pivotal in containing women within the home, then Joy's struggles with her homes mark a resistance to social gender norms. Gayatri Spivak contends that feminist refusals of the value of domestic space, stemming from rejection of its confinements, can actually serve to reinforce the existence of a boundary between inner and outer. As Shands explains it, Spivak's "solution is thus to collapse the strict borderlines between inside and outside or private and public in moving between the two" (65). Such a deconstruction is visible and effective on a textual level, as when Galloway reconceives margins, pagination, and textual layout.

While the spaces of Boot Hill, Michael's council house, and even Joy's own body seem colonized by masculinity, then, the novel manages, through its innovative format, to carve out a space that is resolutely female, recalling the notion of *ecriture feminine*.[20] Much discussion of women's writing focuses on the need for a feminized space, whether a room of one's own or a canon of women writers. What I am suggesting here is that *Trick* takes a somewhat pessimistic view of such space, seeing space itself as implicated in the subordination of women. Rather, the novel seeks to blur spatial boundaries. By making textual experiments, *Trick* forces the reader to approach it as an object. The disruptions of standard prose on the page—the different-sized capital letters, the italics and speech bubbles, Joy's compulsive lists, the words that evoke Joy's own blood by bleeding into the margins— these assert the physical body, the space, of the text, a physicality noted by many critics. For Norquay, "experimentation functions beyond an aesthetic level as a commentary upon the ways in which discursive practices determine the materiality of our lives" (136). *Trick*'s tangibility leads Pat Kane to see it as "a textual materialisation which comes across not as arid experiment but as a necessary emotional device...What makes Galloway even more radical than Kelman...is her materialist fiction—and what makes her virtually unquotable—is the way the actual text itself becomes a material thing, with its irregular typography and variety of forms (factual prose, theatre-text dialogue, concrete poetry)" (105). The body of the text embodies a materialist resistance to abstraction, paradoxically drawing on highly literary techniques to ground itself in the palpable.

And thus it is crucial that the novel recuperate the physical in Joy's life as well as trace the healing of her wounded psyche. While there are no signs of the abatement of the eating disorders, Joy does, as Norquay notes, begin "to function within social rituals" (133). And she makes some significant decisions about her housing dilemmas. Her words about the cottage at the novel's end: "It'll be dark over there. All that peeled-back paper hanging from the bedroom walls. I can always clean away the worst of the visible damage, strip and wash the walls, open the doors to let the winter air refresh. I can leave all the windows open there as well: there's nothing that anyone would come in and steal. I can paint the window frames white again, lift the carpet tile in the hall with a scarf over my nose and mouth. I'll make lists. Things that need to be done for the next week or so. The week after that" (234). With this decision to actively renovate the cottage, Joy rejects the negative space of the housing estate. Its isolation and control are repudiated, its gendered space rejected. Her decision to move back within the realm of reliable public transport and to fight the dry rot speaks to her renewed willingness to engage with society, and, by extension, with her sister Myra and the other issues that the dry rot came to symbolize.

Return to the cottage, then, engages with Scottishness as well, opting to emphasize what Norquay calls the "in-betweeness" of Joy's "dialogic relationship to Scottishness" (139). Scottish identity is yet another boundary that, to draw on Shand's Spivak, is best crossed repeatedly rather than reified through rejection. Galloway's use throughout the text of local language is part of this recuperation. Harvey talks about one of the insights of modernism as its "celebrating universality and the collapse of spatial barriers, [but] also explor[ing] new meanings for space and place in ways that tacitly reinforced local identity" (273). Rather than discarding the very idea of national identity, Galloway uses it critically, replacing it at times with even more loco-specific constructions. Norquay makes a lovely reading of the way that Joy's friend Marianne embraces the nation that she has left through discovering what she needs and misses of Scotland, including, crucially, the right/privilege/ability to have her accent understood. It seems possible, then, to reconceive of Scotland in such a way that, like the cottage that can be rescued from itself, the nation does not need to consume itself with fixed notions of identity; renovation is possible.

Ultimately, Joy's alienation from body, home, and nation remain unresolved. But the tentative efforts at reconciliation, through the projected move into the cottage, as well, on a structural level, through the use of local language, suggest that the suburban peripheral estate is a dead end, a form of containment and control. The gendering of these estrangements suggests a pattern of associating less privileged characters with remote locations, neither urban nor rural, and feminized identities, which Galloway critiques via departures from textual norms, rejecting at the same time the confines of national, gender, and economic constraints. While this conclusion has been reached by sociologists, philosophers, and journalists alike, Galloway's analysis makes the further step of linking literary to architectural practices and supposedly cosmopolitan literary forms to the female, domestic, the local, and the working class.

The Female Body and Public Prose

Like Joy's struggle with anorexia and her alienation from her physical surroundings, her reactions to women's magazines reveal a sensation of nonexistence interacting with pressures to conform to external norms. Helen Malson has pointed out the overlapping and contradictory readings that anorexia encourages, both by its subjects and by external observers: the thin body is both hyper-feminine in its weakness and strong and self-possessed in its independence from food. Malson and Leslie Heywood agree that "The thin female body signifies a multiplicity of femininities *and* a rejection of femininity" (Malson 116),[21] both also asserting a link between the Cartesian mind-body duality and the "inner war" of male and female impulses in the anorexic. "This aspect of anorexia might be better understood, however, not as individual pathology but as the interpellation of the subject by a socially pervasive discourse of Cartesian dualism" (Malson 119). Joy's "anorexic logic," then, relies both on separating her sense of self from her physical body and on reducing that body to nothingness, a struggle for control she must lose if she is to live.

Joy's consumption of fashion magazines gives the appearance of control to her as a reader at the same time as it enforces unattainable body goals, a relationship to mass-market magazines and female cosmetic products that echoes that of Gerty MacDowell in *Ulysses*. Both women suffer from illness that makes their conformity to the norms impossible, and both interior monologues are suffused with collective and institutional languages: Gerty's is rendered in a free indirect discourse—a third person narrative parodying sentimental novels of the turn-of-the-century, while Joy's first person narration reflects her efforts to find a discourse that expresses her condition.

Both *Trick* and *Ulysses* assert that the stream of consciousness—either explicit product plugs or the language of the magazines that are a veil for these products—is explicitly and causally connected to the mindset and techniques of advertising. With the birth of department stores at the close of the nineteenth century, women in particular were issued into modernity by a bombardment of products to be consumed. Like the acceleration of the industrial revolution, the progress of technology, and the development of public urban spaces, the experience of the department store offered sensory stimulation—too much stimulation. Advertising is born out of this same barrage, so suddenly there are words on signs, on fliers, in skywriting. Franco Moretti has argued that the stream of consciousness "is one way—and perhaps the most successful—of confronting this extreme tension" (*Epic* 124) of the overstimulation of the external world. Earlier novels had approached the world with "attention, clarity, and concentration" (134), but a new style, stream of consciousness, is required to cope with the overstimulation outside one's head. This new form calls for "a weaker grammar than that of consciousness; an edgy, discontinuous syntax ... a cubism of language ... simple, fragmented sentences where the subject withdraws to make room for the invasion of things" (135). The link of form to content here is especially interesting given that the stream of consciousness Joyce develops very much resembles what salesmen begin to design as advertisements.

Unlike much of *Ulysses*, Gerty's chapter, "Nausicaa," with its grammatically normative structures and few slang or hybrid words, reads comparatively easily without the aid of annotations, a consequence of her reliance on narrative and on her infusion by advertising. But Gerty's prose is eventually overwhelmed by the weight of its overblown syntax, what Joyce called "a namby-pamby jammy marmalady drawersy (alto la!) style" (qtd. in J. Johnson 204). Her voice is "born of commodified femininity" (Johnson 204), a result of all the products and discourses that permeate and create her consciousness. The relation in which Joyce places Gerty to commodities requires him to develop a different form for her than the "idiolectic distinctness" (Johnson 205) of Bloom:

> Gerty's [eyes] were of the bluest Irish blue, set off by lustrous lashes and dark expressive brows. Time was when those brows were not so silkily seductive...eyebrowleine...gave that haunting expression to the eyes, so becoming in leaders of fashion, and she had never regretted it. Then there was blushing scientifically cured and how to be tall and increase your height and you have a beautiful face but your nose? ... But Gerty's crowning glory was her wealth of wonderful hair. She had cut it that very morning on account of the new moon and it nestled about her pretty head in a profusion of luxuriant clusters and pared her nails, too, Thursday for wealth. (*U* 286)

This passage is suffused with rich imagery, but all of it is inherited, cliché: Irish eyes, luxuriant hair, crowning glory. And we see the syntax of the consciousness, grammatical but not logical: the haircut and the nail-paring both took place "that very morning" but the superstitions and clichés that the mention of the hair inspires run interference. The rich imagery ends up creating an impossibility: the hair that nestles about Gerty's head is also grammatically responsible for paring her nails!

Compare to Joy's makeup session:

> ...just enough makeup to make my eyes seem more, the lips rounder, bleach out the circles growing like a web under the lashes. I have to tint my face because I am pale in cold weather, powder blue. This is unappetising and nothing to kiss. I tint myself Peaches and Dream, stain my eyelids lilac, brush the lashes black. (Galloway, *Trick* 47)

These two passages convey essentially the same messages: women need makeup, the eyes are of prime importance, and the goal is to be seductive. What's changed from Gerty to Joy is the sense that the ability to look good with makeup is something positive about you. Gerty is proud of her brows despite their cosmetic assistance, whereas Joy focuses on the flaws of her face before makeup. Gerty emphasizes the natural aspects of her look, her own coloring, whereas Joy calls attention to the artifice—bleach, tint, stain, brush—and seems to be colorless without makeup. For her, makeup isn't about bringing out her best qualities; it's hiding her worst ones, the gothic webs and blue flesh. Here, as throughout *Trick*, Joy's relationship to products, to commodities, is often one of forgetting or escaping herself, the self that cannot come to terms with her lover's death. Cosmetics can protect you from yourself—with them, Gerty does not limp, and Joy is an alluring woman again.

But for Joy the protection is only temporary. While Gerty seems content, if a little shallow (Jeri Johnson calls her "little more than a tissue of citations to femininity as performance" [205]), Joy never fully escapes herself. Both women use the rhetoric of magazines to shape themselves: "Then there was blushing scientifically cured and how to be tall and increase your height and you have a beautiful face but your nose?" (Joyce, *Ulysses* 286). In this passage, Gerty recalls three beauty articles—probably out of the "Boudoir Gossip" column of *The Princess's Novelettes*, a London weekly magazine for women (Don Gifford 385). All three articles are marked not just by their advice/improvement tone, but also by their emphasis on the reader's current failings: she blushes when she shouldn't, she's too short, and she has an unattractive nose. Moreover, each "flaw" is actually incurable by the likes of the Boudoir Gossip—blushing cannot be scientifically cured, you can't really make yourself taller and increase your height, and certainly in 1904 there was nothing to be done about a button nose. Why would a magazine give advice on such incurables? Herein lies the allure of the women's magazine: if you the intended reader could in actuality be cured, you'd only need to buy one copy of the *Princess*, but because the articles can never succeed in remaking you, you will assume that you are the problem, and you will keep buying the magazine and the products for which "the magazine's beauty and fashion pages [are] thinly disguised plugs" (Don Gifford 386). Indeed, physical beauty is presented in women's magazines "less as an aspirational ideal, more as a holy commandment" (Ferguson qtd. in Malson 111).

The redundancy of the columns—be taller *and* increase your height—echoes the redundancy of the prose style of "Nausicaa" in general: "Many a time and often they were wont to come there" (284), "her mother had raging splitting headaches" (291), "holy Mary, holy virgin of virgins" (290). What's interesting here is not merely a narrative voice that likes to hear itself talk but the sources of the repetitions: beauty columns, sentimental novels, advertisements, and religion seem to blur into one giant discourse of redundancy. They are all, in effect commodities, and Joyce's passage takes pains to make sure that we are aware of the overlaps, that we realize, in particular, that religion uses the same sales pitches as anything else. And indeed, they all share two things: a didactic impulse to improve the reader and need to market themselves. Johnson again: "this is the language of those discourses which tell a woman what she ought (and ought not) to be, which in one way or another attempt to sell her a bill of goods" (205).

There's a formal level here as well. The stringing together of cosmetic solutions with the conjunction "and" makes all three parts of the sentence into main clauses. Of all of the sentences in the excerpt above, this is the only one with no commas, no dependent clauses at all. This makes this central sentence of Gerty's passage grammatically distinct from the ones surrounding it, which are full of balanced clauses and appositives. Here we have something much more like Bloom's passages, paratactic connections: this passage is created by the world of advertising, whereas the others are products of the sentimental novels. Gerty's brain becomes a place for us to watch the transition from the nineteenth century of sentimentalism and order to the twentieth century of chaos and commercialism.

The change to Joy's world of cultural commodification is the change that Fredric Jameson has labeled the move to "late capitalism," in which capitalism absorbs and adapts to critiques of it:

> Diet for a firmer new you!
> Converting a Victorian schoolhouse into a des res!
> Kiss me Quick Lips—we show you how! (Galloway, *Trick* 27)

Here, the same second person address and didactic tone—there are still things wrong with the "old you," but now the magazine has a wider aim and savvier approach. No longer will you try to be taller; you'll aim to be firmer. You won't need a cure for blushing if you live in the right home—ironically, one much like the place where Gerty acquires the mindset above. And best of all, your lips can now generate actions from others—people will want to kiss you quickly, though you do still need to be shown how. Notice that your goals still aren't especially likely—how many people will read this and go out to buy a Victorian schoolhouse? Diets still fail; it's almost as tough to get firmer as to get taller. But now the use of slang combines with the old clichés—des res meets kiss me quick to imply mastery of your language as well. This magazine is written to impersonate a woman's thoughts, to seem like her own ideas in her own language.

Again, both magazines place their readership in the position of ungainly woman in need of help. Moreover, as Thomas Karr Richards points out about the Nausicaa episode, "The superabundance and specificity of those commodities are striking" (759). We get numerous brand names throughout both of these novels. The difference is that Joyce's character, Gerty, buys into the princess rhetoric on every possible level, even adopting its speech patterns for her own, while Joy keeps the magazine rhetoric spatially separate in her text, cannot be satisfied. In this scene, she ends up crying; later, reading a horoscope, she realizes it's "Last month's. No good. But then it's all no good. It's all no fucking good" (39). Her language is profane—perhaps the only expressions not yet appropriated by the magazine. Joy wants to be satisfied and anesthetized as Gerty is, but the magazines fail her. Much as the formal difference in Gerty's sentences indicated the move from one century to the next, the inability of the modern magazines to placate Joy shows us the limitations of twentieth-century rhetoric on the brink of the twenty-first.

Joy's beauty routine merges with the rhetoric of the beauty magazines into an especially dangerous cocktail for her: in the magazines, "beauty figures as a state of salvation achieved through ritualistically following the "step-by-step" instructions, the day-to-day diets for beautification" (Malson 111). The inaccessibility of the ideal, when seen alongside the rituals designed to eternally approach it, resembles Joy's eating rituals: beauty and food become sites for her struggle, the anorexic logic of the magazines expanding the field of her obsession, alienating her from her own body. But while Joy feels trapped and alienated by her cultural consciousness, Gerty feels at one with the magazines and the world that created them and created her. Richards tells us that "no other character in *Ulysses* is so much the product, not of an exclusive persona, but of the collective pressure of the customs and ideology of a burgeoning consumer society" (767). But even if Joy's language is mimicked by the magazines, her consciousness is not; she's still alone.

Richards suggests that Nausicaa's style is a consequence of "the filtration into language of the commodity in its ubiquitous and liquid modern form" and that this calls for "experimentation with a new syntax by which to convey a new order of things through an old order of words" (760). Galloway's prose takes this injunction to convey things via words literally. Galloway turns her text into an object, much as Joy has turned her body into, not an extension of herself, but an object, becoming anorexic and bulimic.[22] Taking words too literally extends them off the page to infect the body, as Ellmann suggests: "Victoria Shahy, another psychoanalyst, has argued that bulimics are acting out the very principle of metaphor. Just as a metaphor 'is a way of "saying" something without actually saying it, so bulimic vomiting provides a means of "eating" food without actually eating it.' According to Shahy, bulimics are 'possessed' by the metaphor of food, because they are compelled to take it literally, translating all their impulses into digestive terms" (M. Ellmann 48). Unlike the novel, which denies anorexia by embracing a bulimic form, here I want to emphasize that Joy's own impulses toward anorexia and bulimia are conflicting, yet equally powerful.[23]

These warring impulses express themselves both thematically and textually. As Norquay notes, "If fragmentation is a theme is Galloway's fiction, fracture is also its predominant technique" ("Mooching" 131). Galloway reveals the limitations of commodification in a world where female minds in particular are so coopted by the language and ideology of advertising. And so we see playscript when Joy feels powerless or when she believes the outcome of a scene is predetermined. So we see words bleeding off the side of the page when a normal narrative would suppress them entirely. Making alienation visible on the page, that is, literal, Galloway uses formal innovations to reveal just how fragmented Joy is by the various subject positions being foisted upon her and expected of her.

Alexis Logsdon notes that Galloway "frequently portrays Joy's body as fragmented, often brutally so" (156), citing scenes where Joy bathes in view of a mirror that "cuts off my head" (Galloway, *Trick* 46) and a photograph where "the camera bludgeons off half my face and the flash whites out the rest" (Galloway, *Trick* 156). This second passage concludes with "It doesn't look like anybody. It doesn't look like" (156)—there's no punctuation ending the thought or the paragraph, a fragmented sentence that reflects the slicing of the body. Such portioning of the body is not unusual in photography, but Joy's narration of it as violent displays how fully she feels objectified by the camera, an objectification she extends in her description of other women she encounters. Logsdon notes that Joy sees all the women around her as overconsuming, from Ellen's efforts to feed her to the health visitor's greedy gobbling of biscuits. Even the magazines that coach Joy in self-starvation show excess as well: "THE BEST MUM IN BRITAIN" has "arms like white puddings hanging on butchers' hooks" (163), an image Logsdon notes is especially unappealing for someone so "averse to eating" (156). Such depictions of women gorging and embodying surplus suffuse a culture in which women are repeatedly enjoined to deny themselves, conflicting messages that overwhelm Joy and are complicit in her disorder.

Just before we witness for the first time Joy in the act of throwing up, Galloway delivers a passage that exemplifies the interpenetration of Joy's mind and the world of advertising: in a paragraph titled "HEALTH UPDATE: ULTIMATE DIET" (85), Joy gives us a second-person, magazine-style inspirational explanation of the how-tos of anorexia: "Allow nibbles of biscuit, the odd cracker or piece of fruit. Feel the tension in your stomach after even the lightest meal as a warning. Drink endlessly to bulk away the craving. You know it'll all be worth it in the end" (85). With larger margins and smaller type than the rest of the page, this moment is marked as an intrusion of consciousness, much as the playscript or magazine articles, but these ideas and this voice are clearly Joy's own. The hyperbole of "ultimate" and "in the end" carries menacing overtones when the recipe is for a slow death by anorexia, calling attention to the extremes passed off as normal register in advertising prose. Narrative inserts here fuse with stream of consciousness, more like Circe than "Nausicaa," yet infused with the cant and ideology of ads.

What's frightening is the extent to which a character conscious of the power of the double barrels of advertising and sexism succumbs to them: "This is where I earn my definition, the place that tells me what I am. [...] I like to be good at what I am" (11, 12). The refusal to eat and the accompanying dynamics of production comprise just one way that Joy attempts to locate herself in a world not structured to accommodate her. A single woman, a lover of a married man, a woman who doesn't want to be nurturing or taken care of, a woman who feels simultaneously crazy and sane—all the ways that Joy sees herself don't fit society. Just as Joy Stone is educated about and critical of social formulations of female identity yet opts to submit to them because she buys into the sane/insane hierarchical binary that acts as a rubric for all of them; likewise, Galloway acknowledges the potential and problems of a double-voiced text.

Alternate Families; Or, "We Could Make a Go of It Ourselves"

Galloway's *Trick* subverts the concern with origins present in so many novels, in particular those dealing with nation. By refusing menstruation, Joy challenges notions of production and reproduction. Moreover, both family and male/female dynamics in *Trick* are revealed to be incredibly problematic. Even in her short fiction, such as "Scenes from the Life No. 23," in *Blood*, Galloway depicts untrustworthy parents: Old Sammy encourages young Sammy to jump into his arms but steps aside to let the boy fall to the ground. Such overdetermined cruelty contests the inherent value of father-son relationships, and Galloway turns her attention instead to alternative families, new categories of relationships. Where Kelman's novels, for instance, stretch toward half-connections, bittersweet family vignettes, and temporary recuperations of father/son relationships, Galloway's make few concessions to blood relations, advocating instead the ideal of family as constructed by choice, not biology.

The other texts I consider in this study all share an element lacking in Galloway's. All of them, among their many other issues and obsessions, are centrally concerned with paternity. Both Stephen's discussion of Hamnet and his conversation with Bloom reveal the centrality of fatherhood throughout *Ulysses*. Kelman's depiction of the relationship of Sammy and his son in *How Late*, like the picture of Pat's stunted interactions with his father in *A Disaffection*, portrays an awkwardness in father/son relations that Kelman sees as endemic in economically depressed Glasgow, belying traditional portraits of the emotional and close-knit-even-in-strife working-class family. We see a slightly rosier but nevertheless preoccupied Doyle explore and critique fatherhood throughout his work, especially in *The Snapper, Paddy Clarke Ha Ha Ha,* and *The Woman Who Walked into Doors.* Not only does he set his narratives in the past, but McNamee also allows Victor's violence to be read by most in *Resurrection Man* as traceable to his unassuming father's weakness and Catholic surname.

These authors are by no means unique in these explorations; their contemporary Dermot Bolger's *Journey Home* and *Night Shift* implicate the squandered paternity of older Irish generations in the problematic offspring of the new. Robert McLiam Wilson tries to evade father issues by systematically eliminating male parents from his protagonists' lives, but their relentless impregnation of women marks the return of the repressed focus on origins. Irvine Welsh, too, is seduced by paternity, linking the pathology of a rapist in *Marabou Stork Nightmares* to a sadistic father. Even *Trainspotting*'s relentless focus on youth culture cedes in its final moments to an examination of the power of fathers: the novel concludes by offering us a "key" to the endlessly irrational and violent Begbie. In an episode entitled "Station to Station," Begbie's encounter with his depressingly isolated and alcoholic father emphasizes the love the older man could never provide and accounts for, even if it does not justify, Begbie's behavior. Clearly, even in these most antiestablishment of texts, the age-old preoccupation with fatherhood endures. As Ellen Friedman has written, "the yearning for fathers, for past authority and sure knowledge... permeates male texts of modernity" (Friedman 159). Friedman suggests that the search for the father hinges on the "profoundly nostalgic conviction that the past has explanatory or redemptive powers" (161), which ties it thematically to the search for origins conducted under the name of nationalism as well. Like the innovative but sometimes backward-looking texts of modernism, those of Doyle, Kelman, and McNamee make a variety of efforts to reconfront personal and national pasts. Resoundingly, Janice Galloway does not.

While Galloway has clear modernist antecedents and influences, she doesn't evince the same concern with fatherhood and origins that her compatriots do. Her interest is not in recuperating a broken family, nor is it in restoring a dashed sense of national pride.[24] Galloway resists these sorts of regenerative impulses, is wary of them and of obsessions with origins. Any time her characters try to do things in some preestablished way, to follow a pattern, failure is ensured. Existing families, words, and formal techniques conspire to shape Galloway's characters, imposing predetermined spaces, structures, and customs that the characters seek to shut down as impoverished or immoral. Joy, for instance, struggles with socially imposed images of her body and her relationship with her mother, destroying both in her efforts to conform. The solutions she and Galloway's next protagonist, Cassie, create as alternatives often strike the reader as inadequate, misdirected, or just plain wrong, at the same time as the refusal of preestablished norms seems brave.

A corollary to this disregard of paternity is suspicion of feminist efforts to recuperate the past. Like a number of recent feminist writings, Galloway's texts also take issue with the insistence that women should inhabit a matrilineal system of inheritance and knowledge in place of or in imitation of the father/son dynamic motivating male authors in the tradition of Harold Bloom's *Anxiety of Influence*.[25] Galloway does more than merely skirt the father/son template, she questions the value of the obsession with and investigation of origins, rejecting mother and sister as means of meaning or support as well.

Novels of family and criticism about novels of family have centered on what Freud called the "family romance." What, then, do we make of novels that deny or truncate experiences of family? And in particular, what is the form of the narrative engendered by such texts? The discussion above touched on issues of motherhood in Joy's own inability/unwillingness to bear children. As we shall see, biological families offer only false answers in the few appearances they make in *Foreign Parts*; rather, Galloway's novels refuse conventional definitions of family, thereby positing an escape from the national family romance that plagues Scotland's efforts to resolve its economic and political quandaries.

Recurrent in Galloway's leading ladies is the absence of any father figure at all.[26] Instead, Joy's family is composed of a distant mother, now dead, and a sister, Myra, twenty-three years older than Joy (and plausibly Joy's actual mother). Joy's mother is of working-class Scottish stock, not investing in a telephone because of the expense, emphasizing common sense above all else. Yet this mother, whom we never meet, possesses characteristics beyond the stock staunch Scottish Calvinist mother: she attempts suicide at least twice, interpreted by Joy as a plea for attention, seeping out from behind the stereotypic hard mother role. "I was very good [at the mother's funeral] because I didn't believe she was dead. I thought she was only pretending to get attention and would jump out of the box later and laugh at me for being a sap if I cried (see footnote*)" (82). This footnote, yet another of the text's disruptive departures from narrative norms, reads "*Love/Emotion= embarrassment. Scots equation. Exceptions are when roaring drunk or watching football. Men do rather better out of this loophole" (82).[27] The inseparability of a woman's status and national identity are again foregrounded here; national identity is in custody of men, who retain an outlet via sport, while women are silenced. The dry sarcasm of the footnote blends with the improbability of a mother staging her own death to mock her daughter's emotions, generating a simultaneous critique of traditional gender roles and national stereotypes.

Yet their genetic and physical proximity is worse than meaningless to Joy; it is dangerous. Joy recalls being "afraid of Myra as long as I can remember. She and my mother/her mother were pregnant at the same time...Myra's baby died. I didn't. Maybe that was why she hit me so much...Hands like shovels" (59). The shovels call to mind the burial of Myra's own baby as well as the conjuring images of earth, making a connection with Myra both indigenous and morbid. As characterized by Joy's memories of Myra, blood relationships are a threatening constraint, an ominous tie to Scotland and to the past.

Even the conversations the two have about their mother, ripe space for sibling-bonding, emphasize the failure to connect. Rather than listening, Myra misreads: "What about your mother you callous bitch? Never gret for your mother" (67) Myra yells at her. The vernacular "gret," for cried, reminds the reader of the stereotypic Scots inability to express emotion that Joy ironically mentions. The family interactions with Myra and with Joy's mother are discomfiting as well, suggesting that contrary to mantras of family, women don't have some special natural connection or innate psychic understanding between them. Joy's eventual rejection of family and the pop psychology that counsels her to rely on blood ties for comfort springs from their inapplicability to her life and implicates them in her continued estrangement and inability to cope.

The months that Joy spends in the psychiatric hospital bring her near an alternate sense of family, one in which people are drawn together by shared problems, but still the prescribed norms remain in place. When one of the doctors at the hospital offers Joy a self-help book on coping with grief following loss, its statements are so clearly inapplicable to Joy that they sting: "Chapter 3 says to get my family around me. My family will be a great source of strength and comfort if I let them. Blood is thicker than water" (171). Twice while Joy is in the hospital, visitors are mistaken for family members, and the one family member who tries to visit, Myra, is not recognized, because "I had no next of kin on the admissions form" (178). Most interesting in this context is the fact that David, a former student Joy is now sleeping with, is mistaken for her younger brother. Ironically, in part because David maintains a certain distance from Joy, their relationship is Joy's first romance in which she is not the caretaker.

It is in this light that we can reconceive of Galloway's repeated theme of sexual attraction (and intercourse) between grown woman and teenage boy, most often in some form of student-teacher relationship. As Magali Cornier Michael puts it, "[s]ince 'the family' is at present 'itself the site of economic exploitation: that of women' and since 'it is within the family that masculine and feminine people are constructed...[and] that the categories of gender are reproduced,' the production of new forms of subjectivity require [*sic*] new family structures and ideologies" (179).[28] What's important about the evolution of these relationships, the move beyond traditional family dynamics into a relationship with a far younger man, is the trajectory from socially acceptable into transgressive.[29] Galloway uses this upheaval of hierarchies much as she deploys disruptions of narrative hierarchies, setting forth new demands from narrative forms, and just as conventional family dynamics fail Joy, so conventional narrative techniques fail the text. And so we have seen the failures of patterns, of following rules, of order. More importantly, Galloway insists that we acknowledge that these failures and disconnections are seldom merely material; rather, they imply and accompany strained human interactions, the inadequacy of existing forms of relationship.

Galloway's next novel, *Foreign Parts*, shows that history cannot be contained by guidebooks, meaning cannot be contained by narrative norms, and human interaction can be contained by neither traditional ideas of hetero- and homosexuality nor normative family structures. While treading familiar ground of personal and political, Galloway recasts the relationship between the two spheres. As in the novels of her colleague, A.L. Kennedy, "... it is not easy to separate the precarious nature of human intimacy from questions of national belonging...the inter-imbrication of public and private does bring to bear on the paradox of Scottish nationality an internal pressure, as though the expansionist gesture of nationalist history and its attendant hauntings were being made to operate in a much more localised but just as intemperate space" (Summers-Bremner 129–130). As Cassie and Rona discuss their attitudes toward the past and forge a new relationship, Galloway looks for the most effective format to express these realizations.

Foreign Parts shows two women traveling to France in part to visit a monument in Normandy, where Rona's grandfather is memorialized. Eluned Summers-Bremner suggests that some characters "only come to rest with their Scottishness by leaving Scotland, literally or metaphorically...the temporally extended equivalent of this journey is the public history of the nation" (129), a tidy analogy that Galloway's novel draws on repeatedly. The physical absence of Scottish soil in the novel and the characters' displacement speaks to their difficulties with expectations of how they ought to occupy space, both personal and national. After witnessing the devastation wrought by war and grand ideas about unity, the women turn away from conventional notions of family, creating their own family unit in a relationship that cannot be filed under any existing stereotypes: they seem somewhat like crabby old maids facing the remainder of their lives together, but a warm physicality combined with the hint of sexual promise, not an out-and-out queer dynamic, asserts an as-yet unexplored form of interaction for the two women. This relationship seems a fuller exploration of the similar intimacy in *The Trick Is to Keep Breathing* between its main character, Joy, and her best friend, Marianne. That novel evades exploration of female friendship in part by sending Marianne abroad. Instead, Joy creates bonds with Marianne's mother and with a much younger man, a former student of hers, splitting the surrogate mother and nonthreatening sexual partner, whereas in *Foreign Parts*, Cassie and Rona may serve both functions for one another. Over the twenty years of their friendship, their lives become increasingly intertwined, and their interactions promise to form the basis of the alternate family Galloway repeatedly seeks.

The opening pages of the novel sketchily describe the disintegration of a traditional family—Cassie's, we can later deduce. This flashback beginning (which bears uncanny resemblance to A.L. Kennedy's opening pages in *Looking for the Possible Dance*, a novel that can be described as a combination of the two I am considering by Galloway) is chapter "none," its page number given as 000. Cassie runs giggling from a bus stop, chased by her mother, who catches up with her and tells her "Your daddy's died" (00). The child doesn't know exactly what she means, not, as we might expect, because she doesn't understand death, but because "daddy" is a contested term: "The man you visit at Aunty Nora's, his sister Nora is your aunty and he is your daddy that you visit on Sundays. That man. Is that the man she means?" (0). The phrasing implies a separation of husband and wife, perhaps a new father figure in the house, a biological explanation of who daddy is, the announcement not making sense without an answer. And no answer comes: the remainder of the episode is filled with noises—of the sea, of the waves, of the cold. The novel begins with a question of who daddy is, the conventional idea of family already put into question.

Cassie's father merits next to no further mention in the novel, deny-ing us the interpretive release of presuming his absence can account for her failed relationships with men or her alienated nature. Even Galloway's page numbers here underline her assertion of the irrele-vancy of fathers. The move forward from 000 to 00 to 0 implies that we're not yet at the beginning, that the traditional family isn't the beginning.

This game with page numbers is only one of Galloway's textual tricks. The novel is composed, like *Trick*, of foreign parts: multiple forms of fragments, both stylistically varied and temporally dispa-rate. We're offered first and third person (and occasionally even sec-ond person) narration, flashbacks, guidebook advice, letters, snippets of overheard conversations, typographic poetry, street signs, and scores of incomplete sentences left hanging mid-page.[30] The effect is somewhat like a scrapbook: one of the first interjections we encounter is a highway sign that says "BRICOLAGE" (13) just off the ferry in France. This instruction for how to read the text guides without being prescriptive, unlike the dictatorial guidebook or the years of failed vacation expectations that Cassie has stored up. The textual varia-tions serve as constant reminders that the text will not conform to expectations of a narrative about "two spinsters on holiday."

Early on, the most textually noticeable fragments, from a visual point of view, are the guidebook snippets, which begin with the site name in all capital letters and are enclosed by rectangles that set them apart from the rest of the page. Generally they provide us with a sum-mary of what is not seen by Cassie and Rona on their trip, giving us a gauge of how far this trip deviates from prescribed norms. (Even their guidebook, which Norquay deems "hopelessly inappropriate to their needs and hectoring in tone" is on the fringe, designed for travelers on tight budgets.) For instance, the book points out that Normandy has a number of lovely cemeteries: "Lovingly tended by the French and often full of summer blooms, they are well worth a visit" (18). This passage triggers in Cassie the realization that the land around them is flat because it has been shelled so heavily. She objects to the unsacred treatment of the gravesites, complaining that "Och just these four lines about the war that are worse than nothing. Sort of offhand. When you think what happened out there and this thing [the guide-book] sticks in something that misses the point. It doesn't even say why it's so flat" (19).

It is within this context that the next blow to prescriptive defini-tions of family comes via the search for Rona's grandfather's grave, paralleling an attack on the processes of history. When Cassie and

Rona finally arrive at one of the cemeteries mentioned in the guide-book, the one in which Rona's grandfather is buried, Cassie feels that any reaction she has to the cemetery is inappropriate because her grandfather is not among the dead there. Cemeteries are places to remember, to commemorate the past, to revisit relatives or notions of nation. Cassie has none of these, feels instinctive horror at the sight of the land but no pull for the thousands buried beneath it. No father, no relatives, no connection to fatherland. She leaves.

Cassie wants the cemeteries to be the repository of the grief of war—this makes sense, seems like the job of cemeteries. The guide-book, by contrast, denies war, denies the physical landscape, focusing on the flowers on its surface instead of on the people beneath, and on the devastation of the land. History is trivialized, ignored. Even the phrase "the French" generalizes, attributing a loving attention to flowers to a national character. Not calling the local people Normans denies the specificity of the front. The guidebook, as one of the most genre-rigid forms, has no way to accommodate more personal or tragic experiences.[31] The presence of restaurant reviews and hotel ratings renders the guidebook inappropriate for what Cassie wants from it. As her own use of the Scots term "och" suggests, Cassie does not seek to an effacement or aestheticization of the past but rather a meaningful progress beyond it. Both her language and Normandy's own peripheral positioning here reinforce the value of moving beyond a metropolitan perspective.

Tourism reduces the war cemeteries to botanical gardens and a chance to essentialize the French, presumably because nobody would want a tour of misery. When Rona does find her grandfather's name on a wall listing the dead, the caretaker highlights the name with chalk so that it will show up in her photographs. This act of kindness is made poignant by the fact that he is unable to speak, has no voice box. His literal lack of voice resembles the silence of the dead soldiers, but his chalking the names gives them presence, privileges the past over the present, and the experience of the tourist over that of the native. As a Scot, Rona's grandfather was part of the British army, and at this moment, the women represent the imperial power, not its victims.

Memory and empire empower the women, but Galloway reminds us that their status will always be mediated by "that wee bit extra: their sex." When Cassie returns to the parking lot to await Rona, a car approaches her, presumably for directions, but in actuality, its French, male passengers want to make lewd gestures and remarks. Cassie falls back on "probably the best-known phrase in the English language:" "FUCK OFF" (55). Her assumption places her in a precarious middle ground: as a native speaker of the world's *lingua franca*, she possesses political and economic power, but as a woman, her own language has been used against her, by "[t]he man who had muttered it at her in the covered bazaar when she hadn't wanted to buy his earrings, the soldier who asked her what fuck meant when it was obvious he knew...the complete arsehole this soldier they were always fucking soldiers licked her neck muttering FUCKYOUBABY they were animals" (55). In this complicated collage of images, given in a stream of consciousness run on, Cassie wields economic power while the soldiers maintain physical power; in calling the aggressors "animals," Cassie constructs a stereotypic association of the colonized (the exoticized word "bazaar" and the presence of soldiers on the street both tip us off to the likelihood that the men in question are in developing nations) with animals, yet their patently invasive and sexually threatening behavior forbids an oversimplified colonizer/colonized dichotomy. Instead, Galloway points out the parallel yet opposing positions of women and "Third World" citizens. Even the acceleration of the prose, the colliding sentences of stream of consciousness, serves to dissolve a rigid hierarchy of colonizer and colonized, of colonial past and postcolonial present, by blurring sentence subject and object and obscuring beginnings and endings. Galloway subverts national norms, gender norms, and formal norms, simultaneously.

As with other prescriptive moments, any time that Cassie and Rona follow the guidebook, it leads inevitably to conflict between the women or to a moment of existential crisis in Cassie, a sense that there's no point to what they're doing:

> Reading the book. It saves a lot of time going to see things. We could do it some more. In fact—Rona rolled her eyes and said oh god—In fact we could have stayed at home really. Got some food and sat in the car, reading bits of this informative book to each other in between spells of map-reading and then had our own beds to go to after. In fact, what are we doing here, Rona? (62–63)

Reading the guidebook replaces the act of looking, substituting words for experience. It is this sense of being controlled by a preprogrammed set of directions that makes Cassie uncomfortable, to the point that "Cassie had asked umpteen times to go somewhere and not have to sun about like hell SEEING things and Rona had said Ok [...] I mean it Rona, nothing as a real possibility" (135). The vacation in France therefore culminates in a week's rental of a remote country house, where Cassie cooks and both women read in a field of sunflowers.

Curiously, Cassie has opted for a vacation of relaxation, not entirely unlike those she used to take to Greece with her long-time boyfriend Chris. "I remember wondering what would happen when we ran out of islands, whether he'd agree to somewhere with ruins or museums: things to look at. Cassie I get two weeks to relax, two weeks: I can do without museums. It seemed reasonable at the time. I didn't say two weeks was all I got too" (90). What has changed is the element of choice; where on the beach vacations Cassie felt forced not to look, on the vacations with Rona she feels compelled to look. In both cases, the genre of taking a vacation is just as constraining as the guidebooks themselves. Cassie must escape the ways that "things are done" in order to visualize a life without a male mate. In a like manner, Galloway "adopts[s] experimental narrative structures which juxtapose different versions of the past" (Norquay and Smyth, "Waking Up" 42). History's reinterpretations, the reconstruction of the World War II narrative, sitting alongside the reconsideration of Joy's own past, require the structure of the novel to evolve to accommodate them.

Stylistically, then, the novel leads Cassie to the breaking of the molds of tradition. The trips with Chris are related via descriptions of photographs, invariably taken by him, of their vacations. Indented on the page, always related in first person and in the past tense, and describing static images, the photo descriptions are especially fixed and unchanging when contrasted with the moments of the text where there are shifts to present tense or first and third person relation coexist.[32] When the women arrive in the town near their rented cottage, Cassie insists that they do some shopping. In a moment reminiscent of Joy Stone's obsession with food, we're given the details of their purchases, notable as well because of the move into present tense, taking place at the moment when Cassie's mood becomes happy:

Cassie pushed back a strand of hair and smiled.

We are going shopping.

We stack

eggs
mushrooms cherries coffee
bread   garlic   tomatoes   onions
cucumber   radishes carrots brie yoghurt
putty-coloured cheese wrapped in leaves parsley

peaches   plums   oil   mustard   vinegar butter
milk   orange juice   two chocolate bars   biscuits
three bottles of wine   a bottle of cheap brandy Grand Marnier

in a trolley

and carry, like a babe in arms,

the biggest lettuce in the world.

It takes up a whole carrier bag on its own. Leaves like seaweed.

I don't care what it tastes like Rona, it's a work of art.
Rona just looks. (119–120)

This passage moves from third person to first, then into a typographic reproduction of what has been stacked in the grocery cart, ending with a moment of looking that feels positive, recuperative, and vibrant after the normative descriptions of photographs. The everyday simplicity of food shopping and of the food itself outstrips the guidebook vacation in both beauty and meaning.

This is not to say that Galloway romanticizes this new form of travel, just that there are glimpses of bliss even on this voyage of mishaps. Cassie is a difficult character to like, her entire vacation marked by discomfort and complaints, a positive development in contrast to the comfortable but vapid vacations she took with her boyfriend Chris over the years. The descriptions of pictures, given new valences by the dangers associated with looking in the text, purport to be descriptions of the scene but tend to talk more about what can't be seen, the hidden tensions and anxieties behind the stereotypic snapshots. Moreover, the photo-memories are arranged chronologically, beginning with Cassie's first trips with Chris, tracing the growing meaninglessness in their relationship, accounting for their breakup, and bringing us up to date on Cassie's few lovers since him. Midway through the novel, we read far briefer, more concrete descriptions of photos of the current holiday. These shorter, less psychological, more scenic descriptions release Cassie from the compulsion to account for her life in snapshots. For Cassie, for whom everything is overdetermined and fraught, the basic descriptions imply a release, their simplicity paralleling the main narrative's discovery of the possibility of a relationship with Rona that will not require the contortions of dating a man.

For Cassie, then, the early stages of the trip underline her disconnection from father and fatherland, though with the side effect of at least being real and challenging. For Rona, however, this first phase of the trip is about connection to family, about a promise she made to her grandmother: "It wasn't for me really. I said to my gran ages ago

I'd go. It was for her, I suppose. Guilt" (113). Rona has brought with her on the trip letters that her grandfather, Peter, wrote to her grandmother from his company in the armed forces. The first letter we read, the last he wrote before leaving the United Kingdom, reveals that he has gone AWOL for the weekend so that he can see his wife and is due to be shipped to France immediately. For Rona, the visit to the gravesite is an acceptance of the tie that father and fatherland have to her. Importantly, she is not overwhelmed by uncovering the family past: she only brings two of the letters with her, and while her eyes mist at the cemetery, she contains that part of the vacation and moves on. It is Cassie who invokes the letter in the final scenes of the novel.

The return to the letters takes place as Rona and Cassie pass back through Normandy; after a novel dealing so much with rejection of family and relationships, it seems curious to position the letters at novel's end. Cassie uses them as a jumping-off point into her analysis of traditional male/female relationships, noting that the poignant promise to do better contains within it a male failure in the past seen as entirely predictable and to be expected. "Now Maggie I will bid you farewell I hope to be spared to come back & to do more for you that I have in the Past" (41, 244), reads the closing sentence of the first letter. Cassie reads trauma as the only means of forcing emotion out of men, particularly out of Scottish men. It is this recognition that the most romantic moment in the letter by definition concedes the inadequacy of male response that allows Cassie to let go of her wish for a man.

This moment of truth leads Cassie to ask Rona why she doesn't "bother with men much?" (246). Rona cites dependency, emotional burdens, and guilt, this last trait being what inspired her trip to her grandfather's grave to begin with. "I don't miss anything," she concludes, then adds a twist to the discussion. "The question is, she says, and I turn, see a delicate face under wet hair; her eyes heavy, lips full. The question is how come you *do* miss them Cassie?" (247). Notable here are both the fact that this scene takes place in the present tense, an indication of Cassie's contentedness (even in the face of this difficult question) as well as the sensual description of Rona. At the end of a tirade about "fancying men and not liking them very much" (250), Cassie proposes that "we could make a go of it ourselves" (251), suggesting that they move in together.

But Rona has along the way dozed off, implying that some women, even those who choose not to pursue men, are not ready to consider an alternate structure. Rona accepts "old maid" life rather than examining options not yet created or sanctioned by mainstream society.

Cassie, however, the narrative experimentalist, conceives of another option: an eroticized but not sexual relationship with Rona, a sisterhood and companionship very like marriage and entirely an affront to it. If, as Engels proposes, "monogamy...was the first form of family to be based not on natural but on economic conditions" while ensuring "exclusive supremacy" (136–137) for the man, then Cassie and Rona's proposed cohabitation simultaneously affirms the economic expediency and rejects the imbalance of power built into heterosexual marriage.[33] As Rona and Cassie drive slowly back to native terrain, Galloway maps out a new means of occupying home. Summers-Bremner suggests that "Scottishness is figured as abiding in more than one region simultaneously" (129) throughout Scottish fiction. If we incorporate as well her suggestion that travel aids Scottish characters in coming to terms with nation and that history itself is such a journey, the neither clearly hetero-, nor necessarily homosexual future of Cassie and Rona represents a means of existing in multiple subject positions at once, and by extension, both accepting of and not entirely compliant with nation.

The remainder of the novel is in present tense: Cassie has made a decision and is happy with it. She tells us at the end, "I know we'll manage. Me and Rona. We'll be absolutely fine. And I know I'll ask her again" (262). The shift into first person seems permanent as well, as though Cassie no longer feels the need to narrate her life from outside of herself. Having found the answer in life with Rona, she can move beyond normal novelistic modes—third person, narrative past tense—and speak from her own perspective.

The final scenes take place on the beach, the coast of the English Channel. The entire novel has taken place in rural France, yet throughout it has centered on the identities of two Scottish women. Their nationality appears in the text largely through their vocabulary and through the reactions of the French who assume they are English. It is this mistaken identity that illuminates Cassie's complicated relationship to her nation. Rona politely replies "Oui. Yes. Scottish" to the question "you are English?" (211). Each time the innkeeper says English, the women mention Scotland, even agreeing while they disagree, understanding the mistake but not acceding to it. But while Cassie was in Turkey with Chris, people also would mistake them for English, which Chris enjoyed, "talking in a drawl about the Houses of Parliament and London Our Capital. It's Edinburgh his bloody capital only he didn't want to risk saying that and have them think he was less important than they thought" (179). Chris exhibits here a textbook postcolonial mindset, for one thing, but also part of the self-aggrandizing male mindset that Cassie rejects in her long speech to the sleeping Rona. To her, postcoloniality is not associated, as so many theorists would have it, with feminization, but with masculinity. Or, as Glenda Norquay has aptly characterized it, "The structures of colonisation lead patriarchy to assert itself more forcefully in men whose political context has disempowered them" (140).

Cassie's sense of nation, then, comes in part from claiming what Chris would prefer to hide. But beyond different accents and the use of the words "wee" and "bairns," what does being Scottish mean to her?

> Mind you, she knew even less about what passed for Scottish history. Macbeth. St. Columba. Your own country's medieval life restricted to an English play and a velcro shape off the felt table at Sunday school. Robert the Bruce. Kings and generals, Men of Letters. Of the mass of people, less than nothing. Women didn't come into the reckoning at all. (165)

We are drawn back here to the point Galloway makes in her introduction to the women's writing volume mentioned earlier. Cassie's knowledge of Scottish history is minimal due to Scotland's assumption into the United Kingdom, and beyond that, what she does know is entirely a male history of the ruling classes. Her critique blends her discomfort from gendered, postcolonial, and class positions. History can only reinscribe these oppressions for Cassie; therefore, she turns away from them in seeking a sense of female identity and of Scottishness. As her most consistently insightful critic, Norquay sees Galloway elevating "the significance of community and family, of personal (rather than national) pasts" (Norquay and Smyth, "Waking" 42).

But for once, Norquay falls short, for it is precisely in this context that the absence of Cassie's family in the novel takes on a meaning beyond the personal. "If James Kelman's fiction resists some of the readings it seems to invite, Alasdair Gray's *Poor Things* and Iain Banks's *The Crow Road* explicitly invite readings as national allegory which they then subvert or complicate" (McMillan 86). McMillan's piece reviews recent Scottish attempts, mostly by male authors, to write a family saga as national allegory that accounts for the life and death of nationalism and for the ravages and benefits, and gains and losses of modernity among castle ruins. As Elizabeth Butler Cullingford and others have done in readings of Irish literature, McMillan identifies the spirit and imagination of Scotland in these novels as feminized. Perhaps not coincidentally, McMillan later mentions that "stable, empowering national allegory and myth in the contemporary Scottish novel are as unwritable as they are unreadable" (97), seeming to imply that unstable categories of nation and of the feminine create this hazy in-betweenness, as well as that a workable form for these novels has not yet been developed.

Because narratives in which the embodiment of the nation is female serve repeatedly to keep women in the role of icon and childbearer, Galloway's novels deal only glancingly with questions of nation. In this way, she and her female characters can escape such containment. Still, her novels do not ignore issues of national identity, engaging as they do with the gendering of it as well as the suppression of Scottish history by an overarching Britishness. Rather, she refuses the link of gender and nation that submerges and maims both even in recent and otherwise progressive national/family allegories. Galloway's new woman is part of alternative, even transgressive family structures, and her new nation is one proud of its identity but not insistent upon its potency.

Galloway rejects the traditional notion of family in concert with calling traditional conceptions of nation and Scottish identity into question. We confront again urban characters disconnected from the idealized rural past; even more explicitly, their inherited conceptions of Scottishness are tied to a Calvinist or Presbyterian inheritance obsolete and ineffective. The value of the past, on both personal and national levels, is repeatedly called into question. History cannot be contained by guidebooks any more than family can be contained by family history; while part of Cassie and Rona's vacation is the search for Rona's grandfather's grave, this task is early eliminated from the plot, much as the marriage it depicts helps Rona and Cassie to eliminate matrimony from their list of possibilities. Their relationship, like the form of the novel, dissolves traditional hierarchies and creates a new possibility for making meaning.

Chapter Five

Eoin McNamee's Local Language

So much of what links the authors discussed up to this point—marginalized dialects, peripheral settings, dynamics of the working class, fragmented form—stems from an aesthetic of reaction. This is not to say that its practitioners are reactionary in the conventional sense of the word; rather, their texts enter into conversation with what has come before them, and for the most part, they feel they must reject, reconfigure, and reinterpret. Neither received narrative techniques nor inherited constructions of nation, class, and region are adequate or satisfying, and I have tracked the sorts of innovations made with an eye to their Joycean antecedents in particular as the modernist era was marked by a similar sense of a need for the new. Given the historical and political contexts of modernism and its critical reception, however, its innovations did not penetrate many literary provinces; stories of working-class characters in particular seem to have generated a rigid genre complete with expectations of authentic representation to a presumed middle-class audience. Kelman, Galloway, and Doyle make interventions in literary history to redress its oversights and inadequacies, writing novels that are beautiful, moving, and thought-provoking. By writing about the Catholic/Protestant "Troubles" in Northern Ireland, however, Eoin McNamee assumes yet a further burden of expectations. If the presumption for a working-class text is of a gritty, realist portrait of a down-on-his-luck character battling an unassailable mainstream, for a "Troubles" novel the stereotypes multiply, precisely because the Republican/Unionist conflict has been so interpreted that it feels possible positions about it have all already been detailed and ossified. Stereotype and cliché and political assumptions would seem to blot out possibility or innovation.

Criminologist Bill Robton sees this exhaustion as a problem only for "factual writers," "because there is no new angle they can find. But for fictional writers it's absolutely perfect" (qtd. in Pelaschiar, *Writing* 27). While he may be right that the pulp thriller thrives on endless recyclings of stock characters and themes, literary critics also bemoan the lack of new angle as restricting the development of fiction in Northern Ireland.[1] Indeed, some of the most powerful voices in contemporary poetry in English come from the North, from the towering figures of Seamus Heaney and Paul Muldoon to Derek Mahon and Ciarán Carson, and while there are a number of strong, active novelists at work in Northern Ireland, only Bernard MacLaverty may be said to have achieved a level of recognition parallel to that of these poets.

Of course, the conviction that there is "nothing new under the sun" certainly predates its inscription in Ecclesiastes; even in the formulaic terrain of Belfast fiction, McNamee creates anew—in his most quoted line, "New languages would have to be invented" (*RM* 16). Ironically, he does this by working within both received genres and received storylines: his three novels to date are all drawn from historical sources, and all are suffused with discourses of film noir, of crime thrillers, of overwrought gothic tales. Rather than fleeing from earlier forms, McNamee draws on them in combination with his own innovations, a pastiche again evocative of the work of James Joyce. The creation of a narrative voice almost without agency derives from the historical and cultural contexts of his stories, as do the challenges to narrative resolution. Through attention to his 1997 novel *Resurrection Man* in particular, a fictionalized account of the crimes of a 1970s Loyalist gang known as the Shankill Butchers who terrorized and murdered Catholics, this chapter will test the notion developed up to this point that the combination of working-class voices with textual experimentation achieves reconceptions of national and local spaces and identities, revealing how shaped by neighborhood and class the use of space is, even in a context normally read primarily through a lens of Unionism and Republicanism.

While the context of the "Troubles" is of course at the center of any account of *Resurrection Man*, I also make comparisons between McNamee's novel and non-"Troubles" texts, in part, to emphasize how the economic situations of the characters, manipulated for political ends in Northern Ireland, offer insight into the issues underlying the angry confrontations and violence, thereby resisting the replication of the isolation of the working classes arising from consideration of them only in the one dimension. McNamee's novel can easily be read to suggest that an individual sociopath is responsible for the violent deaths it portrays, which, at the most immediate level, is inarguable. Aaron Kelly notes the frequency with which the Northern thriller genre and its critics interpret "various rehearsals of the conflict as an intractable yet quarantined and ultimately extractable tumor in an otherwise ordered social body" (15). An alternate and equally prevalent line of analysis sees the problems in Ireland from an essentialist point of view, the actors in the "Troubles" viewed as irreducibly and atavistically violent, shaped by genetics rather than circumstance: in this storyline, the "tragic flaw in the Irish is the result of either their own innate proclivities, the workings of fate or the effects of nature and environment on the Irish psyche....socio-cultural roots are denied" (McLoone 61). In these seemingly opposite scans—the sickness of a single individual versus that of a single national character—a belief in the inevitability of events merges with an enclosure of them in a world separate from the reader's, serving to exculpate outsiders and efface economic pressures underlying the partisan behaviors. Moving beyond the personal psychoses of McNamee's twisted serial killer, Victor Kelly, into an acknowledgment of the role that class and geography play in his killing spree implicates state policy and history in the crimes, while analyses of the discourses used to contain them indict individuals as well.

In a similar vein, I have inserted the role of isolated yet urban housing into analysis of the stylistic innovations of Doyle, Kelman, and Galloway. For instance, I have argued that Doyle's choices to set *Paddy Clarke* and portions of *The Woman Who Walked into Doors* cannot be read, once formal elements are taken into account, as nostalgic for a rurally oriented, homogeneous Ireland, nor do they uncritically embrace the move beyond the mid-century dominance of Catholic nationalism. McNamee's choice to set his novel in the 1970s shows similar nuances. Certainly there is no question of nostalgia for the height of violence embodied by his murderous Victor, but neither does he create a portrait of the "Troubles" horrors as to by implication endorse a period before or after it. The scrutiny of the 1970s suggests that its open violence is merely the most direct expression of a prior and ongoing condition. Examination of the rendering of Belfast's spaces and its interlinked distinctive formal dynamics, in particular the narrative antivoice, with its tensions between heteroglossia and monologism, shows how the interaction of class and geography sustain Victor's behavior.

"Forgotten Outposts against Inner Darkness": Interior and Exterior Belfast

Resurrection Man begins after it ends: "Afterwards Dorcas would admit without shame that having moved so often was a disturbance to Victor's childhood" (3). Beyond the notion of *in media res*, this opening offers analysis of events with which the reader is still unfamiliar; a looking backward that differs from the retrospective of a standard narrative voice in the haziness of the word "afterwards," which declines to specify after what. Such a beginning both disrupts an Aristotelean trajectory of the plot and foregrounds the role of urban spaces in Victor's development. Victor's mother, Dorcas, in speaking shamelessly, declines blame for the multiple moves, and the narrative voice absolves her via grammar, making a gerund perfective, a noun, "having moved," out of words normally verbs and thereby avoiding ascribing agency and rather just stating what has happened as established fact. This sort of evasion of agency by the narrator permeates all of McNamee's novels and marks his most conspicuous authorial signature. Rather than being secured within a single neighborhood, the status quo at the time, Victor and his parents shift from place to place, always to escape trouble with fellow Protestants who assume, based on the Catholic-sounding family surname Kelly, that they are "masquerading," trying to pass as Protestant. The sense of performativity pervades the novel, which suggests that all aspects of identity, whether "inherent" or adopted, spring from role-playing. In trying to live in places that speak to their religious affiliation, the Kellys experience the clash of two sign systems, geographic and linguistic.

For Dorcas and her husband James, a man so self-effacing as to be nearly nonexistent, this tension between word and place is ongoing: they "came from Sailortown in the dock area. Sailortown disappeared gradually after the war. There is a dual carriageway running through the area now. There isn't even a place where you can stand to watch the traffic" (3). Still on the first page of the book, this passage excavates portions of Belfast history for "you." With Sailortown itself as the grammatical subject of the sentence, the narrator casts the demolition in the area as a gradual disappearance, making it sound both peaceful and self-determined. The repetition of the passive construction "there is" at the beginning of the next two sentences reinforces the lack of human agency; the only person in the scene is the second person, placing all activity outside the bounds of the novel. The literalness of the place-name, meanwhile, establishes a world in which there is a one-to-one correspondence between language and knowable reality, the very equivalence that the Kellys's name disrupts. The disappearance of Sailortown thus parallels the vanishing of the language of representation, and while the narrator would appear extremely cautious throughout the novel not to ascribe agency, ever, to anyone, we can read from the choice to mention Sailortown on the first page that slum clearance is implicated in the subsequent "Troubles."

Once a cosmopolitan port of a provincial capital, Sailortown, a primarily Catholic, congested, waterfront district of Belfast, like many other historic concentrations of urban working poor, became the site of overcrowded terraces of dilapidated housing stock, its inhabitants generally menial laborers on the docks or in Belfast's textile industry. With the decline of its traditional industries, and as happened throughout the United Kingdom and Ireland after World War II, council planning authorities and developers saw a confluence in the need for slum clearance and an easy route to the city center for the growing number of cars, so the dual carriageway McNamee mentions, the M2 and Belfast Ring Road, was built and local residents were scattered, with many of the same problematic consequences as I have discussed in relation to Glasgow and Dublin—namely, the dissolution of long-standing neighborhood bonds, the disappearance of jobs, geographic isolation outside the view of most of the city, and limited access to public transit and social services.

Belfast's history, apart from religious tension, is underscored in the novel's early pages as a factor in Victor's pathology. "The city itself has withdrawn into its placenames. Palestine Street. Balaklava Street. The names of captured ports, forgotten outposts held against inner darkness. There is a sense of collapsed trade and accumulate decline" (3). McNamee links economics and empire here via the street names, his choice of present tense for a novel set in the past making it current, ongoing, a stylistic decision which, like the use of second person, closes the distance between reader and story. The decline evokes the disappearance of Sailortown and its employers, reflected across Belfast by the evaporation of business. For Jonathan Stainer, "The implication is made that Belfast was constructed and then abandoned by indifferent and speculative capitalists, leaving behind poverty, unemployment and industrial 'emasculation'" (114). Stainer maintains that Loyalist paramilitaries are a reaction to such emasculation. Rather than acknowledging an alternate narrative of class or the bankruptcy of the modern narratives of progress and economic growth that underlay Belfast's manufacturing trades, those involved in the maintenance of Unionist Protestant identity have drawn on the terminology of progress. In their new teleology, elimination of Catholic impurities replaces shipbuilding and factory work as the project of the Protestant working classes. "*Resurrection Man*'s Belfast seems to be defined in terms of industrialization, modernization and ideas such as progress, work-ethic, materialism and capitalism...positioned within a representative theme of Britishness (or one which seems oppositional to popular, rural or pre-modern constructions of Irishness)" (112).

In this light, the choice of the street names themselves bears symbolic weight. Dermot McCarthy points out that they "recall Belfast's participation in both the rise and collapse of the British empire" (138), though they go even further, the idea of withdrawal evoking entrenchment and associating Belfast not with England but with distant places known for frequent changes of possession. The names evoking the past, the scene set in a narrative present, and the connection to an unspecified future moment of being read thereby dissolve historical time. Beyond such a historical and economic reading of place-names lies a psychological one, connected via their parallel interests in colonization. To Laura Pelaschiar, "the streetnames are a sad reminder of that imperial attempt to hold the 'inner darkness' at bay, an inner darkness which, in a typical transposition of the colonizer's mind, is identified with places and peoples to be seized and subjugated" (119). As for Doyle's characters, whose public lives helped them avoid inner thoughts, place here staves off interiority, with poverty and desolation less frightening than what lies within. But it is not so much location as language that McNamee sees as holding off inner angst; rather than a window to the soul, language here is a defense against it. Still, this language is no longer fixed. As Chris Patsilelis puts it, "McNamee links the ceaseless, violent deterioration of Belfast society to the deformed state of words, the collapse of language itself" (C2).

Such readings, however, posit the relationship of language and city to be one of analogy, whereas, to use Beckett's famous characterization of *Finnegans Wake*, the book "is not about something; it is that something itself." Rather than reading Belfast as comparable to language, McNamee's novel suggests that the city itself *is* language, that space is knowable only via words. There is no reality beyond language, and since language is a series of performances, the implication is that there is no reality at all. Such a syllogism could seem flip were it not for the sheer unreality of the situation McNamee writes about. While he takes as his subject a true story, that of Lenny Murphy and the Shankhill Butchers, McNamee takes pains to emphasize that narrative creates history.

This linguistic dimension acknowledged, it is important to recognize the importance of the physical placement of Belfast within the nation-state of Northern Ireland. Kelly contends that both Unionist and Nationalist mindsets establish what he calls a "rusticative" (83) context that privileges rural over urban in their mythological self-definitions, a nationalist conception much in keeping with those I discussed in my introduction as foundational to Scotland and the Republic of Ireland as well. One of the central characters in *Resurrection Man* is Heather, a woman sleeping her way through the ranks of loyalist paramilitaries and who eventually becomes Victor's long-term girlfriend. Our first introduction to her comes in an enclosed, semi-public, urban space—a bar, one of many in the novel, repeatedly sites for performance and display. Heather is in the office of the Gibraltar bar, which links her to sunnier climes (and possibly, given her voluptuous body type and dark features, to Molly Bloom), and indeed, she is straining to catch rays on her legs through a small window. The narrative voice informs us within a few pages that Heather, whose name evokes the countryside, is indeed not a Belfast native but hails from a seaside town reliant on summer tourists from the city for its survival. When Victor is imprisoned, Heather makes a visit back there, encountering the Catholic journalist Ryan, who falls into an affair with her, unaware that she is the girl-friend of the killer he seeks. (His failure to make this connection is one challenge to the conventional detective form.)

Heather and Ryan share seaside origins, and as though able to read in Victor's face the Sailortown origins of his parents, when she meets him, "The first thing she noticed was his black curly hair and dark skin so at first she thought that he was foreign, a sailor off one of the boats" (42). While Kelly suggests that there is something regressive in the text's function as "malign projection of the inner landscapes of loathing of its depraved inhabitants" (102), I would propose instead that this layering on of externalities casts Belfast as canvas rather than source of the malevolence in the novel. The question of whence evil arises is not academic, as *Resurrection Man* is concerned through-out with borders and identifications; as we shall see, McNamee's prose works to contest the values of his characters. His formal choices interact with stylistic ones in a manner reminiscent of the modernist attention to detail seen in the work of James Joyce.

Questions of Narrative Voice

Indeed, McNamee's prose inspires many critics to see connections to Joyce: reviews of *Resurrection Men* in particular enjoy making the parallel. Seaghán Ó Murchú sees the "homiletic cadences and half-remembered biblical starkness" as reminiscent of both *Dubliners* and "Beckett's street denizens in is carefully modulated detachment." Robert Winder notes the novel ends "with a poetic Joycean flourish"

(16), while Fintan O'Toole sees a stream of consciousness technique that has "turned murky...Randomness, the accidental collisions of thoughts and words that gives such joyousness to Joyce's prose has taken on new, darker meanings" ("Darkness Within" 10). Colin Lacey suggests a link via the urban angle: that McNamee might accomplish for "Belfast what Joyce hoped *Ulysses* would be to turn-of-the-century Dublin; a grand plan by which the city could be recreated with all its sights, smells, moods and menace intact."

This evocation of the hyperrealism of *Ulysses*, an antirealism that looks very much like realism, comes into conflict with the expectations for a Belfast writer in much the same way as it does for a working-class one. John Wilson Foster wrote in the early 1970s, when violence in Northern Ireland was at its apex, that "any fiction writer who wants to illuminate Ulster society has to press realism and psychology into service in the exploration of three things: sex, violence and sectarianism" (qtd. in D. McCarthy, "Babel" 141). More contemporarily, and explicitly in reference to *Resurrection Man*, Colin Lacey writes of the reader's exhaustion after having been "battered by the veracity of the vision McNamee has created" (np). Even John Banville, himself known, in the words of Declan Kiberd, for employing "antirealistic but superficially realist procedures" (qtd. in Kennedy Andrews, *Irish* 23), lauds the "convincing" plot elements, with their "exactness of detail" (22). Here we see the documentary expectations and interpretations McNamee explicitly takes on, complicating his own task in his choice of subject matter drawn from the historical record.[2] In a 2004 interview, he asserts that "One thing that has struck me is that perhaps the traditional novel which purports to be wholly fictional is really the stranger form compared to what I'm doing" (Wild).

As Elmer Kennedy-Andrews has so nicely put it, "McNamee's 'new language' challenges the traditional discursive premises of 'Troubles' fiction,' undermining the 'reflectionist' or realist conventions of literary form and the usual account of history as 'reflection' of a reality which precedes it and determines the form of its representation" (140). But Kennedy-Andrews does not go far enough—his formulation speaks to form but doesn't call attention to McNamee's use of historical material; the two are intertwined. The need for a new form arises precisely to avoid the sort of inescapable reinscription of boundaries that the use of old forms generates. The challenge to realism comes here differently again than it has in Kelman, Doyle, and Galloway. He is the only one of the four, for instance, to use quotation marks. But there are continuities as well, from the denial of narrative satisfaction via conventional resolutions, to the reliance on a narrative flatness, to unconventional grammatical forms (for McNamee, the sentence fragment is especially significant). Although his novels have been compared to all of Joyce's prose by one reviewer or another, at the level of style he might most closely resemble the Joyce of *Dubliners*, with his austere tone and scrupulous, mean word choices.

But the novel does not feel bleak; to the contrary, some reviewers fault McNamee for a baroque overwriting—"unduly inflated," "occasionally melodramatic," "ponderous" (Eileen Battersby, Helen Birch, and Ó Murchú, respectively). Certainly the text revels in language, but these critiques spring, I contend, from an incomplete reading of McNamee's project. To draw on an insight of Kelly's, I begin here noting that the novel "performs *both stylistically and formally* the transgression of filiative, tribal cartographies within the urban context even as it indulges them" (97, emphasis mine). Leaving aside for the moment the discussion of a map of the city, I want to amplify Kelly's point that *RM*'s textual features work, via an engagement with excess, both to give voice to and ultimately contest sectarian stances. The rhetoric of abundance comes into play, lending the vivid word choices a pointed commentary.

In its elegant prose, at odds throughout with the brutality of the murders, *RM* can be said to resemble the film version of *Trainspotting*, with its confrontation of the standard slum-scenes and clichéd depictions of poverty onscreen. The colors in the film are gorgeous, vibrant; the evocative contrasts with received images of housing estates point up the sentimentalism latent within drab, documentary depictions.[3] As Andrew Macdonald, the film's producer puts it, the film sought to replicate the "surrealistic style of [the book], the way it refuses to conform to social-realism…and public health warnings, where people are absolute victims" (*Trainspotting* Web page). Recalling Stam and Shohat's distinction between realism as a goal and realism as a style, we can look at the baroque decor and graceful camerawork in *Trainspotting*, as well as the ornate prose in *RM*, as fashioning a simultaneous pose of realism and sense of estrangement. It is at this level that we can see McNamee as a realist, the point where the detail of the "richly textured" (Patsilelis) prose is no more to evoke a scene than to call attention to the language itself. The rich verbiage, then, can be seen less as self-indulgence or overwriting and more as a conscious comment on the levels of language available to describe violence, from clinical to aestheticized to crude. McNamee refuses stereotypic bleakness, instead opting for a realism of excruciating detail, a realism that bleeds into hyperrealism of estrangement.

The antirealist elements of McNamee's style thereby link him further to Joyce via, for instance, the presence of a pastiche of popular forms. Recalling Bakhtin's charge that heteroglossia distance itself from common language, we can see McNamee's inclusion of various voices as a means of critiquing the norm; that is, the presence of jostling genres presents a direct challenge to the monologic tone. Identifying the destabilizing effect of multiple perspectives, Gerry Smyth identifies the way that "novelistic discourse mixes with other genres, such as documentary, *film noir*, philosophy and crime thriller, making it difficult to settle into one consistent reading position from which to make sense of the narrative" (Smyth, *NN* 121), a multiplicity Kelly links to the novel's urban setting (102). McNamee interjects a confession in the voice of one John McGrath, occupying an entire chapter and without transition to those surrounding it: "This was the first time I ever done anything like that and I hope I will never be involved again" (67), McGrath writes, his grammatical forms marking him as less educated, at the same time as the form of the formal statement to the authorities bears traces of those to whom it is addressed: "I wish to say that I have now embraced Christian values and express repugnance at my deed and that having made a clean breast I am at ease now in Christ" (68), the Biblical rhythms interacting with the clichés to mimic a normative dialect. A juxtaposition emerges here between the presence of a cacophonic polyphony and a recognizable narrative voice, a tension that plays out repeatedly throughout the novel.

This issue of narrative voice requires more attention. Richard Haslam, in his careful and excellent treatment of the question of narration, notes that Victor and Ryan paralleled throughout the novel, and I would emphasize in particular that their introductions to readers take place via mapping their locations. Haslam feels beyond the Victor/Ryan connections, that "the third-person narrator has even more in common with Kelly, in that both are obsessed with the topography of the city, the imagery of cinema and television, and the aestheticization of murder" (207). If we read the narrative voice not so much as a distinct character—evidenced in its vanishing both in the interpolated confession and its retreat during dialogue exchanges—as a pervasive mood, then we can see that this voice is not so much at one with Victor as both of them are influenced by the same set of circumstances. Haslam himself moves toward this insight, pointing out that the free indirect discourse of the many characters sounds identical. The appearance of stylistic unity within the novel can be seen to replicate the "all-pervasive, institutionalized" (Stainer 112) identifications if, as Stainer argues, sectarianism pervades all aspects of Northern Irish life and normalizes hatred and fundamentalism. But when Haslam concludes that voice springs from the city itself, "and the novels' characters are the city's words made flesh" (208), he instead makes an interpretive move that leads him to see the hyperaestheticized prose style as occluding political comment, avoiding "the obligation to do justice, not violence, to one's subject" (208). In adopting the conventional equation of beauty with unreality, Haslam presumes that we must experience the "unglamorous" (208) to understand the horror McNamee depicts. As with expectations that working-class texts offer graphic unsentimentality, this presupposition sets conditions for form based on content. While I have argued throughout this book that certain forms are inadequate to the needs of contemporary narratives of class, I have also worked to resist the imposition of expectations of representational realism, and McNamee's lush language here makes a similar stance.

Crucially in a novel where language has such power, an initial insult to Victor by older boys seems in part to trigger the antagonism toward Catholics that gives way to his murderous acts, the assertion that "Your ma must of rid a Taig" (6). This sentence incorporates the slang for Catholics (Taigs) and for sex (riding) that span the Irish and Scottish regions of the British Isles, along with nonstandard grammar ("of rid" for "have ridden") to locate the speaker within a particular class and region. Interestingly, this phrase becomes a minor refrain in the novel, entering the narrator's consciousness exactly as spoken at times (7) but also shifting form with different consciousnesses; McClure, the force behind Victor's gang, is not speaking but seems to focalize when the narrative states "must have rid a Taig" (137) during a bonding session between Victor and the older man. The move to a more standard grammatical form, "have" for "of," reveals that language is not monolithic within the Unionist community, that no single discourse can accurately represent a group. Despite some common rhythms, then, different characters do evince different iterations of the local language, a move that downplays the narrator's dominance.

In particular, the diminution of the narrative voice during characters' conversations gives those passages of the novel the feel of a screenplay, a sense evoked in *The Commitments* as well, and important for both Doyle and McNamee in its displacement of authorial or narratorial oversight. Though the narrative voice is distinctive, specifically in its use of passive voice and eloquent, the elaborate syntax—the "sensuality of style" often taken for "overwriting" (P. O'Brien qtd. in

Haslam 205), in addition to resisting the expectations of realism, reflects not an effort to beautify violence but to hint that the public discourse itself, the voice shared by narrator and characters, has effected this aestheticization. Local language, then, while present as well inside quotation marks, exists as much in the novel's cadences and style. This is not to say that the residents of Belfast speak in such sentences as "There was a scant rattling in the dry shrubs at the front door, a prowled quiet around the house" (175) so much as to suggest that the prose's lapidary quality merges with the reliance on passive voice to create a detachment from events that resembles the recoil residents have. In offering a comment on the ways in which carnage is simultaneously glamorized and marginalized, McNamee is mistakenly seen to be engaged in exactly this refinement out of existence.

In a similar manner, the unsettling of the reader has a more ideological edge than McNamee is credited with: "All the characters remain enigmatic; the more information we receive about motivation and desire, the more difficult it is to say anything for certain about them. In all these ways the novel resists any straightforward reading, attempting to insinuate at a formal level the problem of alienation which would appear to be the text's major theme" (Smyth *NN* 121). Smyth sees the link of form to alienation, and such an analysis subverts the relentless frame of the "Troubles" that offers simplistic explanations of the motives of the characters, yet this view extends too easily into universal humanist readings, a mindset Smyth himself is critical of but misattributes to McNamee. In assuming that the novel "reveals itself as another reactionary response to the 'Troubles,' interested not in sectarianism" (122) but the human condition, he thus ignores McNamee's indictments of specific geographical and class constructions.

Certainly location is crucial, however, as Kelly realizes in his insistence on the centrality of cartography. The novel's prose incorporates local language in the speech of its characters, major and minor. Regionalisms, often recognizably drawn from Scottish and Irish vernaculars, occur throughout the text, as when Heather tells her lover Darkie Larch "I haven't a baldy what you're on about" (43), meaning she claims not to understand what he is saying. Victor's own speech acts as a signature of his location—"thon" and "wee" (173) making evident via his ambiguous parentage that both Loyalists and Nationalists speak a dialect with Gaelic roots. Profanity is ample, nearly always an inflection of "fuck," like the British Isles slang "fuck-all" (119), meaning "nothing." Victor uses the common term "cunt," a derogatory term for a guy, during a questioning by a detective while he is in prison awaiting trial. To be sure, interrogations by the authorities, as in *How Late it Was*, constitute some of the zones in which we hear the most of Victor's direct speech. As in the novels of both Doyle and Kelman, McNamee declines in this interview scene to offer speech attributions for many of the lines spoken, a technique that has the effect here of even further submerging any narrative presence. When combined with the profanity and other casual speech forms—"how come" (71) for "why" and nongrammatical constructions like double negatives—as well as the regional "I reckon" (71) and "What are you on about?" (70), the result is to give the narrative the appearance of having been ceded entirely to its speakers, who, though bearing opposing agendas, share a common idiom.

This idiom is place-specific, but it is not a fixed, permanent language. Ulster Scots terms crop up, but they bear associations to the past, appearing as faint traces of a now-obsolete tongue: "After eighty-six years forbye the worry of men" (198) laments the mother of one of Victor's accomplices, warning Heather, now Victor's girlfriend, that she has told the police all she knows, finished at the end of her life with accommodating the violence of men. Her age, her reference to the passage of time, and her use of the word "forbye" connect her to a past that Heather is able to recognize and understand but recoils from, literally, as she pulls her hand away from the old lady, who has placed it against the "weightless lineaments" of her "pale skull" while being watched by old photographs (198). The spectral quality of the elderly lady and her past reinforces their lack of impact in the present.

Past and present are blurred elsewhere in the novel, which comments on both aestheticization and the prescription to be realistic via the use of detail. Moment after moment in the novel gives the appearance of description while ultimately not describing. The fixity of objects and the fixity of time are both called into question:

> Big Ivan had only ever had his picture in the paper once. It was when he was eight years old and played in goal for the school team. He had kept the photograph which showed him standing in the back row with his arms folded. The team wore jerseys and shorts intended for older boys. Their heroic stance seemed equally ill-fitting. The back row standing on boxes, the captain with his foot on the ball. The whole composition had a strangeness to it—the smudged, awkward faces, the white fold marks running through the paper, the sense that they are committed to a much grimmer task than football. He longed to have his picture in the paper again. He thought that it would reveal hidden public qualities. (189)

This free indirect discourse from gang member Big Ivan while he is in prison narrates, on its surface, the desire for notoriety that motivates so many of the gruesome actions in the novel, evoking in seemingly realist fashion the worn newspaper clipping of an earlier, more inno-cent Ivan, one of scores of descriptions of photographs throughout the novel, as though the characters are just as interested as the narrative voice they help to constitute in the creation and maintenance of images. But the quoted passage is problematic: it cannot decide if it is describing the cutout or the scene itself, referring to the fold of the paper, for instance, as an element of its composition; the oldness of the picture has become an element of its aura. Accepting this duality does not account, however, for the shift in that same sentence to present tense: "they *are* committed to a much grimmer task than football." Why does the narrator move to the present progressive here? A statement of the timelessness of the image? A comment on Ivan's current grim calling? Ambiguity multiplies even before we get to the oxymoronic desire for the revelation of hidden qualities that are simultaneously public.

Part of what's revelatory about the passage is that this level of involved thought is taken to be the province even of Victor's dumb henchmen. And the self-consciousness of language and the construct-edness of images directs us to questions of performativity. Smyth has critiqued the novel, with Haslam's approval, as ultimately less engaged with responding to problems of sectarianism than interested in "some inscrutable darkness at the heart of the self" (*NN* 123), a reading which, I have suggested, misconstrues McNamee's complex use of narrative voice, and, in addition, contradicts the very foregrounding of photographic and cinematographic representations that Haslam finds so troubling. The novel establishes McNamee's fascination with the contemporary fixation on visual images.

Victor's obsession with American gangster films mirrors the exte-riority other characters sense in him. "With no defined centre of self, [Victor] looks to popular culture for desirable identities, heroic images of masculinity on which he can model himself" (Kennedy-Andrews, "Antic" 134). He uses the films as a script for nearly all his social interactions, from calling his mother "doll" "in an American gangster voice" (228) to his interrogation by a detective in which "they were using the tones of flawed irony employed in the gangster films" (52). But while Victor may be the most extreme manifestation of this need for artistic inspiration in the formation of the self, other charac-ters engage in similar acts of self-construction. Ryan drinks at home because "when he was drinking at home he could work up an impressive sense of ruined dignity" (177). Heather "imagined her naked body being found like a cover from *True Detective*" (172), "She thought that if there was someone else in the room they could see the white of her eyes like a picture of fear" (175). What all of these images share is their need for an audience, suggestive of Belfast's ongoing performance in the world's eye, as well as their reliance on preformed genres, clichés, stereotypes. That which is ossified requires no further interpretation and indeed resists close reading, and so the production of the archetypal drunk, thug, or fallen woman frees its performer from any sense of agency or self-will. Victor, Heather, and Ryan seem impelled less by personal motivations than by enormous, unstoppable social forces.

It is here that the profusion of popular forms becomes ominous, then. Kennedy-Andrews identifies a number of them: "a pastiche of a range of popular forms and genres, including the American gangster thriller (in his use of the figure of the lonely, single-minded investigator, and a narrative voice modeled on a characteristically understated Chandlerese), the comic-strip (as in the comic-strip names of Victor's gang members...), children's television programmes,...*film noir* (from which he takes his imagery of urban desolation and the pervasive atmosphere of doom and darkness), and Gothic horror stories" (134). Each of these genres carries within it a set of expectations and possibilities that preempt other outcomes. In drawing on so many of them simultaneously, McNamee creates a heteroglossia that makes clear that he rejects their inevitabilities and sees his characters' performances as at least in part personal choices. Combined with his refusal to demonize Belfast, this shaking free of the determinism of naturalism shows McNamee himself working to invent and innovate.

Refusals of Genre

At the same time as *Resurrection Man* unearths the complicated agency underlying narrative voice, it resists ossification into any pre-existing generic form, and in particular it functions as a reworking of the detective genre. Laura Pelaschiar notes that Eamonn Hughes

> cites the "Troubles" thriller as the main obstacle impeding a more mature development of the Northern Irish novel *tout court*. The thriller, with its stereotyped generic mechanisms ("goodies" against "baddies") does not allow for any open interplay between characters

and circumstances and leaves very little space for an articulated con-
textualisation of the Northern Irish reality.... "At its most mechanical
the thriller moves to a closure which projects its locale as a closed but
always unresolved system: the Cold War can never end, the forces of
corruption can never be defeated, and the problems of Northern
Ireland will inevitably endure" (Hughes, 1991: 6). (27)

Numerous critics have accurately read the journalists, Ryan and
Coppinger, as hard-boiled stereotypes, noting their awkward fit
within the novel. John Banville sees their presence as one of the
"flaws" (22) of the book, while Ronan Bennett laments that they
"provide insufficient counterpoint and subplot, and are familiar
almost to the point of cliche. Neither is their role quite integrated into
the novel, and, with little else to do, they are reduced to a chorus" (9).
But we can more productively read these characters as yet another
interesting iteration of the need for new languages to be invented.
Ryan and Coppinger (or, more likely, Ryan *or* Coppinger) might have
marked the gravitational center of a more conventional novel, offering an outsider's view of a corrupt world and working within our
oversight to reinstall a sense of order or at least to make sense of the
terror. But here, much of the action takes place outside of the purview
of the journalists, the narrative style rendering their voices nearly
interchangeable with other, seemingly more implicated characters.
RM thereby makes tangible the tensions underlying most thrillers,
which Kelly formulates as in distinction with earlier detective novels,
where "the crime was supposedly the disruption of the ordered, social
totality, whereas the hard-boiled thriller reworked crime as precisely
a means of reconnecting and mapping the social" (22).

The novel abounds with links between the ersatz chroniclers and
their supposed material. Both characters are diseased; Ryan is an
alcoholic and a wife-beater, while Coppinger suffers from throat can-
cer and a nasty sadistic edge, as damaged as the people on whom they
report. Coppinger's language in particular merges local vernacular
with the lingo of the noir detective. "It's like everybody's frightened,
the peelers and all. Even the hard men's worried. Word is you mention
the subject to them they go buck mad" (35). In the somber conclusion,
Coppinger dies, in the same chapter as Victor, his funeral intercut
with Victor's final scene. And the narrative focalization ends with
Ryan's consciousness merged with Heather's as both contemplate the
news that the new corpses will bring. Ryan also becomes one with
Belfast: "He was of the city now, part of its rank, allusive narrative"
(233). Rather than narrating, he is narrated, merging with his subjects

and further blurring any distinction between author and character. Not peripheral to the novel's main themes, Ryan and Coppinger, writers of stories by trade, represent its unnarratability from the outside.

The ending does not come, in the single-solution model that detective and thriller fiction most fully embody but instead stages incompletion, multiple points of view, and unanswered questions. McNamee begins with an explanation by Dorcas, but this effort at possible cause is contradicted by the lack of resolution. Dorcas herself is denied answers at the scene of Victor's death: "Where are they taking him? She asked again without reply" (233). And just as Dorcas does not have answers to all her questions, neither do readers, for whom Victor's death has been less a narrative development than an inevitability mentioned sixty pages before, again in connection with Dorcas. "Of the events leading to the shooting of Victor she could recall only a little" (185). McNamee undermines plot development, denying narrative gratification at the same time as he gestures to the crushing inevitability of violence. Even a character with such power as Victor will fall victim to those with more economic and social clout.

It is this overdetermination of Victor's death that brings us back to issues of urban space. "Evil, unchanging and elemental, is built into the architecture and the landscape" (Smyth, *NN* 122). Yet evil is not a feature of the landscape, so much as the landscape and architecture are obliged to reflect the depravity taking place within them. Throughout the novel McNamee calls attention to decrepit sites of community (notably the bathhouse where Victor murders his coconspirator as well as the debased "Romper Room" in which his executions are performed) as well as proffering images of urban renewal thwarted ("The Harland and Wolff cranes are visible from everywhere in the city. Scaffolding abandoned from the beginnings of the world" [231], we are told, the skeleton of the city exposed as language and the innards of the murdered are). Kelly again is incisive, linking the murders to urban "renewal": "the Resurrection Men allegorize the urban planning strategies of the area, the role of the misnomic Westlink and the systematic ghettoization of working-class communities" (98–99). The systemic and seemingly inescapable poverty and problems are reinforced by the geographic boundaries enforced upon both Catholic and Protestant lower-class communities.

Another level of the lack of optimism for the future, as well as further denial of narrative gratification comes through the fact that the family in the novel is depicted as such a precarious structure. Not only is the marriage of James and Dorcas unfulfilling, but it results in only one child, killed before he reproduces. Heather is revealed to be in her late thirties, past her childbearing prime. McNamee forbids his characters to have children in his subsequent novels as well, again in ways that call into question rather than reinforcing rigid gender identities. The younger generation of characters of *Blue Tango* all remain childless, the murder that sits as its central event sterilizing the future. The victim, Patricia, is portrayed by locals as sexually promiscuous; it may be this very threat to the institution of family that results in her death. Meanwhile her brother becomes a priest, his vow of celibacy merging with his assignment in an exoticized location, Africa, to preclude the possibility of family. Two of the very few female characters in *The Ultras*, Lorna Agnew and Joyce, are both depicted with reference to the unlikelihood of their ever reproducing: Lorna is an anorexic, therefore not menstruating and by implication not fully female, while Joyce is a prostitute running a bordello as part of a covert operation in Northern Ireland, another environment in which procreation is discouraged. All three female characters end up dead—two murders and one suicide, thereby further precluding the possibility of offspring.

Instead of casting women as foreign bodies, McNamee sees the women as caught in the same web of performativity as his male characters. In her suicide note, Lorna lists her regrets, including, " I regret not ever having a husband I would say to him come to me you handsome pouting brute God the lips the eyes the hands. Note. That is not a real regret" (255). Not only does Lorna phrase her regret in cinematic terms, but she also retracts it as unreal, doubly acknowledging the constructed nature of her desires.

Boundaries and Borders

The fact that Victor is at his happiest in prison, one of the places Foucault cites as a heterotopia, is suggestive of his affinity for boundaries, edges, borders. Not only does he trace limits in his car and affirm them with his murders, but they help him make sense of others as well. In jail, Victor is respectful of the fact that the doctor in the pharmacy where he works will not address him, instead devoting himself to small organization tasks, "A fixing of boundaries that Victor understood, an act of seclusion" (74).

In preparation for his acts of terror, Victor learns the names of the city streets, an undertaking requiring both geographic and linguistic control. His bond with place is so intense that he can sit in the backseat of a car, eyes shut, and know, through any number of turns, exactly what street he is on without looking. Later, he opts to court Heather via a subtle display of this fluency, when he takes her for a drive at dawn:

> They drove slowly about the city. At first Heather thought he was driving at random; then she saw the pattern. He was driving carefully along the edges of Catholic west Belfast. She had never been this close before although she had seen these places on television. Ballymurphy, Andersonstown. The Falls. Names resonant with exclusion. Now they were circling the boundaries, close enough to set foot in them. Victor drove up into the foothills until they were looking down on the west of the city, its densely populated and mythic estates, something you don't quite believe in. (45)

Victor's route deepens the grooves dividing different sections of Belfast, just as his killings intensify the antagonism and strengthen the divide between Protestant and Catholic.

It is at this level of cartographies that McNamee's text again resembles those of Kelman, Doyle, and Galloway. While all are intently interested in conveying a vivid sense of lives within specific urban geographies, all of them make clear "the limits of this form of empirical staging" (Kelly 101). While McNamee tends toward Joyce's efforts to render accurately the places in his city—Ryan drinks in the well-known Botanic Inn, for instance—this specific cartography is ultimately undermined by the city's own resistance to fixity, as evidenced by Victor's loss of his early mastery of the city's layout. Where before he had an "enchanted and magnetic imperative" (26) enabling his blind mapping of the city and he "knew the inhabitants of every house and would tell their histories" (26), his command begins to falter just as his mental state becomes hazy. Significantly, he returns to the state of the immobile boy of the early pages of the novel: "Victor had not driven his own car in months" (162), and as a consequence he becomes disoriented, so that he "suddenly discovered that the streets were not the simple things he had taken them for, a network to be easily memorized and navigated. They had become untrustworthy, concerned with unfamiliar destinations, no longer adaptable to your own purposes" (163). Victor's loss of command of narrative or place foretells his death; because the city refuses to remain within one mode of storytelling, to be fixed by his mappings, his control "ultimately breaks down under the strain of change and historical process" (Kelly 100).

And indeed, Victor's death symbolically recapitulates the resistance to fixity that quivers under the surface of the entire novel, from

Heather's permeable apartment to the sense of personal insubstantiality that seems to motivate performance and cinematic self-consciousness in every character. It is crucial to the rupture of boundaries that Victor is killed on the threshold of his parents' house, having closed the door behind him. His murders all took place in secluded, interior, private spaces, whereas he is gunned down on the pavement, failing to find cover and on display all evening. While the Protestant neighborhood would presumably represent safe territory, the implication is that permeable boundaries mean no place is safe. Like his own blurred name, blurred origin, and blurred agenda and motives, Victor's death underlines the dangers of insistence on monologism; its proponents are themselves likely to discover or have seen in them unstable hybridities, challenges to their sense of absolutes.

Ultimately, then, *Resurrection Man* seeks to destabilize monologism on a variety of levels—formally, by means of the multiple genres it draws on; stylistically, through its explorations of the variations of local dialects, thematically, in its depiction of Victor's ultimate failure to enforce his (tribal) vision, an inability stemming from class dynamics of which he is unaware. Bringing together the concerns of class, urban planning, and power, Aaron Kelly persuasively suggests that "*Resurrection Man* evinces such tribalisms in Belfast are not reducible to the intractable persistence of the atavistic" (105) via the novels' connection of McClure's cliché and manipulative sectarianism to "the historical conditions of late capitalism's reification of place, identity and belonging through which the ghettoization of working-class communities in postmodern cities is rationalized" (105). So to return to my opening point, that *Resurrection Man* does not participate in the traditional depiction of evil as distinct from its society, nor in the stereotypic delineation of the Irish character as beset by self-destructive tendencies. Rather, the novel sees how the conscription of the working class into a sectarian conflict serves to obscure the mechanisms of power that have fed the ongoing conflict.

In a novel suffused with disturbing images and events, one of the most chilling features is the occasional shift into second person, generally appearing in passages detailing the intricacies of the rules governing sectarian boundaries and behaviors. As Ryan passes small congregations of young men on the streets, "He could not anticipate their reactions. You had to know the structure of the gang. The implacable codes" (60). Later, after a routine security check by soldiers on the street, Ryan realizes he failed to note Coppinger's address, and the narrator cautions, "Your address was a thing to be guarded as if the words themselves possessed secret talismanic properties. Your name was replete with power and hidden malevolence" (85). In thinking of the effect of prison on Victor's temperament, Dorcas muses that "He was so quiet the first time he got out she asked was it something they done to him in prison, because once they got you to Castlereagh of Gough barracks they could break you like a twig" (143). Also in keeping with the sense of surveillance and power, Heather's recall of her first sight of Victor mentions that he "had these blue eyes could see right through you" (44). In each case, the move away from the third person free indirect discourse arises with the shift into a mode of watchful fear, an anxiety into which the reader is included through the use of "you." The introspection about language that often marks these passages relates the sense of trepidation to the instability of meaning itself.

Even more ominous is a refrain that crops up, again focalized through various characters but shifting into the only first person narration we see. Ryan and Coppinger: "Please. Kill me" (24, 61 respectively). One of Victor's targets: "Please" (119). Heather, or maybe Victor: "Kill me" (174). And then, within quotation marks, while discussing Coppinger's wish to be euthanized, Ryan: "Please kill me" (184). It is as though the collective unconscious of the novel, the narrative perspective that homogenizes, works to make monologic, the voices of all the characters, is groping its way toward an understanding of Victor's underlying motive. In killing the residents of Belfast, primarily Catholics, but also wayward robbers from his own organization as well as random Protestants, mistakenly, indifferently, Victor liberates them from the stifling atmosphere of fear he did not create but does amplify, "beyond the range of the spoken word where the victim was cherished and his killers were faultlessly attentive to some terrible inner need that he carried with him" (174). Once more, we see the connection of the limits of language to violence, and we are told that Victor feels he is fulfilling the wishes of those he destroys. As the narrative voice repeatedly intones "Kill me," then, it articulates a collective desire for escape from this life of terror and bloodshed. The novel itself is begging not to have to exist.

If, as Kelly suggests, "The more conservative modes of the thriller [genre] collude with...a diffusion of human agency" (6), then McNamee's novel would seem to be a reactionary statement of immobility in the face of intractable violence, a stance in line with the construction of Victor as an individual sociopath rather than a product of his environment. But as I stated at the outset, the formal choices McNamee makes render such conclusions untenable; his recurrent insistence on the link of language to place, in tandem with his relentlessly passive narrative voice, implicate history, the present, social conditions, society in Victor's rein. If there is no human agency asserting control, assuming responsibility, this is what happens, and the whole society has abdicated responsibility.[4] McNamee is not faulting individuals—Dorcas may be a bad mother, but no bad mother could single-handedly create a Resurrection Man. Early scenes in the novel juxtapose her bad parenting decisions with tauntings and torture of Victor by older boys—the community is implicated (Elmer Kennedy-Andrews reads this sketch of "Victor Kelly's socially disadvantaged and psychologically deformed background" as "ironic bildungsroman" [133].) But even these malcontents and bad influences are not entirely to blame for the anatomy of a mass murderer—if language itself is scarred and passive, its speakers lack options.

Is the message one of total intractability, then? Part of what links McNamee to Doyle, Galloway, and Kelman (as well as Joyce) is his unwillingness to preach or to offer ready sociological analyses for outsiders. The answers are not easy. In the final words of *Resurrection Man*, bodies "carry news of the city and its environs" to the "lonely and vigilant dead" (233). Since one of the places they are explicitly going to carry news of is the now-vanished Sailortown, it would seem that McNamee is unequivocally linking Victor's tragedy to the destruction of his parents' old neighborhood. His answers are few and certainly not glib, but the cautionary warnings about language and place suggest methods to reduce future conflict.

Afterword

One of the curiosities of writing about living, producing authors is seeing one's ideas verified, refuted, or out and out confused by the appearance of the newest novel or next stage in a writer's career. I have seen all four of my major authors continue to produce into the twenty-first century, each departing in significant ways from the era of peripheral literature I have been exploring, though often, formal techniques or thematic choices recur that hark back to earlier work. I am led to speculate as to the degree to which the acceleration into an ever-more global economy and lifestyle is relevant in these evolutions, as well as the degree to which the onset of an Age of Affluence, its Celtic Tiger heyday now past, but with the rhetoric of economic growth ascendant, has worked to obscure the sorts of economic critiques that underlay the novels of the urban periphery.

Where before they set aside social-realist forms, now Roddy Doyle, James Kelman, and Janice Galloway have moved away from social-realist settings as well. Certainly departures do not efface thematic concerns important to the earlier novels—for Doyle, nationalism is revealed as a class-smothering bête noire forcing emigration, his next two novels set in the first half of the century, both with an Irish protagonist and a historical context. His retelling of Irish history depicts a world much in keeping, politically, with that of his Barrytown novels, but its move to a mélange of historical and magical realist textual features certainly marks a departure, while his scene change to the continental United States serves to amplify his interest in the Irish/U.S. connection that reverberates throughout all his earlier works.

Galloway has turned her attention not just to the past, but to another country, writing a fictionalized version of the life of Clara Schumann. Again, it is clear that the same authorial voice and presence motivate the text, but again, there is a highly visible and conscious decision not to continue writing in the localist vein. In her novel *Clara* she examines in an earlier context the same sorts of controlling and demanding male behaviors that attempt to paralyze her contemporary protagonists.

Kelman's recent fiction may be the most radical departure of the three, as he has left "reality" behind to depict imaginary and postapocalyptic otherworlds. He experiments with new settings, an unnamed futuristic nowhere in *Translated Accounts* and a similarly postapocalyptic America in *You Have to Be Careful in the Land of the Free*, seemingly in an effort to decipher how much of his characters' alienation is universal, how much national anomie, how much class-based—that is, whether peripheral is a physical place or a state of being that is created by language and law. Jeremiah Brown, in *You Have to Be Careful*, might still be Scottish, but direct comment on Scotland has receded distinctly.

McNamee continues to mine real events, further blurring the line between documentary and fiction, though with the 2006 publication of a young adult fantasy novel, *The Navigator*, he, too, steps away from empirical reality. Had these writers begun to publish at some time other than the mid- and late 1980s, their peculiar blend of modernist technique and class consciousness might have been supplanted by an interest in historical fiction. It is to our benefit that despite the hardships of those decades, these novels did come into being.

Notes

One   Introduction: The Poor Mouth

1. While all the authors I discuss have continued to publish after 1997, all of them move in different directions in subsequent work (discussed in my afterword). 1983–1997 brackets a period of extreme economic hardship for the working classes in the UK and Ireland, a time that acts as a backdrop for most novels in chapters two–four. Eoin McNamee's novels depart from my schematic somewhat, in that, not only is he generationally behind the other writers here, but chooses to set his work in prior periods, a decision (as I will discuss) that I attribute in part to the vastly different political context in Northern Ireland.

2. Later in "Discourse in the Novel," Bakhtin distinguishes hybridization from internally dialogized interillumination, saying that "In the former case there is no direct mixing of two languages within the boundaries of a singular utterance—rather, only one language is actually present in the utterance, but it is rendered *in the light of another language*. This second language, however, is not actualized and remains outside the utterance" (362). While he seems to be referring to national languages (the role of Gaelic and Irish is one that has been productively explored), here I suggest the excluded status of the second language resembles the case for working-class voices in literature of the British Isles.

3. David Harvey, David Lloyd, and Seamus Deane, among others, have also expressed skepticism about the potential of the local to effect change. Harvey: "Regional resistances, the struggle for local autonomy, place-bound organisation, may be excellent bases for political organization, but they cannot bear the burden of historical change alone" (303, qtd. in Ryan n91). Contrast this tangentially linked idea of Joe Cleary's: "...peripheries cease to be regarded essentially as passive consumers of ideas of the modern; at certain pivotal moments...they can function as sites of 'alternative enlightenment' where ideas of the modern are intellectually tested, creatively extended, radicalised and transformed, and indeed transferred eventually into the metropolitan centre" ("Introduction" 6). See also Trumpener and Crawford.

4. This is a combination proposed by Derek Attridge in *Peculiar Language* in reference to Joyce's onomatopoeia. Tom Leonard, a Glasgow poet whom Kelman credits as an inspiration, has interrogated the "realism" of standard spelling by rendering accents in the Standard Received Pronunciation on the page via transliteration; for instance, literature becomes "littricha."

5. These historical factors are important background for the sorts of novels and films being produced by and about the Scots and the Irish. Ireland, in particular, can be a troubled term; when I use it here, I refer by and large to the Republic of Ireland. When discussing the island of Ireland, or talking about a unified Ireland as envisioned by those who reject the legitimacy of British presence on the island of Ireland, I will take pains to make my distinctions clear. For more on Scots nationalism, see Keith Webb, Tom Nairn, and Michael Gardiner. For diverse views on Irish nationalism, see Roy Foster, *Modern Ireland*, Frederic Jameson, *Nationalism, Colonialism, and Literature: Modernism and Imperialism*, and Terry Eagleton, *Nationalism, Colonialism, and Literature: Nationalism: Irony and Commitment*.

6. Indeed, Scott comes to be seen as the source of "fake romantic 'tushery'" (Craig, "National" 59), while Barrie, living in London and writing stories of Never Land, often does not seem Scottish at all. When he does write of Scotland, he tells stories of a disconnected past with no bearing on contemporary situations or politics: "Barrie's Kailyard stories are the fulfillment of the historyless world that Scott bequeathed" (Craig, *OH* 39). His use of the working-class dialect presumes a middle-class English as the common language norm.

7. In a poll throughout Scotland in the summer of 1998, *A Scots Quair*, not a commercial success at publication but now a fixture on the school curriculum, did win as the best Scottish novel. Given that the top five also included the notoriously difficult *Lanark* and James Hogg's *Confessions of a Justified Sinner*, it seems likely that the list represents less what people actually read than their internalization of current constructions of a national literature.

8. Such a pronouncement immediately begs some clarification. Flann O'Brien, Brendan Behan, Edna O'Brien—definitely some of the most significant figures of the 1940s and 1950s—do write positively about Dublin. Flann O'Brien I treat briefly, with attention to his linguistic formal departures from his domestic contemporaries, momentarily. Behan, based in Dublin, resembles Flann O'Brien in his reference to the Irish language. Kiberd writes that "Whenever he espoused Gaelic ideas, Behan was at pains to fuse them with socialist principles" (*II* 517). Edna O'Brien's *Country Girls*, with its eponymous locus, treats Dublin as a site that confirms one's inner character instead of offering escape, as well as representing an alternative space in which the constrictions of a Catholic, national identity are relaxed. Grace Eckley's analysis of O'Brien's career excises Dublin altogether: "The two kinds of fiction—the Irish and the urbane—are produced from two life styles in Ireland and in England" (77).

9. Judy Simons sees Braine as one of the Angry Young Men in 1950s Britain, a collection of writers who "asserted an ethic of individualism and of rebellious, amoral youth. ... Braine was in the forefront of the wave of populist writers who, with a contempt for avant-garde fictional devices, rejected notions of artistic elitism and of the refined sensibilities and

unique moral position of the writer" (47). It is this rejection of formal innovation that sets the Angries apart from the authors I discuss.

10. Writing in 1977, Nairn argued that Scotland was less susceptible to this sort of nationalism, having a sense of "historic nation" that Wales, in his example, lacks, including a separate legal system and Church of Scotland, as well as being more recently developed than England, hence a "restive impatience" with "English 'backwardness,' London muddle, economic incompetence, state parasitism, and so forth" (204). Yet, what flourished in 1977 has become an industrial wasteland since, a consequence in part of the denationalization of heavy industries under Margaret Thatcher, so that the Glasgow of a the mid-1980s would very much resemble the muddle and backwardness that Nairn cites.

11. Ryan's list of the "empirical and cultural bases" for the Irish/Scottish comparison is thorough and insightful, including similar linguistic traditions, religious tensions, contested Acts of Union with the British state, and "most importantly, they share an oppressive relation to the English literary tradition" (10).

12. The contemporary demographics in the United States show a similar development, as "Rust Belt" economies decline while profits and population in the "Sun Belt" explode. The even more recent recuperation of the Northeast, and New York City in particular, parallels the renaissances in Glasgow, Europe's "City of Culture" in 1994, and Dublin, now a cultural center in Europe (Belfast's rebirth is slower but certainly in progress). These reemergent cities have shifted focus away from heavy manufacturing and traditional industries, with a concomitant decrease in the visibility of the working class.

13. Gibbons's essay seeks to demonstrate that technology and modernization are neutral forces that can be harnessed by progressive ideologies and reactionary ones alike.

14. See Ryan's *Ireland and Scotland* as well as *Across the Margins: Cultural Identity and Change in the Atlantic Archipelago*, ed. Norquay and Smyth; *Ireland and Scotland: Culture and Society, 1700–2000*. ed. McIlvaney and Ryan, McGuire, O'Toole, "Imagining Scotland," and others. Marilyn Reizbaum in particular deserves credit for pioneering this direction of investigation, one now outfitted with its own institute in Aberdeen and its own journal, *Journal of Irish and Scottish Studies*.

15. In *Modernism and Mass Politics*, Michael Tratner reads *Portrait* as leaning toward fascism, while he sees *Ulysses* as engaging positively with the mass politics of the early twentieth century by allowing for multiple constitutions of the individual subject. Vicki Mahaffey cites the "Evolution" away from *Dubliners*, while Moretti has called *Portrait* a mistake that led to *Ulysses* ("'A Useless Longing for Myself'"); on a slightly different track, Kevin J.H. Dettmar sees the apotheosis of postmodernism in *Ulysses* devastatingly supplanted by a more static *Finnegans Wake* that commits to a single style. The need for a totalizing narrative of right answers and mistakes leads

many critics to overemphasize the "flaws" of the texts less suited to their own theses. Colin MacCabe identifies Joyce's opposition to classic realism as continual, spanning his entire career.

16. While I do want to emphasize that innovation permeates the entire novel, the opening scene of *Portrait* is in many ways its most experimental. Moretti distinguishes between two "distinct strains of stream of consciousness:" one for "exceptional circumstances: fainting, delirium, suicide...waking, drunkenness" (*Epic* 174) and a Joycean everyday stream of consciousness. The use of stream of consciousness for the baby Stephen, soon supplanted by more traditional narration, seems to show Joyce experimenting with and rejecting the "exceptional" strain.

17. M. Keith Booker sees Joyce as unable to escape his petit bourgeois groundings and cites "the failure of Joyce's writing to represent the lower classes of colonial Dublin" as a "genuine shortcoming in Joyce's work" (*UCC* 16). Ryan refers to a "narrow band of petit bourgeois characters...inscribed by an almost exclusively Anglo-Irish history" (156) in *Dubliners*. As I will show, such statements overlook the extreme poverty of the Dedalus women, among others.

18. See my chapters on Doyle and Kelman, in particular, for a connection of this technique to the present. Ignored when Joyce uses it, such diegesis is read in Doyle in particular as evidence of his mimetic, unsophisticated practice.

19. "Joyce's sin was to mingle the codes reserved for pornographic writing with those governing other forms of literature and behavior" (Herr 35).

20. In an uncompleted and totally insane enterprise, I began tracking the frequency of portmanteau words in epiphanic versus nonepiphanic scenes in *Portrait*, finding them totally absent at climactic moments of the text.

21. See Robbins's *The Servant's Hand* for amplification of this sort of reading of the absent or invisible working class.

22. MacAnna is at his most contradictory about the techniques and goals of realism, first berating them in Joyce while lauding them in Dirty writers and later defining dirty writers in opposition to realism as "Zany burlesque" (24) and resisting any comparison to social realism or O'Casey.

23. Among my favorite trenchancies are Conor McCarthy's chapter on Dermot Bolger and the Dublin Renaissance; see also Linden Peach and Ray Ryan. Where my reading of MacAnna departs from these sharp-tongued and intelligent ones is not in seeing the essay as more insightful or less contradictory, but as differently wrong, anti-intellectual, and inconsistent in his misreading Joyce and Doyle and their congenial forms and agendas.

24. In perhaps the most famous episode of the book, the narrator and his grandfather call a census taker "sor," meaning "louse," although they are understood to be trying to say "sir" with a heavy accent. Booker reads this moment as one in which "the Gaels manage a dexterously

double-voiced use of language that rings of submissiveness to the ear of the oppressor but that is in fact highly subversive" ("O'Brien" 173).

25. Colin Graham sees critiques of authenticity as awarding "sacred status" to "established politicized readings of Irish culture" ("Blarney" 26) and calls instead for an evolving, critical authenticity which would embrace urban and rural, national and postnational, a position much like that of the authors discussed here.

Two "Ye've No to Wander": James Kelman's Vernacular Spaces

1. The issue of how to refer to vernacular language is often highly political, perhaps more in the United States than on the British Isles. To American ears in particular, Neuberger's use of the word "dialect" may sound especially charged, as it echoes the marginalization of African American forms of English. Throughout this chapter, I follow Kelman's own practice, as seen in "Vernacular," of using the terms vernacular, patois, and dialect positively and somewhat interchangeably; the terms demotic and slang also come into play in reference to specific vocabularies.

2. In an excellent article, Nicola Pitchford discusses how both supporters and detractors of *How Late* replicate the marginalization of working-class fiction by "sounding more sociological than aesthetic" in their evaluations (701).

3. Ella Shohat and Robert Stam suggest such a classification system in *Unthinking Eurocentrism*. Particularly useful is the proposition that realism as a goal, "is quite compatible with a style which is reflexive and deconstructive" (180).

4. Curiously, however, many of postmodernism's and poststructuralism's critiques of realism's knowable reality, confident metanarrative, and omniscient narrators, valid or not, were not applied disproportionately to working-class fiction, a point that contextualizes the subordination of realism to other narrative forms in the remarks of Weldon and McRobbie.

5. This paradox of mimesis and estrangement is Derek Attridge's in *Peculiar Language*.

6. Kelman here echoes the concerns of George Orwell: "the ordinary town proletariat...have always been ignored by novelists. When they do find their way between the covers of a book, it is nearly always as objects of pity or as comic relief" (qtd. in Robbins 4), moving beyond Orwell's analysis by linking such plot decisions to formal, linguistic ones.

7. The sodjers are also called "polis" in Sammy's vernacular, the interchangeability of the terms suggesting, according to Cairns Craig, the complicity of most of the populace, *polis* in the Greek sense, with near-military surveillance and martial-law style disregard of human rights.

8. This collage of thoughts links Sammy to Bloom. Later in the chapter, I will place Kelman's work within a modernist context.

9. In Glasgow, while "cunt" is still not at all a polite term, its reference to female genitalia is far less common than its somewhat derogatory meaning of "guy" or "bloke."

10. Like Craig and McRobbie, Baker lauds Kelman's ability to draw on multiple traditions, while Crawford's project works to recuperate the term "provincialism"; I prefer the label regionalism, which avoids conflating the political (as implied by the term "province") and the geographical.

11. The connection of realism and regionalism, of course, extends further back, including Scottish "kailyard" stories, which relied on dialect to tell sentimental stories about simple working folk.

12. See Hagan's exhaustive *Urban Scots Dialect Writing* for insightful discussion of the contradictions inherent in rendering accent via spelling as well as a detailed analysis of the conflicting agendas that factor into the decision to weight accent, grammar, and lexis in pursuit of mimesis.

13. In an essay in *Brick*, Kelman recalls a reviewer who referred to Kelman's characters as "'preculture'—or was it 'primeval'?" because of their use of vernacular (68).

14. Foley answers that while formal constraints assert a conservative textual politics, a radical theme often manages to overcome formal limitations. The fact that Arthur does marry and keep his job in a bourgeois capitalist society suggests that in his case, the message of the form may win out.

15. On the other hand, Raymond Williams notes that Thomas Hardy felt orthographic rendering gave a "falsely distancing effect" that reduced characters to types (*C&C* 226). It is the shifts in novelistic techniques over the past century that make Hardy's sensitivity seem misdirected.

16. As a grammatical tool Arthur probably would never use, the colon here seems a literary, written touch and may bespeak a continued narrative regulation of Arthur's thoughts. While Arthur is the focalizer throughout the novel, to draw on Genette's formulation, we can sense the distance between the overt narrator representing Arthur's perspective and the covert narrator whose vocabulary and politics are more self-conscious than Arthur's.

17. Hebdige makes a similar point when he describes his efforts to avoid a Marcuse-like embrace of subcultures as the repository of truth: "Contrary to [Marcuse's] thesis, there is evidence that cultures of resistance actually sometimes serve to reinforce rather than erode existing social structures" (167). Roger Bromley refers in *Lost Narratives* to the British working class as one "normally characterized by its passivity" (139).

18. See my introduction for another take on this quotation, emphasizing a Bakhtinian heteroglossia.

19. The charge of nihilism is often leveled at Joyce as well (see Moretti, "The Long Goodbye"), for his concatenation/profusion of styles, which

replicates on a narrative level what Kelman here achieves on a linguistic one. Griel Marcus's theory provides an alternate reading: the nihilist, "is always a solipsist: no one exists but the actor,...[versus negation, which is] always political: it assumes the existence of other people, calls them into being. Still, the tools the negationist seems forced to use—real or symbolic violence, blasphemy, dissipation, contempt, ridiculousness—change hands with those of the nihilist" (9). This list of qualities resembles the accusations made about Kelman's technique during the Booker uproar.

20. The only problem with Topia's statement here is that it does not take into account the fact that Joyce's rejection of quotation marks dates to the proofs of *Dubliners*, though he was compelled to acquiesce to publishers of early editions of his work. While the absence of quotation marks in *Ulysses* is interesting in the way that Topia suggests, Joyce's polyphony predates the novel where Topia discovers it, implying that the dissolution of narrative hierarchy also predates the novel in which many critics locate it.

21. See chapter three for exploration of Roddy Doyle's adaptation of this technique.

22. Moretti also excoriates the Joyce industry for its reliance on the "facile metaphors" and Homeric frame provided by the "Linati" schemata: "It remains a mystery why on earth these insignificant sheets, which demonstrate only Joyce's high-school fixations ('Menton=Ajax'; 'Incest=journalism'), should ever have been taken so seriously" (*Epic* 184n).

23. Various books have used similar techniques before, *Under the Volcano* being an example especially in its use in an alcoholic context, which provides a connection to essentially all of Kelman's work. Kelman is special in his connection of his chaotic narrative voice with "plotless plots," to de discussed below; in forsaking fully the novelistic progression through dialogue to which Lowry occasionally returns; and in linking of narrative leveling to issues of class. The "chaotic style" is not nearly so chaotic as Joyce's shifts from episode to episode in *Ulysses* (recall Neuberger's feeling that *How Late* "never changes in tone"); rather, it occurs at the level of the sentence, even the word, more like *Finnegans Wake* (suggesting to me a problem with Dettmar's larger argument condemning the fact that the *Wake*'s "initial style is also its final style...[which] remains consistent with itself in a way that *Ulysses* does not care to" [210–211]).

24. For an early rehearsal of this very dilemma, see Wordsworth's claims to authenticity in the preface to the second edition of the *Lyrical Ballads* and Coleridge's rebuttal in his *Biographia Literaria*. Unfortunately, many of Kelman's critics, like Wordsworth, focus on the natural, and not the shaping. Sillitoe's earlier refusals to speak for the working class take on a new resonance in this context.

25. Adam Mars-Jones criticizes Kelman for his literary touch: "in the first sentence of *HL*, for instance, Kelman uses six semi-colons and a single

colon, a near-exquisite piece of stopping that belongs to a different world from Sammy's" ("Holy Boozers" 20). If we recall Kelman's comments about the upper classes issuing perfectly punctuated sentences from their mouths, however, we can see his use of the colon and semicolon as a conscious political gesture made to render all voices and moments equal in their expressive abilities. Sillitoe's semicolon, mentioned above as a literary touch beyond Arthur's reach, is different precisely because the narrative hierarchy of that text remains in place.

26. See the introduction for elaboration of this idea, developed in large part by Robert Crawford in his 1992 study *Devolving English Literature.*

27. Recent anthologies including Burns's poems seem to emphasize the rustic rather than the educated Burns.

28. Sammy's plight is based on Kelman's frustrating efforts to aid asbestos victims alienated by a bureaucracy more interested in avoiding responsibility than in helping them (Wroe).

29. Pitchford discusses the connection that Kelman makes to Milton's Samson as well (719).

30. Patrick Kane refers to "our 'New Beckett'" (126) and credits the "London criterati" with the epithet.

31. They define a "minor literature" not as one that comes "from a minor language; it is rather that which a minority constructs within a major language" (16).

32. Unlike *Ulysses*, Kelman is coy about his exact locations, declining to make clear exactly what street or housing scheme his characters might be in; his pub names appear to be fictional (for which research I am grateful to Paul Gunnion.). This contrast between his hazy map of Glasgow and his studied specificity with punctuation is provocative; both work to resist the tendency to see working-class fiction as "merely" realist mirrorings of the outside world.

33. See *Some Recent Attacks.*

34. Gibbons notes that in Ireland the faith in the rural as a site of cultural authenticity is a notion that seems to have been born precisely out of the modernization that drew people to the cities, a point similar to David Harvey's in *Anomalous States* and in keeping with Tom Nairn's analysis of nationalism, as discussed in my introductory chapter.

35. While this term is rarely used now, its circulation at the height of Glasgow's manufacturing period suggests the analogy draws on industrial parallels.

36. See my introduction for a reading of these quotations in light of national and colonial concerns.

37. It seems unlikely that Pat's fellow conversationalists have ever heard of Heraclitus; his earlier mention of both Heraclitus and the genies in an existential monologue arises as a non sequitur and none of the others actually talk about either, turning Pat's remark about the genie's subservience to a master back to a discussion of class.

38. More recently, in *You Have to Be Careful in the Land of the Free*, Jeremiah is also moving toward a migration that transpires, if at all, outside the boundaries of the novel.

39. By contrast, reading J.J. Bell's notorious 1902 novel *Wee MacGreegor*, "the (modern) reader gets the impression that Bell strove to pack every possible stereotype of Scots pronunciation, lexis and grammar into his novel...[an] exuberance of indiscriminately Scots forms and their unrealistically frequent and consistent occurrence" (Hagan 219).

40. The word "satisfy" is canny here, as it allows for the possibility that not all questions raised by narrative kernels will be answered, although it does still require the text to grapple with them.

41. Moretti goes on to argue that hierarchy is inevitably established on the novelistic level, if not in Bloom's own mind, leading up to his assertion that polyphony, cultural discourse, will triumph over the individual stream of consciousness, only to be beaten back into an anthropocentric mode by magical realism in the second half of the twentieth century. But while certain images may recur in the novel, events themselves do not acquire preeminence, nor do the multitude of discourses arrange themselves into a hierarchical progression. Kelman's texts rely on a similar lack of progress.

42. Craig, *OH* 35. The quote within the quote here comes from Alasdair Gray's *Lanark*, page 160.

Three   Barrytown Irish: Location, Language, and Class in Roddy Doyle's Early Novels

1. Each tower was given the name of a hero from the Easter 1916 rising—a move that gave the act of enclosing the working class the sense of including them in a common patriotic past.

2. My description of the late 1950s and early 1960s in Ireland draws from Tobin, Gibbons, and O'Toole.

3. Similarly, the language of Patrick McCabe's *Butcher Boy*, Francie, is suffused with John Wayne-isms, and the crumpled family structure of alcoholic father and pious-but-crazy mother takes to the extreme the Irish stereotypes of this time, wedding the warped culture to foreign infiltrations.

4. This is the type of sweeping generalization that leads many critics to reject O'Toole's analyses as a whole-scale revisionist break with the past. Still, the preponderance of nonurban writing in the Free State and early Republic is inarguable, even if the supposed nobility of the peasantry in question is not always evident. See Brian Fallon's 1998 *An Age of Innocence: Irish Culture 1930–60* (1998) for a critique of stereotypic

representations of the censored nation. Even in this recuperation, how-ever, all the major authors Fallon discusses are rural, with the exception of Flann O'Brien.

5. O'Toole makes the astute and curious point that Friel, Kinsella, and others do not situate discontinuity in the economic changes (introduction of six billion pounds into republic economy from foreign invest-ment, end to heavy tariffs, hence industrialization and urbanization) but locate it in the distant past (a la 1833 Ballybeg of *Translations*) and in loss of Gaelic. "The 'divided mind'…is no longer the schizophrenia caused by rapid social and economic change in the late fifties and early sixties of this century, but a hiatus between mind and tongue caused by the switch between one vernacular and another in the last century. An economic and cultural problem becomes merely a cultural one" (17). Similarly, G. Gregory Smyth's definition of Caledonian antisyzygy attri-butes duality of mental state to innate Scottishness.

6. Lisa McGonigle's article "Rednecks and Southsiders Need Not Apply: Subalternity and Soul in Roddy Doyle's *The Commitments*" appeared in the *Irish Studies Review* after I chose this subheading; her treatment of Doyle's overlap of neighborhood, race, and class is excellent.

7. This sort of radical aesthetic may account for what is often seen as anti-intellectualism on Doyle's part. By consciously casting himself as equal to his readers, distant from the intelligentsia, an artisan rather than an artist, he equates all forms of production.

8. Chatman defines a pause as when "story-time stops though discourse continues, as in descriptive passages" (74). I am arguing that the exact opposite is taking place here, that discourse stops while story-time con-tinues, the story describing for the discourse.

9. While Chatman's terms can feel limited and rigid, precisely their "falsi-fiability" makes them useful in characterizing how Doyle's novels con-form to and confront narrative norms.

10. In his interview with Gerry Smyth, Doyle observes, "what you think is particular Dublin slang isn't at all. I've noticed the word 'gaff' for house, which I thought was strictly Dublin, used in plays set in Liverpool, and I've heard it used in Glasgow" (*NN* 100). Again, in this list of conurba-tions, we see working-class sites as the basis for comparison.

11. In a country that remains today well over 90 percent Catholic (by birth if not faith), obviously such an identification is based more on percep-tion than demographics.

12. As Timothy Taylor asserts, Jimmy seems to have "'auto-proletarian-ized'" (293); he alone is attuned to the sorts of readings of Ireland long accepted by nationalists, elements of the expatriate community, and academics on both sides of the Atlantic. The film makes his postcolonial consciousness especially clear—explaining why he's still out of work to a dole administrator, Jimmy ironically asks: "What can you expect? It's a third world country."

13. This replacement of race by class critiques a postcoloniality based on skin alone; the new edition of the *Postcolonial Studies Reader* is the first to include Ireland, exploring both the earlier oversight and the limits of postcolonial theory on the British Isles.

14. The scholarship on these issues is vast, as is the debate about the extent of Irish racism, whiteness, and class-consciousness in the United States. See Ignatiev, Roediger, Lott.

15. See Michael Malouf for an exploration of the similarities between Sinn Féin and Garvey's United Negro Improvement Association, discussing the reservations de Valera had about such allegiances.

16. How frustrating that the movie recordings of the "revised" lyrics "ended up on the cutting room floor" (Gorman personal communication). Instead of the regionalistic innovation of the lyrics, the movie chooses a song called "Destination Anywhere" for its reprise, a continual backdrop to the band's unromantic daily lives. The desire for escape in these lyrics contradicts local identification: "Destination anywhere, east or west, I don't care," escapism replacing the positive localism of songs like "Night Train." Instead of the active politics of reworked lyrics, the movie opts to screen a Commitmentette singing an Irish lullaby, a more comfortable nationalistic sentimentalism.

17. I am thinking here of Celtic Revival texts, Bowen's Big Houses, even *Angela's Ashes*, in which the city equals abuse and starvation, while the bucolic countryside provides apples, sexual release, and peace. Most relevant is Dermot Bolger's *The Journey Home*, lauded by Ferdia MacAnna for its Dublin realism, which sets its resolution far outside the city.

18. Doyle's text is published just before the full-scale rap/hip-hop reappropriation of the term would have further altered its valence to foreign consumers of American popular culture. See my article "Why Jimmy Wears a Suit," from which this section is adapted, for a fuller exploration of racial dynamics in the novel.

19. Outspan is the name of a brand of oranges, presumably applied here because the character is redheaded.

20. Hebdige emphasizes the dangers of overly symbolic readings in *Subculture*: it would be "both too literal and too conjectural" (115) to read the punk's pogo dance as a reference to high-rises or dog collars as a reference to working-class entrapment.

21. The working-class white/black connection has been made by numerous other groups and critics, from *White Trash* to declarations of punk musician Richard Hell that "Punks are niggers." In *Subculture*, Hebdige explores the possible valences of white English appropriations of ska, reggae, and Rastafarian ideologies, from a reactionary Teddy boy movement to a relatively progressive punk one.

22. Nehring can demonstrate a Marxist wistfulness much along the lines of most of Kelman's critics. His text is the Sex Pistols, a convincing connection of punk and politics, though many of the arguments that he makes

about punk's potential transfer easily onto The Commitments and their reworking of soul. This is not to imply the divorce of form and content or to suggest that forms have no intrinsic politics, but the scope of such readings must be carefully considered. Punk, for instance, contains a destructive aspect that Dublin soul does not, this negation (in Marcus's sense; see discussion in Kelman chapter) implying a more radical praxis, one which Doyle, certainly, would see as less effective politically than a less confrontational statement.

23. This kind of narrative parallel belies the surface simplicity of the text, creating productive tension between narrative disjunction and the prospect of endless recurrence.

24. In a dizzying array of appropriations, country music originated in Celtic-based bluegrass, evolving, ironically, to its present form through an infusion of African American influence in the form of early rock 'n' roll, which combined blues (known as "race" music) and white country music (see Malone and Stricklin 102).

25. The paperback cover cites critics who laud "wit, candor, and surprising authenticity" and deem it "warm, frank, and very funny...unsentimental," attributions again imposing expectations of mimesis on stories of the working class.

26. See in particular his interviews with White, Foran, and Drewett.

27. In an otherwise astute piece, Adam Mars-Jones cannot get past the idea that perhaps the Catholic Church really doesn't play a role in Barrytown, even in Sharon's decision to keep her baby. Likewise, Stephen Leslie notes, "Religion is—unusually in an Irish novel—also forced to take a backseat," a statement at odds with much Irish fiction but conforming to received stereotypes. Such expectations of a monolithic, authentic Irish identity the novel and movie less take pains to combat than decline to engage with at all.

28. References to critiques of the "Dublin gas" stereotyping of happy working-class Paddys abound; I have found few actual reviews leveling these charges (Denis Donoghue's puzzling comments about the closest: "The Dublin working class don't seem to resort to abortions. Besides, the Single Mother's Allowance is just as good as the wage the girl would earn...There is no sense of sin in Barrytown" ["Another Country" 3, 4]). The presumption that the story would be seen abroad as stage Irish shows a cultural community with concerns that far outstripped the sophistication of non-Irish reviewers, who by and large were so bemused by the absence of the Catholic Church that they overlooked any commentary on Irish identity that the novel makes.

29. Veiled allusions to Ireland's imperial past lurk in Sharon's encounter with George Burgess; that "George" is the name of England's patron saint and four kings during the cementing of England's hold over Ireland is suggestive. Even Sharon's own name sounds more English than Irish—unlike most of Doyle's characters, whose names are clearly Catholic if not Celtic in origin—thus blurring the line between victim and culprit.

30. It is worth reiterating that the Barrytown trilogy, critiqued here as "urban pastoral" (10), preceded the Celtic Tiger by a number of years and hence cannot be a reflection of a complacent prosperity.

31. Similarly, Alasdair Gray renders upper-class Oxbridge speech as deviating from the norm in the "Distant Cousin of the Queen" section of *Something Leather*: "your is 'yaw', poor is 'paw,' literature is 'litricha,' here is 'hia,' nearly is 'nialy' and Shakespeare is 'Shakespia'" (Kravitz xiii).

32. Interestingly, neither Sharon nor Jimmy is part of the scene where we learn that the baby girl has been born; the shift from Sharon's narrative to Jimmy's is concealed in part by the collective ownership of the pregnancy by a close and loving family.

33. The film version of *The Van* received poor reviews in part because of its abundant profanity, a criticism also made of Kelman's *How Late*. The idea of a family movie with so much cussing was seen as contradictory. Social realist texts may have portrayed squalor and linguistic degeneration, but they generally declined to employ profanity, another way in which Doyle resembles yet diverges from the realists who preceded him.

34. Responding to my question at a reading, Doyle claimed not to make reference to Joyce at all: "I don't see why reviewers delight in comparing my passages to Joyce. Just showing off what they know, as far as I can tell." (Union Square Barnes and Noble, April 27, 1996). The (arguable) view Doyle seems to encourage would be that comparisons with Joyce are "a limited critical exercise, so removed are the two novelists in context, method, and intention," as Smyth avers (*NN* 66).

35. Cosgrove in turn is citing Fintan O'Toole.

36. Doyle often reverses the standard functions of scene and summary as part of his destabilization of the conventions of fiction.

37. There is no actual "present" clear in the novel, however, aside perhaps from the moment of composition or narration; Charlo's death is found out to be a year previous, some of Paula's worst alcoholism coming after his death, in the absence of any immediate villain or cause. The temporal ambiguity and the complicated accountability deny Paula or the reader the comfort of narrative resolution.

38. Kiberd points out emigration declined to the point that in the early 1970s, more people returned to Ireland than left it, as jobs were available and the economy was expanding, a condition that emerges again in the (still uneven) prosperity of the late 1990s (*II* 572).

39. Even this image of the end of the rural era contains evidence that the past was never the pure, bucolic origin: the tractor indicates the modernization of farming that had already been in effect.

40. "Supermarkets effected a subtle but decisive change in urban lifestyle. Not only were the intimacy and credit facilities of the neighborhood grocer superseded, but the habit of shopping by day, a strong one in working-class areas, was weakened....transform[ing] shopping from a partly social activity into a purely consumer one" (Tobin 100).

41. Roy Foster: "Again and again in Irish history, one is struck by the importance of the narrative mode: the idea that Irish history is a 'story', and
the implications that this carries about it of a beginning, a middle, and
the sense of an ending." Qtd. in Gibbons's *Transformations* 15.

Four   "Make Out its Not Unnatural At All": Janice Galloway's Mother Tongue

1. For discussions of the postcolonial characteristics of Scottish writing,
see chapters one (Introduction) and two (on James Kelman); Michael
Hechter's *Internal Colonialism*; Robert Crawford's *Devolving
Literature*; Luke Gibbons; Marilyn Reizbaum; Michael Gardiner; Willy
Maley; and Glenda Norquay and Gerry Smyth (*Across the Margins* and
"Waking").

2. This connection of motherhood to deprivation certainly is not particular
to Galloway: "As women, we do not feel entitled to enough food because
we have been taught to go with less than we need since birth, in a tradition passed down through an endless line of mothers..." (Wolf,
"Hunger" 98).

3. When these authors (along with Duncan McLean) gave a reading in
New York, their American editor and promoter, from Norton, informed
me that Galloway would never have the marketability of the men.
Curiously, Galloway's most recent novel, *Clara*, a feminist historical fiction about Clara Schumann that makes no reference to Scotland, has
received positive critical attention, suggesting that perhaps the intersection of national and gender concerns did underlie earlier reluctance to
market her work.

4. The highlands are the locus classicus of tartans and Rob Roy and Walter
Scott novels, while Edinburgh is the acknowledged intellectual and cultural center; Glasgow's industrial profile and mixed immigrant geno-
type are inimical to both.

5. Reizbaum also reminds us that the canon of Scots literature is different
to the British and American audience—readers and scholars—than to
those within the nation (where texts are included partly because of their
exclusion in the general canon).

6. Glasgow's rise was concurrent with its industrialization; if, as Tom
Nairn argues, nationalism is born in part from uneven modernization,
Glasgow, industrial and ethnically "impure," is excluded from the tradi-
tional sites of national identity. See chapter two for more discussion of
Glasgow's identity.

7. See Declan Kiberd's early article "The War against the Past," which sets
up a similar distinction between rebellion/revival and revolution, discussed in my article "But I keep on thinking and I'll never come to a tidy
ending."

8. An avid advocate of young writers, as a proponent of writer's workshops and organizer of public readings, Kelman photocopied Galloway's entry to a short story competition he was judging to help her seek publication. Peter Kravitz sees evidence of Kelman's and Alasdair Gray's "tenacity and...formal and technical breakthroughs" (xxiii) in the writing of Galloway and others in her generation. Galloway herself includes Kelman's name in a list of "important" books her protagonist has read in *Trick* (196).

9. Richard Hoggart, in *The Way We Live Now*, points out that the old class terminologies are no longer operative in Scottish society and makes some curious efforts to reclassify people.

10. As Kerstin Shands has noted, "anorexics sometimes experience them-selves as being outside their bodies" (51). The sense of being external offers early clues to Joy's eating disorder.

11. The development Joy lives in calls to mind Kilmarnock and environs, something of a geographic analogue for Doyle's Barrytown; Kelman likewise places his characters in remote developments. Such housing schemes serve to isolate the poor while leaving inner cities open for eco-nomic revitalization: see the opening scenes of *The General* for a class-based commentary on the forced evacuation of inner-city slums.

12. See Introduction and chapters two and three (note 10).

13. Richard Mabey, *Flora Britannica*.

14. In recalling youth on an estate in Leeds, one resident remarked that the streets had been named after Lake District sights, "with the aim, no doubt, of persuading us that we were somewhere else" (qtd. in Ravetz, *Council Housing* 179). "Some names were chosen to impress residents with local history." (Ibid.)

15. Berthold Schoene-Harwood posits that "in Scotland not only were indigenous place names translated into English but also personal names, with disastrous consequences for the translated" ("Emerging" 61). Schoene-Harwood's argument rests on the conviction that language enforces cultural subjugation; the reverse translation of Boot Hill implies that it could be the mythologizing of Scottishness, a construction likely to elide class distinctions, that needs resisting by the working-class inhabitants of the estate.

16. "At all stages, from design through production and construction to mute consumer acceptance, quality was sacrificed for false economy" (Gibb, "Policy" 168).

17. Joy's place of employment, Cairdwell Secondary, is equally remote, "in the middle of nowhere. It takes over an hour on the bus and then another mile on foot" (Galloway, *Trick* 72). The distance between work and home speaks to the fragmenting of the individual, who, to put it in the most stark terms, is alienated from the means of production by the sheer hassle of reaching the job. D. Gordon has suggested that "the suburban-ization of industry away from the city centers was in part motivated by a desire to increase labour control" (Harvey, *Postmodernity* 191), and

while middle school teaching does not epitomize Marx's proletariat, the choice to situate a school so as to be inaccessible by public transport (a mile would be too far for some younger students or older teachers to walk) belies the purported desire of urban planning to better the lives of those cleared from inner cities and seems rather to indicate the role that economic expediency plays in zoning and construction decisions.

18. It seems likely that Joy's cottage is part of a council development in a cottage estate, a popular construction plan in the interwar years, meaning that while it is not rural, it does precede the inception of Boot Hill.

19. The structural pathology of such confusion of indoor and outdoor spaces is ironically mirrored later in the novel, when Joy enters a mental institution: "The psychiatric hospital's name, Foresthouse, itself signifies a fear of both indoor and outdoor space.... What initially sounds like a pastoral haven proves to be no safer than anywhere else" (Logsdon 151).

20. The word "colonized" seems particularly apt in the Scottish context. Colonized nations are often depicted as female spaces being penetrated by male invaders, linking postcolonial and feminist criticism. But at the same time, Scotland offers Joy little refuge from the masculinized organization of the spaces she must occupy. Norquay argues the interesting point that most critics tend to locate Galloway's style in the orbit of Kelman and Alasdair Gray rather than reading it as a feminist text, suggesting that readings taking nation into account regularly privilege it over femininity, a point Galloway herself has made (see her introduction to *Meantime*).

21. Malson repeatedly cautions against viewing femininity as an "unproblematic, unitary category," reminding us that anorexia may signify "a rejection of this particular denigrated femininity rather than a rejection of femininity *per se*" (117).

22. This literalness connects Joy's project, if not Galloway's, to Kafka's: "Kafka makes his life figurative and his writing literal...His alienated characters, treated like cockroaches, literally become cockroaches, just as the anorexic, reduced to her body by cultural stereotypes about women, literally reduces herself to that body" (Heywood 76). Galloway's crucial move is to make formal innovations not complicit with anorexic logic while she conveys via form the alienation experienced by anorexics.

23. This connects back to Leslie Heywood's arguments, where women fight to become more feminine and more masculine through controlling their bodies. Here, however, the urge to consume and deny consumption are in play. Alexis Logsdon: "The regurgitated text is another form of resistance in the novel as well: a refusal to be a consumer" (156).

24. Feminists and theorists of nationalism discuss the connection of family and nation. Balibar: "nationalism...has a secret affinity with sexism: not so much as a manifestation of the same authoritarian tradition but in so far as the inequality of sexual roles and conjugal love and child-rearing constitutes the anchoring point for the juridical, economic,

educational, and medical mediation of the state" (*Race, Nation, and Class*, qtd. in Yelin 7).

25. See for instance Linda R. Williams, "Feminist Reproduction of Matrilineal Thought."

26. Heather Malson sees sexism in research that repeatedly identifies domineering mothers as the root of anorexic behavior while omitting any investigation of the father's role.

27. There are any number of novels that actually do contain footnotes, from Laurence Sterne to JD Salinger to Stephen King to Wilkie Collins's *The Woman in White*, for example, but these footnotes serve to clarify the narrative and are designed to generate the least sense of disruption possible. Galloway's footnote is closer to those of John Fowles or Edgar Allen Poe, working at some level to undermine the authorial/narrative voice and question the veracity of the text. In the context of Galloway's repeated shifts in tone and type, this footnote—the only one in the novel—signals another generic shift, here to call attention to male ownership of national identity. *Paddy Clarke, Ha Ha Ha* also engages with the authoritative tone of footnotes: the Irish term *amadan* in the main text is translated as "eejit" in a footnote, rendering a foreign tongue into a vernacular rather than a standard English.

28. Michael quotes Christine Delphy, p. 59.

29. Clearly, a student-teacher sexual relationship would still retain serious overtones of power imbalance: it is important that David was never Joy's student and has graduated and gone to college when they consummate their affair. Still, placing David in a student's role preempts the view of Joy as an older woman preying on younger men, a stereotype in its own right.

30. Crucially, the playscript format that comprised such an emotionally charged part of *Trick* is absent here. While the interest in varying the appearance of the page links this novel to the previous one, Galloway's experiments this time are different, stemming from the difference in the personalities of her characters.

31. Examples of this passive and depersonalized voice abound. "St. Dunstan-in-the-East, the bombed-out remains of another of Sir Wren's churches…an unexpectedly [*sic*] verdant garden, the only part of the complex that regenerated itself after the Nazi Blitz of World War II, offers a comforting oasis amid a sea of traffic and masonry" (*Frommer's* 182). As with the cemeteries of Normandy, what is emphasized by the tour book is the peaceful retreat, the explosion of nature, not the explosion of bombs: the reflexive verb even credits the building with agency! For more on the ideologies behind guidebooks, see Spurgeon Thompson's dissertation, "The Postcolonial Tourist: Irish Tourism and Decolonization since 1850."

32. Cassie is always the focalizer of the novel, whether it is in first, second, or third person, which leads me to argue that the shifts in person can be traced to state of mind; the shifts between narrative past and present

tense have a similar function, Cassie being most at peace when the text is in first-person present tense.

33. Engels uses this fact as the basis for his call for the economic liberation of women, and in *The Communist Manifesto*, with Marx, advocates the abolition of the family given that its foundation is "private gain," with women as "instruments of production." Crucially, Marx and Engels are aware that one objection to their aims would be that Communists would aver that nuclear family and heterosexual structures are innate. Such an anxiety is not so antiquated: as late as the 1995 Divorce Referendum in Ireland, a large percentage of the population believed that legalizing divorce would impoverish women by depriving them of their primary access to an income.

Five   Eoin McNamee's Local Language

1. See Eamonn Hughes (*Northern Ireland*), Elmer Kennedy-Andrews ("Shadows"), Joe Cleary ("Fork-Tongued"), Aaron Kelly, and Laura Pelaschiar, just for starters.

2. Critical attention to the historical parallel of Victor Kelly to Lenny Murphy has not noted the ideological significance of some of McNamee's departures from his historical inspiration. Murphy married and had a child, while Victor remains single at his death. Victor lacks Murphy's political edge, his killing using unionism as even more of a pretext than Murphy did. And most significantly, Murphy was gunned down by the IRA (with suggestions that the Ulster Volunteer Force (UVF) might have been complicit), while Victor is unambiguously eliminated by those on his own side whose ends he no longer serves. In such reworkings of his source, McNamee asserts the lifelessness of violence, making it without purpose and without prospects. Though Haslam and others have expressed wariness about McNamee's apparent tendency toward glamorization of his baroque main character, precisely these emendations suggest his desire not to glorify but to excoriate.

3. The protagonist Mark Renton's overdose at a shooting gallery depicts him on a plush red velvet carpet, which sinks several feet below floor level as he passes out. The effect is simultaneously luxurious and death-like: the size and shape of the sunken section is coffin-like, calling attention to the deadly capacity of heroin while emphasizing the luxuriousness of the hit.

4. McNamee's formal reliance on the grammatical passive voice only increases after Resurrection Man, emphasizing the failures of individual agency: "Acts of brutality were referred to on the evening news as senseless and people drew solace from this, random death stripped of meaning" (61), we are told in *The Ultras*. Both the stripping and the referring are grammatically uncredited to humans; presumably, the newswriters

and newscasters are implicated, but their judgments, both reflective and predictive of those of their viewers, deny the possibility of interpretation, making the presence of subjects or agents irrelevant. This unmooring of plot from character is present throughout McNamee's work and hinges on his continual deployment of performance in place of authenticity and questions both the Western philosophical integrity of the individual and the development of the form of the novel in reliance on this idea of an individual.

Afterword

1. With the 2006 publication of *Paula Spencer*, which traces Paula's years since the death of Charlo, Doyle does return to more explicit engagement with and comment on the contemporary.

Works Cited

60 Minutes. "Frank McCourt." Interviewed by Ed Bradley. CBS studios. September 19, 1999. 14 minutes.

Adorno, Theodor. "Punctuation Marks." In *Notes to Literature.* Ed. Rolf Tiedmann. Trans. Sherry Weber Nicholsen. New York: Columbia UP, 1991. 91–98.

Anderson, Benedict. *Imagined Communities: Reflections on the Origin and Spread of Nationalism.* 1983. London: Verso, 1992.

Ashcroft, Bill, Gareth Griffiths, and Helen Tiffin, eds. *The Post-colonial Studies Reader.* London: Routledge, 1995.

Attridge, Derek. *Peculiar Language: Literature as Difference from the Renaissance to James Joyce.* London: Methuen, 1988.

Baker, Simon. "Urban Realism in the Fiction of James Kelman." In *Studies in Scottish Fiction.* Ed. Hagemann. 235–250.

Bakhtin, M.M. *The Dialogic Imagination: Four Essays.* Ed. and trans. Caryl Emerson and Michael Holquist. Austin: U of Texas P, 1981.

———. *The Problems of Dostoyevsky's Poetics.* Ed. and trans. Caryl Emerson. Minneapolis: U of Minnesota P, 1984.

Banville, John. "Ventures into the Belly of the Beast." *Observer.* March 6, 1994: 22. *Academic Universe.* Lexis-Nexis. Baruch College, CUNY, New York. January 24, 2006. <http://web.lexis-nexis.com/universe>.

Barry, Peter. *Contemporary British Poetry and the City.* Manchester: Manchester UP, 2000.

Barthes, Roland. *The Pleasure of the Text.* Trans. Richard Miller. New York: Noonday, 1989.

———. *Writing Degree Zero.* Trans. Annette Lavers and Colin Smith. New York: Noonday, 1968.

Begnal, Michael, ed. *Joyce and the City: The Significance of Place.* Syracuse: Syracuse UP, 2002.

Bell, Ian A. "Form and Ideology in Contemporary Scottish Fiction." In *Studies in Scottish Fiction.* Ed. Hagemann. 217–233.

Bennett, Ronan. "Hearts of Darkness." *Irish Times.* March 5, 1994: 9.

Bhabha, Homi. "Signs Taken for Wonders." In *The Post-colonial Studies Reader.* Ed. Ashcroft, Griffiths, and Tiffin. 29–35. Rpt. of "Signs Taken for Wonders: Questions of Ambivalence and Authority under a Tree outside Delhi, May 1817." *Critical Inquiry* 12.1 (1985): 144–165.

Booker, M. Keith. "Late Capitalism Comes to Dublin: 'American' Popular Culture in the Novels of Roddy Doyle." *ARIEL* 28 (1997): 27–45.

———. "O'Brien among the Benighted Gaels: Linguistic Oppression and Cultural Definition in Ireland." *Discours Social/Social Discourse* 3.1, 2 (1990): 167–182.

Booker, M. Keith. *Ulysses, Capitalism, and Colonialism: Reading Joyce after the Cold War.* Westport: Greenwood P, 2000.

Booth, Wayne C. *The Rhetoric of Fiction.* Chicago: U of Chicago P, 1983.

Bradley, John. "The Irish Economy in Comparative Perspective." In *Bust to Boom? The Irish Experience of Growth and Inequality.* Ed. Brian Nolan, Philip J. O'Connell, and Christopher T. Whelan. Dublin: ESRI, 2000. 4–26.

Brennan, Timothy. "The National Longing for Form." In *Nation and Narration.* Ed. Homi Bhabha. London: Routledge, 1990. 44–70.

Bromley, Roger. *Lost Narratives: Popular Fictions, Politics, and Recent History.* London: Routledge, 1988.

———. "The Theme that Dare Not Speak Its Name: Class and Recent British Film." In *Cultural Studies and the Working Class: Subject to Change.* Ed. Munt. 51–68.

Bruce, David. *Scotland the Movie.* Edinburgh: Polygon, 1996.

Burns, Christy. "Parodic Irishness: Joyce's Reconfigurations of the Nation in *Finnegans Wake.*" *Novel* 31.2 (Spring 1998): 237–256.

Burns, Robert. "Address to the Unco Guid, or the Rigidly Righteous." *An Anthology of Famous English and American Poetry.* Ed. William Rose Benét and Conrad Aiken. New York: Random House, 1944. 190.

Canby, Vincent. "Pregnant, Unmarried and Smiling." Review of *The Snapper,* dir. Stephen Frears. *New York Times.* October 8, 1993: C21. *Academic Universe.* Lexis-Nexis. Baruch College, CUNY, New York. August 5, 2003. <http://web.lexis-nexis.com/universe>.

Caldwell, Christopher. "Revolting High Rises." *The New York Times Magazine,* November 27, 2005: 28.

Carr, Jay. "'The Snapper': Family Values, Irish Style." Review of *The Snapper. Boston Globe.* December 17, 1993: 98. *Academic Universe.* Lexis-Nexis. Baruch College, New York. January 24, 2001. <http://web.lexis-nexis.com/universe>.

Chatman, Seymour. *Story and Discourse.* Ithaca: Cornell UP, 1978.

Cleary, Joe. "'Fork-Tongued on the Border Bit:' Partition and the Politics of Form in Contemporary Narratives of the Northern Irish Conflict." *The South Atlantic Quarterly* 95.1 (Winter 1996): 227–276.

———. "Introduction: Ireland and Modernity." In *The Cambridge Companion to Modern Irish Culture.* Ed. Joe Cleary and Claire Connolly. Cambridge: Cambridge UP, 2005. 1–24.

———. "Towards a Materialist-Formalist History of Twentieth-century Literature." *boundary 2* 31.1 (2004): 207–241.

Cleary, Joe and Claire Connolly, eds. *The Cambridge Companion to Modern Irish Culture.* Cambridge: Cambridge UP, 2005.

Clinch, J. Peter, Frank Convery, and Brendan Walsh. *After the Celtic Tiger: Challenges Ahead.* Dublin: O'Brien, 2002.

Coleridge, Samuel Taylor. *Biographia Literaria.* 1817.

The Commitments. Dir. Alan Parker. Perf. Robert Arkin, Johnny Murphy, and Angeline Ball. Twentieth Century Fox, 1991.

Conboy, Martin. "Postmodern Pastoral: Resisting (En)closure of Rural Representation." *Imperium* 3 (Spring 2002). September 8, 2002. <http://diffie.luton.ac.uk/imperium/>.

Connor, Stephen. *The English Novel in History 1950–1995*. New York: Routledge, 1996.

———. *Postmodernist Culture*. Oxford: Blackwell, 1989.

Cosgrove, Brian. "Roddy Doyle's Backward Look." *Studies* 85.339 (1997): 231–242.

Craig, Cairns. "Introduction." *The History of Scottish Literature*, vol. 4. Ed. Cairns Craig. Aberdeen: Aberdeen UP, 1987.

———. "National Literature and Cultural Capital in Scotland and Ireland." In *Ireland & Scotland*. Ed. McIlvaney and Ryan. 38–64.

———. *Out of History*. New York: New Directions, 1995.

———. "Resisting Arrest: James Kelman." In *The Scottish Novel Since the Seventies: New Visions, Old Dreams*. Ed. Gavin Wallace and Randall Stevenson. Edinburgh: Edinburgh UP, 1993. 99–114.

Craig, David. "The Roots of Sillitoe's Fiction." In *The British Working-Class Novel in the Twentieth Century*. Ed. Jeremy Hawthorn. London: Edward Arnold, 1984. 95–110.

Craigie, W.A. "The Present State of the Scottish Tongue" (January 1921). Excerpted in McCulloch, Margery Palmer. *Modernism and Nationalism: Literature and Society in Scotland 1918–1939*. 14–18. Rpt. from *The Scottish Tongue: A Series of Lectures on the Vernacular Language of Lowland Scotland*. London: Cassell & Co., 1924. 3–46.

Crawford, Robert. *Devolving English Literature*. Oxford: Clarendon, 1992. (revised 2nd edn. Edinburgh: Edinburgh UP, 2000).

———. *The Scottish Invention of English Literature*. Cambridge, Cambridge UP, 2000.

Cullingford, Elizabeth Butler. "British Romans and Irish Carthaginians: Anticolonial Metaphor in Heaney, Friel, and McGuinness." *PMLA* 111 (1996): 222–239.

———. *Ireland's Others: Gender and Ethnicity in Irish Literature and Popular Culture* . Notre Dame: University of Notre Dame Press, 2001.

D'haen, Theo. "Irish Regionalism, Magic Realism, and Postmodernism." In *British Postmodern Fiction*. Ed. Theo D'haen and Hans Bertens. Amsterdam: Rodopi, 1993. 33–46.

De Certeau, Michel. *The Practice of Everyday Life*. Berkeley: U of California P, 2002. Excerpted in *The Blackwell City Reader*. Ed. Gary Bridge and Sophie Watson. Oxford: Blackwell, 2002. 383–393.

Deleuze, Gilles, and Felix Guattari. *Kafka: Toward a Minor Literature*. Trans. Dana Polan. Minneapolis: U of Minnesota P, 1986.

Delphy, Christine. *Close to Home: A Materialist Analysis of Women's Oppression*. Trans. Diana Leonard. Amherst: U of Massachusetts P, 1984.

Dettmar, Kevin J.H. *The Illicit Joyce of Postmodernism: Reading against the Grain*. Madison: U of Wisconsin P, 1996.

Devlin, Kimberly J. "Visible Shades and Shades of Visibility." In *Ulysses—En-gendered Perspectives*. Ed. Reizbaum and Devlin. 67–85.

Dixon, Keith. "Talking to the People: A Reflection on Recent Glasgow Fiction." *Studies in Scottish Literature*, Vol. 28, Ed. G. Ross Roy. U of South Carolina: Columbia, SC, 1993. 92–104.

Donoghue, Denis. "Another Country." *New York Review of Books* 51.3 (February 1994): 3–4.

———. "Kicking in the Air." Review of *How Late it Was, How Late*, by James Kelman, and *The Butcher Boy*, by Patrick McCabe. *New York Review of Books*. 42.10: 45–49.

Doyle, Roddy. *The Barrytown Trilogy: The Commitments, The Snapper, and The Van*. New York: Penguin, 1993.

———. *Paddy Clarke, Ha Ha Ha*. New York: Penguin, 1993.

———. *The Woman Who Walked into Doors*. New York: Penguin, 1996.

Drewett, James. "An Interview with Roddy Doyle." *Irish Studies Review*. 11.3 (December 2003): 337–349.

Duffy, Enda. "Disappearing Dublin: *Ulysses*, Postcoloniality, and the Politics of Space." *Semicolonial Joyce*. Ed. Marjorie Howes and Derek Attridge. Cambridge: Cambridge UP, 2000. 37–57.

———. *The Subaltern Ulysses*. Minneapolis: U of Minnesota P, 1994.

Eagleton, Terry. *Nationalism, Colonialism, and Literature: Nationalism: Irony and Commitment*. Derry: Field Day Pamphlet Number 13, Foyle Arts Centre, 1988.

Eckley, Grace. *Edna O'Brien*. Lewisburg, PA: Bucknell UP, 1974.

Edgeworth, Maria. *Castle Rackrent*. Ed. Marilyn Butler. New York: Penguin, 1992.

Eliot, T.S. "Was There a Scottish Literature?" McCulloch, Margery. *Modernism and Nationalism*. Glasgow: ASLS, 2004. 7–10. Reprint of *Athenaeum* August 1919. 680–681.

Ellmann, Maud. *The Hunger Artists: Starving, Writing, and Imprisonment*. Cambridge, MA: Harvard UP, 1993.

Ellmann, Richard. *James Joyce*. Oxford: Oxford, 1982.

Engels, Friedrich. *The Origin of the Family, Private Property and the State*. New York: International Publishers Co, 1970.

Fairhall, James. *James Joyce and the Question of History*. Cambridge: Cambridge UP, 1993.

Fallon, Brian. *An Age of Innocence: Irish Culture 1930–60*. Dublin: Gill & Macmillan, 1998.

Fallon, Patricia, Melanie A. Katzman, and Susan C. Wooley, eds. *Feminist Perspectives on Eating Disorders*. New York: Guilford, 1994.

Fogarty, Anne. "States of Memory: Reading History in 'Wandering Rocks.'" In *Twenty-First Joyce*. Ed. Ellen Carol Jones and Morris Beja. Gainesville: UP of Florida, 2004. 56–81.

Foley, Barbara. "Generic and Doctrinal Politics in the Proletarian Bildungsroman." In *Understanding Narrative*. Ed. James Phelan and Peter J. Rabinowitz. Columbus: Ohio State UP, 1994. 43–64.

Foran, Charles. "The Troubles of Roddy Doyle." *Saturday Night* 111.3 (April 1996): 59–64.

Foster, R.F. "Knowing your Place: Words and Boundaries in Anglo-Irish Relations." In *Paddy and Mr. Punch: Connections in Irish and English History*. London: Penguin, 1993. 78–101.

———. *Modern Ireland: 1600–1972*. New York: Penguin, 1988.

Foucault, Michel. "Of Other Spaces." Lecture, 1967. Trans. Jay Miskowiec. February 2, 2007. <http://foucault.info/documents/heteroTopia/foucault.heteroTopia.en.html>.

———. *The Order of Things: An Archaeology of the Human Sciences*. New York: Vintage, 1973.

Frazer, Hugh. "Poverty." In *The Blackwell Companion to Modern Irish Culture*. Ed W.J. McCormack. Oxford: Blackwell, 1999.

Freeman, Alan. "Ghosts in Sunny Leith: Irvine Welsh's *Trainspotting*." *Studies in Scottish Fiction*. Ed. Hagemann. 251–262.

Friedman, Ellen G. "What Are the Missing Contents? (Post)Modernism, Gender, and the Canon." In *Narratives of Nostalgia, Gender and Nationalism*. Ed. Jean Pickering and Suzanne Kehde. London: Macmillan, 1997. 159–181.

Furlong, Andy, Fred Cartmel, Andy Biggart, Helen Sweeting, and Patrick West. *Youth Transitions: Patterns of Vulnerability and Processes of Social Inclusion*. Scottish Executive Social Research, 2003. June 11, 2007. <http://www.scotland.gov.uk/Publications/2003/10/18348/27999>.

Galloway, Janice. *Blood*. London: Secker and Warburg, 1991.

———. *Foreign Parts*. 1994. Normal, IL: Dalkey Archive P, 1995.

———. "Introduction." *Meantime: Looking Forward to the Millennium*. Ed. Janice Galloway and Marion Sinclair. Edinburgh: Polygon, 1991.

———. *The Trick Is to Keep Breathing*. 1989. Normal, IL: Dalkey Archive P, 1994.

Gardiner, Michael. *Modern Scottish Culture*. Edinburgh: Edinburgh UP, 2005.

Garvey, Johanna X.K. "City Limits: Reading Gender and Urban Spaces in *Ulysses*." *Twentieth Century Literature* 41.1 (1995): 108–123.

Gibb, Andrew. "Policy and Politics in Scottish Housing since 1945." In *Scottish Housing in the Twentieth Century*. Ed. Richard Rodger. New York: Leicester UP, 1989. 155–183.

Gibbons, Luke. *Transformations in Irish Culture*. Notre Dame: U of Notre Dame P, 1996.

Gifford, Don. *Ulysses Annotated*. Berkeley: U of California P, 1988.

Gorman, A.O. Personal communication, January 21, 2002.

Graham, Colin and Richard Kirkland. Eds. *Ireland and Cultural Theory: The Mechanics of Authenticity*. New York: St. Martin's, 1999.

Graham, Colin. "'…Maybe That's Just Blarney:' Irish Culture and the Persistence of Authenticity." In *Ireland and Cultural Theory*. Ed. Graham and Kirkland, 7–28.

———. "Roddy Doyle: Overview." In *Contemporary Novelists, 6th ed*. Ed. Susan Windisch Brown. Farmington Hills, MI: St. James Press, 1996.

Literature Resource Center. Baruch College, New York, New York. March 17, 2007. <http://www.galenet.galegroup.com>.

Hagan, Anette I. *Urban Scots Dialect Writing.* New York: Peter Lang, 2002.

Hagemann, Susan, ed. *Studies in Scottish Fiction: 1845 to the Present.* Frankfurt: Peter Lang, 1996.

Harte, Liam and Michael Parker, eds. *Contemporary Irish Fiction: Themes, Tropes, Theories.* New York, St. Martin's, 2000.

Harvey, David. *The Condition of Postmodernity* Oxford: Basil Blackwell, 1989.

Haslam, Richard. "'The Pose Arranged and Lingered Over': Visualizing the 'Troubles.'" In *Contemporary Irish Fiction.* Ed. Harte and Parker. 192–212.

Hebdige, Dick. *Subculture: The Meaning of Style.* New York: Routledge, 1979.

Hechter, Michael. *Internal Colonialism: The Celtic Fringe in British National Development, 1536–1966.* Berkeley: U of California P, 1975.

Herr, Cheryl. *Joyce's Anatomy of Culture.* Urbana: U of Illinois P, 1986.

Heywood, Leslie. *Dedication to Hunger: The Anorexic Aesthetic.* Berkeley: U of California P, 1996.

Hilliard, Christopher. *To Exercise Our Talents: The Democratization of Writing in Britain.* Cambridge: Harvard UP, 2006.

Hitchcock, Peter. "Joyce's Subalternatives." In *European Joyce Studies 8.* Ed. Ellen Carol Jones. Amsterdam: Rodopi, 1998. 23–42.

———. *Working Class Fiction in Theory and Practice: A Reading of Alan Sillitoe.* Ann Arbor: UMI Research P, 1989.

Hoggart, Richard. *The Uses of Literacy: Patterns in English Mass Culture.* Fairlawn, NJ: Essential Books, 1957.

Howes, Marjorie. "'Goodbye Ireland, I'm Going to Gort': Geography, Scale, and Narrating the Nation." In *Semicolonial Joyce.* Ed. Marjorie Howes and Derek Attridge. Cambridge: Cambridge UP, 2000. 58–77.

Hughes, Eamonn. "'How I Achieved This Trick': Representations of Masculinity in Contemporary Irish Fiction." In *Irish Fiction.* Ed. Kennedy-Andrews. 119–136.

Hughes, Eamonn, ed. *Northern Ireland : Culture and Politics 1960–1990.* Milton Keynes, UK, and Philadelphia: Open UP, 1991. 1–12.

Hyde, Abbey. "Gender Differences in the Responses of Parents' to Their Daughters' Non-marital Pregnancy." In *Women and Irish Society: A Sociological Reader.* Ed. Anne Byrne and Madeline Leonard. Belfast: Beyond the Pale, 1997. 282–295.

Ignatiev, Noel. *How the Irish Became White.* New York: Routledge, 1996.

Jackson, Ellen-Raissa. "Gender, Violence and Hybridity: Reading the Postcolonial in Three Irish Novels." Irish Studies Review 7.2 (August 1999): 221–231.

Jameson, Frederic. "Cognitive Mapping." In *Marxism and the Interpretation of Culture.* Eds. Cary Nelson and Lawrence Greenberg. Chicago: U of Illinois P, 1988. 347–360.

———. *Nationalism, Colonialism, and Literature: Modernism and Imperialism*. Derry: Field Day Pamphlet Number 14, Foyle Arts Centre, 1988.

———. *Postmodernism, or, the Cultural Logic of Late Capitalism*. Durham: Duke UP, 1991.

Johnson, Nuala. "The Cartographies of Violence: Belfast's *Resurrection Man*." *Environment and Planning D: Society and Space*. 17 (1999): 723–736.

Johnson, Jeri. "Joyce and Feminism." *The Cambridge Companion to James Joyce*. Cambridge: Cambridge UP, 2004. 196–212.

Joyce, James. *A Portrait of the Artist as a Young Man*. New York: Viking, 1968.

———. *Finnegans Wake*. New York: Penguin, 1939.

———. *Ulysses*. New York: Random House, 1986.

———. *Ulysses*. 1934. New York: Vintage, 1990.

Kane, Patrick. *Tinsel Show: Pop, Politics, Scotland*. Edinburgh: Polygon, 1992.

Kearney, Richard, ed. *Across the Frontiers: Ireland in the 1990s*. Dublin: Wolfhound, 1988.

Kearney, Richard. "Postmodernity and Nationalism: A European Perspective." *MFS* 38.3 (Autumn 1992): 590–591.

———. *Postnationalist Ireland*. New York: Routledge, 1997.

———. *Transitions: Narratives in Modern Irish Culture*. Dublin: Wolfhound, 1988.

Kelly, Aaron. *The Thriller and Northern Ireland since 1969: Utterly Resigned Terror*. Hampshire and Burlington: Ashgate, 2005.

Kelman, James. *The Busconductor Hines*, 1984. London: Phoenix, 1994.

———. *A Chancer*. London: Picador, 1987.

———. *A Disaffection*. London: Farrar, Straus, & Giroux, 1989.

———. *Greyhound for Breakfast*. London: Farrar, Strauss, & Giroux, 1987.

———. *How Late it Was, How Late*. London: Secker & Warburg, 1994.

———. "The Importance of Glasgow in My Writing." In *Some Recent Attacks: Essays Cultural and Political*. Ed. James Kelman. Stirling: AK Press, 1992. 78–84.

———. "Vernacular." *Brick* 51 (Winter 1995): 68–69.

Kenneally, Michael, ed. *Cultural Contexts and Literary Idioms in Contemporary Irish Literature*. Gerrards Cross: Colin Smythe, 1988.

Kennedy-Andrews, Elmer, ed. *Irish Fiction since the 1960s*. Gerrards Cross: Colin Smythe, 2006.

Kennedy-Andrews, Elmer. "Antic Dispositions in Some Recent Irish Fiction: Robert MacLiam Wilson's *Ripley Bogle*, Patrick McCabe's *The Butcher Boy*, and Eoin McNamee's *Resurrection Man*." In *Last before America: Irish and American Writing*. Eds. Eamonn Hughes and Fran Brearton. Belfast: Blackstaff P, 2001. 121–142.

Kennedy-Andrews, Elmer. "Shadows of the Gunmen: The Troubles Novel." In *Irish Fiction*. Ed. Kennedy-Andrews. 87–117.

Kiberd, Declan. *Inventing Ireland*. Cambridge, MA: Harvard UP, 1996.

———. "The War against the Past." In *The Uses of the Past: Essays on Irish Culture*. Ed. Audrey Eyler and Robert Garratt. Newark: U of Delaware P, 1988. 24–54.

Kilfeather, Siobhán. "Sex and Sensation in the Nineteenth-Century Novel." In *Gender Perspectives in Nineteenth-Century Ireland: Public and Private Spheres*. Ed. Margaret Kelleher and James A. Murphy. Dublin: Irish Academic Press, 1997. 83 –92.

Kirby, Peadar, Luke Gibbons, and Michael Cronin. *Reinventing Ireland: Culture, Society and Global Economy*. London/Sterling, Va: Pluto, 2002.

Kirk, John. *Twentieth-Century Writing and the British Working Class*. Cardiff: U of Wales P, 2003.

Konstantarakos, Myrto. "The *film de banlieue*: Renegotiating the Representation of Urban Space." *Urban Space and Representation*. Ed. Maria Balshaw and Liam Kennedy. London, Sterling, VA: Pluto P, 2000. 131–145.

Kravitz, Peter, ed. *The Picador Book of Contemporary Scottish Fiction*. London: Picador, 1997.

Lacey, Colin. "Public Enemies, Part Two: Exceptional Writing Marks Otherwise." *Irish Voice*. September 15, 1995. *Highbeam Research*. Baruch College, New York, NY. January 24, 2006.

Lawrence, Karen. *The Odyssey of Style in Ulysses*. Princeton: Princeton UP, 1981.

Lehner, Stefanie. "*Towards a Subaltern Aesthetics*: Reassessing Postcolonial Criticism for Contemporary Northern Irish and Scottish Literatures. James Kelman and Robert McLiam Wilson's Rewriting of National Paradigms." January 25, 2006. <http://www.sharp.arts.gla.ac.uk/issue5/lehner.pdf>.

Leslie, Stephen. "To Probe or Not to Probe?" *TLS* 4577.21 (December 1990): 138.

Levenson, Michael. "Stephen's Diary in Joyce's *Portrait*—The Shape of Life," *ELH* 52.4 (Winter 1985): 1017–1035.

Lewis, Pericles. "The Conscience of the Race: The Nation as Church of the Modern Age." *Joyce through the Ages: A Nonlinear View*. Ed. Michael Patrick Gillespie. Gainesville: UP of Florida, 1999. 85–106.

Llewellyn Smith, Julia. "The Prize Will Be Useful. I'm Skint." *Times*. October 13, 1994. *Academic Universe*. Lexis-Nexis. Columbia University Library, New York. February 21, 1996. <http://web.lexis-nexis.com/universe>.

Lloyd, David. *Anomalous States: Irish Writing and the Post-colonial Moment*. Dublin: Lilliput, 1993.

Logsdon, Alexis. "Looking as Though You're in Control: Janice Galloway and the Working-Class Female Gothic." *Edinburgh Review* 2004. Special

Issue: "Exchanges: Reading Janice Galloway's Fictions." Ed. Linda Jackson. 145–158.

Lott, Eric. *Love and Theft*. New York: Oxford, 1995.

Lyall, Sarah. "In Furor Over Prize, Novelist Speaks Up for His Language." *New York Times*. November 29, 1994, sec. C: 15, 20.

Mabey, Richard. *Flora Britannica*, London: Sinclair Stevenson, 1994.

MacAnna, Ferdia. ""The Dublin Renaissance: An Essay on Modern Dublin and Dublin Writers." *Irish Review* 10 (1991): 14–30.

MacCabe, Colin. *Joyce's Revolution of the Word*. London: MacMillan, 1978.

Mackay, James H., ed. *Complete Works of Robert Burns*. Ayreshire, Scotland: Alloway, 1986. 131–132.

Mahaffey, Vicki. *Reauthorizing Joyce*. Cambridge: Cambridge UP, 1988. Gainesville: UP of Florida, 1995.

Mair, Christian. "Contrasting Attitudes towards the Use of Creole in Fiction—A Comparison of Two Early Novels by V.S. Naipaul and Sam Selvon." In *Crisis and Creativity in the New Literatures in English*. Ed. Geoffrey V. Davis and Hena Maes-Jelinek. Amsterdam: Rodopi, 1990. 133–150.

Majendie, Paul. "Scot Wins Top Literary Prize, Judge Outraged." *Reuters*. October 12, 1994. *Academic Universe*. Lexis-Nexis. Columbia University Library, New York. February 21, 1996. <http://web.lexis-nexis.com/universe>.

Maley, Willy. "'Kilt by kelt shell kithagain with kinagain': Joyce and Scotland." *Semicolonial Joyce*. Ed. Marjorie Howes and Derek Attridge. Cambridge: Cambridge UP, 2000. 201–218.

Malone, Bill C. and David Stricklin. *Southern Music/American Music*. Revised edition. Lexington: UP of Kentucky, 2003.

Malouf, Michael. "With Dev in America: Sinn Féin, Marcus Garvey and Recognition Politics." *Interventions* 4.1 (2002): 22–34.

Malson, Helen. *The Thin Woman: Feminism, Post-structuralism and the Social Psychology of Anorexia Nervosa*. New York: Routledge, 1997.

Marcus, Greil. *Lipstick Traces: A Secret History of the Twentieth Century*. Cambridge: Harvard UP, 1989.

Mars-Jones, Adam. "In Holy Boozers." *The Times Literary Supplement* 47, 48 (April 1994): 20.

———. "Power and the Pint; Pop Culture Plays Its Tune in Ireland in The Snapper." Rev. of *The Snapper*. *Independent* (London). August 6, 1993: 16. *Academic Universe*. Lexis-Nexis. Baruch College, CUNY, New York. January 24, 2001. <http://web.lexis-nexis.com/universe>.

Martin, Augustine. "Novelist and City: The Technical Challenge." In *The Irish Writer and the City*. Ed. Maurice Harmon. Gerrards Cross: Colin Smythe, 1984. 37–51.

McCarthy, Conor. *Modernisation, Crisis and Culture in Ireland, 1969–1992*. Dublin: Four Courts, 2000.

McCarthy, Dermot. "Belfast Babel: Postmodern Lingo in Eoin McNamee's *Resurrection Man*." *Irish University Review* 30.1 (Spring/Summer 2000): 132–148.

———. *Roddy Doyle: Raining on the Parade*. Contemporary Irish Writers. Ed. Eugene O'Brien. Dublin: Liffey, 2003.

McCulloch, Margery. *Modernism and Nationalism*. Glasgow: ASLS, 2004.

McDonald, George, and Darwin Porter. *Frommer's England on $50 a Day*. New York: Frommer, 1992.

McGee, Patrick. *Paperspace: Style as Ideology in Joyce's "Ulysses."* Lincoln: U of Nebraska P, 1988.

McGlynn, Mary. "'But I Keep on Thinking and I'll Never Come to a Tidy Ending:' Roddy Doyle's Useful Nostalgia." *LIT: Literature, Interpretation, Theory* 10.1 (Spring 1999): 87–105.

———. "Why Jimmy Wears a Suit: Black, White and Global" *The Commitments*. *Studies in the Novel* 36.2 (Summer 2004): 232–250.

McGonigle, Lisa. "Rednecks and Southsiders Need Not Apply: Subalternity and Soul in Roddy Doyle's *The Commitments*." *Irish Studies Review* 13.2 (May 2005). 163–173.

McGuire, Matt. "Dialect(ic) Nationalism?: The Fiction of James Kelman and Roddy Doyle." *Scottish Studies Review* 7.1 (Spring 2006): 80–93.

McIlvaney, Liam and Ray Ryan, eds. *Ireland & Scotland: Culture and Society, 1700–2000*. Dublin: Four Courts, 2005.

McLoone, Martin. *Irish Film: The Emergence of a Contemporary Cinema*. London: BFI, 2000.

McMillan, Dorothy. "Constructed Out of Bewilderment: Stories of Scotland." *Peripheral Visions: Images of Nationhood in Contemporary British Fiction*. Ed. Ian Bell. Cardiff: U of Wales P, 1995. 85–105.

McNamee, Eoin. *Blue Tango*. London: Faber and Faber, 2000.

———. *Resurrection Man*. New York: Picador, 1994.

———. *The Ultras*. London: Faber and Faber, 2004.

McRobbie, Angela. "Art Belongs to Glasgow." *The New Statesman & Society*. October 21, 1994: 40.

Michael, Magali Cornier. *Feminism and the Postmodern Impulse: Post–World War II Fiction*. Albany: State U of New York P, 1996.

Milne, Drew. "James Kelman: Dialectics of Urbanity," Vol. 14. *Swansea Review*. Swansea: Swansea UP, 1994. 393–407.

Moretti, Franco. "The Long Goodbye." *Signs Taken for Wonders*. London: Verso, 1988. 182–208.

———. *The Modern Epic: The World System from Goethe to García Marquez*. Trans. Quinton Hoare. New York: Verso, 1996.

———. *Signs Taken for Wonders: Essays in the Sociology of Literary Forms*. New York: Verso, 1988.

———. "'A Useless Longing for Myself:' The Crisis of the European Bildungsroman, 1898–1914." *Studies in Historical Change*. Ed. Ralph Cohen. Charlottesville: U of Virginia P, 1992. 43–59.

Morgan, Edwin. *Crossing the Border: Essays on Scottish Literature* (Manchester: Carcanet, 1990.

———. "Glasgow Speech in Recent Scottish Literature." *Scotland and the Lowland Tongue.* Ed. J Derrick McClure. Aberdeen: Aberdeen UP. 1983. Rpt. of *Crossing the Border: Essays on Scottish Literature.* Manchester: Carcanet, 1990. 312–330.

Munt, Sally R., ed. *Cultural Studies and the Working Class: Subject to Change.* London: Cassell, 2000.

Naipaul, V.S. *Miguel Street.* Oxford: Heinemann, 1974.

Nairn, Tom. *The Breakup of Britain: Crisis and Neo-nationalism.* London: NLB, 1977.

Nehring, Neil. *Flowers in the Dustbin: Culture, Anarchy, and Postwar England.* Ann Arbor: U of Michigan P, 1993.

Neuberger, Julia. "Cooking the Booker." *Evening Standard.* London: October 14, 1994: 27. *Academic Universe.* Lexis-Nexis. Columbia University Library, New York. February 21, 1996. <http://web.lexis-nexis.com/universe>.

New York Times, "Week in Review" section, Sunday, June 21, 1998: WR1.

Ni Dhomhnaill, Nuala. *Selected Poems: Rogha Danta.* Trans. Michael Harnett. Dublin: New Island, 1993.

Norquay, Glenda and Gerry Smyth, eds. *Across the Margins: Cultural Identity and Change in the Atlantic Archipelago.* Manchester: Manchester UP, 2001.

Norquay, Glenda and Gerry Smyth. "'Waking Up in a Different Place': Contemporary Irish and Scottish fiction." *The Irish Review* 28 (Winter 2001): 28–45.

Norquay, Glenda. "Janice Galloway's Novels: Fraudulent Mooching." In *Contemporary Scottish Women Writers*, ed. Aileen Christenson and Alison Lumsden. Edinburgh: Edinburgh UP, 2000. 131–143.

Norris, Margot. "Introduction: Joyce's 'Mamafesta.'" In *Gender in Joyce.* Ed. Jolanta W. Wawryzcka and Marlena G. Corcoran. Gainesville: UP of Florida, 1997. 1–7.

———. "Narratology and *Ulysses*." In *Ulysses in Critical Perspective.* Ed. Michael P. Gillespie and A. Nicholas Fargnoli. Gainesville: UP of Florida, 2006. 35–50.

O'Brien, Flann. *The Poor Mouth: A Bad Story of the Hard Life.* Trans. Patrick C. Power. Normal, Il: Dalkey Archive, 1996.

O'Toole, Fintan. "The Darkness Within." *Irish Times* March 29, 1994: 10.

———. "Imagining Scotland." *Granta* 56 (Winter 1996): 59–76.

———. "Island of Saints and Silicon." In *Cultural Contexts and Literary Idioms.* Ed. Kenneally. 11–35.

———. "Going West: The Country Versus the City in Irish Writing." *The Crane Bag* 9.2 (1985): 111–116.

———. "Working-class Dublin on Screen: The Roddy Doyle Films." *Cineaste* 24.2–3 (Spring–Summer 1999): 36–40.

Onkey, Lauren. "Celtic Soul Brothers." *Eire-Ireland: A Journal of Irish Studies* 28 (1993), 147–158.

Osteen, Mark. *The Economy of Ulysses: Making Both Ends Meet.* Syracuse: Syracuse UP, 1995.

Patsilelis, Chris. "Death in the Shadows Of Belfast." *Washington Post.* September 4, 1995. *Academic Universe.* Lexis-Nexis. Baruch College, CUNY, New York. January 24, 2006. <http://web.lexis-nexis.com/universe>.

Peach, Linden. *The Contemporary Irish Novel: Critical Readings.* New York: Palgrave Macmillan, 2004.

Pelaschiar, Laura. "Transforming Belfast: The Evolving Role of the City in Northern Iirish Fiction." *Irish University Review* 30.1 (2000): 117–131.

———. *Writing the North: The Contemporary Novel in Northern Ireland.* Trieste: Edizioni Parnaso, 1998.

Pickering, Jean, and Suzanne Kehde. *Narratives of Nostalgia, Gender and Nationalism.* London: Macmillan, 1997.

Piroux, Lorraine. "'I'm black an' I'm proud': Re-inventing Irishness in Roddy Doyle's 'The Commitments.'" *College Literature* 25:2 (Spring 1998): 45–58. *InfoTrac.* Baruch College, New York, New York. August 30, 2000. <http://www.galegroup.com>.

Pitchford, Nicola. "How Late It Was for England: James Kelman's Scottish Booker Prize." *Contemporary Literature* 41.4 (Winter 2000): 693–725.

Prime, S. Irenæs. *Fifteen Years of Prayer in the Fulton Street Meeting.* New York: Scribner, Armstrong & Co., 1872.

Raines, Howell. "Glasgow Journal; Thatcher's Music: Is It Off-Key to Scottish Ears?" *New York Times.* September 5, 1987. *Academic Universe.* Lexis-Nexis. Baruch College, CUNY, New York. June 11, 2007. <http://web.lexis-nexis.com/universe>.

Ravetz, Alison. *Council Housing and Culture,* London: Routledge, 2000.

Reizbaum, Marilyn and Kimberly J. Devlin, eds. *Ulysses—En-gendered Perspectives,* Columbia: U of South Carolina, 1999.

Reizbaum, Marilyn. "Canonical Double Cross: Scottish and Irish Women's Writing." *Decolonizing Tradition: New Views of Twentieth Century "British" Literary Canons.* Ed. Karen R. Lawrence. Urbana: U of Illinois P, 1992. 165–190.

Richards, Thomas Karr. "Gerty MacDowell and the Irish Common Reader." *ELH* 52.3 (1985): 755–776.

Riquelme, John Paul. *Teller and Tale in Joyce's Fiction: Oscillating Perspectives.* Baltimore: Johns Hopkins, 1983.

Robbins, Bruce. *The Servant's Hand: English Fiction from Below.* New York: Columbia UP, 1986.

Roediger, David. *The Wages of Whiteness: Race and the Making of the American Working Class.* New York: Verso, 1991.

Rosner, Victoria. *Modernism and the Architecture of Private Life.* New York: Columbia, 2005.

Ross, Stephen M. *Fiction's Inexhaustible Voice: Speech and Writing in Faulkner.* Athens: U of Georgia P, 1989.

Ryan, Ray. *Ireland and Scotland: Literature and Culture, State and Nation, 1966–2000.* Oford: Oxford UP, 2002.

Said, Edward. *Nationalism, Colonialism, and Literature: Yeats and Decolonization.* Derry: Field Day Pamphlet Number 15, Foyle Arts Centre, 1988.

Sbrockey, Karen. "Something of a Hero: An Interview with Roddy Doyle." *The Literary Review* 42.4 (Summer 1999): 537.

Schickel, Richard. Review of *The Snapper. Time* 142.24 (December 1993): 87.

Schoene-Harwood, Berthold. "'Emerging as the Others of Ourselves'— Scottish Multiculturalism and the Challenge of the Body in Postcolonial Representation," *Scottish Literary Journal* 25.1 (May 1998): 54–72.

———. *Writing Men: Literary Masculinities from* Frankenstein *to the New Man.* Edinburgh: Edinburgh UP, 2000.

Scott, Bonnie Kime. "Diversions from Mastery in 'Wandering Rocks.'" In *Ulysses—En-gendered Perspectives.* Ed. Devlin and Reizbaum. 136–149.

Scott, Jeremy. "Talking Back at the Centre: Demotic Language in Contemporary Scottish Fiction." *Literature Compass* 2 (December 2005). PDF pages 1–26. Retrieved from Literature Compass. January 25, 2006. <http://www.Literature-compass.com/viewpoint.asp?section= 11&ref=519>.

Shands, Kerstin. *Embracing Space: Spatial Metaphors in Feminist Discourse* Westport, CT: Greenwood, 1999.

Shaughnessy, Mina P. *Error and Expectation.* New York: Oxford UP, 1977.

Sharpe, Sue. *Fathers and Daughters.* London: New York: Routledge, 1994.

Shohat, Ella and Robert Stam. *Unthinking Eurocentrism: Multiculturalism and the Media.* New York: Routledge, 1994.

Sillitoe, Alan. *The Loneliness of the Long-Distance Runner.* New York: Knopf, 1960.

———. *Saturday Night and Sunday Morning.* New York: Signet, 1958.

Simons, Judy. "John Braine." *Dictionary of Literary Biography, Volume 15: British Novelists, 1930–1959.* Ed. Bernard Oldsey. Farmington Hills, MI: The Gale Group, 1983. 47–55.

Smyth, Gerry. "*The Crying Game*: Postcolonial or Postmodern?" *Paragraph: A Journal of Modern Critical Theory* 20.2 (1997): 154–173.

———. *The Novel and the Nation: Studies in the New Irish Fiction.* London: Pluto, 1997.

———. "The Right to the City: Re-presentations of Dublin in Contemporary Irish Fiction." In *Contemporary Irish Fiction.* Ed. Harte and Parker. 13–34.

———. "Shite and Sheep: An Ecocritical Perspective on Two Recent Irish Novels." *Irish University Review* 30.1 (2000): 163–178.

The Snapper. Dir. Stephen Frears. Perf. Tina Kellegher, Colm Meany, Ruth McCabe. Miramax, 1993.

Snell, K.D.M. *The Regional Novel in Britain and Ireland, 1800–1990.* Cambridge and New York: Cambridge UP, 1998.

Soja, Edward. *Postmetropolis: Critical Studies of Cities and Regions.* Oxford: Blackwell, 2000.

———. *Postmodern Geographies; The Reassertion of Space in Critical Social Theory.* London: Verso, 1989.

Stainer, Jonathan. "Localism, Signification, Imagination: De-stabilizing Sectarian Identities in Two Fictionalized Accounts of 'Troubles' Belfast." *Social & Cultural Geography* 7.1 (February 2006): 103–125.

Stark, Susan. "'The Snapper' is Subversion with a Bite." Review of *The Snapper. Detroit News.* January 13, 1994. *Academic Universe.* Lexis-Nexis. Baruch College, CUNY, New York. January 24, 2001. <http://web.lexis-nexis.com/universe>.

Summers-Bremner, Eluned. "'Fiction with a Thread of Scottishness in its Truth': The Paradox of the National in A.L. Kennedy." *Essays and Studies, 2004: Contemporary British Women Writers.* Ed. Emma Parker. Cambridge: D.S. Brewer, 2004. 123–138.

Swift, Jonathan. "A Modest Proposal." In *Gulliver's Travels and Other Writings.* Ed. Louis A. Landa. Boston: Houghton Mifflin, 1960. 439–446.

Taylor, Timothy. "Living in a Postcolonial World: Class and Soul in *The Commitments.*" *Irish Studies Review* 6.3 (1998): 291–302.

Thacker, Andrew. *Moving through Modernity: Space and Geography in Modernism.* Manchester: Manchester UP, 2003.

Thompson, Spurgeon "The Postcolonial Tourist: Irish Tourism and Decolonization since 1850." PhD Dissertation, South Bend, IN: Notre Dame U, November 2000.

Thornton, Weldon. *The Antimodernism of Joyce's Portrait of the Artist as a Young Man.* Syracuse : Syracuse UP, 1994.

———. *Voices and Values in Joyce's Ulysses.* Gainesville: U of Florida P, 2000.

Tobin, Fergal. *The Best of Decades: Ireland in the Sixties.* Dublin: Gill and Macmillan, 1984.

Tóibín, Colm, ed. *The Penguin Book of Irish Fiction.* New York: Penguin, 2001.

Topia, Andre. "The Matrix and the Echo." In *Post-structuralist Joyce.* Ed. Derek Attridge and Daniel Ferrer. Cambridge: Cambridge UP, 1984. 97–114.

Trainspotting. Columbia University Butler Library. March 21, 1997. www.libertynet.org/%7Eritzfilm/synopsesfiles/trainspot/Trainspo.html. (Site no longer available.)

———. Dir. Danny Boyle. Perf. Ewan McGregor, Robert Carlyle, and Kelly Macdonald. Figment Films/Channel Four, 1996.

Tratner, Michael. *Deficits and Desires: Economics and Sexuality in Twentieth-century Literature*. Stanford: Stanford UP, 2001.

———. *Modernism and Mass Politics*. Stanford: Stanford UP, 1995.

Trumpener, Katie. "The Peripheral Rise of the Novel: Ireland, Scotland and the Politics of Form." In *Ireland & Scotland*. Ed. McIlvaney and Ryan. 164–182.

Valente, Joseph. *James Joyce and the Problem of Justice: Negotiating Sexual and Colonial Difference*. Cambridge: Cambridge UP, 1995.

Warner, Gerald. "Time for a Disaffection from Literary Slumming." *Sunday Times* [London] September 25, 1994. *Academic Universe*. Lexis-Nexis. Columbia University Library, New York. February 21, 1996. <http://web.lexis-nexis.com/universe>.

Webb, Keith. *The Growth of Nationalism in Scotland*. Glasgow: Moledinar, 1977.

Welsh, Irvine. *Trainspotting*. 1994. New York: Norton, 1995.

Whelan, Kevin. "The Revisionist Debate in Ireland." *boundary 2*, 31.1 (2004): 179–205.

White, Caramine. *Reading Roddy Doyle*. Syracuse: Syracuse UP, 2001.

Whitley, Catherine. "Gender and Interiority." In *Joyce and the City*. Ed. Begnal. 35–50.

Wild, Peter. "Interview with Eoin McNamee." *Bookmunch. Google*. September 12, 2005. <http://www.bookmunch.co.uk/view.php?id=1378>.

Williams, Linda R. "Feminist Reproduction of Matrilineal Thought." In *New Feminist Discourses: Critical Essays on Theories and Texts*. Ed. Isobel Armstrong. London: Routledge, 1992. 48–64.

Williams, Raymond. *The Country and the City* Oxford: Oxford UP, 1973.

———. *Marxism and Literature*. Oxford: Oxford UP, 1977.

Wills, Clair. "Women, Domesticity and the Family: Recent Feminist Work in Irish Cultural Studies." *Cultural Studies* 15.1 (2001): 33–57.

Winder, Robert. "Highly Literary and Deeply Vulgar; If James Kelman's Booker Novel Is Rude, It Is in Good Company." *Independent*. October 13, 1994: 18.

Wolf, Naomi. "A Gendered Disorder: Lessons from History." In *Feminist Perspectives*. Ed. Fallon, Katzman, and Wooley. 94–99.

———. "Hunger." In *Feminist Perspectives*. Ed. Fallon, Katzman, Wooley. 247–260.

Wordsworth, William. Preface to the Second Edition of the *Lyrical Ballads*.

Wroe, Nicholas. "Glasgow Kith." *Guardian*. June 2, 2001. Baruch College, New York. June 7, 2001. <http://books.guardian.co.uk/Print/0,3858,4196367,00.html>.

Yelin, Louise. *From the Margins of Empire: Christina Stead, Doris Lessing, Nadine Gordimer*. Ithaca: Cornell UP, 1998.

Index